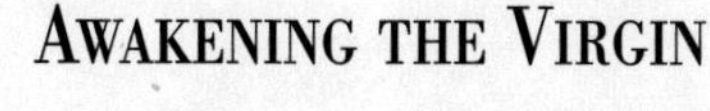
AWAKENING THE VIRGIN

Awakening the Virgin

True Tales of Seduction

Edited By Nicole Foster

LOS ANGELES • NEW YORK

COVER PHOTOGRAPH BY JUDY FRANCESCONI.

MANUFACTURED IN THE UNITED STATES OF AMERICA.

THIS TRADE PAPERBACK ORIGINAL IS PUBLISHED BY ALYSON PUBLICATIONS INC.,
P.O. BOX 4371, LOS ANGELES, CALIFORNIA 90078-4371.
DISTRIBUTION IN THE UNITED KINGDOM BY TURNAROUND PUBLISHER SERVICES LTD.,
UNIT 3 OLYMPIA TRADING ESTATE, COBURG ROAD, WOOD GREEN,
LONDON N22 6TZ ENGLAND.

FIRST EDITION: JUNE 1998

02 01 00 10 9 8 7 6 5 4

ISBN 1-55583-456-6

LIBRARY OF CONGRESS CATALOGING-IN-PUBLICATION DATA

AWAKENING THE VIRGIN : REAL-LIFE ENCOUNTERS OF LESBIANS & VIRGINS /
EDITED BY NICOLE FOSTER. — 1ST ED.

1. LESBIANS. 2. LESBIANISM. 3. SEDUCTION. 4. WOMEN—SEXUAL BEHAVIOR.
5. SEXUAL EXCITEMENT. I. FOSTER, NICOLE.

HQ75.5.A94 1998
306.76'63—DC21 98-6889 CIP

CONTENTS

Introduction

To awaken a virgin to the wonders of sex with another woman—what a delicious concept! As the submissions for this anthology began to roll in, I set about the lovely task of reading all the sometimes naughty, sometimes nice, always very sexy accounts of how the authors seduced—or, quite often, were seduced by—the virgin, inducted her into the hall of sexually accomplished lesbians, welcomed her into the world of women-loving women. Each piece takes my breath away at a certain point, no matter how many times I read it. That's a hot story! The fact that they're true is even more provocative. There's nothing like knowing it really happened to someone, somewhere. And what an eyebrow-raising lot of mini memoirs they are.

If you've ever speculated what it would be like to have sex in a funeral home, Gretchen Zimmerman's "Anything Awful" lets you in on the frightfully arousing details. Charlotte Cooper's "Two Virgins" find each other through the personals, searching for—and finding—a transcendent S/M experience. "Pretty Please" by Debbie Ann Wertheim explores the fulfillment of anal sex. Louye's "Lovely Work" ventures into office seduction, while Marylou Hadditt's "Cowgirl" steps right out of a poster and into a young girl's sensual imagination.

Rosanna Sorella's "Stacked" is a dreamy quest into the fantasies of a bookseller and a beautiful, lonely virgin. "All Tangled

Up" by Paula Clearwater brims with rich descriptions as the narrator is drawn to a mysterious Scotswoman. Kanyon Sweet tap dances, swings, and two-steps her way to a harmonious "Pas de Deux." Soft and romantic define "In My Heart" by Jules Torti, "Every Inch of Her Face" by Shelby Lee, and "My Heart Told Me" by Rebecca Faurer. More bittersweet are the recollections of Paula C. Bowden in "High School Sweetheart," C.J. Place in "Seek and Conquer," and Lou Hill in "My Best Friend's Girl."

Place strongly defines many of the tales. "A Brief Musical Interlude" by Rebecca O'Bryan is set in Los Angeles and San Francisco. "Oh, Dinah!" by Jesi O'Connell explores the pleasures of Dinah Shore weekend in Palm Springs. Bleau Diamond's "Seduction of an Attorney" takes place under the blazing sun of Phoenix. L.A. Livingston's "State of Grace" brings a hurricane-tossed Cape Cod, Mass., to vivid life. The many delights of working at an all-women summer camp are related by Caitlin S. Curran in "The Girl from Kentucky."

I found myself laughing aloud as I read "My Side of the Bed" by Veronica Holtz. The "Tension" related by Alison Dubois had my pulse throbbing right along with all the action, while the blistering heat in Jane Sebastion's "Summertime" made me want to jump into the shower along with the narrator and her virgin.

Some memories revolve around institutes of higher learning. J.M. Beazer's "Peaches and Cream" is set in a New York law school. "The Crush Part" by Jen Moses interprets the relationships of theater students with heated results. "Dinner with Yolanda" by Lori Cardona reveals an unexpectedly sizzling reunion between former classmates.

Women who had already been with men but encouraged pursuit by another woman are the focus of "Eva in the Elevator" by Jennifer Delamer and "Lori-girl" by M. Damian. Some women were truly sexual virgins, including those in "Learning to Swim" by Myra LaVenue, "Rising East" by Fletcher Mergler, and "Silver Marie" by Jennifer Lindenberger.

The virgins and the experienced lesbians who led them into the boudoirs of pleasure share their stories here with passion, joy, exquisite detail, and lots of lust. I invite you to turn these pages and join in their revelations. Most of all, enjoy the journey.

All Tangled Up

by Paula Clearwater

I remember the first words I ever said to her. I'd heard that she had just flown into San Diego from Scotland. I still have no idea how she ended up at our house. I didn't question it at the time because our whole neighborhood was one big commune. People came and went like rubble washed up on a river's shore. Unlike most of the folks who bobbed along between our seven houses, Tara was not a transient at heart. She arrived looking like a newborn colt, thin, glossy, untainted, and curious, needing protection. I immediately wanted to have her.

She was sitting alone on the end of the big couch on our glassed-in porch, writing in her journal. Her focus and concentration were so strong that they seemed to impregnate the space around her with a stillness and fullness that made it impenetrable. I knew not to approach, though I stood and watched her from the kitchen for a moment. Behind her, the poinsettia tree outside was waving gently in the breeze, and shadows from the swaying eucalyptus played across her face, making the sun flash into her eyes in a way I would have found bothersome. But she appeared to relish it. She'd turn her face up to revel in its warmth from time to time, lost in thought. Her skin was as smooth and lustrous as a newly opened bar of soap. The light danced across her straight dark shiny blunt-cut hair. Her lips were small and pouty. She was wearing a pair of wheat-colored bib overalls and a lemon-and-cream striped sleeveless jersey. She sat with one leg wrapped like a vine around the other. I was totally smitten. I had to forge contact.

Quietly I went about preparing two beautiful fresh fruit salads. I sautéed some slivered almonds in butter and placed them in the freezer to cool. I seeded watermelon, scooped out half a cantaloupe, pitted some cherries, and sliced up a half dozen huge sweet strawberries. I diced up apple, pear, and banana, and peeled an orange. Then I picked a small bunch of mint leaves from the garden and minced them into plain yogurt. I transferred the sauce to a pretty bowl and sprinkled the almonds around the edge, garnishing the center with sprigs of mint and a few golden nasturtiums.

Silently I padded out over the cool Spanish tile in my bare feet and set the tray of food down on the low table in front of her. I handed her a cloth napkin, a spoon, and a salad. She took it without saying a word. I ladled some of the sauce over her fruit. She watched with glee, flashing me an engaging smile. Her sable eyes, like wet marbles, gleamed behind canopies of thick dark lashes. She thanked me and then turned her full attention to the food. Selecting one fruit at a time, she swiped it through the sauce and inhaled while she bit in, savoring every morsel. I had to remind myself to stop watching her and eat. She didn't seem to notice. Sometimes she closed her eyes and drank in the flavor. She picked up a wedge of orange with her fingers, sucked the sauce off, and bent it in half, holding the fanned innards up to the sunlight to see how the translucent corpuscles of juice glistened, bursting with life. She sucked a few grapes out of their skins and popped big chunks of watermelon into her mouth with the abandon of a child.

I was happy to be with someone who allowed silence between us; who didn't need the faithless empty chatter that warded off intimacy. We ate slowly. When she was through, she put her bowl down and looked at me. She dabbed her mouth with the napkin and laid it back in her lap, folding her hands and resting them on top of it. "That was lovely," she said in a thick brogue.

The lilt in her voice delighted me, and I started to laugh. She smiled at me. I don't know what prompted it, but I came up with the most curious question in response. I was feeling adventurous and daring, wanting to win her over. I skewered a piece of cantaloupe and said, "What are you most afraid of?" Startling myself with the question, I expected a quizzical look from her. Instead, she studied me for a moment. Then she unwrapped her long colt-like legs and pulled them up to curl beside her on the couch. She looked off across the room in careful consideration and then back at me.

"I'm afraid of love," she said.

"Why?"

"Because you can't see it coming."

She told me about the relationship she'd left behind: a much older Scottish artist who had taken her to France with him, and who had always seemed just out of reach. He had sent her back to Scotland when she'd gotten depressed and anorexic. She talked about how she would've given every part of herself to him. She felt unloved because he didn't want it all.

The next morning, I made *chiles rellenos.* Just about every morning after that for weeks, no matter where she was staying, she came for breakfast. We never talked about it. I didn't know much about what filled the rest of her days. We talked instead about our nocturnal dreams. We both kept journals of them.

Sometimes she would read her poems to me. Often, they were in French. I loved to hear it, especially since I could bask in the sound of her voice, unhampered by having to listen to the meaning. She'd translate: betrayal and loss, love unmet.

One day I had a very disturbing dream. It was one that had been hard to talk about. She had not dreamed. I felt uneasy when we parted.

That night she came to my room. When she walked in, I was sitting on the floor in near darkness. A small spotlight was trained on the area in front of me. All around me were magazines and scraps of paper, paints and pens. I couldn't see who had entered until her feet were within the circle of light. It was then that I realized that I'd been working under inadequate lighting for a couple of hours, having gotten so absorbed in my project that I hadn't noticed nightfall. She carried a basket, which she swung into the light just long enough for me to see that it contained a variety of delectable foods and a bottle of wine, a couple of glasses, and a small wrapped gift.

I motioned for her to turn on the floor lamp. I tried to get up, but I had worked myself onto a tiny island of rug space amid the sea of paper and magazines. Instead, I cleared a place for her, and we sat cross-legged with the basket between us. "It's to thank you for all the breakfasts you've made for me," she said. "You've been a one-person charity club for this poor indigent immigrant." She spread some brie onto a hunk of crusty bread and gave it to me. "Besides, I've been thinking about you, and when I called, Willy said you'd been up here all day." I was amazed that my roommate had even noticed, and flattered that Tara had cared.

I explained what I'd been doing, trying to depict my dream in collage form. I'd gotten the idea after she'd left that morning, and I had walked down to the Goodwill to buy up a stack of *National Geographics.* I hadn't considered that I'd have to carry them all back on foot. She marveled at what I'd done so far. It was powerful seeing different parts of my dream connecting in a unified visual whole. It portrayed a woman, representing me, standing with her back toward us, her arms outstretched over her head. She is surrounded by soil; buried beneath the earth. Above her the roots of a large plant end just out of her reach. Above the surface a sunny day washes over the vegetation, nurturing life. Underneath, part of the woman's body is beginning to decay, return to the soil. I already cannot see her feet.

Tara was enthralled. She decided to do one as well. She pulled the lamp closer and sat up on the bed. We worked until early morning. I expanded the richness of color above the earth's surface, and the tangle of roots, burrowing animals, and an increasing descending of darkness below. When we finished we propped the finished pieces up on the chest at the foot of the bed and cleared away just enough room to stretch out and look at them. We studied them for a long while without speaking.

Her collage depicted a large clay pot overflowing in a heap full of all kinds of stuff, some of which I could easily recognize as parts of her, others of which I knew nothing. The things at the top of the pile were precariously perched, looking as though they could topple over at any minute. An old woman with a deeply pained look of desperation was breaking through a crack near the bottom of the pot. A child's hand poked through under the old woman's armpit and held out an uprooted flower. A man and woman in a lovers' embrace had already fallen from the bowl, landing on their heads, crumbling apart.

We talked about our work for a long time. She remarked that she had borrowed some of my theme. She said we were alike in our search for fulfillment and in our need for expression. She wondered aloud whether either of us would ever find a man who could appreciate our depth.

I felt like I'd been stung. Nausea and numbness swept through me in waves. I had long since stopped looking for a man to fulfill me, having been out as a lesbian for several years. It seemed inconceivable that I wouldn't have mentioned that to her somewhere along the line. Perhaps I thought that my desire for her had been obvious.

The wine had made us both heavy with sleep. I looked over to see her eyelashes, like awnings over the windows of her soul, trying desperately to stay open. "Tara," I said. "You're not going all the way down to Quince Street tonight. Get up and let me clear off this bed and you can slip in under the covers." She didn't argue. I threw scissors, glue, and magazines off onto the floor. The scraps of cut-up paper remained. She stood up just long enough to step out of her clothes. She slid like a reed between the sheets. I pulled the covers up around her, turned off the lights, and crawled in beside her. The darkness curiously refreshed me. I lay staring into it while the shapes of my walls slowly came into focus, illuminated by the streetlamp outside my window. I felt thirsty. My legs tingled, going numb.

Tara turned on her side, facing me. The darkness had awoken her too. She thanked me for being her friend. With her words, I realized I had to let her know that I was in a different place. I wanted to be more than friends. My heart pounded with fear as I reached over to drape my arm over her. I whispered, "I love you." She said she loved me too. She had meant it, but she hadn't meant it as I had. I wanted her so badly. My desire was torturous. I thought I'd explode if I had to contain it any longer. I had to risk. Sliding my other arm under her head, I pulled her up to me and held her close. She snuggled up to me, holding on, and said good night.

After a while I fell asleep, wallowing in her embrace. When I awoke, the sun was bright against my window shade, casting a golden glow on us. She had just roused and was attempting to free herself from my arms. The cool of the morning chilled me as her warmth unfurled along with her body. While she headed for the bathroom, I stared at the ceiling, worrying about her reaction to what I'd done. She returned and I went to freshen up. I expected her to be dressed when I came back. To my surprise, she was lying on her stomach on top of the bed, facing the foot of it, still in her underwear. "Look at these things in this light," she laughed. "Aren't they amazing?"

I sat on the edge of the bed. Bits of paper stuck to my legs, itching. The collages were amazing indeed. In the golden softness of the morning, the cut edges of each image disappeared, and the collages looked seamless, as though they'd been painted on a canvas. The roots of mine looked alive. The woman appeared to be suffocating. We could feel her panic, her depth, the closeness of the air around her. Tara's bowl took on a three-dimensional quality, brimming with life spilling out toward us, uncontainable.

Without allowing myself to think about it, I grabbed her shoulder and turned her over on the bed. She gasped. I thought she was going to push me away and run off. She appeared to consider it. But I placed both my hands on her shoulders, gently. "Please stay," I choked. "I love you. I want you so badly. Please."

Tara's body tensed. I let go. But my hands would not retract. They lingered at the base of her neck. Slowly I began to trace her clavicle. I massaged the tops of her shoulders. She was leaning on her elbows. She focused on the window while I touched her. Her eyes looked like pools of melted chocolate kisses in butter. Her tension evoked a fierceness in me. Normally, I felt protective of her. But I could not protect her from myself. My body steeled against itself. I pulled her elbows from under her, lowering her flat onto the bed. She didn't resist. I placed a hand on her hip and pressed down while I buried my face in the softness just below her rib cage. With my teeth, I hoisted her T-shirt up past her breasts, letting my chin graze her nipples. I kissed around her neck and earlobes and ran a hand through her hair. It was as silky as I'd imagined. Her skin was cool, like glass. I began to plant tiny kisses along the ridge of her collarbone and down her arms while I moved a leg between her knees. She stiffened. She pushed against my shoulders. I slid my hands beneath her back and arched her toward me, swirling my chin in a big soft circle around her belly.

"Tell me to stop," I said.

She said nothing. I knew what she wanted. She wanted to let go, to spill over. But she wanted me to temper her flow, to contain her. I had not usually been so unyielding an aggressor in bed. But I trusted my instincts. I flattened my whole body against hers. My weight alone held her down. She wriggled beneath me, but I remained pressed against her. I reached down and caught hold of her arms, one at a time, pulling them up over her head and locking them by the wrists into my left hand. That's when I saw the first real glimmer of passion in her. Her breathing quickened. Her face flushed red. I kissed her, tenderly at first. She squirmed under me, sealing her lips tight. I nuzzled her neck, breathing hot into her ears. When she gasped I covered her lips with mine and sank my tongue inside her mouth, pushing past her teeth, forcing my tongue deep inside. She breathed wildly through her nostrils, heaving her chest open against mine.

I kissed her over and over, gently and then savagely. My gentleness made her bristle. My aggression made her hot. In a whim, I snapped her T-shirt up to her wrists and twisted it, making it easier for me to hold her down. She struggled against the ties and growled. I moved down to her neck, pressing my lips into her jugular, feeling her quickening pulse. I smoothed along her armpit with my cheek and rested my head on her chest, then flicked her nipples with my tongue. She writhed. I bit down lightly on them. Every time I began to move off of her, she rippled, straining against me. I wanted to explore her whole body. But I knew I couldn't let go of her wrists.

Kneeling between her legs, I lifted her and pulled the bedsheet up around her sides. She cooperated. Keeping it taut, I twisted it around her arms and folded it underneath her back. The bulge of its bulk had the added advantage of arching her toward me. It worked. As long as I kept her pressed down, she was bound. Sliding my hands along her sides, I brought my face to her pelvic bone and bit down softly. My two arms were rested along hers. My hands were clamped around her forearms. She surprised me, flailing her legs and then digging her heels into the mattress and pushing herself along, loosening the sheet's hold on her arms.

I reached under her, grabbed the cheeks of her ass, and pulled her back sharply. She yelled out so loudly that I thought my roommates would be alarmed. The weight of my arms and torso alone would not be enough to curtail her movement. I assessed the situation. If I could get her feet pinned, I could have my arms free. But how? Tiny scraps of paper jabbed into my legs. I looked down to where my pillows were propped up against the headboard. I grabbed them quickly, keeping one hand pressed into her stomach. I yanked off her underwear and then stacked the pillows along the insides of her legs, forcing them wide open. Two of the pillows were heavy bolsters. They rested against her knees, preventing them from bending.

Trussed to the bed, she lay open before me. I flattened against her again. I kissed her very sweetly, tentatively. "Do I have to find a way to keep you quiet?" I whispered.

She whimpered, "No."

"You'd better behave," I warned.

"I will. I promise," she said.

My blood was boiling. I wasted no time. I knew she wanted me to take her quick and hard, to make her surrender to me without reservation. I wanted to feel her ass again. It was small and firm, like holding a set of water balloons filled to near bursting. I lifted her mound toward me. A tangle of wet, dark moss met my mouth. She smelled like pungent earth. I let my knuckles furrow along her inner ridge. She squealed. I lifted up and saw that she was arched with her head looking far behind her. "What did I say?" I warned again. She cooed.

She was so wet that I needed no extra lubrication. I found an opening and plunged all five fingertips in. I felt her tighten. I pumped, penetrating her more deeply with every stroke. She bucked in tandem. My left hand still held her ass, which was driving me mad with its rhythmic clenching. I kneaded my palm into her fleshy gluteals while I drove my fingers like a piston. I needed to go harder faster. I drew back first, teasing. She cried out. She was ready. I wanted to make her beg. Feeling meaner by the minute, I commanded her. "If you want it, you're going to have to ask for it."

"No!" she cried.

"Yes," I countered. "You're gonna beg for it. Or I'll stop right now."

"No, please don't make me beg. I do want it."

I pulled out slowly, which made her arch deeper, furiously. "No, don't. For God's sake, don't stop." She twisted like a worm on a hook.

"All right, then," I taunted. "I'm going to have to take you hard, right now."

She groaned and whimpered some more. I squeezed her butt and plunged four fingers into her with full force. I left my thumb ridged upright so that it would graze and jab her clitoris with every plunge. This drove her wild. She rocked and bucked, acting like she was trying to escape but riding my hand with precision all the while. I let her work for it, making her fuck herself on my hand. She fought against her restraints until her legs were nearly free. Bucking madly, she came in a shiver of spasms, bearing down past my knuckles, massaging my hand as she throbbed, folding me inside her container gushing with wetness. She came over and over again. Just when I'd think she was done, she'd move just a twitch and shudder in orgasm once more.

Afterward, she curled up in my arms. We lay in silence for an eternity, until my stomach growled, signaling breakfast time. I suggested that she relax while I fixed us something. I'd bring it up to her.

When I returned, the room had been straightened. The magazines were piled in a stack, the bed was made, the window opened to the new day. She sat, still naked, in the center of the bed, smiling shyly. She had something in her hand. When I set down the tray, she handed me the small gift-wrapped package I'd seen in the basket the night before. I sat down on the edge of the bed, wanting to unwrap her again instead but curious about what was in the box.

To my amazement, it was a hand-tooled sterling ring of delicately twisted roots. She must've paid a fortune for it. "I saw it yesterday right after you told me your dream. I thought you should have it," she said. I wanted to cry.

Instead, I kissed her. In my best Scottish brogue I said, "It's lovely."

Pas de Deux

by Kanyon Sweet

PROLOGUE

I dance.

My mother says that when I was very little, I spent hours posturing and cavorting for grandma and grandpa, twirling and whirling in their living room to music that grandma played from the concert grand.

Everyone in my family dances.

Dance is what we did for hours in the long living room on Granger Street, the furniture shoved to the edges of the room and the oval braided carpet rolled up. Cousins and playmates are captured as whirling dervishes on the old eight-millimeter film that my dad shot at birthday parties with the Kodak Brownie.

Dancing is what my father and mother did to the full-blast stereo sounds of Glen Gray and the Casa Loma Orchestra. My dearest memory of my father is watching him glide across the living room, the windows rattling from the bass reverberations, lost in his recollections of his younger adulthood on the dance floors where Benny Goodman played, leading my mother in his arms, she laughing and crying, "Oh, Frank!"

We did it all on the living room stage. We tapped. We tried to balance on our toes. We tripped over each other's feet learning to "boy girl" dance. We learned to rock and roll to Dick Clark's *American Bandstand.* We twisted and shouted through all the changing choreography as we danced our way through adolescence, and all of us eventually exited the dance floor stage in search of the perfect partner.

In looking back it is evident that dance is the medium of the metaphor that choreographs whatever new step I need to learn to help make it through one of life's passages. Dance is love's aphrodisiac at the start, or a balm to soothe a wounded heart at the impasse. Dancing is whatever my soul requires for establishing peace or for waging acts of love. The Womyn's Dance Saturday night would provide the score for rocking and rolling away remains of my last heartbreaking affair.

I.

Climbing from the seat of the pickup, I fingered the rolled-up sleeves of my T-shirt and pushed the tails into my Levis. I stomped the heels of my boots together to make sure my pant legs fell over the instep. I tugged at the silver labrys around my neck. Finally, I took a deep breath, adjusted into my most formidable butch posture, and walked into The Dance, alone.

Allow yourself a fantasy, dear reader, and imagine, now, that here, before the lead assumes her position on the dance floor, the action stops. The dancers pause, holding their positions in midair. The orchestrator and choreographer put their heads together. They argue the details, their voices rise, and then whisper. The choreographer gesticulates and waves the sheet music. How to stage a grand entrance? How to capture the audience with the rising tension? How to stage the ultimate rise to the fall? The prima donna is waiting in the wings. Her lead is posing and stretching from the other corner of the stage. The maestros come to an agreement, and the dancers are called to the stage.

It was merely part of the choreography that the prima donna simply danced into my life, and my heart, that night. From my vantage point across the floor, clearly this woman was different from every other lesbian dancing or lining the walls waiting to dance! She was not in costume. No blue jeans, no tux, no tie, no cowgirl boot-scootin' attire, no rolled-up sleeves, no white shirt and vest, none of the standard cruising-the-dyke-dance-scene action wear. What she had on moved with her when she danced, was soft and silky, and she was bare-armed and barefooted. She could dance, and I was going to dance with this lady.

I watched from the door, waiting for her to leave her partner, and when the disco beat faded into the next track, I moved across the room and wordlessly held out my hand to take her back to the floor. Wheat colored, bleached bangs fell over her eyes. With a moment's hesitation, she pushed back her hair from her face, and began to move in assent. When she looked at me, the rhythm of the dance rolled from the speaker vibrations through her and into me. The seduction began. This woman moved right and I followed to the right. She moved left, and I followed to the left. She danced back and drew me with her. With every shift of course, I flowed with her, feeling the growing swell of an emotional river. Shoulder roll right and shoulder roll left, and closer still until our breasts touched and we were swaying together so close that I could look into her eyes and feel a current pulling me irretrievably from any safe shore. And so swept, we danced until the night was over and I held her tentatively close for a few bars of the last dance and released her into the night, not sure that I'd ever have the courage to call the number on the business card she left in my hand. I looked down at her name: Regan.

II.

How many days could I wait? Four. I called. Regan says to come Saturday for breakfast! "My house is the one with the pink front door. You can't miss it."

What kind of woman has a pink front door?

A dancer and an artist. A woman who has a flowing waterfall in her back yard and a pond with water lilies and goldfish. A woman who paints floral sprays from a watercolor palette of sun-washed pastels. A woman who whips up pancakes from a gourmet recipe, who brews coffee so strong and rich that it changes my whole breakfast palate. A woman who says, "I should tell you, I'm not really sure I'm gay. I only just left my husband a few weeks ago."

But there, the next day in Sunday's paper, is the ad for the Russian ballet performance of classic pas de deux! Undaunted and determined to find a place on this lady's dance card, I ask once again. Through the phone wires I can feel her brushing the yellow shock from her forehead, and with that same moment's hesitation I felt on the dance floor, she says, "Yes."

III.

The ballet, however, is weeks away. What do I do in the weeks before the ballet? Waiting patiently is not my forte. What better place to act out this metaphor than to take her to the bar, to join in the press of sweating bodies and throbbing pelvises that pump and sway to disco music pounding out the drum beat of the mating ritual of the lesbian dancers.

The bar is new to her, and I like to show that I know my way around. I feel like such a butch to this female! So I slide up to the bar and come away with her white wine. But the music is cued up and the rhythm is too primitive, too seductive to resist. Glasses down, we are again on the dance floor, lesbians all around us pulsating to the same beat, all Eros and foreplay. I dared to pull her close and push my pelvis into her pelvis and turned her to hold her butt to belly and put my lips in her hair and on her neck. We throbbed together until sweat poured from every pore and mascara ran down her face, until I swear that I could feel her melt into me through the wetness. We closed the dance floor. The lights went on and we were thrown into the dark outside where the night air blew a cool breeze between us, breaking the spell. With a hug and a promise she sent me into the night, alone.

IV.

Tonight is the ballet. How I had badgered the ticket seller to make sure we could get the best seats still left in the house! Center floor is nearly perfect. Together we are nearly perfect. Me in a tux and Regan dark and sophisticated in hunter green and cream, the most handsome couple in the house. As the ballet unfolds on the stage, next to me I can feel Regan sway and count rhythm. She leans and whispers that this ballerina is exceptionally strong. She leans and tells me to catch the beadwork on the tutu. She leans and hands me the opera glasses. She leans and pulls me to her—magnetized. Once again I feel myself being mesmerized by the magic of the dance, caught up in the choreography. But it's over so soon and into the crisp air that I worry the spell, like at the bar that night, will be broken. But then Regan is telling me about her shoes, her toe shoes and her tap shoes and her trunk of dance costumes that were hers when she danced professionally.

"You'd love tap," she tells me. "It's a great workout, you're a natural, and you'd love it! Come home with me and come see my shoes. We'll smoke a joint and then we'll put the shoes on you and let you tap on my hardwood floor."

So Regan opens a closet and pulls out the box of dancing treasures and tells me details about how shoes are tied and taps screwed on to have the perfect resonance on the floor. And there are the shoes, all patent and pink bows, and satin slippers with grosgrain laces. We sip wine and we smoke dope and move to the living room with the wood floor where she puts the magic on my feet, carefully lacing the bows so that they don't drag on the floor.

Here I am in my tuxedo, in tap shoes, and if only I had a cane and a top hat! At first a tentative click and tap. Then the other foot, less tentative. Regan shows me how to make the tap brush, how to make it whisper. I fantasize a roll and a rhythm that can't possibly be coming from my feet, but she says I'm a natural. Of course I'm a natural! I've been dancing all my life. Right here and now is the living fantasy of all the dance lessons I never took, the stages I never graced, all the performances I never gave, the embodiment of style and movement in athleticism that I secretly harbor in the private recesses of my heart! I am totally seduced by the fantasy of dancing into the wings of romance and passion!

I am totally loaded.

It's Regan's turn. She ties on the shoes. She postures. She brushes and clicks and taps, losing herself in her own fantasies while I find my way to the sofa and slowly sink into the recesses of too much dope and too much wine.

I sit there on the sofa, somehow sensible enough to know that if I can't stand up on my feet any longer, I'm not driving home. I watch Regan slip off her dancing shoes and disappear into the hallway. It gets colder in the house as the night takes over. Somewhere I think I hear a clothes dryer turn. Bewildered by the incongruity of hearing laundry being done, my worry begins to mount. Needing a place to stay is beginning to feel very awkward. I hadn't even kissed this woman yet! Somehow that reality confuses the whole issue of where I will sleep. The dryer sound stops, and Regan reappears in the doorway with a fresh blanket. She tosses it over me, hot from the dryer. "You know I can't drive," I apologize. "You're fine," she tells me as she snuggles next to me, pulling the warmth tight around our shoulders. The dancing shoes are forgotten, as is the question of where I will sleep.

After a few moments, Regan picks up my hand and begins caressing my fingers. We compare the size of our bones, the length of our fingers, and wonder at the fragile thinness of our wrists. A new dance begins. She strokes my arms and strokes my fingers. I shiver and tentatively stroke back, not knowing where or how far this will go. Then I am trembling with the realization that this woman has begun caressing my lips with the tips of her nails, that she is brushing the side of my forehead with her lips and smoothing the hair back from my face. Regan places her hand on my cheek and turns my face to meet her gaze. She parts her lips and pulls my mouth to hers. I had barely quit worrying about where I was going to stay when she stands and pulls me to the stairs to her bedroom. She takes me up the first few steps and asks, "Is this OK?" I briefly flash on the dancing shoes, and the ballet, and the bar, and the rhythm of our bodies on the dance floor. When she asks me again if it's okay, my heart laughs out loud.

The hardwood stairs to Regan's bedroom are steep and narrow. They creak conspiratorially as she beckons me upstairs. From the corner of my eye, I glimpse watercolored flowers blossoming from frames that trellis the stairwell. A closed door at the top signals me that this is a room of her own. When Regan pulls me through the door, I am enveloped in shades of subtle soft pink and feminine florals everywhere. Thoughts race through my mind, curious images of this former husband of ten years. I wonder where he fit amid all this female pulchritude with no evidence of male inhabitance. But never mind—Regan pulls back the sheets and lays herself on the pillows, lowers me to her side, and orders, "Take off my clothes." The music has changed from an ol' soft shoe to something more like *Bolero.* Hours of foreplay in the living room have culminated with urgency.

Regan's silky evening clothes are hooked with intricate little fasteners and small pearly buttons. She whispers, "Let me." Regan unbuttons the top and arches her shoulder to help me slide the silken fabric from deeply suntanned shoulders. Her breasts are barely covered by a wisp of lacy brassiere that unhooks from the front. As I slip the clasp, Regan arches her back, tilts her head, and bares her neck in an archetypal ritual of submission. Her posturing fires a primitive, instinctual frenzy that contracts the walls of my vagina and floods me with wetness. I inhale the fragrance behind her ears, rim my tongue around her earlobe, and then teasingly sink my teeth into the soft flesh between her collarbone and the taut muscles of her arched neck. Suckling and nuzzling her neck and shoulders, my hand finds small, hard breasts. I take her nipple between my fingers, roll and stretch the skin until her tit is erect. I verge the sensation just to the edge of pain, listening for her breathing to increase, gushing inside myself even more when she parts her lips with a promising moan of anticipation. Then I cover her lips with my mouth, drinking deep inside until she pushes my head down to her breasts and arches for me to suck them. I pull away to study her breasts and dark nipples. There are no white tan lines marring these breasts that kiss the sun in worship. I lower my head and roll my tongue around the dark outline of the areola. I suck and pull her nipple with my teeth until a gasp escapes from her lips. Fueled by the sound of her breathing, my responses are primal and urgent. Quivering from excitement and frustration that I am still dressed, I disengage long enough to unpeel the layers of my evening clothes. Standing there naked in front of her, looking down at this golden female, I am filled with amazement at the perfection of her body. Yet she gazes back and tells me, "You are beautiful."

I lie down next to her again. I find her breasts with both my hands, cupping them into firm mounds, and run my tongue from one erect nipple to the other. Then I slide down the middle of her chest with my face to the rippled belly muscles and to the edge of the clothes that she still has on, vainly protecting her from the certainty of penetration. I lift Regan's butt from the bed to pull off her dress pants, and I let them fall to the floor.

Regan is wearing no panties. Her dark hair pushes through nylon hosiery. I blow into the triangle beneath the nylon with long, deep hot breaths. She moans and thrusts upward. Trying to be slow and careful, I roll the elastic down to her belly button, under her butt, and over the angles of her hipbones, while brushing my lips across her stomach. I glide the stockings from her legs, one at a time, down hard dancer thighs, off her toes and drop them with the other silken pieces in their unshaped folds on the rose carpet.

Now naked and fully exposed to me, Regan's deep breaths force muscles to contract across her stomach, urging her pelvis to arch toward me. I cry in wonderment, "You're perfect, you're so perfect." I squelch my cries with the salt of her sweaty belly rolling across my tongue. Her raw femaleness, without a trace of political correctness, without a hint of butchness, evokes a state of sexual urgency from the depths of my loins. I marvel in this urge to thrust, to penetrate. I know that what I want to do more than anything is to crawl on top of her and plunge inside and fuck this woman until she wraps her soul around me and comes, taking me with her.

I think it's impossible to quell the urgency rising up in me, but a voice inside warns, "Wait, wait! Go slow!" Barely reining my desire, I lower myself down to her hips and bury my face in the tendrils of her hair, while I firmly, slowly, and hungrily spread her legs to tease and caress that hairless smooth place on the inside of each thigh. Regan's fingers run through my hair to pull me closer. I take this as assent to go down between her legs. I reach under her butt and lift her mound to my lips.

There I drink thirstily of all her deep rose and purple female wetness. Lapping and sucking and rolling her clitoris around on my tongue, I inhale deeply of her mossy smell until I am so intoxicated that I am conscious of nothing but the pounding of my vagina and the wet juice sliding down my leg.

Regan's voice then whispers from somewhere above me, "Come closer. I want you closer." She pulls my face to her face and I let her savor the bouquet of her own wine.

She rolls over on top of me and tentatively moves her hand down my hips. Regan has never done this before. I put my hand over hers firmly and push away the nervousness coming through her fingers. I guide her to my opening, signaling to her that yes, I do want you to do this. Her middle finger finds the wetness between my lips. Regan inhales with surprise. Parting the folds, she slips into me. Slowly at first. Regan slides in and out, over my clitoris, and back inside, building confidence until she is fucking me rhythmically. I can feel that she is still a little uncertain. I should give her more reassurance. I should tell her I like this. I should let her know that I'm dying from lust, but I can't breathe, I can't talk, and my head is spinning me somewhere outside this reality. As she is pumping her fingers in me deeper and more insistently, the thought crosses my mind that I don't come this way. But I am, now, anyway. I feel my body ebb and flow with the currents of chardonnay, cannabis, and cunt juice coursing within me.

"There," I whisper to her between gasps of breath, "there, there..."

Fighting an urge to drift into unconsciousness, I roll her over and pull her to my body, cupping her butt in my hand, rocking with her to bring me back to myself. I pull the covers up to keep her warm, brush my lips over her eyelids, to her cheeks, and lay my lips on hers, while letting my fingers trail their way to her hips, her butt, and to the inside of her thighs.

"Make me come, please!" She is begging me.

Sliding my hand between her legs and nudging them open, I feel her breathing speed up again. She rolls back submissively to give me access. I trail along the crease of her thigh and push her legs farther open. Her knees rise up in anticipation and she lets her legs fall fully apart. All the folds, one by one, I push aside to unleash the flood of wetness.

"Look at me," I insist.

I make Regan watch my eyes as I pull wetness from her with the tips of my fingers and rim my lips with her come. I watch her face, making her keep her eyes open, as I slide but one finger inside, and gently part the walls preparing them to take more of me. I can feel her tension mounting. Sliding one finger out, I put two together, and slither in and out slowly, until she is nearly crying in desperation to be fucked. She closes her eyes and gives way into my arms so that I can fill her over and over with all my fingers. In measured sequence, her breathing stops and her body stiffens with the struggle to come. I let her suffer with passion for a few moments, drawing her closer, until it's time for mercy. I trail my fingers to her clitoris and stroke firmly until her breaths become gasps and she comes pounding underneath my fingers. I cup my full hand over her triangle, rub swollen lips together, teasing out the last tremor, and then massage her belly to release one final contraction from her womb.

Rolling Regan to her side, I swaddle her in the blankets and pull her close to me, butt nestled inside the curve of my belly. I realize that the lamp beside the bed is still on. I reach over and turn it out. As I drift to unconscious depths, I hear her whisper to me.

"You know you're the first woman."

V.

In the morning Regan is silent and turns her head when I try to kiss her. "I'm afraid that I didn't do it right, that I didn't please you," she murmurs. I am amazed and hurt that she even questioned my response to her. There was no reassurance for her that I had been carried to heaven with her touch. Her silence filled the spaces and pushed me to the door. It was time for me to leave. My evening clothes were in a pile on the floor. Regan went to her closet and pulled out a pair of men's slacks. "These are a pair my husband left here. You can wear these home." She hugged me good-bye. There was a chill in the morning air as I stepped outside. I called later. The answering machine clicked on. She never returned my calls.

EPILOGUE

I think about Regan sometimes. I recall the brush of the bangs from the forehead, the moment's hesitation before saying yes, the disclosures from the first, a husband whose pants were still in the closet. We had never danced to the same song. I should have been listening all along.

Lately I've taken to listening to country music. There was a time when no country station would cross my radio dial. I guess I can change my tune when I need to.

Country is so simple, so straight, so straightforward. You live some, you love some, and you lose some. Heroines don't have "issues," they have broken hearts. Heroes settle their scores with good, clean acting-out. Somebody steals your gal, you wallow in your beer for a chorus or two and shoot out the jukebox when the song is too sad and the heartbreak too much to bear.

You know, I've been wanting to learn to two-step. I imagine a butch in 501s bringing me a beer from the bar and leading me around the dance floor on country night. Tap dancing never was my style.

The radio is playing right beside me. A new tune beats out through the speakers, and I break momentarily from my reverie to catch the singer.

Love is a slow dance.
Love's rock 'n roll.
Hate bein' a wallflower
Cuz her dance card is full.

The metaphors in country are clean and simple.

THE GIRL FROM KENTUCKY

by Caitlin S. Curran

Phoebe reminded me of a dancer, with her long flowing hair like a waterfall and her eyes laughing, wise, smiling as she leaned in to kiss me, slightly uncertain, like me. Long legs like a ballerina, legs that grabbed onto the sides of a horse when we took off down a dirt road, whooping and hollering like there was no tomorrow, like we needed to make today last forever.

"Caitlin!" she'd call out. "I'll bet Colt and I can beat you and Whiskey! Let's start at the tree, go to the stone wall. Loser buys dinner in town the next night out!"

And I would agree, and off we'd go, thundering down the road on our two buckskins, mine the savvy old ranch horse, hers the youngster we were training up to be a good mount for the wranglers. And Phoebe's hair would fly out from under her hat, and it would stream back in the wind all honey and maple syrup-colored, and I would race after her from one boundary of the camp to the other and never even notice how far we were going.

I was Phoebe's supervisor at a summer camp, at times humbly and occasionally arrogantly ruling over her and four other wranglers and hordes of children and, of course, the horses who were the big draw, the lifelong fantasy for children and young staff alike. When Phoebe asked to be my fifth wrangler, saying she knew a bit about horses and wasn't afraid to try, and the job she'd initially been offered as a plain old counselor wasn't as exciting as she'd hoped, I said yes because of her waterfall hair and her crystalline green eyes and the delicate hearts-and-flowers shape of her face. Oh, and she could ride a little, she said. With qualifications like that, how could I possibly refuse her?

My friend Megan, the waterfront director, teased me about the "hottie babe" (our term for a sex goddess) I had chosen to complete my staff of wild horsewomen. I laughed at her and looked longingly at Phoebe's gentle, slightly mischievous blue-green eyes and the soft pink lips she often turned my way in a smile. I was hooked.

Phoebe was from Kentucky. *Kee-in-tucky* was how she would say it, drawling her voice to a ridiculous degree, making us all laugh at the little southern gal, out in California seeing the sights, setting her life straight, figuring things out, exploring the world with the hippie-bohemian eyes her parents gave to her. She was born in San Francisco, in the freewheeling Haight-Ashbury district, and lived on a commune the first ten years of her life. When she first told me about the commune, all I could think about was her walking around naked, and it made me weak in the knees. Now she went to college in Lexington. I asked her if she had ever been to the Kentucky Derby, and she said no, but she was going to see it one day and get all dressed up, which apparently was the thing to do, drink mint juleps, and scream herself raw cheering on the prettiest horse. I told her to drink a mint julep for me if she ever made it to the Derby, and she awarded me a teasing smile that gave me stunning hot flashes.

Phoebe came to camp to work with kids and live with all women for two months, like she'd been aching to do, although she had a boyfriend back in the bluegrass state. She spent insane amounts of time on the phone with her boyfriend that summer. After the kids were tucked away at night and we could breathe a bit, she would saunter off to the old building above the pool that had the pay phone none of the kids was supposed to know about. She would talk sometimes until 1 in the morning, and when our alarms went off at 6 the next day, I would allow Phoebe to sleep in a little, knowing that she was tired from those nonphysical trysts with her boyfriend, a thousand miles away. Sometimes the other staff grumbled at me and cast hard looks Phoebe's way. But I was in love with Phoebe's quick laughter and her sexy walk and my nightly fantasies that involved just the two of us, so I carelessly brushed aside their complaints and let Phoebe do pretty much whatever she pleased. Besides—I had Megan to tease and whisper to and play with whenever I wanted.

Megan was one of my closest friends and my new lover that year—her fourth summer at camp, my fifth and last. I first met her when she was 17 and I was 20. This entanglement with her was new and exciting for me: being sexual with an old friend who'd been coming on to me for the past two summers; who was, in fact, my first female lover. That last summer I just up and crawled into her sleeping bag during a night off that we were illegally spending together in the big meadow (while in camp, even during time off, staff were not supposed to sleep anywhere but in their own beds, alone). I shocked the hell out of her and surprised myself, but I had been itching to find out what lesbian lust was all about, and she had been itching to find out what I was all about, so it ended up fine.

We played discreetly all summer, or as discreetly as we could. The kids weren't supposed to know the staff were at all sexual, of course. It being a women-only place, there were always a lot of flirtations and sex and little dyke dramas going on. But policy's policy, and none of us eager little bunnies wanted to get fired just for having fun at the wrong time. So Megan and I were very careful, even though her position as waterfront director and mine as head wrangler gave us pretty good job security. I was excited by this new aspect of my life, and it occupied my thoughts much of the summer.

But then there was Phoebe—she of the long honey-colored hair and aquamarine eyes, and I just couldn't shake off the bedazzling effect she had on me. I fell in love with her when I first saw her, in love with the dreamy possibility that a ridiculously beautiful and strong woman could want me as a friend and maybe even as a lover. She had that irrepressible je ne sais quoi that made my head spin and put a hot spot in my crotch, and sometimes when I was with Megan I dreamed that it was Phoebe under my lips and tongue, Phoebe begging me for more, Phoebe who was grabbing me and kissing me and biting my earlobes and nipples and thighs.

And surprise, surprise—Phoebe was wondering what it would be like too. This is how I found out.

At the end of one long and dusty day, all the wranglers were showering in our community bathroom. Phoebe and I went last, since there were only four showers and there were six of us. Phoebe always went last anyway, which I attributed to her languid Southern ways. I was in a changing stall, drying my hair, when Phoebe said, "Caitlin, are you done with your shampoo? I forgot mine in the cabin. Can I use yours?"

I said "Sure" and slipped it through her shower curtain.

Uh-uh. None of that modesty stuff for little miss here. She

whipped open the curtain like she was making a grand entrance into a ballroom and stood before me in all her naked glory.

I must've stared a tad longer than was strictly necessary, because she actually posed for me: head slightly tilted to the side, one leg cocked up with only the toes touching the floor, breasts flung toward me like an offering. And what an offering they were: perfect, round, full, beautiful, with rosy nipples. My eyes boggled, my mouth drooled, and my crotch snapped to attention with a clench that sent this really groovy tremor down my spine—you know, the one that tells you sometime soon you're going to have earthshaking sex with this person.

"The shampoo, Caitlin," she reminded me, extending a hand for it. Her eyes were on me like lanterns, all bright and focused, a beacon for the ocean of desire within me. She wasn't hiding a thing from me, neither body nor lust, and she was telling me as plainly as she could, without actually giving voice to the words, that she wanted me.

I handed her the shampoo. Our fingers met for an electrifying instant, wet sliding across dry, and I nearly lost my balance. Then she smiled a thank-you, withdrew both hand and shampoo, and closed the curtain over her melting loveliness.

My wobbly legs almost didn't take me down to dinner, not a hundred feet away. That night, alone in my bunk but listening to Phoebe's sleep-sighs and tossings in the bed right above mine, I almost imploded keeping myself quiet when I came, imagining her lips on me, teasing me with those deep blue-green pools that passed for her eyes.

When I repeated the incident to Megan the next day, she exclaimed, "*Whoo-ee!* She wants you bad! Damn, I'm jealous. She is beyond hottie babe. She is queen o' lust incarnate." Megan fanned herself and panted. I lightly punched her arm and she grinned at me. "I would *definitely* do her."

Megan and I had a sort of open relationship, in which we could and often did give grades for level of sexual turn-on by the women at the camp. I was gratified to know that Megan had given me a high grade the first summer she met me, and it hadn't gone down since. I wondered how Phoebe would mark me.

Phoebe had been watching me and Megan all summer, seeing our relationship unfold, waiting, wondering, and slowly going crazy from sexual starvation, separated from her man. She knew what kind of girls we all were, and though she wasn't one, she wanted to find out. And I finally let her.

On break for a few days at my apartment about a hundred miles northwest of the camp, during which Meg and Phoebe had said they would help me move since my lease was up, Phoebe and I went shopping at the local mall. We each tried on all the girlie outfits that made us look sexy and very womanly, and we giggled a lot, something we would never do at camp, where we slung 100-pound bales of hay around like they were so much fluff and had the strongest arms and thighs of all the staff from riding and tussling with cranky horses. Each of us bought a new dress, and we arrived back at my apartment jazzed up and ready to show off our newfound femininity.

I called Megan, who was staying at her mother's house about 20 minutes away, and demanded that she come right over to take us out to dinner. She hemmed and hawed, but I played up the new outfits and sounded all come-hither over the phone—Phoebe had been fixing me Southern drink creations and I was heading toward the fly-to-the-moon phase of drunkenness. Megan heard the giggles of two women—one of whom she had, one of whom she wanted—and said she would be over *tout de suite.*

Over dinner at a nearby Claim Jumper restaurant, we flirted with Megan until she blushed from the attention. I called her a butch with her two femmes (being a bit unclear on the concept but thinking it was somewhat accurate), and her eyes about popped out of her head as she frantically shushed me and looked around to see if anyone in this bastion of breeders had heard my comment. When we finally made it back to my barren, box-filled apartment, we talked and teased and played let's-discover-one-another's-sexual-history drinking games. My roommate, who also worked with us at camp, was thankfully visiting her family for the break.

At one point we got to talking about threesomes. Megan, being an old hand at that activity, of course, told tales of her frisky exploits with friends beneath the sheets. Looking from her to me, raising her beer bottle to her delicious lips, Phoebe asked, "But if you and Caitlin brought someone else into your bed, wouldn't you be jealous?"

"Not if she's as sexy as you are!" Megan yelped, and tackled me to the ground in a steamy kiss. I saw Phoebe gulp her drink in one swallow at both the revelation and the kiss, and I gulped myself.

I remember disappearing with Megan behind the door of my room later amid sly smiles when we finally said good night, leaving Phoebe to bunk alone in the living room, attempting to be quiet during the sex. I fiercely imagined my golden woman in the room right next to me, her beckoning smile and her unsubtle advances toward me—but I still didn't figure that she would *really* want to be in here with us. I fell asleep dreaming about her smooth skin and her rose-colored lips, but I firmly told myself to spend the remainder of the summer doing only that.

The next day at about 1 in the afternoon, Phoebe and Meg and I were sitting on my balcony, drinking Ten High Kentucky Whiskey mixed with Coca-Cola, lolling around in the melting July sun like a bunch of dimwits, going crazy during this sorely needed distance from children and animals and other grumpy staff.

We mixed the bourbon and coke into huge shots, using the very large plastic cups you get at Burger King or McDonald's as part of a promotional gimmick. Some male basketball star stared back at me from my cup as I downed the godawful mix, and I let out a shriek like a train whistle.

"Phoebe, this stuff's hideous! Damn, woman, it's disgusting—what the hell do you Kentuckians do, raise babies on this crap?" She had given me a cup that was exactly half bourbon and half Coke, and Megan was falling over herself laughing.

I sputtered and gagged while Phoebe primly drank hers down, not spilling a drop. She gave me a sweet smile, wiped my chin, laughed, and tossed an ice cube at me. Megan grabbed another few cubes and tossed them back, grinning devilishly with the expression I recognized as her unleashed wild child. Phoebe shrieked and arched her back, exposing her front side to me in sharply outlined detail as she strained away from the coldness sliding down her back into the soft fuzz above her neon-bright bikini bottoms.

That's how the whole little balcony party thing started. Phoebe was wearing her shocking yellow-and-orange bathing suit, the one with the stiff cups in the top for which she received merciless teasing from everyone when she was at the camp pool. She picked up another ice cube and ran it sort of suggestively across her breasts, not quite daring to look at us. I could see her pulse hammering in her neck, glistening under a sheen of sweat, and I knew right then what was going to happen. I remember lowering my sunglasses to look at Phoebe with my eyes, uncovered and real, trying to make sure that what I was seeing was what I was seeing and that she really wanted it. At that point, I certainly did.

Megan looked at me with raised eyebrows, grinning wickedly, and she reached her hand to Phoebe's hair and ran her fingers through it. Phoebe smiled at me and lobbed another ice cube my way that hit my legs and landed in my crotch, and she reached over to retrieve it. I remember the way her fingers trailed over my skin and the dark cloth of my bathing suit, and how I inanely thought of fire and ice and how I was thanking God that my roommate wasn't home, because how would she ever understand this?

I was half-sprawled next to Megan, and she leaned over and began unabashedly kissing me on the brilliant, sunny balcony in this redneck town, home of IMPEACH CLINTON bumper stickers on the backsides of plenty of tough black Ford trucks, which were also equipped with KFRG stickers portraying the inanely smiling green frog who promised the best and the most country music. We must have given the neighbors a good show on that hot, muggy summer day.

Watching us kiss, and of course having all the alcohol sloshing around in her system, had apparently finally gotten Phoebe's motor revved so high she wasn't going to turn it off. A few moments after Megan finally let me go, Phoebe leaned over and delicately, curiously, trustingly kissed me. I remember her lips, tasting strongly like raspberry lip balm with SPF 10 and faintly of bourbon and Coke and of her own sweet skin, and her mouth that spoke so eloquently of the need, the need for me and my touch. I remember how excited and shaky and yet somehow loose and calm I was, sitting there on my hot balcony with her, my wondrous Phoebe dancer, the woman who had been haunting my dreams every night all summer in that little cabin in the mountains, as she tossed in her sleep in the bunk above me. I was awestruck that she had chosen me to be her first, and I vowed that it would be magical.

We stayed kissing on the balcony, Phoebe alternating from kissing me to being kissed and fondled by Megan (who saw no sense in pussyfooting around and liked to cut to the chase), soothed by music from Megan's portable boom box (my stereo was already packed up), until I eventually realized that this was really and truly becoming a ménage à trois and that we had best get ourselves out of the gaze of our surely dyke-hating neighbors. I vaguely understood that not only was I (and Megan, I somewhat jealously conceded) introducing Phoebe to sex with another woman, Megan was also giving both of us our first threesome. I was in the dual role of seductress and innocent, and it was both titillating and confusing.

Once inside my room with the curtains drawn over the balcony doorway, we somehow managed to undress, but I don't recall if we undressed each other or if we took off our own clothes. I remember kissing long and slow and sweet, and I remember Phoebe reclining on the floor, her hair waving silky around my face as I traced her perfect pink lips with my tongue and nibbled on her earlobe. I recall her sigh and her closed eyes as she tilted her head back to expose her slender tanned neck to me, and I remember the tangy taste of her skin as I skimmed my teeth along her collarbone and licked the hollow just above her breasts.

The long sheer curtains over my sliding glass door billowed lightly in the breeze as we three lay in a naked heap on the mostly empty floor of my room. Phoebe, the beautiful, innocent virgin being offered up to the carnal unicorn, was the focus of our ministrations. While Megan was kissing her mouth, I was stroking her belly and hips with hands that were still trembling at this mind-blowing event. When I moved up to kiss Phoebe's soft mouth, Megan moved down to nuzzle her belly button and run a tentative hand over her silky, tangled hairs. I felt Phoebe shake at that touch, and I wanted to be the one causing it.

I gently moved Megan aside and laid myself on top of Phoebe. I placed little butterfly kisses along her collarbone, I teased her ear with my breath, I darted my tongue between her soft lips and dove into her mouth with abandon, tasting and exploring, listening to her hiccups of air between the little cries and the quiet moans. She opened her eyes and pushed me back a bit, but it was only to study my face for a moment and to touch it with curious fingers. She traced my jawline, then dropped her other hand down my back and ran it along my ass. I tensed in surprise, and both she and Megan giggled.

Megan settled herself against a pillow so that she was behind Phoebe, and Phoebe was resting against her. Megan moved her hands over Phoebe's breasts, over her head, and smiled at me. I could almost hear her thinking, *Good girl, you're a quick study.*

With Phoebe, I felt like I had been making love to women all my life, rather than having just experienced my own first time a month earlier. My lips knew exactly how to please her and my hands knew just the right touch to make her shiver in my arms. As Megan held her and stroked her and murmured encouragement to us both, I licked my way over Phoebe's body, pausing over the hard planes of her hips. She moved sensually under my tongue, and I took my lips up one side of her rib cage and down the other. She breathed in sharply and grabbed my head.

"Kiss me here," she whispered, and drew my head to her breasts in a gesture that was oddly reminiscent of a mother giving her child the milk of her body. I latched on to one pink English-rose nipple, rolled the bud around in my mouth, gently bit until she squealed, softly, like a kitten. "Yes," she said, tipping her head back against Megan's ample chest. Megan took full advantage of that move and rubbed her chest against Phoebe's face, kissing her and squeezing her beautiful breasts.

With my other hand, I reached between Phoebe's thighs, the same ones that could grip a horse in full flight or provide the strength to leap on bareback, now soft and pliant and aching for my touch. She willingly parted her legs for my questing fingers, and I briefly traced her slick inner lips.

"Caitlin," she moaned. It was so sexy hearing her say my name, usually spoken only in the squeaky-clean atmosphere of children, with such husky longing that I felt a new wave of heat roll over me.

"Do you like this?" I asked. My voice was low, raw with my desire. Eyes still closed, she nodded against Megan's breasts, arching her pelvis toward me. Turning her head slightly, she danced her tongue around Megan's left nipple and licked with long, swirling strokes, eliciting a sharp intake of breath from Megan.

I half sat up and continued my exploration with my fingers. After circling my forefingers on her thighs for several minutes, which caused her to tremble and breathe so fast I thought she might pass out, I slowly inched upward into the curly dark gold hair between her legs. My fingers delicately found their way into her, and every bucking move she made, every little sound that fell from her mouth, made me so wet I thought the top of my head would blow off. She tilted her hips toward me just a bit, and my fingers slipped in naturally and found a rhythm we both liked, and I spent several minutes just sliding in and out of her, matching her movement for movement, gasp for gasp. Megan was practically going crazy watching all this from above, and I knew she wanted to come as badly as I did. When Megan finally reached for my hand and pulled it toward her, down toward her own dark patch, I let her, adjusting myself somewhat so I could touch both of them at the same time and not lose my hands to cramps.

With my right hand twitching and tensing inside Phoebe and my left rapidly stroking Megan's clit, I alternated movements between the two of them, fluttering gently on one and stoking furiously on the other, then abruptly switching motions, causing both of them to gasp in unison. I was getting into this. I had sexual power over two incredible women, and it felt damned good.

Still keeping my fingers on Phoebe's clit, I leaned over her face to kiss Megan and nip at her neck. Phoebe suddenly reached up with her tongue and began lapping at my breasts, and I nearly fell on both of them from that touch. As her tongue moved more quickly over my hardened nipples, accompanied on occasion by her teeth, so did my fingers. Megan began panting, emitting these little squeaky breaths, and I knew she was on the verge of coming all over my hand. Then she abruptly moaned deep in her throat and fell back, pulling the lone pillow over her face to muffle the rest of her cries as her thighs closed about my wrist and hand in spasms. Her wet slit pulsed beneath my slowing fingers, and her legs tightened and loosened over my hand.

After a moment, Megan gently disentangled herself from us, and we both sat back a moment to admire Phoebe. Her golden hair spread out over the pillow and her creamy thighs opened wide for us, she looked like a sacrificial offering to the lesbian goddesses of lust. My cunt throbbed in time to my banging heart.

We worked on Phoebe for a long time, using all the resources at our disposal: tongues flicked and licked and left wet trails from vulva to ass cheek and back again; fingers tweaked nipples; moistened lips grazed sensitive ears; mouths murmured torrents of encouragement, lustful exhortations, begging and pleading cries. Beneath us, Phoebe writhed and twisted and threw her limbs about in the most appealing way. Her breath caught and hitched in small gasps that almost made me come on the spot. I stroked her golden thatch until I thought I had permanently lost all feeling in my fingers. Megan bit Phoebe's earlobes, sucked on her neck, slurped at her breasts, and we both took turns nestling our mouths into her delicately fragrant pussy folds, which were plumped out and threatening to burst but stubbornly holding on to that last explosion.

Finally, after we had somehow managed to work ourselves halfway across the room yet had gotten no closer to our goal of making Phoebe see stars and hopefully even faint with the joy of it all, Phoebe caught at my hair and gently tugged my face down to hers.

"Lotion," she said in a ragged whisper into my ear. "Lubriderm. In my bag. Living room."

Ignoring Megan's questioning look, I got to my feet and staggered into the living room. Groping through Phoebe's bag,

I found the large bottle of lotion and brought it back to her, like a prize from a hunt. I dropped back down beside her and watched.

She squeezed some out onto her hand and began vigorously massaging her clit with lotiony fingers, moaning deep in her throat and tossing her head around, eyes closed. Her fingers were coated in white Lubriderm and her own sweet juices, and her mouth was opened just a bit, the tip of her tongue nudging at the corner of her mouth. Megan and I watched this apparently familiar ritual in fascination.

My own clit began vibrating in anticipation, and I grabbed Megan's hand to my breast, urging her to play with it. I reached over to take Phoebe's free hand and placed it against my crotch. I was so wet lotion was definitely not a necessity. Phoebe's eyes opened, and my breath caught in my throat at the shimmering clear green of their color. She smiled at me for a fraction of a second, then closed her eyes and began circling her fingers on the both of us with urgency, the same tempo driving us both mad, making my head spiral up and spin around, sending hot tremors down my legs, a fiery stampede beginning in my thighs and traveling to my toes in a tingling rush. The top of my head felt staticky, and I was seeing white points of light behind my closed eyelids. Phoebe moved her hand around and played my pussy with her fingers as though playing a concerto, skimming her fingers over herself and over me in a deeper frenzy, building up to the rushing climax. I could smell her light sweat and the lotion and the wild animal scent of both of us rising up from underneath her hands, and my own hands flexed convulsively on Megan's arm, and Phoebe breathed faster and harder and hissed against her teeth, and suddenly she cried out in a mewling sound and then shrieked in a full-bodied voice, and I felt my own orgasm rise like molten lava and erupt and spill over the brink, and I cried out in some unintelligible language. My breath came out raggedly as I collapsed over Phoebe, and I lost myself in the raw sex-smell of her hair and her skin and her breath.

After some minutes of slowing our heartbeats and lazily running fingers over cooling flesh, Megan propped herself up on an elbow and regarded Phoebe curiously. Phoebe looked back at her with clear eyes and smiled, stroking my arm as she did.

"So," Megan said. "The lotion. Do you always use it?"

Phoebe brushed some hair from her eyes and glanced at me, still lying atop of her. I pushed myself up a little so she could look in my face. My pulse was still doing double-time.

"Well," she began, in the Southern drawl that drove me wild. "Gets a bit dry at camp. My skin's fragile. You know how I always shower last, Caitlin?" she asked me. I nodded. "You ever wonder why?" she said with a small grin, tapping the knocked-over lotion bottle down by her leg and trailing a finger over her hipbone.

I could only stare at her as Megan began to laugh, and then Phoebe began to laugh too, and finally I was chuckling along with them.

I have not seen Phoebe since that summer, though I think of her now and again.

A few years later, long after I saw Phoebe to the airport at August's end to greet her boyfriend and show him around California before they headed back to Kentucky together, I received one letter from Phoebe, postmarked Lexington, Ky. It was written in brightly hued crayon on purple construction paper. I smiled at this whimsical touch and read it. She told me she went to the Kentucky Derby and because it was a big social event in the South, all the ladies had to wear these outrageous hats and pretend to be stylish. So she and her friend wore crazy hats and walked with thousands of other people on the grass by the racetrack, and they drank mint juleps, the cool green drink sliding down their throats in a mixture of fresh mint and smooth bourbon. Then her letter abruptly broke off, as if she had been interrupted in the middle of writing it and had to mail it at once, or more likely had been a bit tipsy from all those mint juleps, simply forgot she had not finished the letter, and dropped it in the mailbox without another thought.

Reading her description of the mint juleps once more, I thought I could almost taste them myself. I recalled her sweet kisses on the balcony and her sensuous touch and the hitch in her voice as she gasped when I ran my tongue along her bare skin. And I smiled and held on to that memory.

Eva in the Elevator

by Jennifer Delamer

The first time I saw her, she was kissing a man.

The doors opened on the elevator in my apartment building and revealed a scene of fiery passion. They hadn't noticed me at first and were very surprised to see me standing there. *That must be some kiss,* I thought to myself. They broke it off, and she giggled. He bent down to tie his shoe. Over his rounded back, she smiled at me. It was an inquisitive, not quite shy smile—definitely a more-than-hello smile. I think I smiled back, but I'm not sure, because I was stunned by her deep blue eyes that held my gaze. The elevator whooshed to a stop at the fourth floor. He stood up; she widened her smile a little and then turned to look at him.

I fumbled with my keys and out of the corner of my eye watched them walk down the hall. They stopped at an apartment just two doors down from mine. I could hear her laughter even after I shut my door. I leaned against it and dropped my bag. I took a deep breath. "Who is she?" I wondered out loud. "It doesn't matter, she obviously has a boyfriend," I answered myself.

For the next few days, I tried unsuccessfully to put her out of my mind. I kept thinking about the way our eyes had locked, her smile, how my hands would feel in her long hair. "Stop it," I chastised when I caught myself staring again at the door down the hall. For whatever reason, I couldn't get her to leave my head.

Over a beer I confided in my friend about the strange meeting. I told the whole story, including how she had locked eyes with me teasingly behind her boyfriend's back. "I don't know anything about her, but she is captivating—"

"Bullshit!" Heidi cut me off. "You know lots. You know you saw her kissing a man, for chrissakes! Just quit thinking about her. Look—" she made a sweeping motion with the hand that held her beer "—at this room full of beautiful lesbians. Why do you want to go on obsessing about some straight chick you saw one time in an elevator?"

Heidi had a point.

"I don't know. It's her smile, I guess." A couple of friends came up and joined us at the bar and saved me from more of Heidi's acidic, albeit well-meaning, advice.

When I dropped Heidi off at her house that night she slurred some final words of wisdom. "You know that thing about all the fish in the sea, right, kid?"

"Yeah, I know. Thanks a lot."

"Well, remember it, OK?" She punched me lightly in the arm and then got out of the car. Despite her advice, I thought about the mystery woman all the way home.

My thoughts were still on her when the doors to the elevator opened and there she was. Alone. She was coming from the basement with her laundry. She was wearing a T-shirt with no bra and shorts. Her feet were bare, but her toenails were painted bright red. Recognition flashed across her face when she saw me, and she smiled.

"Hi, I'm Eva," she said as soon as I stepped into the elevator. I yanked my eyes away from her nipples to look at her face.

Her eyes caught mine. They pierced me.

"I'm Jennifer," I said, extending my hand. She balanced her laundry basket on one hip and gave my hand a firm squeeze. I had to remind myself to let go. The elevator stopped and we got out.

"We should go for a walk sometime at the lake. It is only three blocks from here," she said, smiling.

I replied "Sure," returned her smile, and then, trying to sound calm, added, "It would be nice to know some of my neighbors."

"I know, it seems like it can be hard to meet people here," she replied. "People keep to themselves."

"Well, a walk sounds like fun. See you later," I said while finding my key. She smiled one more time. I felt the heat rise to my face.

"Bye," she said and walked off down the hall.

A few days went by. I didn't see her. Heidi's advice was to let her come to me. "*She* mentioned going for a walk, right?"

"Well, yeah," I replied.

"Well, if she meant it, she'll ask you. Besides, what's her boyfriend going to think if a dyke knocks on the door and asks if his girlfriend is home?"

"You got a point there," I admitted reluctantly, and then added, "OK, OK. I'll wait."

I didn't have to wait too long. The next night I heard a knock on my door. When I looked out my peephole and saw Eva, I panicked. I looked down at my SOME OF MY BEST FRIENDS ARE STRAIGHT T-shirt and grimaced. I held my breath and watched her through the peephole. She looked at her watch and then knocked again. *Carpe diem,* I said to myself and opened the door.

"Hi. I hope I'm not bothering you," she said.

Oh, God, how she bothered me. I pulled her into my arms and planted slow, burning kisses on her lips and neck. Then I snapped back to reality.

"Hi, Eva. Do you want to come in?"

"No, but thanks. I just came over to see if you want to take that walk tomorrow morning."

"Tomorrow? Sure, that sounds fine. What time?"

"Well, how about 10, is that too early?"

"Ten o' clock is great for me." I replied.

"OK. I'll see you at 10. Bye," she said, smiling at me while she reached out her hand to push the down button for the elevator. A grin slowly spread across my face. I shut my door and watched her through the peephole. Her long dark hair was loose around her face. She was wearing a skirt with a slit up the back, and one taut calf muscle was barely peeking out. Draped casually around the neck I had imagined kissing was a floral scarf. She was smiling to herself.

"Gorgeous," I said under my breath. The elevator came and she disappeared.

Ten o' clock took forever to come the next morning, but once we began talking and walking, time leaped by very quickly. I learned that despite the kiss I had seen, she and her boyfriend were not doing well. And I learned that the reason for this was because she couldn't stop thinking about and dreaming about being with women. The mystery was beginning to unravel.

"Does your boyfriend know any of this?" I asked her gently.

"Yes, and he is dealing with it pretty well. We were going to try out a threesome with another woman, a friend of ours, but it didn't work out. So far I've only kissed another woman. Sorry! I can't believe I'm telling you my life story."

"That's OK, really. Does your boyfriend know we're walking today? I mean, I assume he, that you, well, that you know IÕm a lesbian?"

"Let's just say the T-shirt you had on last night confirmed my assumptions," she said teasingly. I blushed and looked at the ground. "Hey, don't worry, he is not the jealous type. Anyway, he's out of town this weekend."

"Oh, really?" I asked.

"Really," she said, arching one eyebrow mischievously. We walked a few moments in silence, and then she started asking me questions about myself. I don't remember answering her, but I do remember noticing the sensuality of her lips and how she threw her head back a little when she laughed. Too soon we were back at the building.

"Well, thanks for the walk," I said as we left the elevator.

"You're welcome. Let's do it again."

"OK, sounds great." I said as I pushed the door of my apartment open. I sat down on the couch feeling dazed. I knew more about her, but I was feeling more confused. *Damn, I should have asked her to do something tonight.* When would I see her again?

A few hours later I heard a knock on my door. I knew it was her. I was beginning to like this. "Hello, would you like to come in?"

"Thanks anyway, I'm on my way out. I just talked to a friend who canceled on me for tonight. We were supposed to go see that movie *Boys On The Side.* I just came over to see if you might want to go?"

"Actually, I did kind of want to check that one out," I said, hoping I didn't sound too excited.

"Great, can you be ready by 7?"

"Sure, 7 it is."

"OK, see you later." She winked at me and put her hand over mine where it rested on the door frame. With that she took off down the stairs and denied me the pleasure of watching her wait for the elevator.

One ring, two, three. *Come on, Heidi, pick up, I need your advice.*

"Hello?"

"Thank God you're home. I need your opinion!"

Heidi listened quietly to the whole story.

"Are you done?" she asked.

"Yes."

"Is that *all* that happened?"

"Yes, " I said, a little annoyed.

"*Woo-oo-woo-oo-ooh!*" she howled into the phone. "You are one lucky lesbian!" she yelled.

"What?" I asked her.

"Can't you see, she's practically throwing herself at you. She wants you to be her first! Duh!"

"What? Are you sure?"

"Yep," Heidi said smugly. "I know it."

"I don't know." I hesitated.

"What the hell do you need, an engraved invitation?"

"No, I just...."

"Go for it, champ. Carpe diem and call me in the morning, *after* she leaves." The phone clicked dead.

"Carpe diem," I whispered to myself as I hung up. I couldn't stop smiling.

We stared at each other wordlessly. The elevator stopped and opened.

"Do you want to come in for a while?" I asked. "It is only 10 o'clock."

Eva looked at her watch, then looked at me. "OK."

Remain calm, I reminded myself silently while I opened the door. "Would you like a glass of wine?" I asked while she wandered around my living room looking at pictures.

"Yes please, that would be nice." She smiled at me briefly and then looked away, shyly. I poured two glasses and walked into the living room. The glow from a streetlight played on her hair and lit up one tan shoulder. I set my glass down and strode up to where she stood, staring out the window. Lightly, I ran the tip of my index finger down her arm.

"Here is your wine." I offered it to her.

"Thank you." We were quiet for a moment. She turned away from the window and looked into my eyes.

"It is funny," she said.

"What is?"

"Us meeting like this, being neighbors, the whole thing…" Her voice trailed off.

"Why don't we sit down and you can tell me how funny it is." I took her hand and led her to the couch. We laughed, talked, and finished the bottle of wine. "What do you want out of life?" I asked, suddenly feeling philosophical.

"I want you to kiss me," she answered quietly.

"What?" I teased her, thinking, *Who is seducing whom?*

"You heard what I said," she answered, and put her hand over mine. Tiny sparks raced up my arm and exploded behind my ear.

"Eva, I don't know, I—"

"I know, you don't want to be my first woman. But ever since I saw you, I knew you were the one. I don't want anything else. I am not trying to get you involved in my messy breakup. It's just that I haven't been sleeping at night, knowing you are down the hall."

"I...I don't know what to say," I stammered, shocked by her revelation.

"You don't have to say anything. Just show me," she whispered.

"OK," I said, smiling. I put my wine glass down and stood up.

"Where are you going?"

"I'll be right back." I returned with a soft blanket, which I spread on the floor in the patch of light from outside. "Come here," I commanded her in a low, hungry tone. Her eyes grew wide and she looked scared. I wondered amusedly at what had become of the confident Eva who had pursued me with so little subtlety. Silently she joined me on the blanket. I took her chin in my hand and lightly kissed her lips. Then I placed a tiny promise of a kiss in her palm. She still looked mildly frightened, so I drew her close to me and whispered in her ear. "It's OK. I will be very gentle. You don't need to be afraid."

"I'm not," she murmured against my ear.

I smiled at her bravery and eased her down on the blanket so that she was lying on her back. I began to kiss her very delicately at first. Then I straddled her hips and kissed her more passionately. Sighs escaped her lips between kisses. I grazed my lips over her face and down her neck, biting there very softly. She moaned "Jennifer" in an excited, sexy way that drove me crazy and dug her hands into my hair. Even though she was scared, I could tell that she was essentially uninhibited and very passionate. Taking this slowly was going to be difficult, but I wanted her first time with a woman to be special. I planted rows of kisses on her collarbone and one long one in the hollow of her throat. I continued kissing down her chest until I reached the first button of her blouse. I undid it slowly and kissed the newly-exposed skin. I paused for a moment and looked up at her. She seemed more relaxed. "Is this OK?" I asked, as my hands went to work freeing the remaining buttons.

"Yes," she said and stroked my hair. I opened her blouse and gazed at her smooth stomach and her breasts, still hidden from me behind the lace of her bra. At the top of her jeans, with my tongue, I flicked a trail of fire up to the clasp of her bra. Eva moaned and squirmed under me. I placed my mouth over one hard nipple that was poking out at me. I breathed heat onto it, and it responded by growing harder. I gently sucked it, making the lace wet. Eva continued to stroke my hair. I gave the same loving attention to her other nipple before I released the clasp. I uncovered her breasts and sat back a little to admire her.

"Do you like what you see?" she asked tentatively.

"Yes, very much," I assured her. Her skin was smooth and olive-toned. Her breasts fit perfectly in my hands. Their color reminded me of roses and fresh earth. "You are beautiful, Eva," I growled in her ear and then kissed her. She kissed me back feverishly. Once again I thought about the kiss I had seen in the elevator.

"Do me a favor?" she asked.

"Anything."

"Take off your shirt."

"OK," I said and complied.

"This too," she said, reaching around to unhook my bra. I flung my shirt and bra aside and slid my breasts over hers slowly and lightly, barely touching her. She arched her back. "Oh, my God, this feels so good," she exclaimed breathlessly. I smiled to myself, thinking that it must feel much better than a hairy man's chest.

"Turn over," I ordered her. She did as I asked, and I remained straddling her. I held the hair away from the nape of her neck and gave her a hot sucking kiss right there. I imagined it was her pussy and felt myself get wetter. I sucked her harder and then took nibbling bites down her neck.

"Oh, my God, oh, my God," she moaned as I ran the tip of my tongue down her spine to the waist of her jeans. I lightly blew on the wet trail I had just made. She shivered and giggled softly.

"Turn over again, please," I said. She obeyed, and I kissed her lips. In her ear I whispered, "Are you wet?"

"I didn't know I could get this wet." She smiled up at me. We kissed for a long time. I could feel her passion rising as I kissed her mouth as if it were her pussy, giving her an unknowing preview of all the ways I would make her feel good. I moved down to her breasts and sucked on her nipples. I spread her legs with my knee and put my hand over her. Even through her jeans I could feel her moist heat.

"Are you ready for these to come off?" I asked her while grinding my knee into her.

"Yes," she answered between gasps. I undid the button at her waist and kissed her there. Slowly, I drew down the zipper. I smiled when I saw her lacy panties. I slid the jeans off her toned legs and took a long look at her beautiful body. She had a little mole by her right hipbone. Her nipples taunted my mouth with their erect excitement.

"What are you thinking?" she asked. I must have been staring too long.

"Honestly?"

"Yes, tell me honestly."

"Well, I was just thinking that because this is your first time, I want it to be really special. I want to go slowly."

She smiled, reached up to squeeze my nipple, and said, "I don't have to be anywhere until Monday morning." I groaned and pulled her to me. The kissing started all over again. I was going mad with the desire to feel her wetness on my hands. Finally, I laid her down and straddled her again. Licking and sucking, I worked my way down her body, leaving a wake of scorching kisses.

When I reached the top of her panties, I moved off of her hips and said, "Spread your legs, sweetheart." She spread them a little. "Wider," I gently commanded her. She obeyed, but I could tell she was feeling shy. I stroked her stomach lightly and tenderly and said softly, "It's OK. Don't be shy. You are beautiful, and I am going to make you feel very good." I sat down between her legs and draped them over my knees. Her breathing became faster and shallower. With the back of my hands, I faintly, excruciatingly faintly, caressed the insides of her thighs. She began to moan, and I noticed she was biting her lower lip.

With one fingertip, I traced the elastic of her panties between her legs. I caressed her stomach and breast with my other hand. She sighed, and her hips began to undulate slightly. I brushed my hand between her legs, allowing my touch to become more forceful with each stroke. She was soaking wet, and it seeped through the fabric and onto my hand. "Can these come off now?" I asked her huskily, my hands poised at the top of her panties, awaiting her reply.

"Yes, please," she replied. Slowly I pulled them down over her hips and off. I repositioned her legs over my knees and treated myself to a long look at her. She was glistening pink and exquisitely shaped. I needed to be inside. It took all my strength not to dive into her wetness. My fingertips played with the hair on her mound.

"Eva, are you ready?" I asked her.

"Uh-huh," she sighed, arching her hips toward my hand. I bit the inside of her thigh sweetly, and she squirmed. My fingers played in her hair, and I let my thumb slide delicately over her clit and down to her opening that seeped wetness. My thumb pushed just inside of her. I coated it with her honey, and then I drew it up over her clit with firmer pressure. "Oh, God," she sighed. I smiled. Lightly and slowly, I dragged my thumb over her clit. Her hips began to rock with my rhythm. While my thumb tended to her swollen clit, I entered her with one finger. I began to move inside her softly at first. "Oh, my God, you are so gentle. It feels so good." She breathed out. I wanted to bring her along at an achingly slow pace; I wanted to drive her a little crazy.

I fucked her tenderly for a long time, until I was the one going crazy. She began to cry "More, more" between her moans. I eased another finger into her sopping pussy and fucked her a little faster. Eva sighed deeply. She was breathing faster now. Her pussy sucked on my fingers. I never wanted to stop. I was soaking. She arched her back and threw one arm over her forehead. Her breasts floated with my strokes like anemones in the tide. "I am getting close," she announced.

"I know," I said and smiled down at her. She was beginning to have little contractions in her pussy, like tremors that warn of an earthquake.

"Fuck me harder, please," she pleaded with me. I gave her three or four forceful strokes and then slowed down again. She groaned in exasperation. She was very near orgasm, but I wasn't done with her yet. I withdrew my hands from her, and she moaned in a hurt and surprised way. I stretched myself out over her body. "Why did you stop?" she pouted.

"It's OK, baby, I'm going to give you something better." I kissed her smile and then sucked on her breasts. I kissed her stomach and each hipbone. I kissed the insides of her thighs and the wet mass of curly hair. I brought my mouth very near her pussy and breathed hot air onto her. She buried her hands in my hair, and her legs quivered. I ran my tongue up and down the outside of her lips. Her honey flowed out, and I took some of it on the tip of my tongue. I licked her softly everywhere. I wanted to taste her for hours.

"You taste wonderful," I said to her and reached up to caress her erect nipples. She sighed in response and stroked my hair. I covered her clit with my mouth and began to suck it softly. Eva moaned and pressed into my face. I slid two fingers into her melting pussy and continued to suck and lick her clit. I fucked her like this slowly, in and out, for a long time. Every time she got close to coming, I backed away. I was enjoying her tight wetness and her taste too much to let it end.

I slid a third finger into her and she cried out sharply, "Oh, yes, please fuck me hard, please!" When I heard the desperation in her voice, I knew I couldn't deny her any longer.

"OK, Eva, anything you want, honey." My tongue flicked more insistently. I fucked her harder and faster until my hand and arm started to throb.

"More, more," she chanted between gasps. Her juice flowed out and covered my hand. Suddenly she bucked wildly, and her hips rocked in a frenzied dance. I fought to keep my mouth on her clit. "Don't stop," she begged me. I fucked her as hard as I could. Finally she came again and again, grinding her saturated pussy into my face, contracting around my fingers many times and moaning my name. Her whole body quivered. When she quit writhing, I took my face away and smiled up at her. She returned my smile dazedly, closed her eyes, and inhaled deeply. I kissed her clit sweetly and softly. It made her tremble and set off a new round of contractions. She sighed a satisfied sigh, and I felt the tension leaving her body. She gasped in pleasure when I withdrew my fingers.

I laid down beside her and pulled her into my arms. I kissed her forehead and then her lips. She lifted my chin and stared at me with those magnificent blue eyes. “When do I get to do *that* to you?” she asked teasingly, smiling at me.

I kissed her forehead and answered, “I don’t have to be anywhere until Monday morning.”

Learning to Swim

by Myra LaVenue

Ironically, I never even noticed Kelly the night we met. In a crowded room, she was one of three baby dykes dancing to a song by Crystal Waters. Her Hispanic-American friends were both exotically beautiful, which contrasted with Kelly's blond, blue-eyed loveliness. Despite her pretty face and sexy 22-year-old body, with her quiet voice and shy demeanor, she did not immediately grab my attention.

I went up to Josie, a woman in the group I had met recently on a strange double date. "How's it going?" I yelled over the music. She smiled excitedly and motioned for me to join their dancing.

"Myra, this is Kelly and Marie," she introduced me, with a cupped hand over her mouth. I waved to the other two, and let my eyes wander over Marie, the other Hispanic woman. Her delicate features were sensual and so feminine, which contrasted nicely with Josie's androgynous energy. I noticed Kelly watching me shyly, and I smiled politely.

The four of us became friends that night and formed a kind of clique. We shared a few things in common: a newness to the New York lesbian community, a pursuit of fun that was free from drugs and excessive drinking, and a basic respect in how we treated people. Respect was rare in that insulated community where gossip, drugs, and philandering were rampant.

One weekend soon after meeting Kelly, Josie invited me to a hike in Connecticut. I eagerly accepted. Like most New Yorkers, I felt my outdoor activity was limited to city walks where my lungs filled with exhaust fumes instead of good, clean air. As we rode in Josie's Bronco to the trailhead, I was sitting close to Kelly in the backseat. It was then I first noticed just how captivating her sweet smile and responsive laugh were. My mind formed the notion that here, single and attractive, was a woman I could truly enjoy dating. I shifted into major flirt mode.

To kill time on the long drive, we all swapped college stories. Since I'd just turned 30 and college was a faint memory for me, I decided to share my coming out story instead. I assumed my story would be quite different from the others. Like them, I had come out a year earlier, only I had left an eight-year marriage to a man. Prior to meeting my ex-husband, I'd dated many men in college. I was never really satisfied with men, and my husband always complained of my controlling nature. Through conversations on-line with women, I met someone and had an affair with her. This directly caused my separation from my husband.

Since he left I had met and slept with three women in three months. My sex drive was unquenchable, and I felt as if I had awoken from some debilitating illness: paralysis of the clitoris. Thank you, Jesus, I am healed! I used the skills I had acquired picking up men to seduce women and had a much better time doing it. I was honest with everyone I dated, telling them that I enjoyed sex and really wanted to avoid a relationship right now. I hoped my honesty made my intentions clear and communicated to my lovers that our intimacy was purely for fun.

As for telling my friends and family, that went fairly smoothly. My parents were both dead, leaving me a family of three brothers and a stepdad, all of whom took the news fairly well. And I had yet to hear a disapproving comment from any friend, although a couple had needed time to adjust to the "new" me.

While telling my story, I saw a variety of looks, some supportive, some shocked. Kelly was warily looking at me with a kind of thoughtful curiosity, which she tried desperately to hide behind her slight frown. I was giving her my best "ain't I a devil" smirk.

She shifted a bit away from me. Her tall, lithe body was so close in height and weight to mine that my attraction to her seemed almost narcissistic. We both had blue eyes, stood about 5 feet 9 inches, and weighed close to 120 pounds. My brown hair brushed my collar in a kind of messy shag cut while Kelly's dirty-blond locks were swept back off her face.

We finally arrived at the trailhead, and as we hiked that day, my jokes were flying faster than the pebbles flung from our boots off the trail. Still, I wondered if I should pursue Kelly; she was, after all, very different from me. With the first chance I got, I walked next to Kelly to find out more about her. Her coming-out story at first amazed me and then inspired great admiration in me.

Kelly had dated men in college but had not slept with any of them. Since she was young, she had felt stirrings within her that she finally identified as lesbian crushes on her childhood girlfriends and female teachers. Coming from an extremely close and religious family, her realization was much more dangerous than mine. Finally, in a move so brave I myself could not contemplate it, Kelly came out to her family before ever even dating a woman. The result was pure poison. Her father and mother were destroyed by the news and forbade her to tell her sister. Kelly's mom stopped speaking to her. Meanwhile, her father would meet her for dinners in the city, during which he vacillated between begging her to see a therapist and crying over the state of his little girl's life. Her story was startling because it revealed to me that this virgin knew she was a lesbian without ever confirming it sexually.

I watched Kelly thoughtfully for the remainder of the hike and during the ride home. I liked the way she carried herself. Her proud independence and confidence in her sexual identity increased her attractiveness to me. I was looking forward to seeing her again, but I decided to wait on asking her out. The timing had to be right.

Two weeks later we all took a weekend trip to New Jersey, which would prove to be a monumental turning point for Kelly and me. Why we ever let Josie convince us New Yorkers to journey to southern New Jersey for a lesbian party in a local hotel, I'll never know. But to this day, I would not exchange that trip for a date with k.d. lang. Well, on second thought, better make that a date with Tammy Faye Baker.

The seating arrangements for the drive there were a repeat of our hiking trip, only with one major difference. As Marie and Josie spoke to each other in the front of the Bronco, Kelly and I were facing each other in the back, totally engrossed. I had rested my hand along the back of the seat we were sharing, and occasionally would let it brush against her shoulder after a bump in the road. I caught her blue eyes staring at me every once in a while when I would shift my head to see the road or inquire about the distance remaining to our destination. The attraction we were both feeling had created a palpable tension, which I hoped was sexual in nature but also feared could be explained away by Kelly's shyness.

The hotel party was awful in a way that only a dance thrown in a hotel conference room can be. A shapeless disc jockey, spinning records that skipped when anyone passed by, was situated at one end of the room, while a beer and wine bar anchored the other end. In between, a number of round tables covered with pink tablecloths were scattered about. The crowd of women at these tables looked like they'd rather be home watching TV. These southern New Jersey lesbians were not quite the same as the Manhattan women I was used to watching. Needless to say, after a brave attempt at dancing in front of the group, we fled.

A friend of ours had joined us at the hotel; she was from the area and knew of a mixed gay bar on the coast. We all quickly agreed to try it out, and drove to our new destination, which was considerably more acceptable in two respects: the music was great and the place was virtually empty. There was just one drunk, lurching dyke on the dance floor when we arrived, and assorted gay male couples scattered throughout the place.

At this bar I wanted to somehow get close to Kelly, but for some reason, my usual courage for seduction had left my body. I think that her inexperience and quiet nature petrified me, so the move I finally made that night on that dance floor goes down in my book as one of my bravest. As a Madonna song came on, I closed the distance between our two dancing bodies, and, after a couple of unsteady breaths, slid my hand around her back and pulled her body close to mine. She curled into me willingly. My excitement only added to my already overflowing case of nerves.

Our slow, sexy swaying went on for another hour or so, until the others pried us apart and drove us to the house of our New Jersey friend. The sleeping arrangements were dictated to us by our hostess, without a single knowing glance: Josie and Marie on the pullout double bed downstairs while Kelly and I could fight over the floor and the twin bed in the guest room upstairs. My heart and nether regions throbbed in unison! She and I were in the same room, and everyone else was yards away behind their own doors.

I changed clothes first in the bathroom and washed my face. Kelly and I then shared the sink as we brushed our teeth together. God, could she be any more inviting with those shy glances my way in the mirror? We were both intensely aware of the mood from the bar, the way our bodies had felt pressed together and our breasts had lightly brushed each other's.

When I finished in the bathroom, I returned to our room and immediately chose the bed on the floor. I sat down, pulled my legs up to my chest and hugged them, waiting for the inevitable moment when that sexual tension monster would rear its beautiful and powerful head with her entrance. I was wearing a T-shirt and panties. As she walked in, I saw she had chosen the same sleeping apparel.

My nervousness tripled as she sat down on the floor next to me. "I don't know why I am so nervous," I told her. But I knew why. This woman, this sweet innocent woman, was about to experience her first sexual encounter ever, not just with a woman! This made my every move feel amplified, as I knew she would remember this for the rest of her life. I wanted everything to be right for her, to be memorable and perfect. I was walking unfamiliar ground, because I could not treat her as a casual encounter.

Kelly just smiled at me. She seemed so relaxed, as if she had been waiting for this moment for years. "Don't be nervous," she whispered as she moved toward me, and we kissed for the first time. Her soft lips were incredibly willing and slightly open at my touch. *Our first kiss was finally happening,* I thought as our lips touched and breaths mingled in a delicate and intimate dance.

We kissed again, and this time I moved a little closer to her kneeling body. I pulled her next to me, felt our breasts touch between thin layers of cotton, and my nipples got hard. Her light kisses were a bit unsure, so I led the movements of our mouths and tongues. Like an eager child learning to swim, she began to mirror my movements as she took on the role of my amorous student.

Then I heard it. The sound that will always be Kelly's alone: a subtle, soft breathy sigh. That sound epitomized what I knew of her; that sweet little exhalation of sound filled me with a gentle protectiveness and a deep sense of responsibility for her pleasure. I slowly slid my hands under her T-shirt and felt her inhale with exquisite anticipation. My hands brushed over her back and caressed her stomach, before slowly reaching upward. Her small breasts fit into my hands perfectly, as my thumbs lightly stroked back and forth over her nipples.

I felt her pulling her T-shirt over her head, and I stopped to look into her eyes. Her blue eyes stared back at me, so trusting and full of desire that it took my breath away. I kissed her once again, before bending my head to take a breast into my mouth. Her hands slid around my head and pulled me closer before trying to reach my breasts under my T-shirt. As I sucked her nipple in and out of my mouth, I ran my tongue around its base. I paused and let her remove my shirt, before resuming my exploration. Those soft sounds coming every few seconds from between her beautiful lips were driving me wild. I leaned back for a moment, and Kelly moved immediately to my breasts to let her hands and mouth explore this new landscape. She placed her mouth over my nipple and ran her tongue around the tip of it. She seemed oblivious to my gaze as I watched this sweet woman do things she had only dreamed of before this night. Her eagerness to please me and hear my excitement was enormously exciting to me.

I don't know how much time passed, but there came a moment when our intimacy reached a natural stopping point. I did not want to rush into sex with Kelly that first night, and I could tell she was limiting our explorations to areas only above the waist. I smiled at her, stroked her cheek with one finger, and asked, "Are you OK?"

Kelly nodded, smiled shyly back at me, then leaned forward for a quick kiss before moving to her bed. A few moments later, her voice drifted to me from across the room, "I really can't believe I just kissed a woman. It was wonderful, Myra."

"I feel the same way," I replied. I lay there for a while, listening to the sound of her gentle breathing as she fell asleep.

In the morning the group split up. Because of our pressing schedules, Kelly and I took the train back to New York City. I was thrilled to get her to myself for a solid two hours. We spoke quietly about what had happened the previous night, and I asked her how she felt in the light of day. I knew that last night had been a significant step forward for her. She blushed slightly at my question, and I felt my stomach do a flip. Then, to my delight, she told me she was as interested as I in continuing our budding relationship. As we traveled through the suburbs of the city, we spoke of when we could get together next. We exchanged knowing smiles and a hug before catching our separate subways home.

And so began the cat and mouse period of dating, with her desires and pacing leading the way. We met for a movie one night, and made dinner for each other the next. With each meeting the physical attraction between us revealed itself in longer and more significant ways.

Then it happened. Her roommate made plans to leave New York for the weekend, and Kelly asked if I wanted to stay over. I knew what this night would bring, and I prepared with extreme care. Kelly had spoken of safe sex and using protection for any sexual contact. Knowing this, I thought of the easiest solution: Saran Wrap. I tore a couple of sheets off and wrapped them in paper towels. I packed some candles and soft music. I was ready.

She made me dinner that night, and I brought the wine. As she cooked I stood near enough to smell her perfume. At one point, a bit of pasta sauce splashed onto her finger, which I quickly drew toward me. I put her finger in my mouth and sucked and licked the finger clean. Her eyes stared intently into mine, as her breathing grew short. The boiling water snapped us out of the mood, and I handed her the pasta for the pot.

During the meal I watched her laugh at my jokes and heard stories of her childhood. We talked about the pain the separation from her family was causing. I could feel anger rising up inside me at the thought of her family's insensitivity toward her.

To change the mood she asked me if I wanted to dance. I nodded, and she rose to put on some slow music. We danced very slowly around her small living room. I pulled her so close that I could feel her chest rise and fall against mine. I rubbed my cheek against hers, smelled her wispy hair, and caressed her neck with one hand. Our bodies moved slightly to the rhythm as our hands slid to places now grown familiar. As my lips touched hers, I felt her shudder, and then I heard that soft sound again.

Our kissing grew more intense, and I danced her toward her twin bed in the corner of the next room. As I undressed her, kissing and tasting the skin on her neck and chest, I felt her fingers run through my hair, urging my lips to her nipple. I don't remember how she removed it, but I remember realizing I had no shirt on. My hardened nipples rubbed against hers as I pulled her into my arms, our bodies lying side by side with legs entwined. Her body was so soft, and the light hair on her skin gave off a faint yellow glow under the dim light of the streetlamp outside and the candles inside. I could wait no longer—the moment had come for me to feel her excitement. I had to know if I was arousing her to the level of passion I felt. My fingers slid quietly down her flat stomach, and through her blond pubic hairs. When my fingers felt her wetness, my body exploded with an intense hunger.

My lips left her mouth and began to move down to join my hand. I could feel her nervousness, so I began stroking her body with both hands, moving them up and down and over her torso to soothe and warm her. My head got so close to her, I could smell her delicate sweet smell. One of my hands reached below the bed, where I'd previously placed the Saran Wrap. I pulled out one of the sheets and laid it over her, before moving my tongue back and forth. Her sharp intake of breath made me pause, then her fingers on my head urged me onward. My lips began to open and close once I knew my efforts were being felt through this protective sheet. As my movements became more rapid, I could feel her squirming increase and her moans grow louder. Suddenly she moved her body away from my mouth, and her arms pulled me up her body. As I moved towards her head, I placed a leg between hers and wrapped my arms around her. Pulling her close to me, I saw the tears in her eyes and felt her clinging to me. I held her for quite awhile, stroking her back with one hand and holding her tightly to me with the other while she cried softly. Her face was beautiful in the candlelight, and her eyes shone from the tears as they looked into mine. We spoke about the experience in that quiet voice lovers use in bed, as if they will be overheard despite being completely alone. She spoke of her passion and the feelings I had evoked in her with a miraculous awe. Her tears were from the joy of experiencing such intense new feelings in her body. Her kisses and caresses that night told me she had no regrets.

As we fell asleep, wrapped in each other's arms, I felt she had helped me as well, in reaching a new place for myself. She had inspired in me a desire to nurture a relationship with one woman. I knew that whatever our future, Kelly would always be special to me as would this amazing night where intimacy, passion, and respect all mingled into a lasting memory.

STACKED

by Rosanna Sorella

Her face was one you could possibly forget. It was small and round and hadn't changed much over the years. But her body— now that was an entirely different matter. It was, in a word, memorable. Her legs ran full and muscular; her arms stretched smooth and strong; her thighs straddled her particularly buoyant hips; and her skin rested quietly over the whole of her like the color of coffee in the morning after you've poured in the cream.

She had, as I have explained, a beautiful body. But she had no idea of the ways of this body. She only knew that people had wanted it but that she had never been able to give it away. She had tried before, been in love and out, in love and out. But then her relationships had always been purposeful, uninspired, not at all what you would expect from her. Not at all what you would expect from a woman with such a beautiful body. Not at all what you would expect: She was, to be precise, 33 years old and still a virgin.

She couldn't tell you how it happened exactly, only that it had something to do with needing a book and something to do with dialing her old rotary telephone. She preferred making her calls along the dial because she liked to feel her fingers travel through space around the numbers. It made the journey to speech more important somehow. It was after 10 one night, and she was having one of her usual bouts of insomnia and couldn't find any of the words she needed to lead her to rest in any of the books on her shelves, so she called the bookstore at the other end of town, the one that stayed open past midnight.

She carefully dialed the numbers and watched each one make its deliberate revolution along the dial until she heard a ring. Someone answered.

"Hello," she heard, and the voice confused her. It wasn't the regular, official-sounding one that usually answered, giving the name of the bookstore and its location. No, this voice was different, deeper, much more…crucial.

"What can I do for you?" the voice inquired.

"Well, I need a book, on—um—plants, uh, horticulture. It's called *Making Music With Your Gardener*—I mean, *Garden.*"

"Oh," the voice responded, "plants, I'm good with plants. And I think I know just where to find it." After that the virgin expected, as usual, to be put on hold and to have to wait awhile on the other end of the line. But instead, she, this voice, said, "Let me take you with me…I've got the portable." And just like that, they walked through the aisles.

"Let's see," she said, "Biography, Mystery, History, Self-Help, Children's, Cultural Studies, Women's Studies, Gay and Lesbian Studies, Fiction, Psychology, Philosophy, Cooking, Romance, Travel, Poetry, oh, yes, here it is, Gardening." She paused for just a second. "Do you want to come for it, or something?"

"Oh, I'll, um, could you have it sent to me?"

"Sure," she said, "but I'll have to transfer you to the person who does those sorts of technical things." And then the woman was gone, lost, gone forever from the reach of the beautiful virgin.

(You know, I don't know a single thing about gardening. I was just flustered hearing this woman's voice, and I had to think fast, so I remembered my grandmother and how she used to tell me that "there should be some kind of book, or something, about music and plants; my plants," she would say to me, "they love to listen to Mario Lanza... You should write a book about how plants should listen to him." In case you haven't figured it out, this story is about me, and, well, it's true, but I figured you probably wouldn't believe it unless I stopped and sort of told you a few things. Fantasy is one thing and reality—well, it's another. It's another kind of thing entirely when you know it's real. So let me keep going.)

The beautiful virgin found herself calling the woman at the bookstore back and letting her know her telephone number. Soon the woman began calling the virgin regularly herself. It became a nightly ritual just to hear her deep voice carry the virgin around the bookstore with her. At first it was fun. Then it started to become dangerous. The woman would dial her up just before closing, when it was almost time for her to restock the shelves. She would be all alone then and have all night to talk if she wanted. At first she would ask general questions that had something to do with the particular book she was shelving, and the virgin would have to guess what section she was taking it to. At some point her questions became suddenly personal, and the guessing game shifted.

Out of the blue, one night, she asked, "So, what's your favorite way to come, anyway?"

"Oh, that's an easy one," the beautiful virgin said quickly, "you're going to the Self-Help section."

"No, no," the woman answered, "I mean it. I don't have any more books to stack tonight; I'm asking you this question for real." She continued, "Do you like it on top, bottom, sideways, by yourself, with two other people, a vibrator, dildo, what?"

Paralyzed with fear, the virgin managed to say "I'll have to get back to you on that one" and hung up.

(Look, I had no idea what she was talking about, and I didn't catch on for a very long time. You know, I couldn't tell her the truth. I wanted her to think I was worldly, sophisticated, elegant, smart; that's why I liked the guessing game we would play every night; I was well-read, so I could figure out where she was going—with her books. With this, I couldn't say anything because I didn't know anything. I didn't know how to tell her that growing up we lived in a crowded house with lots of kids, and after my dad left, I was the oldest and shared the space in the big bed next to my mom. Mom was totally into being Catholic and into me being a nice Italian girl, so she made sure I never went anywhere near my underwear, ever. So I just didn't, couldn't, wouldn't. I grew up not knowing how to make myself do anything. And the women I had tried to be with couldn't figure out how to make me do anything either. Who wants to tell her all of that? Why would I want to give myself away like that?*)*

A few months went by, and the woman never mentioned anything like that again. Until one night when she said to the virgin, "Hey, it's been months, and I still never got an answer to my question."

"Um, which one is that?" the virgin fumbled.

"Your favorite way to come. Let's see, maybe I can find out," she said. "What are you wearing right now?"

"Well, I've got a pair of jeans on and a black silk shirt."

"Oh, in or out?"

"What?"

"Is your shirt tucked in or out?"

"It's in."

"OK," she said, "now, pull it out, your shirt, untuck it, and stick your right hand over the front of your jeans and unzip them."

"But they're buttons," the virgin said.

"Oh, even better. Slowly rip open those button-flies," she said. "OK, are you done?" "Yeah."

"Good. Now, what's under there; I mean, what color is your underwear, and what kind is it?"

"Um, let me see—gray, the Jockey kind."

"Gray. OK, now, I need to know the rest of the wardrobe. Is your shirt long- or short-sleeved, and are there buttons there too?"

"Yeah, and long sleeves."

"Good. Now slowly undo whatever buttons are there, open your shirt a little bit, and tell me what kind of bra you're wearing and what size it is."

"Well, I'm not wearing a bra."

"Oh, my, no bra, huh."

"Sometimes, they get a little tired at night, so I give them a break by taking them out."

"Them? What size are them anyway?"

"Well, I normally wear a 38D."

"Oh, my God! You've been keeping things from me. What else don't I know?"

(That was the new beginning. After that she would routinely invite me to have phone sex with her, and I could come all sorts of ways now. Just the sound of her voice was enough to get me aroused, wet, soaked, in fact. And I developed a whole new vocabulary with her. She taught me how to masturbate myself to orgasm, to fuck myself into delirium. All over the telephone.

Gently, kindly, hotly. She taught me about my body. And in response she would get totally turned on at the other end of the line and make herself come all over my rotary dial. I was never happier, never more sexually satisfied, never more at home with myself or anyone else. And we had never even met. And it was time that we did.)

The beautiful virgin decided it was time to meet this mysterious woman who she had spent so much time with, who had become in fact the virgin's true love. The virgin thought it was best to surprise her just before closing time. She thoughtfully put on her gray Jockey underwear, her button-fly jeans, and her black silk shirt. (She also put on her new black lace bra because she thought her lover might like that.) And she headed to the bookstore.

It was almost midnight, and there was a warm summer breeze outside that calmed her as she walked from the parking lot to the store's entrance. It was strange to see the books all lit up like that, so near to her; these many months the whole thing seemed to exist only in her imagination because she never actually made this journey before.

She entered the bookstore and went directly to the information desk. She knew precisely the layout of the store from all her portable-phone visits. There were two women behind the counter, one facing her and one with her back to her. The one facing her was young, blond, thin, and the virgin had a momentary sinking feeling.

"I can't help you right now; we're about to close," this voice said.

Overjoyed, the virgin knew instantly that this was not her. And the beautiful virgin found herself saying, "That's OK. I'm waiting for someone else."

Within an instant the older, dark-haired, fuller-of-figure woman turned around and simply said, "I knew you would come." The virgin had never seen anyone more beautiful in her life. Here she was. This body and this face that went with this crucial voice were stunning, and the sea-green eyes that looked back at the virgin told her more wonderful stories than all the books she had ever read. "I've been waiting too," the woman said, "my whole life."

(You know, I could never describe this meeting accurately. You have to try to hear it. Turn your ear to the page and listen intently, almost breathlessly, for a long time, and you'll understand. It was that we already knew each other so completely, had forged an undying trust over these many months of vocal intimacy. I knew every nuance of her voice and knew every inch of her body from the countless sounds and words she had offered me. Everything I knew, I knew from hearing her tell me. And it wasn't just fantasy anymore. She really was real. And she wasn't finished with me yet.)

"I'm Val," the woman said, "short for Valentina—Sicilian, on my mother's side." The virgin paused just long enough to realize that this woman could have had any name, any name at all, and she would have known her.

She replied, "My full name is Rosanna Angela Sorella but to you I can just be—"

"Angela," Val interrupted, "just Angela." No one had ever called the virgin by her middle name before, and she began to sense that whatever had gone on in her past could no longer be relied on.

The virgin thought she needed to be formal for their first meeting, so she used the longer version of Val's name. "Um, Valentina," she hesitated, "I came here tonight to meet you because I thought that, uh, maybe we could get to know each other better." There, she'd said it. Val's face brightened, and a wonderful, sexy smile emerged.

"Oh, Angela, my sweet dove, it's a little bit late for that." And she laughed and came from behind the counter, and slipped her arm deftly around the white band of gray Jockey underwear just showing a little over the virgin's jeans, and pulled her closely, tightly, swiftly to her. "I've got things to show you," she whispered into the virgin's ear. "Someone else can close the store tonight," she announced, "tonight won't be like any other." She took the virgin by the hand, and they left through a side door. They walked into the night together—all the while the woman holding fast to the virgin, and in this way leading her forward.

(OK, I hate to break up the narrative, but you need to know that I was terrified out of my mind. I just thought we would stay there; you know, in the store, and I would be protected or something by all the books and the familiarity of the place. Maybe, just maybe, I thought we would kiss a little in the garden section where it all began. I never could have imagined anything like this.)

"We're almost here," she said, as they turned one last corner. And there was Val's building, with several outer doors lined up across the front of it, the sight of which caused the virgin to feel momentarily panic-stricken. What if they entered the wrong door—the virgin's life would be ruined forever. She gathered herself for the possibility of doom, when the woman calmly opened the very last door standing before them. Once opened it revealed a series of inner stairs leading to the actual door of the apartment. On every third step in front of them, to the virgin's astonishment, was a burning votive candle inside a holder of colored glass: green, cobalt, amber, and copper. The virgin had never had such a greeting in her entire life.

"They're for you," Val said, "for your arrival. Let me show you." And she took the virgin inside. There was a desk, a chair, a rug, some plants, a bed, all the usual things in someone's living space, but all around the apartment there was something different: drawings. Some framed, some not, some as small as 1 by 2 inches, others as large as 8½ by 11, and each one, without exception, had a title and date at the bottom.

"These are extraordinary," the virgin said. "I didn't know. Are you an artist?"

"Well, I draw things. I mean I draw our conversations: how they feel, what they mean to me."

"What?" At first the virgin didn't understand. And then she stopped and looked at each picture again and realized that the whole history of her and Val's relationship had been chronicled, preserved, in the most unexpected and beautiful of ways. Angela ran her fingers carefully over each line that Val had made across these pages and understood, for the first time really, what she had heard all along these many months of hearing Val's voice—that they were meant to be together.

(I have to tell you. Never had I experienced anything like that before. Never had I felt so loved as I had climbing up those warm stairs and seeing those drawings—that is, until Valentina took me to bed.)

The virgin was nervous but half expected Val to start to joke or laugh or smile and talk about how big her breasts were going to be. Instead, Val said seriously, "It would be an honor, Angela, to be able to spend this night with you." Val's eyes fixed the virgin's present and future in this precise moment as she took her hand and led her, led her down onto the feather bed waiting for them in the corner of the room. "I want to take you and make you mine," Val told her, "I want to give you everything you've never had before, for real, here, right now. No distance, no phones, no more need for talk."

At first Valentina was almost systematic in her lovemaking and moved, quite literally, from head to toe all over the virgin's body. She gently pulled at the virgin's dark hair curling over her dampening forehead, whispering, "Naked, you are more beautiful to me than stars." Those were the last words Val spoke before she continued by sweetly caressing the virgin's long thick eyelashes with her own and digging her nails confidently across her shoulders, waiting a moment, and then dragging them down her back. As the virgin became increasingly aroused, Val pulled hungrily at her upper lip, while swiftly moving her own hands from behind the virgin's back, up across her belly, and squeezing her breasts to overflow. Sucking, tugging, moaning over her ample nipples, Val knew in exact measure what the virgin could not tell herself: how best to knead the breadth of her inner thighs, to tantalize each toe across the roof of her mouth, and just when it was precisely time to extend her hand into the far reaches of the virgin's pussy. After making sure she had carefully made love to every part of the virgin's body, Val let go of all sense of order and began, quite frankly, to ravage the virgin.

(I felt as if Valentina had garnered all the passion of the universe and presented it to me as some kind of offering, like her drawings. They represented her talent for seeing things both as they were and as they could be. After all of this, I think Valentina was knowingly creating a future, a me, the Me of me, the woman I had kept myself from and from all others all these years. She didn't just take me; she took me someplace better.)

"Your body is a place for me," Val told Angela, "and now I want to fill you up. Wait here." The virgin stayed warm under Val's covers and waited for her to return. When she did, she had on a black leather vest and a black leather harness surrounding a burgundy dildo. "Can I please," Val asked her, "can I please..."

Angela was a bit uncertain how to respond to this entreaty with anything else but an emphatic "yes," except that part of her was hesitant. She was unsure that she could be to Valentina the kind of lover that she deserved; she looked up at Val and said softly, "I'm a little afraid."

And Val said the unexpected but most right words possible back to the virgin: "So am I." And Valentina began to cry, slowly at first, in pace with the rhythm of her fucking, and then she began to sob into Angela's ear, rocking into her, deeper and deeper and deeper, until Angela became hers completely.

They rested together like that a long time, until Angela, the virgin no longer, spoke: "I know now," she said, "my favorite way to come."

You should know now what happened after. Val made love to me again long into the night, and has continued to do so for countless more. Our phones have gathered dust, our books have gone unread, but our lives have grown together, intertwined, like a garden my grandmother would be proud to sing to.

PEACHES AND CREAM

by J.M. Beazer

I met Megan the second week of law school. She came up to me in the crowded hallway in front of the law library. "Hi, I'm Megan McCarthy," she said, extending her hand. "I'm in your Crimes class." She had one of those "map of Ireland" faces. A peaches-and-cream complexion with a spot of pink high on each cheek. Blue eyes and a slice-of-watermelon smile. She wore her blond hair in a boyish cut, short at the nape of the neck and long on top, with a cowlick that dangled a sun-bleached forelock over her forehead.

The handshake introduction struck me as a little formal and old-fashioned, but I was shy about meeting new people and felt relieved someone else had taken the initiative. I took her hand, and we exchanged a firm handshake. "I think I've seen you in Civil Procedure too," I said.

I'd noticed Megan before, but I hadn't pegged her as a likely friend. By the end of the first week of school, our class had already divided itself into several cliques, mostly because—as recommended by everything from our professors to the novel *One-L*—we'd gathered ourselves into study groups. Megan and I had each fallen in with very different crowds. She hung out with the "just-out-of-college" crowd, a group of about eight students who shared the same fresh-faced, suburban look as Megan. They all wore a mix and match of khakis and brightly colored, patterned sweaters; one of them, Karen Mc-Donald, could easily have filled in for Donna Reed in *It's a Wonderful Life.*

By contrast, everyone in my study group had taken at least a year off between college and law school to work in New York City. This alone made us worldly and sophisticated by law school standards, and to Megan's crowd perhaps even a little dangerous. We counted three native New Yorkers in our crowd and two heavy smokers. One of the New York natives, Eric Al-theim, bore a striking resemblance to John Lurie, the actor who had given several Jim Jarmusch films their look of down-town hip. Eric called Megan's group "the Pampers set."

So I was surprised Megan would seek out my friendship. But I'd hated the idea of cliques since junior high school, and I was happy to cross any boundaries they posed. Besides, I knew I wasn't worldly. I'd grown up in the suburbs myself and had my own collection of patterned sweaters.

When Megan approached me, I was talking with my Civil Procedure professor. By the second week of school, I'd already developed a huge crush on this professor, mostly because I'd heard she was a lesbian. I had realized I was gay only recently, during my year off after college, and thanks to a combination of reticence, missed opportunities, and a raging romantic streak that rendered casual sex an impossibility, I hadn't man-aged to act on it yet. I knew exactly one other lesbian, a college friend named Tammy who'd rebuffed me after one kiss because she said we looked too much alike. And so it seemed a stroke of good fortune that my Civil Procedure professor was gay. Un-fortunately, she already had a long-term lover, but I figured I could adore her from afar with impunity. At least it would make studying for one class a whole lot easier.

Although it was a decidedly uncool thing to do, I'd made a point of answering the Socratic-method questions Professor Bonno posed in Civ. Pro. as well as staying after class to ask her questions about the cases we were studying. And so by the second week of law school, I was already known as Professor Bonno's pet. When she was widely rumored to be gay, this was enough to raise questions about me among my classmates, but I was also more or less out as a lesbian. I'd come out to everyone in my study group, and I'd made it clear I didn't expect them to keep my orientation a secret; I therefore assumed the word had gotten around school. And Megan's crowd was particularly well situated in the loop of law school gossip.

We started hanging out together: going to movies after studying in the library, grabbing a bite for dinner at a restaurant. Then Megan included me in one of her charitable activities, handing out meals to the homeless on Thursday nights.

She also started giving me rides home after these activities. After college Megan had returned to live at home with her parents in Bronxville, N.Y., a tiny town about a half hour's drive from the city. She commuted to school each day in her dad's Nissan Stanza or Honda Accord. I was living in a downtown apartment, a long trip by subway because of the connections, but only about a ten-minute ride by car.

She told me she had a boyfriend, Tommy, and that they were on the verge of becoming engaged. But she was plagued with doubts. She thought he was "too noble" for her. He'd once considered becoming a priest. He'd never pressured her for sex; he'd wanted to remain a virgin until he married. (For Megan, it was already too late.) When she finally initiated sex with him, he cried for his loss of innocence. They'd gone out together their last two years at Holy Cross, but now she was thinking of breaking it off with him. She'd already cheated on him twice, with two different guys at law school. She felt she'd ruined her relationship with Tommy. She also felt it just wasn't meant to be.

Not long after that she told me she'd broken up with Tommy. She'd told him she'd cheated on him, several times. Although deeply upset, he was willing to forgive her and go on. This wasn't the response she wanted. She told him she thought it was a sign something was fundamentally wrong in their relationship—or really with her. She was just too wild, and he was too good.

One time after handing out sandwiches to the homeless, we went to a bar. It was a place called Keats, one step up from a standard Irish bar. We each got a pint of Guinness and gossiped about the other students and professors at school. After a second round, she said she had something to tell me. She asked me to promise I wouldn't freak out. I promised. She said she thought she might be a lesbian. I blinked. My mouth dropped open. That was such a coincidence, I told her. Because, well, I'd known for some time I was gay, and I'd been planning to tell her about it soon.

Really? she said. She was so surprised. I didn't look like a lesbian. Did I have a girlfriend? No. But I'd had one in the past, yes? Oh, yes, I said. A short-term thing. She was straight, just experimenting with me, and she'd ultimately gone back to her boyfriend.

I'd lied before I'd even realized it. And I knew why: I just felt like too much of a fool to say I'd never done it. It seemed more aesthetically right, somehow, that I should already have had some experience. I was supposed to be the sophisticated one, after all. And it was just too complicated to come out to someone and then explain that so far you'd only been a lesbian in your head.

I told her I'd play lesbo big sister for her. I'd be happy to show her around the lesbian clubs in New York, answer any questions, and introduce her to my lesbian friends—fudging the plural "friends" from the few lesbians I'd met who were friends with Tammy.

One time we sat talking on the steps out in front of the library. She told me she had a "wild crush" on someone, and the person had "melting blue eyes." I figured she meant Brian Mahoney, a blue-eyed second-year student I'd seen flirting with her. She asked if I could guess who, so I mentioned Brian. She said no, he was a jerk.

I had blue eyes, and the thought crossed my mind she meant me. But that was too scary a thought so I banished it. I was the older "big sister" who was supposed to be taking care of her, not preying on her for my own selfish purposes. And how could I guess she meant me? It would be too mortifying if I were wrong. After a few more wrong guesses, I asked her who it was.

"Not telling," she said.

She kept giving me rides home after school, and we fell into the habit of having long talks in the car just outside my apartment building. I often invited her up, but she always said no, she had to get home.

After talking for about an hour one night, I unhooked my seat belt and said I'd better get going. She grabbed me on the shoulder. She said, "Jolie Beazer, if you don't kiss me I'm going to kill you."

"Oh!" I said. What could I do? I kissed her. I touched my hand to her cheek and gently pressed my lips to hers.

After a few moments, she moved across the seat and on top of me. She pressed the length of her body down against mine. She pressed hard, and her mouth was wet and open, her breath bated and hot.

We kissed for a long time. Then I needed to talk. I shouldn't have done that, I told her. I was supposed to be playing big sister dyke, not snapping her up for myself. She wasn't even sure she was a lesbian. I didn't want to push her into anything. I didn't want to corrupt her.

We hashed that out for a long time, but eventually she convinced me I was being too scrupulous. Silly. A jerk.

"Does this mean we're going out?" I asked.

"We could try it," she said.

We started having sleepovers at her house. No sex, just sleepovers. We rarely stayed at my apartment, partly because I had a roommate with whom I wasn't getting along, partly because we both thought it was more fun to get out of the city. And her parents were often away; they spent several months of the year in Florida. She introduced me to her parents as a friend. I figured that made sense, since she wasn't even sure she was gay. It wasn't like being closeted. On Saturday afternoons we sometimes played golf with her mom. On Sundays I'd go to mass with her even though I wasn't religious.

One Friday night she invited me again to her house. This time she had her dad's station wagon. She apologized for "the bomb;" some mix of sisters and brothers had beaten her to the other cars.

While we were still on the parkway, a thunderstorm broke. When I mentioned I loved thunderstorms, she asked if I'd like to go for a ride before going home. I said sure; she said she'd show me her parents' country club, where we'd play golf with her mom in the morning, weather permitting.

We pulled up at one corner of the parking lot. The rain had turned into a downpour. A streetlamp's arc illuminated the pouring raindrops against the backdrop of the green mesh on the tennis courts' chain-link fence; its lower reaches shone an orange glare on one godforsaken Saab and the white lines of the parking spaces.

We made out in the front seat. She asked if I'd like to stretch out in the way back. It was the one good thing about the bomb, she said. I said sure.

We climbed into the way back of the station wagon. A 20-pound bag of dog food lay in one corner. The floor was covered with a thin, feltlike carpeting that provided next to no cushioning. She lay back and pulled me down on top of her. We went back to making out. Her lips were warm and sweet; they felt small, feminine, and soft. Our legs fell into an interlaced pattern, and her thigh felt firm and warm between my legs, as solid and comforting as a mountain. Soon I found myself pressing rhythmically against her, and she rose up to meet me each time. She slid her hands under my layers of bra, turtleneck, and sweater to feel my breasts. I did the same and unhooked her bra. I felt myself edging close to orgasm, but I held back, embarrassed by the idea of going over so quickly.

Then she reached down and started unbuttoning my jeans. Panic set in. Now I was supposed to know what I was doing. She would be looking to me. I considered confessing but rejected the idea. It wasn't the time. I'd just have to wing it. How difficult could it be? I wanted to go down on her, and I'd imagined it so many times before, in such minute detail. I'd read *The Joy of Lesbian Sex* from cover to cover, and I'd studied all the drawings. Wouldn't the same principles apply as for kissing?

The problem was my nervousness had killed all my feelings. Instead of needing to hold back, I was wondering how I could possibly have an orgasm. Would I have to fake it my first time? I'd faked it a few times with my one boyfriend in college, but I didn't want to have to fake it with a woman. That would be such a letdown, especially after all the hours of daydreaming I'd invested in it.

But at least I could do whatever I could to bring her to an orgasm. That would be something. I helped her out of her jeans. I'd already bunched her turtleneck and sweater up by her neck, and she'd pulled her arms out of the sleeves. I kissed her breasts and moved slowly down her stomach. Her back arched as I reached her belly button. She had her legs spread on either side of me, as if she had no doubt what I had in mind.

And then I had it right in front of me. The darkness inside the car left the colors grayed-out, but I could still make out the slip of smooth, wet pink nestled between the darkness on either side. The slip of pink was her clit, I knew, and I followed it down to place where it tucked itself away into the shadows. I wanted to plunge my face into it and lap it all up. I'd been waiting so long.

But I decided that would be maladroit. I decided to tease her a little bit. I nuzzled forward with my nose and lips, just grazing the hair and letting my breath stroke the flesh. Her pelvis was rocking up and down, and she let out a series of small sounds. She started gyrating beneath me. I touched the tip of my tongue to her clit right at the top, where the folds joined together. She bucked against me, let out a groan.

With a growl I sank into her. Nose, lips, and chin; my tongue slid down into the mouth of the tunnel at the bottom. I was surrounded with the soft, puffy folds; everything was gooey and warm and wet. And mine, all mine. I sucked and nuzzled and kissed, letting out a repeated rhythm of eager, murmuring sounds—mmm, mmm, mmm, mmm, mmm. I slathered my face with her wetness. I was feasting on her; gobbling her up. I smacked and slurped to make sure she knew what she was getting. And that I liked nothing better than to give it to her. Pussy, pussy, pussy, pussy, pussy, pussy. Oh, pussy. Been waiting so long. She gyrated wildly beneath me, one hand alternately gripping mine and then pressing its palm flat against me.

Without realizing it, I'd been squeezing my legs together again and again. I was surprised to find it could be so arousing to service someone else. And when I felt her building to a climax, I was right there with her, mirroring each escalation in the pitch and intensity of her moans and gyrations with my own. When she let out a guttural scream, the mere sound of it sent me over the edge with her. I squeezed and squeezed while she bore down against me. We were joined into one grinding, bucking, and groaning machine.

As we were coming back down, a brief worry flashed through my mind: Should I have held back so she could go down on me? But just then light illuminated my eyelids with an orange glow. My eyes snapped open. A double beam of white light panned over the car, sparkling the water streaming down the windows.

"Shit, the cops!" Megan said, scrambling out from under me.

"What?" She was already climbing into the back seat, naked except for the sweater and turtleneck hanging around her neck. I pulled up my jeans and followed. The other car stood facing us from the side, its headlights staring straight at us. All the windows were fogged up. The fogging might have prevented them from getting a good view of us, but the mere fact of it also probably gave them a good idea what had been going on inside.

I fell into the passenger seat. Megan turned the ignition and started backing us up. "I can't believe they shined us," she said. She straightened us out and pulled out of the parking lot, nice and slow. The cops followed us a few feet behind. "You don't think they could tell it was two women, do you?"

"No way," I said, although I wasn't sure. I was more concerned with her evident familiarity with the ways of the town police. Somehow I had the feeling this wasn't the first time Megan had been "shined."

This business with the cops distracted me, to say the least, and so it wasn't until much later that I realized we'd succeeded in "doing it" for the first time. When neither of us had ever experienced lesbian sex before. Two ingenues, with our patterned sweaters and our law school textbooks piled in the back seat. Virgin-to-virgin, all peaches and cream. I liked that. I liked it a lot.

Oh, Dinah!

by Jesi O'Connell

I held Renée close to me as we danced, surrounded by hundreds of other sweaty, sexy, excited women in a hotel ballroom in the desert. I put my leg between Renée's legs, and she began to grind on it—still dancing, of course. She was wearing her black velvet jeans, which she knew were my favorite because of their softness and the casual elegance they projected. I was aroused, a bit tipsy, and a lot confused. This was my best friend I was holding in my arms. My *married-to-a-man* (but separated) best friend, who in the past six months or so had become most interested in my lesbian life.

Of course, this was also the weekend of the Dinah Shore golf tournament, that annual springtime sapphic conflagration in the desert. This was the big time, baby. Twenty thousand lesbians (so they said) had descended on Palm Springs, Calif., that weekend, turning the geriatric, rich, very white town into a melee of swarming lesbians from every walk of life who threatened to consume everything in their "out and damned proud of it" path. This was manna from dyke heaven.

In other words, if you didn't get laid, you were pretty pathetic. With 20,000 women to choose from, how could you *not* get lucky at some point during the three days of bacchanalian revelry under the sun? There were topless women-only pool parties, sumptuous evening affairs with babes dolled up to the teeth, luscious ladies everywhere strolling the streets. Opportunity knocked from all sides.

So here we were, me and my straight best friend Renée (who had transformed herself into quite the little lesbian-in-training the more she hung out with me), dancing up a sexy storm under the multicolored lights of the packed lesbo extravaganza to which we had chosen to fork over $35 apiece. We were getting closer as the night got wilder. My opportunity, it seemed, might be coming from a most unexpected place. As I placed a hand on Renée's thigh and tentatively caressed the velvet, I tried to recall how things had progressed to this very sensuous moment, ripe with the promise of forbidden sexual adventure amid the libidos in overdrive in the desert.

I first met Renée when we were 18-year-old students at college, new and raw and exposed to the big world for the first time. The school is a small liberal arts women's college in California, near several other colleges that admit both men and women. During our four sun-drenched years there, I had a boyfriend for two and a half years and an increasing curiosity about women. Renée had boyfriend after boyfriend, eventually culminating in her fiancé. By the time we graduated, she was a year away from marriage, and I was a few years away from firmly declaring myself a lesbian.

After commencement (my school did not "graduate" students; it commenced us on our next adventure in life), Renée retreated farther south to attend graduate school. Never very close friends during college, we lost touch until her wedding, a rather dour affair during which her other friends quietly expressed among themselves amazement that she was actually marrying the guy; they considered him to be completely unworthy of her. After the wedding Renée and I again drifted out of one another's lives, not to reconnect for more than a year.

In the autumn two years after college, I was jobless, living at my mother's house, reveling secretly in my newfound lesbian sisterhood, and bemoaning the fact that most of my friends lived improbable distances away. Then Renée and her husband moved to a town ten minutes from my house, and suddenly she and I were the best of friends.

Renée threw herself into all the activities dear to my heart: horseback riding, hiking, camping, photography. We indulged in our cherished riding when we could, took a photography class together, joined the gay and lesbian Sierra Scouts (only because she had friends in it, of course) to go camping in Big Sur, and hiked in the local mountains every chance we got. Once, heading down a trail on a typically warm fall day, we heard what I could swear was a very loud sprinkler system, except that sprinkler systems in the middle of a national forest are, to my knowledge, a rarity. We rounded a corner and a man shouted, "Be careful up there! There's a rattlesnake right on the trail." Renée clutched at my arm as we gingerly stepped closer for a good look, and I remember swelling with some ridiculous emotion like pride at the thought of protecting the little golden-haired maiden. Already dangerous signs of attraction were appearing, but I was blind to them. Or keeping them under very tight wraps, at least.

The February after the rekindling of our friendship, she urged me to make a surprise Valentine's Day visit to my current flame, who was attending school up north. Renée joined me for the ten-hour drive; in fact, we took her car and she did most of the driving. Katherine, my adulterous love of the moment, was busy seeing about five other women at the time, but naturally she took the time to roll around with me during the weekend we spent up there. Hey, there was a willing woman in her bed all weekend!

On the second evening the three of us prepared dinner in her apartment prior to going dancing. During the meal we all flirted with one another somewhat mildly. Katherine knew about Renée's burgeoning interest in the world of Dorothy's sisters and was encouraging it. Later, at "gay night" in the local disco, we shimmied and drank and got wild with one another—Katherine and I, that is. Renée was shy during the dancing and hung back, watching closely but not participating.

Later still, after we were back at Katherine's apartment, Katherine and I started to get hot and heavy on the floor in the living room in front of Renée. At this point things took a distinctly *Twilight Zone*-type turn.

"Mmm, Jesi's kisses are really good." Katherine, who was totally ripped, said this in a sort of woolly voice from the floor to Renée, who was watching us out of the corners of her eyes from her perch on the couch. "Isn't she hot? Don't you think she's the sexiest thing when she's dressed up in her riding clothes?" Katherine had seen me in my riding clothes quite a lot the previous summer when we worked together at a riding academy for rich kids. "She has this really cool little English crop. And her black riding boots. And those chaps—" Katherine could barely go on from remembering our summer nights of debauchery, which included episodes with said chaps, and she began kissing and sucking my neck. I futilely patted her away and complained of hickey marks. "You know, I called her Chaps all last summer. In private, of course. But, *wow,* when she walked around in them! I could hardly keep still."

Katherine was getting that gleam in her eye, the one that always preceded sex. I looked at Renée. She avoided my eyes but sort of grinned in an appealing, femme-y girl way. Katherine noticed this and said lecherously, "Come down here with us. Come on, we won't bite."

"*I* won't, at least," I said, as reassuringly as possible. Renée looked torn, like she was ready to either flee out the front door or leap down to join us. She stayed frozen.

"Jesi," said Katherine, her voice teasing and giggly and pseudo-top the way it got when she was really turned-on. "Go put them on. The chaps. You brought them, didn't you?"

"Oh, indeed," I replied simply, disentangling myself from her and getting up.

I stood in Katherine's room for several minutes after I had slipped on the soft black leather chaps. I was not wearing underwear and my ass hung out the back, like the well-toned gay boys who "dress up" for pride festivals. I protectively put my hands over my exposed, furry mound in front, the lips already pouty, juiced up from Katherine's kisses earlier, and edged toward the living room. Showing off to and playing with Katherine was one thing. But that was Renée in there. My straight friend. My married friend. I did not stroll around naked in front of my friends. Especially not while wearing riding chaps and nothing else. Good old puritanical American values at work there, but that was that, and I couldn't do it. But this—this was feeling different. Renée was crossing the line from friendship to—something else. What she was crossing over into, I was not yet sure, and I wasn't sure I could handle it.

Much later, Renée told me that when she saw me walk into the living room in my leather attire, she literally could not breathe for a second. When she finally could breathe and think again, she realized that she was both very turned on and very scared by the implications of her arousal. She really wanted this: the sexual lesbian relationship, the bonding with women, sex and safety with women. But when the reality of it approached, encased in black leather with silver zippers up the legs and little brass buckles in the back and the front, she couldn't deal with it.

Katherine made me prance around the living room a bit, laughing and leering and stroking me when I got close to her. I pranced, got hotter by the second, and watched Renée. She was watching me too. Katherine was whooping and encouraging Renée to touch me. Suddenly, Renée got up.

"This is too much for me. I need to go to sleep," she said, rising and turning away from us. She went down the hall to the bathroom without a backward glance and closed the door, and we heard water running a few moments later.

Katherine looked at me. "Guess she's not ready yet," she said, her party mode slightly deflated.

"Guess not." I glanced toward the bathroom door. I was wondering if Renée was going to be ready for this ever, if this was *really* what she wanted. And why on earth would she want me? I was a friend, not sex-with-a-woman-for-the-first-time material. Renée was cute in a pixieish, little blond way, but she was my friend, and I drew the line at sleeping with someone I considered only a friend. Hah! Not only blind, but stubborn.

When we drove back to Los Angeles, we barely discussed the incident. Our brief conversation was enough to put me at rest about her intentions, however.

"Jesi, whatever happens between us, ever, I always want to be friends. So if we ever start to do something that will mess up our friendship, I want to stop. OK?"

I agreed and that was that. For a little while, at least.

So I denied the whole attraction thing to myself for another month and a half. We were merely friends, and besides, she was a married woman. (The fact that married people regularly cheat on their spouses, which is what Renée's husband had done to her and the reason for their impending divorce, somehow did not enter into this neat little equation of mine.) But then here we were in Palm Springs at the end of March, dancing so close Saran Wrap couldn't pass between our sweaty flesh.

Well, fine. I was a *bit* interested in her. She was pretty, she was totally safe, she was showing the signs of being physically attracted to me (uh, gee, Jesi, you think?). I was surrounded by shimmying lesbians displaying an abundance of sweat-sheened flesh, I was a bit drunk, and I really was turned-on. The erotic stars were in alignment that night.

When we got back to the condo were staying in for the weekend, the rest of our party dispersed to their various rooms, and there was the requisite amount of either giggling or total silence from behind each door. Renée and I were staying in a room together, which did not dawn on me for a number of years as being preplanned. Not only was I in denial, I was simply plain dense about the entire matter at the time. The realizations hindsight can bring are amazing.

I remember Renée was wearing a white nightdress that flowed loose and sleeveless from her shoulders to her ankles. There may have been lace around the hem and small blue flowers sprinkled liberally across the fabric. I have no idea what I was wearing—probably my usual bedtime outfit of sweat pants and a T-shirt. The room itself was unremarkable: a typical condo bedroom, fully carpeted, with white walls and bookshelves filled with paperbacks from the 70s. The queen-size bed, covered with a dusty rose-colored throw and several plump pillows, was the focus of attention.

We crawled into the bed, the same one that had held us chastely the night before. I did not move, practically did not breathe, and waited for her to turn out the light. We lay in the dark for several minutes and discussed mundane details of the weekend, carefully not touching one another. Finally there was a silence, and I could almost hear her gearing up for an announcement.

"Jesi." She stopped and stayed quiet for another minute. I was suddenly so afraid of what she was going to say that I almost blurted out something stupid to make her stop. But I managed to rein in my idiocy and listened as she slowly went on.

"Well, Jesi, you have to know how I feel about you. I'm totally attracted to you, and you can't be blind to it."

Sure I could. I was terrified as she spoke; terrified yet aware of her cute, small body right next to me, about to be mine for the taking, it seemed.

"I've been thinking about you and wanting you for a long time, and this opportunity seems ideal. You know I've thought about sleeping with a woman, and you're safe. I trust you." Her voice was soft and tentative. "Can I kiss you?"

"Uh," I replied gracefully. She took that for a "yes" and moved closer to me, sliding across the sheet in a cotton rustle. When she leaned over, with me flat on my back and in shock, I smelled girlie things: scented lotion, clean hair, a dab of mango perfume on her neck. As her face came toward mine in the semidarkness, I was barely breathing.

Soft, gentle, curious lips on mine. She kissed like a naive beginner at first, closed mouth and little pecks. As my pulse started going faster and my mind spun to catch up with these interesting events, my mouth began responding, and I soundlessly encouraged her to slow down, take her time and explore. One arm stole over my chest, planted itself beside my head, holding me firmly as she kissed with growing confidence and passion. Tiny noises escaped from her throat, and she kissed me more fiercely.

I finally moved my arms around her and pulled her on top on me. My sole impression of her that entire first time was of a little bird, so much smaller than any woman I'd ever slept with, almost fragile. But I sensed the steel inside her and wondered fleetingly if it would reveal itself that night.

"Show me," she murmured, but it was she who was showing me with every move of her mouth, her hands, her body atop mine.

Our lips and tongues tangled together with increasing urgency. She tasted like a piece of sweet, ripe fruit. I licked her neck, her chin, kissed her lips over and over, nibbled on her small ears, hungrily nuzzled that little hollow at the base of her neck. In return, she moaned and whispered my name, breath panting gently against my skin. She stoked the sides of my face, touched my breasts, shivered with delight as my nipples hardened under her ministrations. I was still lying flat on my back, still not completely comprehending that this was happening—*I'm in bed with Renée! My best friend! She's kissing me! She's doing more than kissing me! She's never done this with a woman before!* Etc.—not quite sure how to react to it all. Except to lie there and take it and get really turned-on.

As Renée kissed me and explored my stomach with delicate fingertips, inching up under my T-shirt to my bare breasts, I sucked in my breath. Though a virgin to another woman, Renée knew how to arouse a body, no matter what the gender.

My fear that something weird was happening here with my best friend began to fall away with every touch of her skin against mine, every groan that was pulled out of me from her lips and fingers. I was still on my back, however, and wasn't yet inclined to suddenly top her and prove who was the lothario of lovemaking in this situation.

Renée gently tugged my shirt over my head. In the dark, her blond hair was a faint gleam as she bent over my breasts and began to lick them.

"Renée," was all I managed to get out, stunned by her tongue circling my nipples, her teeth gently biting the areolae, her fingers massaging and pressing and exploring. I was turned-on in a slightly muffled way; an incomplete arousal hidden behind my startlement at these events. But I could feel the wetness between my legs as I ran a hand through her hair, skimmed my fingers over the back of her neck, touched her lower back.

Slowly, but with all the eagerness of a kid on Christmas morning, she left my breasts and sat back on her knees. Her hands grasped the waistband of my sweats and she pulled them down, sliding across my thighs, gathering at my ankles, tugging them off with a bit of impatience. My breath caught in my throat at this move, though my hips lifted willingly enough to let her proceed. I was certainly not going to stop this now, not at this delicious point.

With gentle hands she pushed my legs apart and ran her fingers along my inner thighs, down to my feet—that tickled, and I squealed a bit—back up to my knees, higher. Her fingers lightly touched my hipbones. My breath filled my chest in a long, controlled inhale and stayed for an eternal moment, suspended as I waited for her next action.

She maneuvered herself down on the bed, rubbed her face against my legs, licked some shaking skin, put her head between my legs. My breath loudly left my lungs in a whoosh.

"Renée, are you sure you want to…oh, God," I moaned as her mouth landed on my clit, my wet inner lips, the throbbing point of desire that abruptly leaped and pulsed with pent-up tension at her touch.

She lifted her head for a fraction of a second to deliriously exclaim, "It tastes like I always thought it would!" before returning to the task at hand. I was so far gone I couldn't possibly reply beyond an overwhelmed groan.

Her sweet virgin mouth and daring virgin tongue were not at all unskilled as they descended on me. She licked like a pro, knowing exactly what to do, when to focus intensely on my clit with short, sharp strokes, when to swirl her tongue all around every fold and crevice and cover me with heat and wetness. I was *still* flat on my back, legs spread wide now, reaching down to touch her rhythmically bobbing head between my thighs. I was in such a state of delighted disbelief that any hang-ups that might have manifested between us had this been more planned were wiped away by her wet tongue, my inner vision of her pixie head planted firmly over my burning pussy, my excitement at the feel of her virgin lips on me. I came so quickly, so easily, that I almost missed it. It rolled over me like a tiny wave at low tide, breaking on my vibrating clit and moving on through my pussy walls, across my belly and up to my chest, unconcernedly passing through my head and out my mouth in a long sigh.

Either she did not realize I had had an orgasm or she knew full well; either way, she continued on, her lips making little sucking sounds and her fingers daring their way through my wild bush, drumming lightly on my ass, inching up toward my aching hole, and then quickly leaving as her mouth fastened on me more determinedly. She pulled the heat out of me and into her mouth, reached and bit and licked my clit until I was trembling all over, my fingers grabbing her head and lightly pushing it farther down onto me, making her lips smash into me, working fiercely and with serious intent, making me whirl up and go blind with the force of it, until I came, and I came, and I came.

When I stopped moving beneath her and only exhausted little noises left my throat, she wiped her face on the sheet and crawled up my body until her face was at mine. She lowered her lips onto mine and kissed me, and I could taste my juices in her mouth, mixed with her own delicate scent and her still-rising excitement.

Renée clearly wanted reciprocation at this point. She rolled over and lay there beside me, gently circling her pelvis against the air, trailing questioning fingers down my arm. I was somewhat in a daze from the completely unexpected orgasms she had teased out of me, I was still in a tiny bit of shock from the entire thing, and I was terrified she would think my lovemaking prowess was pathetic. Team a bottom with a virgin lesbian/straight girl who wants to learn, and you've got a problem. So while I lay there, mind racing over what I should do next, I merely slipped my hand onto her smooth belly and down to the curly golden hairs between her thighs, fluttering my fingers along the way, guided by her breathy sighs of encouragement. My hand nestled itself over her wet folds and began to stroke. Her hands grasped my arm and started a seemingly unconscious rhythmic action of pressure, monitoring my movements, speeding me up, slowing me down. I rolled my thumb over her clit, massaged my index finger in her slickness, and rubbed her as steadily as I could.

Her voice chanted musically in the otherwise still room, noises that were not language, only sounds coupled with light breathing and the squeezing of her hands on my arm, her hips circling and rising under my fingers, until she finally gasped and shook a bit, and then gently moved my hand away.

"How was it?" I asked fearfully after a few minutes, pulling her close to me.

"Baby bang," she said back, still breathing quickly. I grimaced inside, wondering if a "baby bang" was enough. But she petted me reassuringly, and drew me to her for kisses, and I held her close and touched her skin everywhere and inhaled that sweet smell of mangoes and girl and sex.

I was too scared to do more that night, and we merely held one another and talked and finally drifted off to sleep. She was giddy in the morning and managed to be physically close to me, touching my hand, my shoulder, pressing against my back, all day. I was confused and alarmed at what I had allowed, and I was distant. I fled from her and the delights of Dinah Shore with hardly a good-bye that weekend, fled in a resurgence of fear at what those turn of events would mean to our friendship. Renée was justifiably upset with me.

Eventually we made up. Eventually we were lovers again. Eventually others came between us. Eventually what I knew in my gut would happen did indeed occur: Our friendship disintegrated into jealously, lies, betrayal, spiteful words and actions that left us each bruised and silent for more than six months as we tried to lick our wounds and heal in peace, alone.

We finally did patch things up, and we even slept together one last time; in Palm Springs, ironically enough, although not during the wildness of another Dinah Shore weekend. What I recall about that last time together was Renée's sweet, uncomplicated rocking back and forth on top of me, and her long slow sigh as my fingers lazily played over her, and the absolute wonder of her hands when she finally collapsed on me and stroked my face. And her words: "I finally understand, Jesi. I finally know what it's really like with a woman. I saw the light." And I was simply content that I had finally pleased her.

Silver Marie

by Jennifer Lindenberger

I lived in Gaithersburg, just half an hour's commute from Georgetown and downtown Washington, D.C. I'd earned a degree in American literature, and I put my BA to use by working at an express lube on Rockville Pike. It wasn't all bad. I had my evenings free to go clubbing, and unlike most grads, I didn't mind rolling up my sleeves and ending the day covered in grease.

All of my coworkers were guys. Given my buzzed, tomato-red hair and choice of occupation, they had an idea that I was gay, and I've always been open about it. So when a new girl applied as a cashier on a hot August morning, some of my grinning associates elbowed me and pointed through the office window.

"Idiots," I jokingly called them. "Get back to work." But I have to admit, I'd already noticed her. Maybe she looked a bit like a princess with her short denim skirt and frilly blouse, but she had a nice way about her. I was glad when she got the job.

Her name was Marie. Each time I finished a job, I handed her my work form, and she rang up the customers. For three weeks, we never said much more than "Here you go" and "Thanks." She seemed kind of quiet and sad, but I was too busy to ask why. I'd had my heart broken by princesses and breeders before, so what was the point in getting involved?

One day she came right out and asked if we could talk. "After work," I told her, and we met at my place. I would have gladly met her somewhere else, but after ten hours of playing in motor oil, it's smart to get a shower. It didn't matter, though. She was anxious and came early, so I answered the door in my overalls and looking like a certifiable grease monkey.

"You found the place all right?" I said, stumbling over my words. It's hard to explain. I'd seen her six days a week for nearly two months, but that was work. Things are different on the outside. She looked so pretty now, the waning sunlight sparkling in her long dark hair, small breasts pert beneath her white blouse. She'd taken off the bra she usually wore, and her chocolate nipples shone through in the light. Even her skirt was shorter and more revealing than was typical, and I wondered at her choice of attire. That's when I noticed her hazel eyes, glistening with tears.

"Can I come in?" she said.

"Of course," I told her. I sat her down in the little den of my apartment and fixed us some tea. We got to talking, and it soon became clear that she was having trouble with her boyfriend. *Here we go again,* I thought. All my life it had been attractive friends telling me their man troubles. The more I helped, the more alone I felt, and meeting strangers at clubs only went so far.

I sat down on a towel to protect the couch from my greasy clothes and told her I didn't know how I could help. I'd seen her boyfriend around the shop. A punk, about ten years older than her, in his 30s, unemployed, and laying rubber everywhere he went in his black Firebird. I knew the type. I wanted nothing to do with this.

"He's angry that I won't have sex with him," she said.

I rolled my eyes. "Sounds like that's his problem," I said and sipped my tea.

"I haven't had sex with anyone," she confessed, leaning close. Her eyes were serious and soft, but what I noticed was her hand on my leg. Was she so naive that she didn't realize what she was doing to me? Already my cunt was smoldering, my clitoris full of blood and tingling. Every time she moved, I swore I almost caught a glimpse of her bare nipples between the buttons of her blouse, and the subtle seduction drove me crazy.

"Don't do anything you don't want to do," I said, mind wandering through a myriad of sex fantasies. I'd had enough one-night stands in college. But I missed lovemaking terribly. The fact that she was a virgin only added spice to my lust, and I suggested she talk to someone else. She seemed not to hear me. As she looked out the window, her hand moved up my leg.

OK. So now I really didn't understand this chick's trip. I could easily have put my lips on that slender neck of hers, but the last thing I needed was rejection. Or a virginal tease, for that matter. I was just starting to get my shit together, and I didn't want to lose it again.

How would you like to lose it, Marie? I heard myself wanting to say. Enough. I needed out, and I made up an excuse that I felt icky in these clothes, and that we could talk after I cleaned up. Truth be told, I had a toy or two waiting in the shower for me. Maybe she'd hear the vibrating motor. Maybe she'd even hear a moan or two. But I didn't give a fuck. Let her deal with it. I told her to make herself at home, and I went to the bathroom where I stripped down faster than ever in my life. It sure felt good to get those overalls off, and even better to peel my undies from my moist crotch. I got the water good and hot and jumped under it. No foreplay today; I put my vibrator on high and stuffed that little bitch right in there. Fingering my clit, I came just as princess tapped on the door.

Shit!

I froze. My legs were shaking, my mouth salivating. And I just knew she'd come in uninvited. That seemed to be her style, and what luck—I'd put in a new, transparent shower curtain because I thought it was (of all things) sexy.

"Can I come in?" she said.

"Of course!" I called back. How about that? I let my pussy do the talking, every time. How I must have loved torturing myself, and I pulled my pink vibrator out so fast that it hurt, fumbled to turn the dial off, and dropped it just as the door opened. I snapped around, put my hands behind my back like a kid hiding something. I felt so silly. Just two girls in the bathroom—why was I acting like this?

"Is something wrong?"

"Not at all," I said, doing what Mother used to call my "nervous dance." I grabbed up the soap as though to prove that I was just cleaning myself. I swear, I even held it up so she could see I wasn't up to anything. Like, *Look! Just soap! Nothing going on here!*

Marie sat down on the only seat available and started talking. Pretty soon, I'd relaxed enough to not only wash, but to make a bit of an exhibition of it. I couldn't help it. I saw her through the curtain as plainly as she saw me, and I liked the way she looked at my rotund, womanly body. Once or twice, she glanced at my bush, dyed as fiery red as my hair. I washed it slowly for her, and she seemed to like it.

"I've always had stronger feelings for women," I heard her saying. "Even as a kid. Maybe that's why I have intimacy problems with men."

"Maybe," I said, hardly hearing her. I was washing my ass now. I slid the soap along my crack, delighting in the slipperiness of my skin. Marie was looking away at the moment, and it sort of pissed me off. I mean, I was putting on a good show here!

"But I can't be a lesbian," she said. "I mean, I've never had sex with a woman, either."

OK. Now I really was pissed. "Listen," I said. "Sex is just a way of acting out desire. Fucking women doesn't make you a dyke. What's inside does!"

That's about how I put it. Maybe even more strongly. The way I figured, she'd either listen to me, or she'd leave. Either way, we were both better off, and I've found that it's better to cut through the bullshit in these matters.

Marie didn't say a thing. She turned her chin up slowly, and her eyes held me. The silence lasted forever, our eyes locked and my heart racing. I was so nervous. Minutes might have passed, the water splashing on my shoulders and back, massaging me. My hand came alive. Like it had a mind all its own. It slid slowly down my belly, and Marie watched as my fingertips reached through my red mound of pubic hair. My throat nearly closed up, dry with anxiety. She could look away. She could get up and leave. It was all up to her, but knowing that didn't stop the pounding in my chest as I took things a step further.

"Feel anything?" I breathed as my fingertip brushed my swollen clit. I was so sensitive that I jumped and my thigh muscles twitched. I almost came again, just from that one touch!

"Yes," she said, and she got up and came to the shower curtain just as I parted my labia. She looked down, her eyes sultry as I slid my finger inside my vagina. It was happening! I was so damned excited, because I knew it was happening and there was no stopping it now. Marie was entranced as she knelt down and watched me slide my fingers in and out, massaging the smooth walls inside of me. Steam billowed all around. It was cold compared to the hot oil inside my cunt, and I closed my eyes and put my head back as I masturbated for her. I loved the way she watched with such innocent fascination. Almost like a child, but I could feel her hunger too.

The next thing I knew, Marie had pulled the shower curtain aside. She leaned into me, her mouth touching my fingers as I masturbated. I let out a groan and caressed her dark hair with one hand while I pleasured myself with the other. She licked my knuckles so delicately, sometimes slipping her tongue between my fingers and teasing at my flesh. She knew how to drive me crazy, that's for sure. Sometimes I wasn't sure if it was my hand or her soft tongue that rubbed against my clit, but it sent shock waves through me either way.

She pushed my knees apart, slowly. Then she went all apeshit. Maybe the long wait had gotten to her too. She yanked my hand away and buried her mouth in me, all her years of denial shed away at once. I almost fell over at her aggression! She ate so forcefully, licking deep in my hole and pushing me with her face. I might have come if she would have relaxed a little, but I got off on her lust. If she was inexperienced, her ambition certainly made up for it!

My eyes shot open just as the hot water ran out. I shivered, my large nipples turning painfully hard in the cold. Marie reached back under her skirt and was playing with herself as she ate, and I remembered that the best pleasure awaited.

Stepping from the stall, I took her by the arm and led her up. We kissed, and I tasted my juices all over her mouth. My teeth chattering from the cold, I led her into the bedroom and put her down on my bed. There was a drawer in my dresser. From it I removed a thin, silver dildo in the elegant shape of a woman. I set it beside Marie and leaned over her, dripping on her clothes, and we kissed again as I unbuttoned her blouse. I licked her nipples, so dark that they were almost black. I never heard a woman howl with such pleasure at having her nipples sucked, but this was all new to her. Her chest heaved like mad. I could hardly keep my mouth on her, but I put up a good fight trying! Her hands ran over my shoulders and pushed me down to her belly. I pulled her skirt and panties down, inhaling her aroma. Oh, how she moaned and breathed with such anticipation! I couldn't help myself, and I dove on her as eagerly as she'd gone down on me.

This virgin tasted fresh and salty, and quite ready for love. Her labia were tiny, almost nonexistent, her pussy a mere slit that invited me to squeeze my tongue in. Her clit was round and full, though. My nose rubbed against it as I ate. She squealed again and again. Her legs shook. I knew she was about to come, and I reached for my Silver Lady.

The Silver Lady: the slender, chrome dildo, beautifully cast in the likeness of a woman. She was a virgin herself, bought on a spring break trip to St. Petersburg three whole years earlier. I found her with another woman at a sex shop while we vacationed there. I'd waited for a special time to use my Silver Lady, but we split up before I ever got the chance. I knew that this was it, and I licked her from head to toe and slipped her inside Marie's awaiting vagina.

I had to keep control. I was so ready to just fuck. You know the feeling, right? But Marie needed some delicacy. I wanted her first experience to be as gentle as possible, so I eased the chrome dildo back and forth, just slightly deeper each time. Marie rotated her hips. She slid down the bed, engulfing more of the dildo than I intended. Maybe she was as eager as I was, and she lifted her head and wrapped her hand around my wrist. She pulled hard, taking the sex toy in deep and sudden. Then she let out a squeal and dug her nails into my wrist so hard that I bled, pressing her face against mine so that our lips mashed together. Her body shook like she was possessed. She cried out again and finally let go, collapsing on the bed and groaning with pleasure. Thin blood ran gently from her, down the crack of her little ass and onto my bedspread.

"Oh, my, oh, my" I think I said. For a moment, I was shocked. Then I was greedy. I tossed my Silver Lady aside and mounted sweet Marie. Legs spread like scissors, I pressed my slit into hers and held onto her ankles. She had this satisfied, womanly look on her face, but also looked like she wasn't quite sure what I was up to. I bit my lip, and I rode her, pumping and grinding, and pretty soon, she more than caught on. My inflated labia massaged hers, juices flowing as her virginal blood painted my thighs. This was what pleasure was all about, her nipples exploding as she pinched them and screamed with her first orgasm. I came too. At last! Her blood stimulated me, and her clit felt burning hot as it slipped against mine. We fucked until the sun was down and we couldn't see each other anymore, then collapsed, aching, in each other's arms. I never felt so spent in all my life.

The perfume of our sex still hung in the air as we held each other in the dark. This was the part I would have worried about, if I'd had the time to worry. What would she say? What did she want? Hell, I didn't even know what I wanted, lying there all sticky from sweat and our juices. She was all over me.

Oh, no, I thought. I was heating up again just thinking about her, and I tried to come up with something to say.

"I liked it," Marie whispered in my ear before I got the words out. It was a hard question to ask, and she'd beat me to it. "It was just what I wanted."

"I liked it too," I told her, and we held each other awhile longer, listening to ourselves breathe and smelling each other's skin.

Later Marie said that she needed a shower. I said "OK" and dug out a towel for her. I felt awkward again, but she kissed me and told me not to worry. How about that? Here I was, a dyed-in-the-wool dyke with more lovers in her youth than I cared to count, acting like I was the one who'd just lost her cherry! Well, maybe that was natural. When I opened Marie, I opened doors for her. But just as much, she gave me a new experience and the chance to see through fresh eyes.

I put on a robe and made fresh tea while she showered. We drank leisurely, and then we kissed and said good night. I felt really good. I looked forward to seeing her the next day, and when I did, things weren't as uncomfortable as I might have expected. I learned quickly to give this seeming princess a bit more credit.

We didn't make love again for a long, long time. We worked on our friendship, and we both saw other people. The jackass with the Firebird was quickly out of the picture, and I took Marie to readings at some of my favorite bookstores and sometimes dancing on the weekends. Other than an occasional kiss good night, it seemed that the sexual part of relationship had passed. She became my closest friend.

More than three years have gone by. I've moved since then, northward to Pennsylvania on a scholarship, and I just obtained my MA. Marie writes and calls, and sometimes we visit. Things between us have heated up again, but the long-distance stuff is hard. She says she's moving to sunny Miami, and she wants me to come with her. Marie is so impetuous these days! Her offer is almost tempting as it's the dead of winter here, and the people in this town are as frigid as the weather. All the same I don't think I'll go. Not with her, anyway. And not to Miami. I'll find my own path, and I plan never to forget my virgin princess.

In My Heart

by Jules Torti

I had never loved a virgin before. Her warm flesh untouched, a blank canvas, a colorful palette…eager and desperate for knowing hands and an experienced tongue. She begged me with wide-eyed innocence, golden hair spun of silk cradling her soft features. Blue eyes like the distant Pacific and skin the color of butterscotch pudding. She said she was an art student, a sculptor, and that she'd love to do my body in clay. Would I mind posing nude for her?

I wondered who was doing the seducing. She was the virgin, I was the experienced one. I wondered why I hadn't used the sculptor line before. Probably because I didn't sculpt. I was a painter, though, so I decided to offer my nude body to a work in clay if she returned the favor. I was tempted to do her in oils; it takes longer for the paint to dry, and I could extend the length of time needed to study and indulge in her lovely, naked body.

We met in a little café on Commercial Drive called Josephine's. I often went there after work to sip a couple of black coffees on the patio. They make the flakiest blueberry strudels, and when she approached me, I had a mouthful of berries and pastry. She strolled onto the patio with the grace of a butterfly, long legs taking confident strides. Dressed simply in a gray cotton T-shirt and a faded pair of jeans, I noticed her immediately. She looked so healthy, like she drank lots of water and ate oatmeal every day. The chair beside me was empty, and she asked if I would mind if she joined me.

No.

Her eyes penetrated my own, and my heart beat faster than the wings of a hummingbird. She had ordered a strudel too. We talked about strudels, the mild autumn weather, Picasso, and sex. She gave a guy a blow job last summer and quickly decided her gender preference. Women. In particular, me. She had seen me once before, walking my dog in Canarvon Park, and decided then and there that I would be the first woman she would sleep with.

I worried that she was one of those bi-curious types, that she would break my heart after a night of champagne kisses in the hot tub. Part of me was convinced that she was genuine after hearing her blow job/lesbian revelation story, but I still hesitated. I was used to being the seductress, not the seducee.

Our coffee mugs were soon empty, anticipation making us incredibly thirsty. We talked until the sun cast shadows and the streetlamps flickered on, illuminating the busy sidewalks. Josephine's was closing, now what? We spoke at the exact same time, blushing in the darkness, exchanging excited smiles. "You go first," she insisted.

Her hair fell across her shoulders, cradling her pert breasts. I imagined the fine curves of her waist, the firm flatness of her abdomen, the rosy color of her sweet nipples. I imagined all of this as I looked deep into her eyes, knowing that she was undressing me at the exact same time. She would taste like all of my favorite things. Her velvety skin on my lips would be like fudge still warm from the oven. Fudge that would melt with my knowing touch, my deft tongue, and my overwhelming desire to make her cheeks flush strawberry-red with ecstasy. Beads of sweat would glisten on her brow as I teased her with biting teeth. Biting teeth nibbling the insides of her thighs.

I watched as she placed her hands on the table, folding the yellow serviette into a smaller triangle as she waited for my response. I knew she would do anything I asked her to. Her eagerness was obvious, and it made my heart thump in excitement as I stripped our bodies down and imagined the positions, the taste and smell of her pussy as she straddled my face. Her hips pushing down, her vulva riding wildly across my tongue and chin. The come spilling out of her as I teased her clit with my hot breath.

She would do it on the carpet, on the hood of the car, on the roof...anywhere. She'd lick and nibble and drum my insides until I screamed. Until I begged for mercy in a soft kiss. She was all of my fantasies, waiting and wanting. She wanted my experienced hands and mouth as much as I wanted her innocence and virgin lips. Her tight little cunt enjoying the thrust of my fingers deep inside her walls. Her pink little clit swelling with arousal. I could feel myself getting wet, my boxers damp between my legs. I knew she was wet too. I wanted to rip her panties off with my teeth right there.

"I'd be lying if I said that I wanted you to come over and see my studio. I don't think I have to impress you with my Picasso and Carr collection, either. And you probably don't want another coffee, so why don't you come over to my place for..." I paused, a devilish grin on my face.

"Sex?" she inquired, returning my devilish grin.

Definitely sex. Virgin or not, she was a goddess in denim with gentle curves and perfect breasts. I watched as her nipples bumped out in the chilly night air and suggested that we leave;

I lived only a couple of blocks away. Her arm brushed against mine, purposely I think, as I pushed my chair out from the table. Steps away from her, I could smell the warm scent of vanilla that she had splashed on her skin.

Walking down the sidewalk, I had to remind myself she was a virgin. I was amazed. How could she be? Why didn't she have lesbians begging for her attention? She grabbed my hand reassuringly under the canopy of maples as we cut across the front yard to my house. Ripley, my black lab, greeted us with much enthusiasm and immediately stuck his wet nose in both our crotches. Embarrassed, I apologized for his behavior. "Probably a lesbian," she joked. "I wish I could get away with that."

"Do you wanna have a beer?" I offered. She accepted, resting the open bottle sensuously on her hip, as though she were posing for a calendar. "You're a very attractive woman," I smiled, feeling my damp boxers clinging to me. "How come you're a virgin?"

"I'm picky."

"So, why me?" I asked with great curiosity.

"When your heart pounds like a jackhammer, and you feel all dizzy, like you're going to throw up, and your pussy is wet from just a smile, that's when you know."

She was so damn eloquent with her words. I, on the other hand, struggled in my attempt to be alluring and enticing. I should have been the virgin, stuttering and tripping over my thoughts as I imagined her perfect body, kissed by the summer's sun, her captivating scent, her soft, damp curls brushing against my cheek. I drank my beer thirstily, like it was some kind of potion that would make me brave.

"Look, I know that I've never loved a woman, but I know how to touch myself. I've seen *Desert Hearts,* you know," she explained defensively.

I laughed aloud and pulled her close, my fingers tugging on her belt loops. She ran her slender fingers through my shortly-cropped hair, admiring how it felt like the bristly skin of a kiwi. I leaned closer and whispered, "You smell delicious." My hands gave way to desire and slid underneath her cotton shirt, greeting her erect nipples with my fingertips. Her hands followed my lead and dipped into the back of my jeans as I approached her lips, gently brushing against them. She didn't kiss like a virgin. Her warm tongue greeted mine, not with wild abandon or carnal force, but with tender passion.

I pushed my pelvis into hers, wrapping my arms around her strong back as she snaked her tongue along the nape of my neck. I watched as she removed my shirt with careful hands and lovingly took my nipple into her mouth. Obviously she had seen more than *Desert Hearts,* as I felt her seemingly practiced hands undo the buttons on my jeans. "Hey, slow down," I whispered. I wanted to go slow, to enjoy her tongue exploring my skin. I wanted her to take my nipple in her mouth and suck on it, her hands squeezing the fullness. I brought her head back up to my lips, our tongues diving into each other's mouth until our skin burned with desire for more.

My nipples stood on end, inviting her warm mouth to swallow them whole. With guidance she rolled their firmness between her lips, her teeth biting as I leaned back, pushing my breasts forward. Her hands traced over my body, rubbing hard against my other breast, racing down to my nipple, sneaking into my open jeans. She discovered the wetness in my boxers and smiled with satisfaction. She begged to kiss me, her fingers running through my hair.

"Please let me make you scream. I want to love you until you beg for me to stop. Tonight you are mine."

I gave in, nodding my head in approval.

Lowering my jeans, then boxers, she told me to sit on the counter. I obliged, enjoying the feel of her novice tongue skating across my skin, lingering and traversing all of my erogenous zones with her strawberry lips.

"Remember, this is my first time," she reminded me. She inhaled deeply as she followed her tongue from my navel to my bush. She buried her nose in my wet curls, her chin rolling in the slipperiness. "You smell wonderful." Her fingers ran through my curls as she traced small figure eights around my vulva, dipping just below my clit and just under my opening. She pulled my labia back, watching as my swollen clit jumped out of her hood. Her breath sent shivers racing across my body. Her tongue so close to my clit made me crazy. Now I was the one begging her.

"Love me, kiss me, I want to feel you inside me."

She raised her eyebrows between my legs as only her hands moved across my skin. I felt like one of her sculptures, my body a mass of clay being reworked in her hands. She shaped me and formed me with strong, deliberate squeezes. Pushing and pulling my skin with open palms, covering the whole expanse of my body. Her sculptor hands transformed me into a burning, desperate mass.

"Please...." I moaned immediately as the tip of her tongue traced my wet vulva. Her hands pulled back my labia again, and with the full breadth of her tongue she lapped up my sweet cream. I tossed my head back with dizziness as her teeth tugged on my fat clit. I spread my legs wider on the counter, moving a loaf of whole wheat bread from behind me. She devoured me like a ravenous cheetah, licking and sucking as I abandoned my body as delicious prey. Fingers glided along my lips, circling my lubricious opening. I didn't remember this part in *Desert Hearts.* Shit, my ex-girlfriend of three years couldn't pleasure me like this.

I played in her long honey hair, loving the rush of ecstasy that coursed through my veins. Her teeth nibbled, her tongue fluttered…but when she entered me, two fingers massaging my walls, thrusting in and out, I almost came. Her tongue was relentless as she pulled my lips back and concentrated on my sensitive clit. Thrusting and pumping, three more fingers pushing deep inside me. My body rocked into her mouth and absorbed her fist. My body was hungry. My feet wrapped around the insides of her knees to brace myself.

I forgot that she was a virgin in that moment as I moaned loudly, almost falling off the counter as my back arched and my muscles clenched, my throbbing clit resting on her lips. She removed two fingers from inside me and rubbed my anus. I responded, eager for her entry. I tightened around her fingers as she plunged inside me. The fullness of her in my cunt and up my ass made me breathe heavily. My body shuddered as she continued gliding and sliding, in and out. I watched her eyes, blue as the ocean, open and close with a smile. My muscles contracted around her fingers, holding her tight inside me. *Stay inside.* I pushed my pussy closer to her face. Closer to her warm tongue, grabbing handfuls of her hair as I begged her closer. She pulled her fingers out, wanting me to come in her mouth. She wanted to taste my come after the rush, to lick it from my soft, pink flesh.

She pulled at my nipples with her fingertips, like a robin tugging on a stubborn worm. My body turned into a liquid mass. She devoured me, and I succumbed to the orgasm, shuddering and shaking on the counter as she sucked harder and my whole body clenched. I slid off the counter and into her arms, breathless. She kissed me with gentle lips, like the wings of a butterfly, and I laid my head on her shoulder, the scent of warm vanilla on her neck.

She was my beautiful virgin lover, fingers and tongue responding to her beating heart and lascivious lesbian desires. She gave me the sculpture before she moved to Seattle. Flesh or clay, her hands were always gentle; she could create beauty in a smile.

Years may have faded the memories, but I was the first to love her the most. Underneath the images of the past, and memories of lovers gone, I hope I remain. The painting I did of her was lost in the move, but she remembers it exactly. I remember her exactly.

I made a batch of chocolate chip cookies yesterday, and smiled as I stirred a teaspoon of vanilla into the batter. She remains not in clay or on canvas, but in my heart.

Anything Awful

by Gretchen Zimmerman

"Anything awful makes me laugh. I misbehaved at a funeral once."

—Charles Lamb, 1775-1834

"What was it like with that virgin?" Gail asked as we sat at Serafina that night, sipping wine and eating calamari.

"Pardon me?" I said.

"You know. That woman you slept with a couple of summers ago. What was it like?

"I don't suppose they're any different than anyone else," I replied.

"Oh, come on," she said, lowering her voice to a whisper, "you know there's nothing like sleeping with a woman who's never slept with another woman before." Leave it to Gail to cut right to the chase.

On the drive home from the restaurant, I thought about what Gail said over dinner, and my mind drifted to thoughts of Tarin and the time she seduced me.

The Bonney-Wilson funeral home is just like any other funeral home: quiet, serene, lavishly decorated, a place of comfort for the bereaved. It is the largest funeral home in the area. From the outside it looks like a castle: large, gray, and ominous, with tall black wrought iron railings surrounding its perimeter. The railings are so high that they look like security bars. I wondered, the first time I saw them, who would want to break in to a funeral home. Certainly no one was trying to escape. The prison-like feel was certainly not the place to foster an erotic encounter.

The home itself is made of red and gray brick, with white trim surrounding two prominent turrets. From the street it looks like someone's house, albeit a very large, cumbersome house, but a house nonetheless. Once inside it looked less like a home and more like a traditional place for the bereaved, soft and welcoming. There is plush, dark blue carpet in each room like a square sea and delicate flowered wallpaper. Well-appointed ferns dot the hallways here and there. It was in this house of the dead that I first met Tarin.

I had gone to Bonney-Wilson for the funeral of my longtime friend Richard. *Richard looked better dead than he did when he was alive,* I thought as I stared down at him in the coffin. He'd chosen a white coffin to fit his "virginal personality," he'd said. He wasn't about to meet his maker in something black.

Richard's face seemed more colorful than it had in his hospital bed. I felt a certain sense of relief to meet him again here, his pain absent from the room. I smiled at him and placed a pink rose on his chest, also a last request. Roses were his favorite flower.

Richard's lover of 15 years, Patrick, graced the room greeting guests with large hugs and even larger thank-yous. There was a sadness in the room that accompanies most any death, but there was also a zest for life that surrounded each one of us. Richard wouldn't have wanted us to sit around in black suits and boo-hoo into our catered drinks. He'd want us to dance around his coffin and make merry the way we did when he was alive: joyously and fully.

I'd gone to the funeral alone but knew I would see many of our mutual friends, some from the hospital the day before. We milled around the grand foyer until it was time for the service to begin. Snippets of laughter could be heard over the whispering crowd. Richard was always a joker, and it was clear today his jokes continued even after he was not around to tell them.

As I made my way to the beverage table, my eye caught the figure of a woman I'd never seen before. She stood alone on the other side of the room by a table full of calla lilies. She fingered a full glass of water and had that look that people get when they don't know many people around them. She wasn't normally my type, but I found myself drawn to her anyway. She was much more femme than any woman I'd ever found myself in bed with.

Through the shuffle of guests I continued to watch her. Formal black jackets punctuated my perusal of her body. From where I stood I was only able to catch snapshots of her, partial pictures in between people passing. Her shoes: black, velvet, crossed at the ankle. Her dress: a subdued red, tight at the shoulders and the waist. Her neck: soft and pale in the muted funeral lighting. Her lips: slightly parted and touched with a hint of lipstick. She turned her head to survey the room, flicking the length of her curly brown hair over her shoulder. She took a sip of water, and I watched as the muscles in her neck moved ever so slightly.

Guests continued to arrive, blocking my view of the stunning new woman. I found myself moving closer to where she stood to get a better view. I was drawn to her, had to see more of her. My vantage point changed somewhat, I could now view her with greater ease. I stepped slowly just behind the fully open parlor door and watched her through the crack where the door joins the wall. Through the crack I could see slivers of her quite clearly: her broad shoulders, the full, small curve of her breast. No bra. My own nipples got hard as I pictured myself above her on the table full of lilies, the flowers tipping over at our embrace, spilling water all over the floor. Wetness everywhere.

I leaned forward slightly to see more of her. The cut glass panes of the glossy white door showed me a picture of her I would have otherwise not seen. It fragmented her into pieces of red and white, her dress and her skin arrayed like an impressionist painting. I wanted a clearer picture of her. I wanted an uninterrupted image. I wanted to explore her body. I wanted her. Right there in the middle of my friend's funeral, I felt myself getting wet.

Just then some friends from back East came over to talk to me. They demanded to know why I was hiding behind a door. I reluctantly took my eyes from the new girl and forced myself to engage in conversation. We talked about Richard as though he were still alive: his horrible taste in movies, his excellent taste in clothes, and the time he fell into his indoor pool after too much birthday champagne. I began to remember the Richard I used to know, the one full of life and love, the one who was no longer with us, and as we spoke, my thoughts drifted back to the new girl. Guilt began to settle over my desire like a layer of dust. But I knew Richard would rather have me chase a girl at his funeral than feel guilty and morose, or "Catholic" as he called it, so I forced myself to find out who she was.

Then I lost her. I looked back at the table full of lilies, and she was gone. She seemed to have disappeared from the funeral home entirely. I kept shaking hands and nodding to people, some of whom I'd just seen that morning, some I hadn't seen for more than ten years and whose names couldn't recall if I tried.

There is something extremely comforting about funeral homes. There is a security and a sense of unity that doesn't exist anywhere else. There is also an ease with which people greet each other. We are united in our continued existence, and we greet each other through our sorrow. Our loss holds us together across time and space. It's our desire that keeps us moving forward, as I found myself searching through the crowd for that gorgeous woman.

I perused the room, looking for her already familiar form. I discovered her again near the rest rooms. The same heat rose within me as I laid eyes on her once more. She was chatting with several other guests, all speaking in their best funeral voices. I strolled past them slowly, giving the entire group a nod, all the while keeping my gaze fixed on the girl I'd never seen before. She did not look at me but kept talking to the group of people. I entered the bathroom, shook my head, and leaned forward to steady myself.

I'd fucked in washrooms many times before, and as I stared down at my hands on the edge of the sink, I pictured the new girl with her ass on the edge of the counter, her head thrown back into the mirror, her wetness gracing the marble-colored ledge. The image flashed so quickly in my head I felt a rush of heat overtake me. Suddenly the washroom felt too warm. I began to look around the room as though I'd lost something. My remorse. Where was it? Once again I began to feel guilty. Here I was at Richard's funeral, with sweaty palms and a wet pussy, yearning for a girl I'd never seen before. It felt perverted and odd, like a pleasurable trip to the dentist. It felt so kinky it had to be right.

I turned and stared into the large, well-lit mirror and saw my own face gazing back at me. I laughed at the reflection staring back at me. I was in my early 30s, but I could still pass as though I were in my early 20s, or at the very least, a late teenage boy. I had very few wrinkles around my eyes and no gray hair as yet, but I still felt too old for the beauty on the other side of the door. She'd surely never look twice at me. She looked young, maybe just in her early 20s. I haven't been attracted to someone born in the '70s, ever. Her face had a freshness to it that my own had not had in years. There was clearly only one thing to do: hit on her before she left the building. I straightened my tie, pulled down on my shirt sleeves, made sure there was no food in my teeth, and prepared to face her once again.

As I left the washroom I realized the group she had been talking to had dispersed and she was standing there all alone. "Hi," I said, pretending I had just noticed her.

"Hello," she said, her large brown eyes looking deep into mine. "You knew Richard?" she half stated, half asked.

"Yes, he's one of my closest friends. I mean…was."

"I know. He talked about you often."

"How did you know him?" I asked, curious to know what the bugger had said about me.

"We had a lot of conversations about you. He really liked you. I work in the floral shop near his house. We talked lots, about stuff, you know, movies, flowers, the latest in fashion."

"So you're a fag too," I said, hoping she would get the joke. She laughed, just as the lights dimmed for the ceremony to begin. I looked at her chest while she turned her head in the direction of the grand foyer. A light brown birthmark running down the side of her neck and disappearing into her breast enticed me. I longed to know how far down her body it ran and if I could trace it with my tongue.

"The flower shop where I work did all of the arrangements for the service. Richard wanted me to make the bouquets myself," she said. Watching her breasts but thinking about the flowers, I commented on how exquisite the arrangement was.

As she spoke I watched her mouth. Her lips moved around her teeth in a dance I longed to be part of. Every word she spoke enticed me, every syllable an invitation.

"Are you sitting with anyone for the service?" I asked.

"No. I actually hate funerals. I just came to say good-bye to Richard," she said. "And to meet you. He talked about you so much I figured you'd be here."

"I hate funerals too," I replied. "What exactly was that old fart saying about me anyway?" I asked. I could feel my brow wrinkle as I asked the question.

"Oh, it was all good, believe me," she said, smiling widely. "My name's Tarin," she said next, holding her hand out toward me.

I looked at her hand as though it were a gift she were giving me. I reached out and held her long slender fingers, squeezing them gently. I longed to pull her toward me, to get closer to her body, to feel the weight of her against me. "Gretchen," I said. My hand released hers and fell reluctantly back at my side.

A small, delicate chime sounded from the front of the funeral home, indicating the service was about to start. Tarin and I started to walk down the gold-trimmed hallway toward the large room where Richard's body lay. I placed my right hand lightly on the small of her back in what looked like a gesture of support but was just an excuse to touch her. Just before we reached the entranceway of the large room, the white double doors now closed, we reached another, smaller room, an antechamber. It seemed like a quiet room of sorts, the kind of room where a hysterical mourner could be rushed off to in order not to startle the other mourners into their own version of extroverted grief. The room would not be needed at this funeral. All of Richard's friends were hysterical to begin with and did not need confinement.

Tarin glanced into the room as we approached it, flicked her curly brown hair once more, and turned to enter the room at the last moment. I followed her scent into the room. She was either about to become hysterical, or she wanted something. I had the feeling it was the latter. "There's something kind of sexy about funeral homes, don't you think?" she whispered over her shoulder at me, dropping her clutch purse on a low chair and running her fingers along a waist-high table.

"I've never really thought of them that way," I said, pushing the door almost all the way closed behind us. "I think you're kind of sexy, though." The quiet of the air stood between us. I watched her hips sway as she stepped deeper into the room. Several small baroque-type paintings with wide-eyed women and men were hung in the room, making it seem like we had an audience even though we were all alone.

"Kind of?" she said, turning around. I could hear the minister's voice over the microphone addressing the crowd. "Friends, family, loved ones. We come together…" his voice trailed off as I stared at Tarin. The freshly cleaned room smelled like a forest. Somewhere someone got the idea that the smell of cedar could surround your grief and perhaps ease the pain a little. A faint hint of eucalyptus peppered the room, and the aroma of pine surrounded us. Tarin walked toward me as the minister continued speaking. She walked softly and gracefully, like a dancer. "I've wanted you ever since the first time I saw you," she said. Her breath hit my chin, and I could hear her tongue ring click in her mouth.

"You mean 20 minutes ago?" I said, slightly nervous that we were missing the ceremony.

"No, six months ago in my shop. You were in there once with Richard. He bought two dozen pink roses for his piano. You were with him. Don't you remember?" I didn't. I remembered going into the shop where she worked, but I did not remember her. I'd been too preoccupied in a breakup at the time to notice anyone. We could have walked into the Jodie Foster Flower Shop and the only thing I would have noticed would have been the tiles on the floor, my head was hung so low from sadness.

"It's OK if you don't remember," she whispered, her breasts approaching mine in a house of the dead. It felt slightly creepy to think about pinching her nipples when I should have been in the other room saying my last good-byes, but I went with it anyway. I thought earlier I could ask her back to my place after the service, but like the saying goes, there's really no time like the present.

"I've never fooled around in a funeral home before." I said, as my hands found their own way around her firm waist.

"That's OK. I've never fooled around with a woman before," she said.

"You're kidding," I said. Just as the words left my mouth she kissed me long and hard. I could feel her tongue ring as we kissed. The hardness of it excited me. Her mouth met mine, and my tongue eagerly explored her mouth. Within seconds my hands were on her breasts, pulling at the dress above them. The soft fabric gave way with my touch, revealing the birthmark that I had seen earlier. I bit her neck and placed both of my hands on her ass and pulled her toward me. She felt small compared to what I was used to in a woman. Her dress was silky and slipped over her hips with ease. I lifted the skirt of her dress slowly until I found her skin. The muscles in her legs were hard and firm. I slid my hand up her thigh. She had no nylons on, no panties—how perfect and perfectly planned out. I didn't care whether she planned it or not. She was hot and I wanted her.

Her right knee rose and placed itself on my hip. She ground her hips slightly into mine. "Fuck me," she said, "right now." It had the sound of a command. She didn't have to tell me twice. I continued to kiss her and bit her shoulder. I turned her body slightly and leaned her backward over the table she had fingered moments ago. I held onto her tightly as though she would disappear again if I let go. The hard oak of the table met the softness of her thighs as I bit the flesh above her breast.

Her hands on my jacket pulled me into her, grasping at my back. A small vase of tulips shook and almost tumbled to the floor as I rocked my hips between her open legs. I found myself face-to-face with the faintly flowered wallpaper and Tarin's heels digging into the back of my thigh. The fullness of her hair seemed to take up the entire room, catching itself in my fingers and my mouth. I grabbed a handful of it in my fist and held her head still against the wall as I sunk my teeth into her chin. I stared upward into her eyes and saw that her gaze lay somewhere on the ceiling. I listened to the soft moan that came out of her mouth as it entered my ear.

I slid my right hand between her legs and placed the back of my hand against her open lips. She'd shaved her cunt so that there was only a tiny racing stripe in the center. Her public hair scratched my hand gently, and I felt an old Pavlovian itch above my upper lip. I knew her cunt would rub my skin raw if I went down on her.

Cunt licking was not what Tarin had in mind. I put all of my fingers together and lay them at the opening of her cunt. Then slowly I entered her as gently as I could, watching her every move for signs of discomfort. We fucked silently, carefully, but with a roaring intensity. All I could hear was the sound of the minister's voice and the shuffle of clothes around me. The smell of pine and cedar seemed to increase around us. I could feel beads of sweat roll between my shoulder blades and collect in my boxer shorts. She gasped as I fucked her and buried her face into my dinner jacket to muffle her moans.

Tarin continued to thrust her hips onto my hand, and bit my neck so hard I thought I would faint. She fucked my hand. My hand fucked her cunt. I heard a small, muffled thud over my shoulder and realized without missing a thrust that one of her shoes had fallen off and hit the floor. I turned my head slightly and stared toward the door for signs that someone had heard us. When it was clear that no one had, I turned my head back toward Tarin and kissed her. Her lips met mine as the table rocked beneath us. I reached farther inside her, her pussy sucking at my hand. I knew from experience that she was the kind of woman who would turn your wrist numb if you let her. And I would let her, but not here, not now. There simply wasn't enough time.

Once again in my head I had a cock, and for a moment I was plunging it into her as she pulled me inside. I closed my eyes and buried my face in her neck and floated inside her. My cunt ached as I imagined my flesh entering hers. I momentarily forgot that we were supposed to be the bereaved. The only thought in my mind was of her body and mine joined together.

I began to slow down as the image faded and slowly took my hand out of her. Her thrusts slowed as well, telling me she'd had enough. She sighed heavily and held on to me as though she might fall. I held her and the table at the same time. We stood silently with the antechamber surrounding us. We bumped noses clumsily, kissed gently, and decided it would be best if we gathered ourselves together.

I straightened my tie in a mirror on the wall and made sure none of my very short hairs stuck out. I could smell Tarin on my hand as I ran my fingers through my hair. Tarin adjusted her dress and reapplied some lipstick before we left the room. I re-opened the door and stuck my head out to see if anyone was watching. The hallway looked a great deal brighter to me as I checked to make sure the coast was clear. I nodded to Tarin to follow me out. She took my hand as we tiptoed back across the plush carpet and sneaked into the back room of the service.

The large room felt hot and stuffy. The well-oiled door failed to announce our late arrival to the service, for which I was glad. A Bette Midler song had just started playing, signifying to me the end of the ceremony. My mind came rushing back to the task at hand, as I remembered Richard dressed in drag as Bette for one of his party's. I smiled to myself as I leaned against the back wall and tried to act inconspicuous. Tarin leaned in next to me with her shoulder next to mine, and we listened quietly as the music finished. She gave my hand a little extra squeeze just as the song ended.

I stared at the rows of heads before me in the room. Here and there hands full of tissue darted up to blot tear-stained eyes. I felt myself get choked up along with the rest of the guests. The minister said a few more words, and there was a shuffle of chairs and coats as mourners stood to leave. I could see Patrick at the front of the room shaking hands with the minister. Reverend Stinson was a gentle man and the only minister we knew who performed gay and lesbian weddings against the advice of his church. He loved Richard just as much as the rest of us.

After several minutes of seeing people off, Patrick walked down the cherry-red carpet and approached Tarin and me. My boxer shorts were twisted around my waist and were wedged snug between my ass cheeks, making standing slightly uncomfortable. I smiled, however, as though they weren't driving me crazy. "Nice necklace, you shouldn't have," he said, commenting on the mark Tarin had obviously left on my neck. "What you doin' with tears in your eyes, girl? You want Richard to roll over in his coffin? He's upstairs in full drag with the big man, dancing up a blue streak, and you back here all feelin' sorry for yourself. Get thee to a nunnery," he said with a big laugh. "Get this girl a tissue," he said to Tarin, placing his hand on her arm. He gave me a big Patrick hug and made sure we would be coming back to their place for the post-funeral extravaganza, as he called it. "And bring your date," he said over his shoulder in our direction.

I pulled into my driveway just as my thoughts of the funeral ended. I wondered briefly where Tarin was and if she had seduced any more women in peculiar places. The Bonney-Wilson will never look the same.

Cowgirl

by Marylou Hadditt

My best friend, 11-year-old Phyllis, had already gotten her period and had visible signs of breasts beneath her white school blouse. She was everything I wasn't: blue-eyed, pale-pink-skinned, a blond whose never-been-cut hair trailed to the small of her back. She was a princess in a fairy tale, a source of admiration and envy.

Sometime between fifth and sixth grades, Phyllis and I became enamored of "Petty" girls. These were airbrushed drawings of seminude women, which appeared in full color in *Esquire* magazine, the *Playboy* of the day. These illustrations took their name from the artist, George Petty. All the women had large, high breasts, small waists, full hips, and long blond hair, like Phyllis's. Petty girls were seductively dressed in skintight skirts with slits, décolletage, short shorts, negligees showing every possible cleavage. Each always had a telephone at her ear while the cord teased her breasts or crotch. When she wasn't a gatefold in *Esquire*, she was posed on three-foot high cardboard posters advertising Old Gold cigarettes where, instead of talking on a phone, the Petty girl was smoking.

Phyllis's big brother, Sam, regularly bought *Esquire*, which he carefully hid under his bed. In short time we discovered both *Esquire* and the almost-naked women within the pages. We were fascinated by the Petty girls. Phyllis threatened to tell on Sam unless he let us cut any pages we wanted from the magazines. We wrapped the Petty girl pages in Phyllis's pajamas and hid them in a Rich's department store box under the bed.

Every afternoon after school, we hurried to Phyllis's house, raced up to her room, announced, "We've tons of homework," and loudly slammed the door. We huddled on the floor beside that treasure box, and her long blond hair brushed my short dark curls. She smelled of Ivory soap. Our shoulders touched. We giggled as we arranged the sensuous Petty girls in neat piles as if we were playing an erotic version of paper dolls. I gave Phyllis a red leather scrapbook for Christmas and, with great care, helped her paste Petty girls on the pages. Our fingers caressed their curves as we flattened them on the page.

One afternoon, on the way home from the dentist, I wandered into a store that carried used books and magazines. Near a stack of ragged *Saturday Evening Post* and old *National Geographic* magazines, I found a dusty pile of *Esquire* magazines for a nickel apiece. I began to build my own sub-rosa Petty girl scrapbook and soon had a collection almost as large as Phyllis's. Since I've never been good at keeping secrets, one Saturday, instead of going to the movies, we headed straight for the used bookstore. We spent the afternoon clustered in a dark corner leafing through old copies of *Esquire,* stifling giggles while we read the risqué cartoons. When we made our purchases, we told the bookseller that they were for our big brother.

Like boys with baseball cards, Phyllis and I traded Petty girls.

"I'll swap you the one in the black dress with the slit skirt for the girl in the red lace panties and bra."

My coup took place one Wednesday afternoon after school when I'd gone to town to meet Mother and Dad at our family's jewelry store. When I got off the streetcar, a three-foot high

Petty girl wiggled her behind right in my face. She was a brazen Old Gold poster flirting from the window of Jacob's drugstore. Wearing a ten-gallon Stetson, black high-heeled spurred boots, a bright green bolero that barely covered her nipples, and a short fringed leather skirt, she twirled a lasso in one hand and held an Old Gold cigarette in the other.

I could hardly believe what I'd seen. I heisted my school books from one hip to the other, looked and looked again. Taking a deep breath, I walked into the drugstore. Right up to the woman behind the cash register.

"Hey, there." I spoke with a pretty little smile my mother would have adored. "My daddy is Lawrence Holzman from the jewelry store next door." I lowered my Southern belle eyes.

The cashier smiled. "How can I help you, honey?"

"Well, my daddy thought it'd be mighty sweet of y'all if he could have that cowgirl cigarette poster there in the window when you're through using it. He says it's just right for his rec room."

"I don't see why not. Here's a pencil. You just write your daddy's name on the back. In small letters, you hear? And you tell your daddy Edna says she hopes he enjoys the cowgirl."

"I sure will, and thank you, ma'am."

When my father saw that the framed satin-and-lace paper dolls, which had been hanging over my bed since I was four, had been replaced by a three-foot high poster of an almost naked woman, he exploded.

"What the hell is that doing there?"

"It's my new room decor, Daddy. I wanted something nice and bright instead of everything pink and blue."

Daddy sputtered and stomped out of the room to seek my mother's opinion. She was amused and mumbled something about me growing up.

Phyllis's envy was severe. She refused to go to the used magazine store anymore and our after-school visits were curtailed. One day she informed me she had given her collection to her cousin in Birmingham, then she shook her pale yellow hair at me and pronounced, "Who needs those old Petty girls anyway, when you can see Tyrone Power or Van Johnson every Saturday at the Fox Theater."

Lonely, I comforted myself with Cowgirl, who every night kept faithful watch over me. Her long legs, spike-heeled boots, luscious breasts, barely covered by that green bolero, were a challenge to my sweet little-girl, pink-and-blue flowered wallpaper. She dared bring a touch of zest into my life.

One night as I was drifting off to sleep, Cowgirl stepped down from her wall poster, sat beside my bed, and began to take off her cowboy boots.

"Well, you don't expect me to crawl into bed with boots on, now do you?"

I giggled.

Plop! Plop! Boots bounced on the floor.

Her bare legs stretched the length of my bed. Cowgirl was almost a head taller than me—I could tell by how far down her feet went. She let her golden hair fall on my shoulders. It tickled deliciously.

Cowgirl whispered something, but I couldn't understand. Only her breath was against my cheek.

Her hips, her thighs, her long legs were warm beneath the covers. I wanted to touch her all over. She tossed away the quilt, threw off the bolero jacket. In the moonlight I saw the whiteness of her magnificent round breasts, the pinkness of her nipples begging me to touch them.

"Go ahead," she whispered. "Feel how soft they are."

I reached out, cupped a breast in each hand, felt the exquisiteness of her hard pink nipples on my palm, coaxed them into my mouth. Cowgirl took off my nightie, wrapped her sweaty thighs between my legs. I held her so tightly her breasts swam on my chest.

"Have you ever touched a grown woman?" she asked.

I shook my head, mesmerized by the curls of her pubic hair. I didn't dare ask her to part her legs so I could see what a grown-up looked like. Instead, I gingerly slipped my hand into her crotch, but was too shy to reach deep inside.

"Don't be afraid," her voice soft and reassuring. She took my hand and put my fingers in my mouth. "This is what I taste like.

"Now, let me show you."

She propped me against the bed pillows, put her tongue in my mouth, then started sucking my nipples so they got hard like hers. I was startled when her mouth was right smack between my legs. Cowgirl squeezed my nipples while her tongue flickered my clit, swirling me into a frenzy.

I was wet, wetter than I'd ever before been.

I couldn't hold still.

I couldn't move.

I was throbbing inside.

I was shuddering outside.

Cowgirl's cheek rested on my thigh. Her blue eyes smiled at me.

"That's how it's done, Sweetie." Her light laughter rippled through me.

I lay absolutely still, holding my fingers on my clit, relishing every heartbeat, tasting every breath.

I wanted to hold this moment—

Sluff. Sluff. Sluff. I heard my mother's bedroom slippers outside my door. She invaded my room, an enormous dark shadow looming over my bed in the moonlight. Her voice pierced the heavy air.

"Miss Priss!" (That's what she called me when she was really angry.) "What are you doing? Take your hands out of the covers this minute."

She patted my arms against the quilt as though she were patting down a pie crust. "Nice girls don't do things like that. Come on, it's way past your bedtime."

She kissed me lightly on the forehead and *sluffed* back to her bedroom.

Meanwhile, Cowgirl, in her ten-gallon Stetson, black high-heeled boots, green bolero, and fringed leather skirt had returned to her vigil on the poster above my bed. As I began to drift off to sleep, I couldn't help but wonder if those pale breasts of Phyllis's, hinting at me under her blouse, would grow up to be full and round like Cowgirl's.

My Best Friend's Girl

by Lou Hill

Jan was my best friend. She had been dating Darcy for only a couple of weeks, but I could tell she was already hooked. When I finally met Darcy I saw why.

I invited them to dinner at my house. After dinner we planned to hit the bar. I heard the car pull into the driveway and met them at the front door. When Jan introduced me to Darcy we shook hands. I wondered if the tingle I felt was mutual and immediately felt guilty. I found Darcy extremely attractive. For a moment I found myself unable to speak. All I could do was stare, a dumb grin on my face, while Jan rambled on. I don't know if Darcy realized I was studying her. She seemed to hang on Jan's every word.

Darcy had long black hair and clear, fair skin. Her eyes reminded me of a cat's, green and mesmerizing. She wore tight black jeans, which revealed a firm ass and no visible panty line. I could see the outline of her nipples through her thin white T-shirt. I wondered what she saw in Jan. I mean, like I said, Jan was my best friend. But Darcy looked like more woman than Jan could handle. Jan's a good person, but lovemaking had never been her forte. She was a one-woman woman and didn't date much.

"How about the grand tour?" Darcy asked. She smiled. I swallowed hard and tried not to let the attraction I felt show.

We made our way through the house. I gave a running dialogue, pointing out the little quirks and flaws of the house, trying to be witty. Darcy laughed, and each time she did, my stomach did little flips.

When we got to my bedroom I hesitated. I opened the door and flipped on the lights. Darcy brushed by me and strode toward the middle of the room.

"If these walls could talk, what kind of stories would they tell?" She turned and stared at me. Her eyes glowed brightly.

"What's Jan been telling you?" I asked. My mouth felt dry.

"That you're a wild woman," Jan answered, with a laugh.

Darcy continued to look at me for a moment, then glanced toward the bookcase. "Private collection?" She wandered over to the bookcase and studied the titles. I have an extensive collection of lesbian literature. My tastes are eclectic. I devour mysteries. I own everything by Rita Mae Brown, Katherine V. Forrest, Lesléa Newman, and Mary Wings, as well as several collections of short stories and volumes of erotica. Darcy slid her hand along the books, then stopped at one book and glanced back at me, a strange look in her eyes. "Mind if I borrow a book sometime?"

"No, no problem," I said, noting the position of the books that had caught her attention.

The tour completed, we ate dinner, and then it was time to head out. I went back into the bedroom to grab my jacket. I remembered the bookcase and checked the titles: *no other tribute, Leatherwomen I and II, Private Lessons;* stories about women in submission. These stories aroused me like no others. I wondered what Darcy had been thinking when she read those titles.

The bar was crowded. I saw several familiar faces and spent most of the evening on the dance floor. A couple of times during the evening I thought I caught Darcy watching me. I pushed the idea from my mind and tried to concentrate on available women.

I made my way to our table and dropped down into the seat next to Jan. Darcy was in the rest room.

"Dance with Darcy," Jan said.

"You dance with her," I said. "She's your girlfriend."

"You know I don't dance. C'mon," she pleaded, totally oblivious to the fact that I wanted to do more than dance with Darcy.

Darcy returned to the table. I waited for a couple of minutes, then asked her to dance. She agreed eagerly. We moved to the dance floor and danced without speaking. The music changed to a slow song. I stopped. She pulled me closer. I glanced back toward Jan. She smiled and waved.

"I love slow dancing, don't you?" Darcy asked.

"Yeah, sure," I answered stiffly. I felt her breasts rub against me. Her hands were soft and warm. "So you and Jan hit it off, huh?"

"Yes. She's the sweetest thing. I've never met anyone like her."

"Yeah, she's a great person. I don't want to see her hurt."

"She won't be. I'll make sure of it," she said. "That's quite a library you have. Several of them looked very, um, interesting."

"Anything in particular?" I smiled smugly.

"Yeah. *Private Lessons.*" She raised one eyebrow.

"One of my favorites. I've got others you might find interesting. Maybe you'd like to take a look sometime?" I looked into her face. Our eyes met. We both knew what I meant.

She nodded. "I'd definitely be interested. Maybe I'll come by tomorrow. If you're free…"

"I'll be there."

The rest of the evening passed. Jan and Darcy dropped me off at home. I stood on the porch and waved good night, wondering if Darcy would show up.

I waited around all the next day, afraid to leave, afraid I'd miss her. Around 6 o'clock someone knocked on the door. It was Darcy.

"I didn't think you were going to come," I said. We moved to the couch.

"I spent all day working up my courage."

"Courage?" I asked. "It didn't have anything to do with feeling a little guilty?"

"No, no guilt. Jan will never know I was here. Not from me anyway."

"Why courage then?"

"I want something from you," she said. "Something I've never found with a woman."

"Something Jan can't give you?"

"Something I wouldn't ask for. I wouldn't want Jan to think less of me, and what I want she can't give me."

"What are we talking about, Darcy?" I didn't want to assume anything.

"I want someone to take me. I want hot, aggressive, down-and-dirty sex. Just once I want to be totally dominated." She looked at me. I studied her quietly.

"And you think I'm the one?"

"I hope so."

I stood at the foot of the bed and gazed at Darcy's naked body, spread-eagled and fastened to the headboard with bungee cords. Her eyes were covered with a scarf of black crepe.

With her arms spread wide and her back arched, her breasts jutted upward, nipples erect. The breeze of the ceiling fan had created goose bumps on her milky white skin. She shivered slightly, perhaps in anticipation. The room was dark, the only light coming from the shimmering candles I had placed in front of the mirror.

I listened to her breathing. She turned her head, straining to hear me, knowing I was in the room, but not where.

I made the final adjustments on my leather harness. The large pink dildo fit perfectly. The base bumped against my crotch. I looked down, thinking how strange it looked but how good it felt. I ran my hand along its length, squeezing the smooth head, the bumpy shaft.

I moved to the side of the bed. Reaching down, I ran my finger from her shoulder down to her breast. I cupped both breasts with my hands and squeezed. Her nipples were like candy kisses. I straddled her, leaned over, and sucked on her nipples, licking and biting them like a small hungry animal. She moaned softly. Her hips arched toward me.

I moved down and pushed her legs apart, settling in between them. I placed my palm on her crotch, stroking it. I separated her lips with my thumb and pushed my way into her warm, wet cave. I reached over to the bedside table and took an ice cube from the glass. I pushed the ice cube into her darkness. She moaned.

I pulled a pillow from the head of the bed and pushed it under her hips. I could see her firm, round ass. I took another ice cube and pushed it inside her asshole.

I could feel my own wetness growing. I wanted to be inside her. But I didn't want this to be over too quickly.

I leaned forward and kissed her hard on the mouth. I pushed my tongue inside her mouth, flicking my tongue against hers, biting it slightly. As I pulled away she sucked on my tongue.

I moved up, straddling her chest. I ran the head of my dick across her mouth. She pulled away slightly. "Open your mouth," I commanded. "Suck my hot cock." She opened her mouth, and I leaned forward, inching the dildo between her lips. She twirled her tongue across the head, closed her lips around it, and sucked.

"Get it good and wet. Suck it hard." My clit grew harder and throbbed. I watched her suck my cock and couldn't wait to be inside her. I pulled back and slid down along her body. I bit her neck. I bit her nipples. I reached down and slid my hand under her ass, squeezing her cheek. "I'm going to fuck you," I whispered. She moaned.

I positioned the head of my cock against her wet slit and slowly slipped inside. Inch by inch, I entered her until the full length of my cock was hidden. As I began to move my hips, forward and back, sliding in and out, she pushed up to meet me. Her hips undulated to match mine.

The dildo became flesh, my flesh, and I could feel each movement. I was on fire. *Not yet,* I thought. I pulled out, slowly, and sat back on my heels.

"Don't stop," she moaned.

"Quiet," I said.

I ran my hands over her crotch, parted her lips with my fingers, and flicked my thumb across her swollen clit. Again, she moved to meet me, arching her hips. I ran my thumb down across her asshole, massaging it, and slipped my thumb inside. She squirmed, trying to expel it. I moved my thumb in and out. She began to relax.

"Fuck me," she moaned.

I pushed the head of my cock against her slick slit. It glistened with her wetness. I moved it down. She felt it against her ass and tensed. I pushed against her until the head popped inside her, then leaned into it. She pushed against me. I reached down and kneaded her clit as I inched my way inside. She arched her shoulders and pushed her head back. "It hurts," she moaned.

"Take it," I said. "You want it." I pushed the full length of my cock into her ass. I began pumping, in and out, in and out. I could feel my own orgasm waiting, ready to explode. I could see the blood in my head, boiling red-hot, then white-hot. I fucked her harder and harder. I could no longer see the person on the other end of my cock. I could feel only the tsunami sweep over me from the depths of the ocean.

My body convulsed with aftershocks. I pulled out, collapsing onto the bed. I didn't know if she had come or not. I didn't care. I lay next to her and felt the tiny contractions inside my body. Once they stopped I felt as though I was coming back into my body from somewhere else.

I rolled over and reached down to her crotch. She was still swollen, hot, and horny. I picked up a bottle of oil and drizzled it over her and over my hand. I shoved two fingers, then three, inside her. I moved rhythmically, slowly. Now four fingers. She opened wide to me. Her hips rose to meet my hand. I slid my hand in and turned it, willing it to be pliable. I massaged her clit with my thumb.

As I slid in and out, her breathing became uneven. The harder she breathed, the more excited I grew. I moved my thumb to my palm and pushed my fist inside her. Her cunt swallowed my hand. As I fucked her I felt myself growing hard again. She bucked against my fist, thrusting her hips against my wrist.

"I'm coming," she said, low and guttural. "God, I'm coming." I felt her contractions clamp down on my hand, her clit jumping with each wave. I pulled back a little and ran my thumb across her clit. She moaned and shuddered.

I was throbbing. I pulled the harness away from my body. I straddled her chest and pushed my cunt against her mouth. She licked me like she was parched and I was cool water. I moved against her tongue, letting it flick across my clit. I pushed her head hard against me. Her tongue slipped in and out of my slit, and I fucked her face until I exploded. I pushed hard against her tongue, leaning my head back, arching my back, rocking, rocking, rocking.

It was late when Darcy finally left. We didn't kiss good night or even speak. She walked up the driveway to her car. She opened the car door, turned and smiled at me, then climbed in and drove away. I took a long hot shower and sat in the recliner, reliving each moment of our evening together.

It never happened again. Darcy and Jan are still together.

I'd like to say I don't see them very often. But the truth is, I do. When we go out together I laugh too loudly, my gestures become a little bigger, and I find myself trying too hard to look happy with whomever I'm with.

Sometimes, late at night, I think about Darcy and am aroused by the memory of that night. I gave her everything she had longed for. And she responded in a way I had only imagined.

And I ask myself, why is she still with Jan?

Dinner With Yolanda

by Lori Cardona

I'm going to have to admit it, right here and now. Back in 1984, I was 26 years old and one hot, seemingly heterosexual Latina woman, working hard for time to play even harder on the stimulating streets of New York City. I kept my hipbones in motion even without a salsa tune playing, because I had rhythm in my soul and a man whose eyes were meant to stay focused. On me. Little did I know that the time would soon come when I would be the one with eyes that wandered off and opened wide while falling deep into the charms of my old high school hanging buddy, Yolanda C.

When Yolanda called and said she was coming into the city for a brief visit, I got more excited that I ever remember being over this man I was thinking about marrying. I hadn't seen Yolanda in about seven years and had lost track of where she was and what she'd been up to. One phone call to my office got us all caught up and got me all confused. She told me this story about how she'd fallen in love with a woman and that the woman had just left her after four years of what Yolanda thought was the best thing that had ever happened to her. Her tales of this great love of hers reminded me of all the crushes and fantasies I'd had for several women over the years; crushes I tried to ignore and dismiss as nothing more than sexual curiosity, fantasies I used to enhance my sexual excitement when fucking men.

But the men were hard when I longed for softness. I remember feeling almost jealous at their delight for hands on a soft, full breast, their satisfaction for having inspired wetness and throbbing. I wanted to feel what they felt, I wanted to hear the sound of a woman's breath in my ear, increasing in rhythm, sighing my name. I wanted the strength to move another body, equal in density to mine, across the bed in frantic fucking, lost to desire. I wanted to strap on a dildo and watch a woman arch her back to receive me, her breasts swaying with our movement, her legs spread wide, her hands holding onto my ass, bringing me closer to thrust harder, deeper. I watched couples walking arm in arm and would envy the man who ran his hand over his woman's curves as they spoke. Yolanda got me thinking that it didn't have to be just fantasy or longing from afar. Yolanda got me thinking hard.

She told me that she used to run home "in a rush of gladness," that's what she called it, just wanting to get her hands all over that woman of hers. She told me about how they'd get to kissing, about how their clothes would get all peeled down from their shoulders and thighs in no time at all before that woman would give my girl some serious fucking. I mean, to hear her tell it, you'd think that woman had some kind of heaving cock, to keep her all open, screaming and thrashing about like she was.

She said it was like they'd just turn themselves into a couple of insatiable, hungry animals getting hungrier by the minute, tearing at each other and leaving scratch marks that they prized. She said there were times when she got up to find welts on her ass and grooves on her arms from being held down while her woman gave her some hot slamming for tasting so good. That's what she told me. And I said "Really," and she said "Well, yeah, it was great," and I said "*Really*?" and she just sort of laughed, like she knew I was missing something and that I knew it too. I felt pangs of jealousy creeping in through my reserve.

Finding myself at a sudden loss for words and with a strong desire to see her immediately, I asked her if she wanted to get together for dinner that very evening, and she said, "Yes, I do," in a voice that sounded more like a seduction than an acceptance to a dinner invitation. We spoke for a few more minutes and made arrangements to meet at her hotel.

Then, before saying good-bye, she started to cry. It seemed like she was truly missing that lying, cheating hedonist who had walked out on her without an explanation while moving in on someone new. Yolanda said she felt such pain at having been so easily replaced and then discarded, like crumbs flicked off a buffet table without a second thought, and I found myself anxious to comfort her. The rest of the day moved much too slowly, and all that mattered to me was dinner with Yolanda.

I knew my life was about to change as I searched my closet for the clothes that would mark the transition from my world to hers. I changed my clothes so many times I was beginning to sweat from the stress and thought I might have to make time for another shower. Choosing just the right outfit is so very difficult in the middle of a sexual epiphany. I just never knew! With the final decision, I stood in front of the mirror and observed the message of my short, black silk, sleeveless dress. In anticipation of her reaction, I decided to remove my panties. Then I strapped on a garter belt, rolled sheer black stockings onto my legs, and breathlessly attached the hooks. The silk of my dress caressed my bare upper thighs, arousing my imagination as well as my cunt. My heart began to beat faster as I called her hotel to let her know that I was on my way. Her voice registered an unspoken understanding, that yes, I was on my way.

Walking out to the car, I ran one hand over the length of my body, feeling the silk of my dress rub smoothly across my skin. I pressed in, briefly, subtly, over the mound of my pelvic bone and then down onto my clit for a moment's touch. I wondered if I looked like a cat in heat, slinking, stretching, striding across the parking lot. I could feel the different fabrics that touched my skin: silk, nylon, lace, all arousing me, sparking my imagination for my time with Yolanda.

In the car my dress slid farther up my thighs, and I imagined that she was there to lean across the seat, to run her hand up between my legs. I imagined the feel of her skin, her breasts. I imagined her nipples hardening under the flesh of my tongue, her breath deepening into the sound of desire as she moved her hips against mine. I imagined not going out to dinner at all.

Standing at the door outside of her hotel room, I was suddenly filled with panic and fear and an urge to run away. I held on to the door frame and leaned in to see if I could hear her inside. I wondered if she were on the other side, watching me through the peephole. I took deep breaths. I tired to imagine what a 19-year-old Yolanda would look like as a 26-year-old lesbian. I wondered if she had trouble deciding on what to wear. Maybe she was in jeans and a T-shirt, and I was overdressed. Maybe she would laugh at me, scoff at the idea of my seduction plans. I needed to go back outside, to find a phone, to call her and cancel. I could tell her I had an attack of some kind. Asthma, maybe. But then I found myself knocking.

Lust has no logic, so it's best not to think too much about it. Just knock.

Yolanda opened the door to show me that the pretty young girl I remembered had indeed grown into a beautiful woman. She was captivating, sophisticated, and full of curves and skin and heat. All of this I noticed before we even said "hello." I don't know how much time passed as we stood there in the doorway, looking at who we had become, remembering who we were. To bridge the gap between then and now, Yolanda reached out to pull me into a warm embrace. Then we laughed, held on to each other's hands, touched each other's faces, questioned the years that passed without a word. We sat on the bed, knee to knee, taking turns to say "you look great" and noting our changes with glowing compliments. We had occasional nervous silences and awkward glances, but we kept our bodies close as we exchanged brief stories about our lives.

Yolanda's neck was bare and brown, her blouse's neckline distracting my eyes away from her face and into her cleavage. The scent of her perfume drew me closer as I tried to breathe her in. She asked me about my love life, and I told her not to ask. She sat back, curious, an eyebrow raised in question. I took a deep breath, shifted in my seat. And, looking away, I told her about the nagging agitation that hampered my day as I couldn't get her off my mind, my excitement at seeing her, at being there with her, my desire for her.

In the silence that followed, I closed my eyes tight enough to see the image of myself jumping out her sixth-floor window. But then she leaned in close to me, took my face in her hand, and turned my head so that I was looking into her dark brown, penetrating eyes.

"I'm not sure you know what you want," she said, softly.

I took her hand from my face and pressed it to my lips, saying, "Oh, yes, I do know what I want."

Yolanda stood up, and for a moment I thought she was going to ask me to leave. Instead, she walked over to the room's little refrigerator and pulled out two tiny bottles of red wine. Her body moved with a sexy, graceful confidence. I got up to follow her, stood behind her, put my hand on her back as she slowly turned to face me.

"Do you really think you're ready for this?" she asked in a quiet, husky voice. Without words to answer, I kissed the softest, most delicious lips that had ever been created. I felt as though I were about to lose my breath as I swooned in shock at the bliss I had just fallen into.

Yolanda wrapped her arms around me in a strong, tight grip. Moving from my waist to the small of my back, her hand pressed me forward, forcing our bodies to grind against each other. Then, pushing me against the wall without allowing space to come between us, she moved her hands up my waist, over my ribs, and onto my breasts. I was thrilled, electrified. Her kisses were tender when her hands were rough. When she slowed to gentle caresses, her kisses were hungry, insistent. I held on to her shoulders and pushed farther back into the wall, afraid of falling from the weakening of my legs. She pulled me away from the wall while kissing deep into my mouth. I lost my breath. I lost my mind. She grabbed my ass as if to squeeze me with all the strength of her hands, then stopped for just a moment as she too seemed to weaken while she moaned into my ear.

Her touch softened as she moved her body slightly away. I held her head back to watch her face as she looked down over my body and ran her fingers over the area of my dress where she could feel the outline of the garter belt's strap. With deep breaths and no words, she took my hand and led me to the bed. I watched her restraint as her eyes told me of her desire to rip off my dress to see what I had brought for her underneath, to thrust her hand into the cunt she knew was longing for her thrusting. And in knowing this, she began to move slowly.

She seemed to revel in the delicious torture of bringing me to this new experience of previously unknown, exquisite pleasure. She lifted my dress to touch the lace of my garter belt, she swallowed hard and took a deep breath as she laid me down on to the bed. I had to resist an urge, on the edge of ravenous craving, to grab her head and force her mouth to eat the hunger out of me. I held back, as she held back, the touch I was about to beg for.

She ran her hands over my stockings, up to the flesh of my thighs, and on to my hips. She unzipped my dress and pulled it down off my melting skin. She touched my breasts and pulled down the lace of my bra to suck my nipples, leaving my garter belt, stockings, and heels to remain. Then, slowly, she removed each item, taking time to caress every inch, even down to the strap around my ankle as she unbuckled my heels and dropped them to the floor.

When she finally touched my now desperate cunt, we both cried out in raw, naked need. She took me, then, for all that she needed to fill her mouth, her hands, her skin. She bathed herself in my come and in my sweat. She watched me move against her, under her. She gave me her body to take for myself the sensations of her hot, soft skin, the wetness of her seemingly insatiable cunt, the amazing movement of her vaginal walls as she took me in and released me, took me in, and took me in. Her clit grew hard as if reaching out for mine to press against it, and I felt myself falling into the core of my desire for her. She took me to the depth I sought, as I became mesmerized by the hunger within me.

I wanted to tell her that my heart was as full as my cunt, my clit, my brain, and my lungs as she pounded against me, allowing a throbbing need to escape from restraint, for release, for relief. My every cell was swollen with a pulsating resurgence of fantasies finally coming to life. I wanted to tell her that I felt reborn when I pulled my fingers from her cunt and watched the fluids run down over my hand, as I listened to the cry escape her throat, as she called out my name, as I watched her move, control, submit. She reduced me to primal expression, she took away my human voice, leaving me with no more than the growls and gasps and screams and moans of her doing, and I wanted her to know. I tried to speak, but then coming came, and all was lost to the ecstasy of her mouth, her heat, her hands, her body, her orgasm, mine.

Even the momentary stillness that followed had its rhythm. Our breaths intermingled, our fingers entwined, maybe our hearts were beating in sync. The rising steam from our skin joined to skin created a blanket of heat and sweat. I knew I was forever changed. I reached for her and held on tight. She whispered "I know" as if reading my mind.

Good-bye was an instant, a running away. She seemed to fear me in the world outside our hotel walls. Our night together was for my initiation to a world I was then to seek out on my own, as she turned away and headed for home. But, *ay, mi amor,* I think of you now, even after all these years, and I wonder how you are. Remembering your story of heartbreak and your use of me to soothe it, I send you a kiss, *un beso de recuerdo,* for making me the kind of woman who doesn't mind being torn in two. I walk with pride while folks who can't seem to understand whisper and point behind my hip-swaying back. I walk with pride and remember you.

Tension

by Alison Dubois

I'd never been a player. So it felt weird when I responded to an ad in the singles section of the local paper. I wasn't really looking, I told myself. I just needed a "friend" to talk to, while Jade and I worked out the kinks in our relationship and reunited.

That's how I met Jeanie. She was 20 years younger, which in and of itself would have been a deterrent, but there was something in her ad that intrigued me. Maybe it was because, like myself, she was struggling to regain her so-called "girlish" figure. Or maybe it was her genuine, youthful innocence. I wasn't sure—I was only sure that there was something there.

We agreed to meet at Ram's. It was hard not to be pensive. I mean, what did I really know about this person I'd only exchanged a handful of letters with, and a few phone calls? Yet when she entered the restaurant, I "knew" her instantly, without a picture, without a formal introduction. It was that youthful vibrance showing itself beneath her formfitting attire: tight Giovani's and a pinstriped tank top.

She walked right past the hostess prepared to seat her and stopped directly in front of me. Her blue eyes were sparkling with a mischievous spirit.

"Kate?" she said less as a question but more as a statement, as she smiled broadly. I started to stand, but she put her hand up. "Don't get up. I'll sit down," she said smugly. She was exactly as I'd imagined: cocky, gorgeous, and self-confident.

"Well, at long last, eh?" I could feel my nervousness showing in the way I nearly stuttered just making a casual remark. Her eyes met mine with such an intensity that I had to look away.

"Yeah, I was beginning to think you were going to fudge out." I looked into those baby blues that were so dark now. Wondering if I should have canceled. What was I doing here, really?

"Care for coffee?"

"Of course. And let's have some pie. What's good here?"

We both laughed. A woman after my own heart. This had been the attraction. Her brassy, yet sincere style. It reminded me of days gone by and, in a small way, of my own youth.

"Well, the chocolate mocha is to die for," I offered.

"So let's have two of those and two of the apple, á la mode." She matched my suggestion.

"I thought we were supposed to be planning our strategies to conquer the battle of the bulge," I reminded her.

"Absolutely, but we can't do that on an empty stomach, can we?" she quipped. I was smiling in spite of myself.

"Certainly not!" I said, as we laughed again. I knew then we were going to be friends. Something had been cemented between us.

I watched her walk away that first day. A big girl like myself, she carried her weight well, confident and sassy in her step, her youthful bosom bouncing with each stride. A nagging whisper inside me kept hissing: *What do you think you're doing? What about Jade?*

Now when I look at her, I remember that first moment, remember that first impression. Sometimes she will catch a hidden smile and inquire, but I always decline. Some things are better kept to oneself.

As summer blossomed, so did our friendship. I discovered I had more in common with Jeanie than I ever would have imagined. The routine became ritualistic.

We weighed ourselves, checked in whenever the urge to "binge" would hit, and slowly, over low-fat dinners, weekend workouts, and daily walks, we were transforming our pillowy midriffs into more streamlined versions.

One afternoon the conversation drifted to sex. Jeanie was a smoldering volcano who hadn't connected with the right woman to make her erupt yet. Sometimes I wondered if she was secretly hoping I would be the woman to give her that first bite from the apple of passion. I wondered if my own innocence and naïveté had showed on me like it showed on Jeanie.

Feeling particularly uncomfortable, I excused myself to hide out in the kitchen. I needed to regain my composure. I didn't want Jeanie to see my hot cheeks and be left open for her to wonder what was going on.

"Hey! Where'd you go?" She came into the kitchen just as I was heading back out. Our eyes met, then I averted my gaze. "What's going on?" She followed me into the living room. I plopped on the couch, feeling overwhelmed.

One thing about Jeanie, she wasn't shy. She loved to talk about sex and brag about her orgasms, which she told me she had perfected while waiting for Ms. Right to enter the picture.

Tonight I didn't dare imagine that youthful body achieving climax. Usually I just felt amused, enjoyed being entertained by her fantastic tales, but there was something different about tonight. There was an edge to her voice. An urgency in her story. Was she sensing something?

"What gives?" She landed on the couch beside me, her breasts brushing my arms in her haphazard landing. I shook my head, unable to dismiss the sensation. A chilling dose of reality jolted me: I was attracted to this woman, no mater how much I tried to deny it. My body was betraying me, making me perspire. Did she know? Could she see my excitement?

"Nothing," I finally managed to stutter.

"Nothing, my ass!" she shot back. I looked at her, embarrassed by her bluntness. Her eyes were fiery marbles searching mine for some indication of what I was holding back. I looked away, looked out the window.

I saw Mr. Whittleston weeding his petunias from his flower bed. I remembered thinking it was a "good day for it," for such tasks. Remembered feeling there was safety in such banality.

Suddenly I felt her fingertips brush my arm.

"Hey!" I said. The word was out faster than I could think. Immediately I was up, pacing the room.

"Kate, what's going on? I wasn't making a pass, you know better than that." Her young face, framed by long, flowing blond tresses, showed her surprise. But it was in the way that her eyes held mine, just a little too long, that told me we were in trouble.

"I'm sorry…sorry." I touched her arm, then settled into the La-Z-Boy across the room from her. I could feel her eyes upon me, knew she was studying me.

"I think I'm going to have a drink. Want one?" I scarcely looked at her, quickly heading back into the kitchen. I was fumbling with the ice tray when I noticed her standing by the table.

"Do you need one?" I stole a fleeting glance at her, but I didn't answer, I couldn't answer. Instead I turned away, pretended to be busy mixing the drink.

Suddenly I felt her arms slide around my waist and felt her full bosom pressing against me and her hot breath against the nape of my neck. I shivered, reeling with desire yet feeling overwhelmed by guilt. I didn't know what to do; only what my heart wanted and my body begged for.

In a moment that seemed like it was in slow motion, as if it were someone else, I was in those arms that were holding me so tight. Kissing those lips that I had wanted to kiss and taste for so long. Pressing my body against hers, singing the song of my soul, and feeling all the pent-up passion between us suddenly flowing freely.

From the quick, curious, dry kisses, to the wet, long, probing ones that were the language of lovers, we experienced them all. Our bodies bending, blending, like two trees intertwined, a thousand branches interlocked, a thousand kisses spent, a thousand thoughts and feelings fused; we were one.

But then it was as if, by the sheer intensity of the moment, I was suddenly more cognizant of the situation and the truth of our circumstances. I was not free. I pulled away.

"Kate...." Her voice was a breathy plea. I looked into her eyes, those same eyes that only moments before had been so sharp but now showed hurt, confusion. I could not be passion's apple. I could not speak, only shake my head and manage to find my way to the couch. Jeanie followed.

"Kate...." I looked at her, then away. "Kate...."

"Jeanie...that shouldn't have happened." I only dared a glance, afraid to look at her.

"I want it to happen!" she shot back, the hurt and anger reflected in her eyes. "I know you want me as much as I want you. I know you do," she insisted, but in her voice, I heard that fear of doubt. "Admit it," she pressed.

"OK! I do. But it can't happen," I sputtered, trying to quell my own frustration.

"Why?"

"Jeanie...please...you *know* why. I'm not free!" I stammered.

"But you're not with her, are you?" she pointed out. I knew, of course, that she was right, but it didn't change things, didn't change the fact that I'd made a commitment to another.

"Come on. Let's drop this, OK? I don't want us to have a bad evening."

She sat across from me. I watched her expression change. Slowly her buoyant youthful resilience seemed to kick in, and she was smiling again.

"Want to watch a flick?" I suggested, trying to keep the mood light. She looked up. I looked back, then away; it was still too much to hold that gaze.

"In a minute...." She got up, vanished into my bedroom. My mind raced. She had pushed the door behind her, but it hadn't closed entirely.

I sat there wrangling with my own curiosity. Finally I went to the doorway and stopped. Through the crack I could see her stretched out on my bed, totally naked, playing with my vibrators!

My mind was not as concerned with how she'd found them but rather what she was doing with those toys. I pushed the door open, and it squeaked...she looked at me, gasped, and smiled. She'd been waiting for me, knew I would come.

I just stood there, feeling the blood rushing to my loins, then back into my face. Feeling the excitement of naughtiness coursing all through. A voice inside my head told me to leave while another screamed for me to stay. I stayed, unable to leave.

I delighted in watching her fingers caressing her nipples, rolling one between her fingertips, then the other. Watched the way she performed for me. Taunting me as she slid the biggest vibrator in and out of herself.

I was in awe. I'd never been able to accommodate it personally, but she thrust it all the way in, until only a nib of white winked from her love tunnel, and she did it seemingly with ease. It made me blush just to watch.

"Like what you see?" she asked, sliding it out, knowing I did. It glistened from her juices as she extracted it, sending a shiver all through me.

"I shouldn't...."

"Be watching?" she finished for me, shoving that spear back in. A new wave of desire swept over...my legs felt like rubber, but I couldn't get them to carry me out of there. Something was keeping me bound.

She opened herself to me, exposing her femaleness and a clitoris that was larger than any I'd seen, and I'd seen quite a few in my day. It looked like a crystal with a rounded tip, jutting out from the arms of her labia.

But when she opened herself to me, her clit seemed to be looking at me, smiling at me. She was beautiful. I had always liked to watch, look, see. In that way I was a very visual woman. Combine that with her need to "show," and you had a very dangerous mix.

The more I saw, the more excited I grew. She pinched her clit playfully, tugged on it. I gulped, closed my eyes, reeling.

"Open your eyes..." she instructed. I obeyed.

She had stuffed one of her nipples in her mouth and was sucking on it, shimmering as one hand continued to thrust the vibrator in and out, in and out, while her free hand kept busy kneading her clit. I could feel my own loins growing hot and wet, aching to be satiated.

I was too mesmerized by what she was doing to care how she was managing to do all of that at once. My eyes were held captive with each thrust she made, drawing it out to the very tip before once again plunging it back into her depths, and hearing the reverberations of her saturated womanhood spilling juices over herself, on my down comforter, and coating the vibrator with yet another layer of her female nectar.

Her body was rocking and arching to the rhythm of her own strokes and building with each pulsating plunge. Suddenly she released the left nipple from her mouth. It rebounded in place, looking a bit like a mangled purple grape blinking at me, as her two breasts cascaded against each other in unison with her stomach and thighs, also gyrating in harmony to the intrinsic beat of her passion.

"Ooh...Kate...." She groaned in a way that I knew meant she was getting close to catching that elusive butterfly. I started to leave, suddenly feeling the need to depart, overcome with the guilt that I had watched as much as I had. Had watched this woman sexually exploring herself.

But she beckoned me back.

"Kate! Stay, please..." her voice trailed off into a raspy plea. "Watch me..." she begged.

I stayed, unable to refuse her request. Watched her shove the toy back in, watched her face contort in that all-too-familiar way, knowing she was reaching her pinnacle of desire. Suddenly she cried out. In unison, her woman cavern spit the vibrator like a torpedo, followed by a gush. Her youthful body writhing and spasming, jerking. Followed by the heady, pungent odor of sex, of female sexuality, permeating the room, filling my senses. It was too much. Goose bumps had formed on my arms, sweat on my brow. I watched her finish. Needing to know, to see her magnificence. Her rosebud a dark crimson red, engorged and slick.

Her thighs clapped together as her head flopped back against the comforter, the throes of her ecstasy still holding her. Slowly, somehow, I'd found my feet again, and had managed to leave.

My own desire blazing through me, I fell into the shelter of the big chair. My hand automatically found that throbbing bead. And was working it at a furious pace, feeling my own lather all over my fingers and hand, as I got closer and closer to that clandestine mountain.

Then, just as I was reaching the top, I heard Jeanie's voice, cheering me on. Briefly I opened my eyes, long enough to see her standing in front of the chair, watching me with a broad smile on her face.

Unable to hold back, to contain my feelings any longer, I exploded, submitting to that world of wonder as I shuddered, gasped, sputtered…then pulled back, fell into my own fantasy, nirvana, whirling about in the introspective cosmos. A mix of ecstasy and embarrassment fused together on my journey.

Until alas, I became aware of her stroking my hair. Slowly I returned. Opened my eyes. My face was beet-red, and I was left totally speechless.

"Did you say something about a flick?" she asked.

What could I say? A movie would never be the same to me again.

My Heart Told Me

by Rebecca Faurer

"Are you OK? Your message sounded like you were dying." I had panicked when I heard Kate's message, demanding that I come over right away.

"I'm OK. I'm just s-o-o-o excited. I couldn't wait to tell you. We finally found someone to rent the extra room!" Kate's face was lit up like the Fourth of July. Her eyes had a twinkle that I had not seen in quite some time.

'You're telling me I drove like a bat out of hell for that? I'm happy for you and all, but is this really life or death?" I found it hard to ever get really mad at Kate, but this was starting to look like a good time.

"Beth, she's a fellow spook! But if you're going to keep up that crabby-ass attitude you can just go home."

I deserved that. "Sorry. I was expecting a death in the family or something. Let me adjust here and dump some adrenaline. Do you have any Pepsi?"

"Yeah. I'll get it."

Kate returned from the kitchen and handed me an ice-cold mug of my favorite drink. "OK, so fill me in."

"She answered the ad we put in the queer paper. She moved her stuff in yesterday and left this morning for some school for three weeks."

"So what makes you think she's a spook?"

"When we asked her where she worked she said, 'I work for the government.' Do you guys learn that in training or what? So anyway I said, real matter of fact like, 'You work for the CIA?' You should have seen the look on her face. I am good!"

"Yes, you are, but that's beside the point. So..."

"After an eternity of 'yes, you do,' 'no, I don't,' she swore us to secrecy and confessed. We asked her if she knew you. I didn't know 20,000 people worked there." I suppose it's just one of those things people do. Forgetting how big cities or organizations are, when they ask if one of 500,000 would know a Jane Doe.

"So—what else?"

"Beth, you have to meet her when she gets back."

"Gets back from where?"

"She's at Quantico for three weeks for some kind of spook training. She left us her address. I can't tell you why, but I have a feeling about this woman. I think you should write her."

"Is she single?" Oh, shit! Why'd I ask that? I had sworn off women—at least until I couldn't remember every torturous detail of my last breakup. Six months ago I packed up a U-Haul trailer, attached it to the bumper of my hamster-powered Nissan, and set off from Colorado Springs, Colo., to McLean, Va. I left behind a lover who had informed me I had to forgive her for having a four-month affair and deciding to move in with "the love of her life." It had taken a full week to drive those 1,500 miles at 40 miles per hour. I listened to hog reports when I got bored with the 30-plus tapes I had brought along. I was more balanced when I finally pulled in front of my parents' house, but I knew then, and I thought I still knew, that more than anything I needed time alone. Time to screw my head on straight. The last thing I needed was another woman.

"Beth. Beth. Where were you?"

"Uh. Oh. Just thinking. Sorry, Kate, what'd you say?"

"I said yes."

"Yes what? What the hell are you mumbling about now?"

"Yes, she's single. Are you going to write her? Never mind. Here's her address. Take a chance. This one is special. I can't tell you why. Like I said, I just have this feeling." Kate handed me the paper.

"I'll think about it, OK?"

"'K. what are you going to do to celebrate after midterms?"

"Kate, that's like three weeks away."

"I know. But the Hung Jury's having their 'At least you're halfway through' party. Wanna go?"

"Is Jamie going?"

"Hell, no. She's still behind at work. I feel her crawl into bed at night and leave before I get up. That print shop is going to be the death of Wanda." Wanda was the name Kate had given her vibrator. Her honesty and lack of inhibition were two of the qualities that had attracted me to her.

"You're such a pig! I guess. Let's see what happens. OK?"

Midterms had gone well, and it was to be a night of celebration and flirtation. I was in a funk but thought I could blow it off, so I went to pick up Kate. "Damn, Kate, look at you. Gorgeous *and* on time! Miracle of miracles!"

"Thanks. You look great too. Are those new?" She wiggled her eyebrows and twinkled her eyes in the direction of my tight black jeans.

"Yeah. Ordered 'em from L.L. Bean's. Ready to go?"

"Yep. Watch out world! Two hot girls, loose on the streets of D.C.!"

I always loved the drive from McLean into the big D.C. city. But tonight especially, driving felt good. Too good. The rhythm of the road and the beat of the radio were helping to ease my mind. Along the river the trees and ivy were starting to show swatches of their fall colors. We crossed the George Washington Bridge, drove alongside the Washington Monument and around the White House. Then made the infamous turn into the slums. Global standard, unfortunately, for most queer bar locations.

"So'd you do it?"

"Do what?"

"Did you write her?"

"It's classified."

"Oh, Beth, don't give me that shit. She comes back tomorrow. I want to know."

"You are such a pain the ass."

"Thanks. Did you write her?"

I had reread her letters so many times I could almost recite them from memory. Sarah's first letter was pretty standard agency paranoia: "How'd you get my address? How'd you get on at the agency? What's your position? Clearance? Age? Life story?" I answered honestly and much more openly that I had intended. I had preferential hiring status at the agency because my parents worked there. The agency logic is that they've already done the security clearances on a good portion of my family, and I couldn't possibly be a security risk. So they only had to do a short investigation. No one told them I was queer, and fortunately they hadn't asked.

I worked nights and weekends as I wished, "watching" nonagency people as they entered and moved about the facility. For this I got paid big bucks as college jobs go. I told her of my joys and fiascoes in Colorado. I explained that I had moved here to take advantage of my parents' offer of paid tuition and free room and board if I lived with them. I told her of my dreams and desires. I bared my soul to a piece of paper that I prayed wouldn't be intercepted by "them."

Reading her second letter was like meeting a whole different person. She wrote that she also felt driven to tell me—a total stranger—her life story. She was 25 and has been working at the agency for six months. She had moved here from Ohio, where she went to school. She had gotten an associate of science in criminal justice and had worked as a college police officer until she got this job. She loved music, wine, the outdoors, clothes, and most especially water. She had done some synchronized swimming in college. She'd tried out for the swim team but was too slow. She often drove through the night so that she could wake up literally on Rehoboth Beach.

The way she wrote came as a cherished song to my heart. Although we were sharing, like two inmates on death row, there was still an undertone of caution. We were both reaping the benefits of our unencumbered lifestyles. We were sculpting what I was to discover much later was an unparalleled bond and friendship.

Remembering our letters was again igniting a feeling within me that I could not put to words. Something was driving me to keep our divulgences secret. Hidden. But I had to tell Kate something. "I wrote."

"And you didn't tell me. You shit!"

With intentional calm, in an effort to derail her, I said, "Kate, when you get all riled up the veins in your temples pound. It's not very attractive!" Before I could react, the flesh of my thigh was being pierced by razor-sharp talons. "You know, if you had actual *human* sex, those nails would shred! Stop it! I'll hurt you!" Retraction accomplished, I went on. "Jamie's still putting in the hours, huh?"

"Yes. And don't change the subject."

"All right. Her first lett—"

"FIRST letter! There's more than one? You shit fucker! Give me details or risk a permanent limp!" Kate showed her angry face.

"If you shut up, I'll tell you." In fact that was the last thing I intended to do. Perhaps I could stick to the safe details.

"FINE!"

"Fine. Her first letter was a little paranoid. She's only been at the agency for six months—yeah, I know, same as me. She's a federal special police officer. She thinks she knows who I am. I, of course, don't have a clue. The second letter was a lot more relaxed. I guess she figured, since she was still employed, I wasn't going to blow her cover. Anyhoo, long story short. As you know, she gets back tomorrow. She said she's beat and needs to catch up on some sleep. She'll probably call Sunday. That's about it. No big deal."

"No big deal, my ass! Beth, there's one thing that has always endeared you to me: You can't lie for shit! Look at you! Your face is glowing just talking about her! I won't pry. Shut up! It is not the first time I've said that! Anyway, I'm so very happy for you. I pray this turns out to be good for you."

"Thanks. I want to tell you more, but I don't. Know what I mean? I'll tell you this, though—she does seem to be someone special. I haven't been able to put my finger on it, but there is something that is, like, driving me to her. Oh, Kate, keep me from falling in love. I don't think I'm ready."

"Lighten up, you haven't even met her yet. Maybe she has no teeth or bug eyes or something!"

"Somehow I don't think that matters. Know what I mean?"

"Yeah, I do. And Beth..."

"What?"

"She doesn't. She's very cute. No, not cute. She's...captivating. Yeah! Captivating!"

"Thanks, Kate."

"No problem. You don't much feel like going anymore, do you?"

I shook my head no.

"Me either. To be honest, I was taking you out so you wouldn't sit home and fret. So how 'bout we turn the Hamster Mobile around and head back over the bridge."

I loved Kate. She often knew what I needed. Sometimes even before I did. I was glad to turn the car around. I put Jim Chappell in the tape deck and quickly found that comfortable groove again. What a gorgeous night. It was as if sharing what I had with Kate had made the "us" of paper more real. I was loving life and the road and the music and the trees.

"Beth, you just missed my exit. Or are we driving to Quantico?

"Oops. Sorry." I took the next turn off and in minutes we were sitting in front of Kate and Jamie's three-story brick house. I didn't noticed the blue Blazer before, but I blew it off.

"Hey, I got an 88 on the midterm. What'd you get?"

"Oh, uh, a 96."

"Oh, Beth, that's great! Can you help me figure out a way to remember the muscles? All the points I lost were 'cause of them."

"Sure!" I was beginning to feel claustrophobic. I wanted to leave.

"Can you come over tomorrow? *She* won't be back until after midnight, right?"

"Yeah, sure, OK. I'm going to the Falls tomorrow. I'll come by around 6. OK? Bye, babe."

"Thanks. See you then, and Beth—get some sleep." She winked as she flashed me an embracing smile.

It was a gorgeous day. Not a cloud in the sky. "Unseasonably warm temperatures," as the weather guy had predicted. I was so at peace I actually fell asleep on the shores of the Potomac, listening to the water race itself for the trophy. Last night I'd reread all the letters, searching for a phrase or word or undertone that could change my feelings toward this "paper" woman. I was unsuccessful. She was becoming more and more real, and yet sometimes, I couldn't believe that she even existed. I was glad she was coming back tonight. Soon I'd be able to put an end to my dreams. But maybe the dreams were better!

Dear God, why did I have to write her? Why didn't I leave well enough alone? I was happy. Doing well in school. Enjoying my job. Maybe we'll see each other and say, "Oh, hi," and move on. Yeah, that's it! Quit worrying. I lay back and watched a bunny chase a carrot across the sky. I tried to imagine she was chasing away my fears.

I reached to turn off my alarm clock. "Where is that damn thing?" I opened my eyes but couldn't focus. As my vision cleared, I realized I was still lying on my polar fleece blanket in the park and the sun was setting. My alarm had been a Harley heading home. I focused on my watch. "Shit! It's 5:30!" I quickly gathered my things and crammed them into my backpack. I ran to my car and drove like I'd just won the lottery.

I offered a quick "Hi, I'm late and need to shower," to my parents and ran upstairs. I showered, dried my hair, and dressed in a record 20 minutes. As I ran by my parents' laughing faces, I heard, "Hot date?"

"No, I was supposed to be at Kate's at 6 to study for A&P, fell asleep in the park. Love you. Bye." I'm not sure they ever were young themselves, and they were certainly never this frantic to study. But they embrace my biology and support me in my gallivanting. The deal is, I bring home good grades for their financial investment, and they'll let me do as I please. Mom's fridge is always full, and I have my own huge master bedroom, so I figure, even on the worst day, it's better than sharing a room in the dorms and eating cafeteria food.

It's 6:45 and I sit for a minute in front of Kate's house in an effort to catch my breath and slow my heart. As I glance around the street, I see that same blue Blazer from last night. Again, I let the observation go without great thought. I amble to the front door, mind blank. In a daze I glue my finger to the buzzer. That nagging feeling returns. After my acrobatics, if she's stood me up I'll kill her. So focused on my irritation, I jump when the door opens.

"Hey, you," she said with a smile.

"Hey." I'm confused. Who…wait. Oh, shit! She's gorgeous! In my rush to get here, I'd forgotten. Dear God, let me look OK. Did I brush my teeth? "Sarah?"

"Come in," she ordered gently. "What's with the schoolbooks?"

"Kate asked me to come over to help her study. What are you doing back? Thought you didn't get in until late tonight?" Then it hit me. The Blazer's hers! She was here last night! I'm feeling set up. But by whom? "I think we were set up. Kate's not here, huh?"

Sarah shook her head no as she flashed a soul-melting smile.

"I don't want to bother you. Let me just go, and you can call when you're more settled." I was halfway out the door when the screen and its frame fell into my arms.

"I'll let you go, no need to destroy my house." Sarah laughed with a glow in her eyes.

I laughed a belly laugh too. My words stumbled over themselves as I spoke. "Sorry. Do you have a screwdriver? I can fix it. It won't take long. Or I could do it later. Really. I don't want to disturb you. Why don't I just come back later?" Never in my life have I done such a perfect impression of a babbling idiot. *Come on, Beth it's just a woman. An absolutely gorgeous, blond-haired, blue-eyed, big-breasted woman, with a voice that could melt an Alaskan glacier.* I silently direct myself in hopes of gaining some self-control. *Any* self-control. *Breathe, Beth…in…out…in…out…in…Bad mantra.* Visions of taking Sarah right there flash before me. *Control!* I scream inside my head, but I'm not listening.

Sarah, unsuccessfully trying to stifle a laugh, says, "Beth, just lean it against the wall and get back in here."

After depositing the door in its new resting place, I let her take my hand and guide me to the couch. "Sit. Relax. What would you like to drink?" She headed to the kitchen, providing me the opportunity to soak in the view of her solidly muscular legs, small, perfectly packaged butt, broad shoulders, and beautifully sculpted hair. *I'm in trouble.* My silent words fall on my own deaf ears.

From the kitchen I hear, "There's water, orange juice, beer, Pepsi, and wine. What's your pleasure?"

"You!" I mumble, intentionally trying not to be heard. "Uh…whatever you're having'll be great. But no beer."

"White OK?

"Sorry?" Losing! Hell, I'm lost!

"Wine. White wine. Is that OK?"

"Yes. Great! Thanks. Can I help?" There we go. I'm finally starting to regain my composure.

"No thanks. Are you hungry? I was just getting ready to make myself some dinner."

"Actually I'm starving. I went to the river today and fell asleep. I raced to get here. I didn't have time to grab anything. Are you sure I can't help with anything? I'm pretty handy."

Handing me my wine, she looked at the door and giggled. "No, really. I'm witness to your handiwork already."

I smiled.

"To tell you the truth, I've missed being in the kitchen. It won't be long. Is there anything you don't eat?"

"Celery! Can't even stand the smell!"

There's a *thud* in the kitchen. "That takes care of that then. Can you put on a CD?" Sarah said from the too-distant kitchen. "There weren't many creature comforts at Quantico. No kitchen, and I forgot my radio. With the exception of the drive there and back, I've heard only jarhead rap. Not that there's anything wrong with that, it's just that 24 hours a day gets old. So play anything but rap!"

Laughing, I head to the stereo. "OK."

"What were you supposed to be studying?"

"Muscles."

"Mmm. One of my favorite subjects. Anything I can help with?"

More than you know. Sarah's running shorts revealed areas I wanted to study. "No thanks. Kate had asked me to come over here to help her."

I finally found a CD and with trembling hands managed to get it to play. On my way into the kitchen I heard Sarah whisper.

"Ooh, baby."

My heart skipped several beats. "Sorry, didn't hear that. What'd you say?"

Startled to see me standing in the doorway, Sarah jumped. As she turned toward me, her face revealed what she had tried to keep hidden. Clearing her throat, she squeaked, "Oh—uh—n-o-o-o. I, uh—was just talking to myself. Nice choice, that's Suzanne Ciani, *Velocity of Love,* right?"

"Very good. You sure I can't help?"

"Actually, you being in here is more of a distraction than a help."

My head vibrated. She is just as taken by me as I am by her! By the hand, she led me once again, to the couch. She gently pushed me down and began walking back to the kitchen. I started to rise. I wanted to reach out to her. Feel her body against mine.

As if on instinct, she turned and instructed me. "Sit. We need to eat. I'll be right back."

I did as I was told. She was, after all, a cop. An intelligent, gorgeous, feminine cop, who right now was fixing me dinner.

Sarah returned with a tray of sliced cheese, melted Brie, crackers, fresh apple and pear slices, grapes, strawberries, and chocolate seashells! There was the bottle of wine and a crystal glass. As a finishing touch, two long-stemmed red roses lay atop the feast. She began walking up the stairs.

I sat still. In a daze. Waiting for instruction.

From halfway up the stairs, she called, "Bring your glass."

On shaky knees I rose, talking silently to my legs. *One in front of the other…come on, legs…MOVE!* Wearing sweat on my brow like a medal, I had conquered Mount Everest. Sarah was waiting for me in front of a closed door. I stood next to her, holding my breath.

With the face of an angel and lips sweet and soft, she kissed me. My knees wobbled but held. My heart, on the other hand, was doing laps around my stomach and crotch. Once sure I was not going to fall, she kissed me again. I focused my eyes and realized the door had been opened. I was speechless.

The room was bathed in the glow of dozens and dozens of candles. Tall candles, short candles, fat candles, skinny candles. All white. No reds. No blues. No greens. White. A hypnotic, embracing, soothing, seductive melody swam from flame to flame. Against the far wall was a masterful work of art. Blanketed by hundreds of rose petals was the place I knew I'd discover the depths of this gift. Off-white flannel sheets barely peeked themselves from under this fragrant blanket. On another wall was a poster with the words from the song "The Rose." Another wall held what looked like a window, revealing an unobstructed view of the ocean stealing sand from the beach, one grain at a time. Sand-colored curtains covered a hidden window on the remaining wall. A gold cloth covered the bedside table that held our feast.

Having acknowledged the room's contributions, I sought to praise its orchestrator. I felt arms embrace me from behind. I turned, lips parted, to embrace this goddess. I had never danced as one with a woman. Until now. We swayed to the music we heard, and to that which was coming from the black box. If there was a world outside that room, I no longer cared.

As the song ended I asked, "How did you know?"

"Your letters touched feelings within my heart I didn't know I could have. I took a chance you were feeling the same way. Don't be mad at Kate. She helped get you here, but it was at my request. She and Jamie are enjoying a much-needed night alone together at the Fairfield. Talk to me. Tell me I did OK."

"You've done much more than OK. I have been trying to tell myself not to feel the way I've been feeling. I can't explain. I simply…need you. I want you. I want to make love to you, Sarah." I had to hear myself say her name. I had to know this was the woman who had been the source of my torment. I reached for her and kissed her for the first time, as mine. Gliding down from her ears to her neck, I smelled heaven. "Um. What are you wearing?"

"KL." Breathy now, it was Sarah who had difficulty with words.

"Dear God!" I exclaimed, as I buried my nose in the nape of her neck.

I began unbuttoning her silk, long-tailed shirt. With only four buttons left, I stole a glimpse at her breasts where they tried to escape their captor.

Sarah pulled away. "You first," she requested.

I wasn't going to argue. I quickly removed my pants. Then my underwear. Hesitating momentarily, I glanced into her eyes. Encouraged, my hands discarded my modesty and my shirt. I slid back the covers and eased my wetness into the bed. HER bed! With eyes alone, I instructed her to do the same.

With a look borrowed from a nervous child she began. Slowly. The shorts were sacrificed. She slowly stood with hands at her side. A shirt tail graciously stepped aside to reveal a few strands of hair below her belly. As if they were glued, she struggled to undo the last buttons of her shirt. Although now free, she clasped the two edges together. She appeared frightened, but a look in her eyes told me not to move. To let her do this herself. I complied. She helped the shirt fall from her shoulders.

"Oh, dear God!" was all I could manage. Her beauty was beyond words. I reached out for her to embrace me. To feel me as I needed to feel her. She inched forward. With my heart bursting, I lunged to her. Bringing her down heavily on top of me. A whispered moan involuntarily escaped our lips.

Expertly I slid out from beneath her and was at once lying on my side, facing her. I could see her. Know that it was her. I caressed her face, her neck, her shoulders, her breasts. Forcing myself not to linger too long, I continued my exploration. Her silky soft stomach, her thighs, her knees, her calves, her ankles, her toes. And in reverse, until I again felt her breasts. I guided my lips toward her. Slowly, I let the heat of my mouth engulf her hardening nipple.

"Um." Brushed my ear. I'm not certain of its source.

Around and around. I played my tongue against her nipple. I pressed my face into this soft pillow. Sarah's hips thrust upward. Rhythmically rising and falling. Her hand, pressed firmly against the back of my head, forced my face deeper into her breast. Gasping for air, I pulled away. My hand continued where my mouth left off. I slid my body atop hers. I tasted the sweetness and felt the moisture of her lips. With urgency, Sarah smothered my lips with a kiss that began in her toes. With hips firmly locked I mirrored her rhythm, while our tongues danced to a rhythm all their own.

I needed more. With eager regret, I forsook the lips and searched for the neglected breast. I gently sucked and tugged at her nipple. Over and over I devoured and released. Circling around and around. With growing intensity her hips pressed themselves into my stomach. My tongue deviated. I tasted a hint of salt in the sweat that glistened on her stomach. Lower and lower my tongue searched, slowly heading for heaven.

I smelled sweetness. I was close. My tongue brushed the coarse hairs aside, and suddenly I tasted the sweet nectar. I plunged deeply inside! My arms fought for their hold on her thighs. Deeper and deeper I dove, searching for the source of this sweetness. Slowly I pulled my tongue out. But I hadn't had enough. I plunged again. Tasting. Teasing.

"Oh, God, please! Oh!" Sarah prayed.

I slowly retreated from her depths. "Oh, Sarah! You are…" There wasn't a word created to express as much as I could show her. I easily slid my face between her wet thighs, opening my lips ever so slightly to take her in. I sucked rhythmically. Gently. Harder and harder and harder and—

"Ooh, Beth… I—I—I—I—I…Ooh!" Sarah tried to find words but failed.

By thighs of steel, I was trapped. Rolling, thrusting, rising. sucking, moaning! Sarah released a deep, forceful scream. Suddenly there was calm. No noise. No movement. Nothing. Just Sarah and me, consumed by an embrace.

I'm not sure how much time had passed when I heard Sarah say, "I—I—I've never felt like this before." Tears filled her eyes. "I'm sorry. It's just—I've never—done this before."

My fingers tried to quiet her lips as my words tried to console. "Shh. It's OK. It's just been a long time." I believed the apology was for her tears and the strength of her emotions. I could not accept it.

In time her embrace relaxed, and she spoke again. "I want to do the same for you."

Knowing that all she had to do was *look* in the direction of my crotch and I would come, I said, "I'm fine. Really, I'm OK."

She ignored me. The next thing I knew we were dancing to my music. I came for this woman as I had never come before.

Sarah ran her fingers through my hair as she revealed her secret. "What I was trying to tell you was that…I've never done *this* before. I've never made love with a woman."

Recalling my heaven only moments earlier, I was not a believer. Sarah had a warm, loving, mischievous smile on her face. She added, "In fact, I've never done this with anyone."

"You're a—were—a virgin?"

Sarah responded simply. "My heart told me you were the one."

The Crush Part

by Jen Moses

We have the same birthday, my friend Hannah and I, October 6, 1962 and 1969, respectively. We met doing theater at the University of Iowa; she was a grad student, I was an undergraduate. The first time I saw her she was onstage, in Maria Irene Fornes's *Conduct of Life.* Her character was that of the wife of a Latin-American military dictator. The costume designer envisioned her as an Evita and spent $30 a yard on the silk for her robe. She was beautiful, and she was a great actress. The minute I saw her I knew we would know each other. The scene shop is dark and empty at night.

"What are you doing?"

"I don't know."

My best friend Hannah has her hands on my tits. She's giggling and nuzzling my ear. Everyone else in the theater building is either in rehearsal rooms or in the main stage theater, where *Twelfth Night* is on. I'm in it, playing Antonio in our cross-cast, sexed-up version of Shakespeare's play. Obviously my costume is having quite an effect on my heretofore platonic friend. It makes sense as the whole thing is pretty much see-through, the frame of a period sailor coat, with a deep blue leotard accentuating my breasts underneath it, and knee-length suede britches. I look like a lovestruck, swashbuckling androgyne. She gently pinches my nipples; I can feel them harden under her fingers. I'm shocked and speechless. She had convinced me she was totally straight.

"Your hands are on my breasts," I exhale, the realization surging through my body. Fire engulfs my cunt, and for an instant Hannah says nothing but faintly kisses my neck. Suddenly I'm aware of a ringing in my ear, and I remember that I was in the shop to use the phone. My friend Steve arrives tonight from out of town to see the show in its final weekend, and I am expecting him at my house sometime before my show is over. My lover and former best friend is also coming, tomorrow morning. No answer. I hang up. The clock says 9:30. I still have ten minutes before my first scene in Act Three.

Wait, Hannah is standing behind you, Jen, with her arms around you and her fingers on your breasts. What does that mean? I can't answer the question, but I know enough to reach my arms around before she lets go. Of course, as soon as she feels my hands on her virgin ass she wakes up scared and pulls away, saying, "OK, let's go."

"Wait!"

"No." Without thinking I flex my muscles around her.

Suddenly it all comes back to me: A year ago when we first got to know each other, I did develop a terrible attraction to her, but she was older and straight and my director so I forgot about it. Not, however, before one night in The Mill over a table of Dickel shots and beer, when I grabbed her feet and was nibbling her toes while she shrieked and laughed. I felt I made my point, then I let it go. And so Hannah became my beautiful blond older best friend. I love the friendship so much I really don't remember the crush part. Until now, this moment. Now, it's all I'm aware of, as if her surreptitious hands have opened some long-forgotten window.

The intensity of my and Hannah's relationship had been forged in an atmosphere of crisis that had permeated the winter. The Gulf War was in full swing, and we all knew people getting bombed in Israel. In my private life, my lover was in another state having a breakdown, going in and out of the hospital. Hannah had been there with me through that situation, and together we watched her boyfriend lapse into an alcoholic binge. Chaos was everywhere, and all we had was our companionship and the warmth of our theater department friends. It made the bonds strong, and by spring we were all ripe for some release, some mirth. And that night we were going to get our chance at the cast party, the blowout that occurs in the final weekend of most plays. I made sure Hannah was invited.

It is now 12:30, and the party is in full swing. Our friend Louis brought us some kind bud and we are all sweetly high, dancing and drinking and hugging. Theater people are always touching each other. I feel elated, surrounded by my good friends, Richie and Kim, and Jennifer and everyone else from the show. I'm dressed for the prowl, in boots and my black lace see-through shirt with a black bra visible underneath. All night people have been complimenting me, and I'm turned-on by the attention. Hannah just walked in. She sees me and smiles. We kiss and laugh. This is strange. We know each other so well, we love each other, we are so familiar. Now something else is happening, and we keep laughing and laughing, unable to believe or speak words on the subject.

"Hannah, do you like my new shirt?" I lift my arms and rotate to the music, showing her my new see-through blouse. She's biting her lips and making a faint groaning noise. I do look good, my supple torso in black bra gyrating underneath the lace. Other people have been putting their hands on me all night, but it's time for her to. I've been waiting. She started it in the scene shop, but now, high and dancing at this party with our friends, I can't forget about it; it keeps rushing back through my mind, and I find myself kissing her every few moments. The kisses are so easy. Our lips are softly drawn together and then we look at each other in disbelief. Is this really happening? She's panicked, I can tell, but laughing and excited. She's scared but there's nothing to be done now except go with it. And it feels good. I'm in heaven, oozing with the sweetest anticipation.

Somebody calls for a game. It's Kim. Our friends want to play a game called Truth Circle. OK. Sounds perfect. We all lay around on the floor, telling our deepest secret at that moment. Everybody's hedging because they're not really up to it. It's my turn. Suddenly I'm terrified because there is only one truth for me at that moment, and it is so pervasive that I can't admit it out loud, even though I have no denial of it within myself. I want Hannah. I am wet with desire for her. I want to scream it, but I am not able. My mind travels back for an instant to her squeezing my nipples in the scene shop. Hannah flashes me by lifting her skirt. She's laughing like a beautiful devil, "Come on, Jen. Come on, you wimp! Tell the truth!"

"I'll tell Richie, but only alone and in the other room."

Richie and I go into the bedroom.

"OK. I think I want to sleep with Hannah."

"Of course you do. Is that it?"

"I'm scared!"

"Don't be scared, everyone knows you guys are gonna do it."

"They do?"

"Yeah, it's totally obvious."

Oh. We go back into the other room. The rest of the circle is sitting there smoking cigarettes. Why does he seem to think it so easy? Why isn't it easy? Actually it seems to be quite easy for my body, which is crawling back to Hannah from the bedroom. My mind is way behind. It won't catch up until tomorrow.

How did we get on the floor like this, lying in each other's arms? I don't remember getting here, but I feel like I've melted in some kind of delicious lava pool. I can't speak. Somewhere in the annals of my consciousness a voice says *quelque chose au sujet de mon amour, qui arrivent ce matin.* But I can't at that moment remember my four years of French. Someone just took a picture of us. I barely hear Jennifer saying, "Wow, you guys."

Hannah gets up and runs into the bedroom. After a minute I follow, and I find her on the phone.

"Who are you talking to?"

"It's Louis. Go away."

"Louis? I know what you're doing."

"What? I'm not doing anything."

"I know what you're doing." I start moving toward her, toward the bed. I keep saying it, because I do know what she's doing. She's calling this guy Louis that she has a crush on, and it's gotta be 2:30 in the morning. She's calling him desperate for some way around the fact that she made a pass at her best girlfriend in the scene shop. I'm scaring her now, like I did that night I was nibbling her toes at The Mill. But this time is different. She's laughing into the phone and apologizing over and over again to him. I'm chanting "I know what you're doing" as I crawl on top of her on the little twin bed. Finally she hangs up the goddamned phone, and suddenly we are grinding together, kissing more. We pause and look at each other.

"You're beautiful," she says.

"You are," I say.

We get up and stand together in the full-length mirror, moving to the music from the other room. Again, like in the shop, she is behind me, holding me. We're looking at ourselves and writhing and laughing breathily. The door opens. It's Kim and Richie and Jennifer.

"What are you guys doing in here?" Richie flops onto the bed. Kim stands next to Hannah and me in the doorway. We look at each other and Kim smiles at us. "How's it going?"

Hannah looks at me. "Let's go." She's got my hand.

I look at her meaningfully and clarify, "Let's go?"

"Let's go."

I look at Kim. "We have to go now."

"OK. Have fun," Kim says, grinning like the Cheshire Cat. It's three-something in the morning. No one is tired, at least not me. Still in daze of pot and lust, I wander with Hannah into the other bedroom for the coats, and we fall down on the floor looking for her purse. She's cradling me in her lap saying words, saying, "What did you tell Richie about me? What did you tell him? Hmm?"

Her voice is like candy velvet, almost a whisper. Her lips are damp and hovering over my ear, and I can feel acutely the breath of her words. Every time she utters a new sound I melt. I am a delicious lava pool now. Every part of me feels like it's wide open. This is why falling in love with best friends is so good and so dangerous. She's still asking, urging me to say what I said to him, but I can't, and my voice is raspy and weak with feeling. I think I'm trembling.

Finally we make it outside. The cold snaps some sense into me, and I take the lead to Hannah's car. We get in, and she starts driving. "Where am I going?" she asks as if there's any doubt.

I am no longer hazy. I turn to her with a smirk. "To your apartment. Where the hell else would you go?"

"Oh, I'm scared."

I look at her, put a hand on her arm. "Don't be scared."

Hannah's apartment is beautiful. There is plenty of light from the streetlamps. The door is never locked. We go in and I head for the bathroom. By the time I make it back to the bed, Hannah is already in it with the covers pulled up to her chin. It's very funny to me, and I laugh. "Are you naked?" I ask. She doesn't answer me. I'm taking my clothes off in the streaks of silver light.

She says, "You're so beautiful."

When I get under the down comforter I find her naked except for her underwear, which are the hilarious, up-to-the-neck variety. "You left your underwear on!" I exclaim. Her skin is cool and smooth. We slide against each other until we fit together. Like everything else in our relationship it feels remarkably familiar, so much that it's thrilling to discover it. We linger, touching each other, not kissing yet. She is under me, her blond hair sprayed on the pillow. Her noise is a sort of coo and purr, and comes with the breath. We push together and moan. I can feel her wetness on my hip. I can see my own silvery profile in the streetlight as I slowly lower my face to hers. Instinctively I rub my cheek softly against her cheek and drag my lips across her skin. She gasps and murmurs a tiny high-pitched noise from her throat. Our bodies begin to wind together, like snakes, and the movement intensifies to a writhing. We both begin to breathe harder, and finally our lips meet in a hungry kiss. When our tongues touch, a bomb drops so heavily I think the floor is going to give way underneath the futon. Oh, my God.

We pull apart and lie side by side, enveloped in an unexpected calm. Hannah runs her hand over me gently. She says, "It feels like I'm touching myself. Really, exactly."

"It feels that way to me too, as if it was my hand touching myself."

"Wow. Wow." Hannah looks at me, so close, as close physically as we have become mentally and emotionally, karmically. We smile at the same moment, free from worry, from everything. "This is amazing," she says, almost laughing, but quietly.

Out of the stillness a new wave of passion swells and breaks upon us, and we end up wound together again, kissing relentlessly. We are completely matched. She moans, and I hear myself moan with her. It's like we are two strains of one melody, blending with no calculation but total precision. My fingers move into her wet pussy with utter knowledge. I stroke her clitoris and then dip down inside of her, just inside, then a little deeper, making circles. She is overcome, and I am being driven from some core. I can't believe it. It's like there's a fire in the bed.

A rhythm emerges and my hand is following it. My forefinger is moving in and out of her vagina while my thumb rubs her button. Her pussy is beginning to really stir. Her hips begin to bump into my hand, and I can feel these sympathetic waves in myself. Oh, oh, oh. She's calling. So am I. We are moving together like a beating drum, pushing higher and higher, until she cries out and I can feel her cunt clutching at my fingers. Her head is going side to side, and she is grimacing and laughing at the same time. When the fury subsides we lie in each other's arms, panting and sighing. We fall asleep this way. It won't be until the sun comes up that I will remember my out-of-town lover who arrives today. It won't be until the sun comes up that Hannah and I will begin to understand what we've started.

Summertime

by Jane Sebastion

You know those days that are so cold your ears or nose could fall off? Well, this wasn't one of them. Calling it the hottest summer of the decade was an understatement. Everywhere people seemed to hang like sweaty rags on the street, barely moving. If I remember correctly, some of those human rags dropped for good. All day the sun poured its unforgiving heat down on us hapless air conditioner-free souls. Its slow trek across the sky was pure torture; the whole town waited for the great ball to fall, to sink behind the mountains and into the sea. When it did, however, it brought no relief, for the heat had cooked the day, leaving the night hot and sticky.

It was a night like this when I left work and slowly fought my way home through the heavy evening air. Home was no better than outside, worse even. All of the windows faced the sun's onslaught.

I need a shower, I thought. Leaving a trail of sweat-soaked clothes behind me, I made my way to the bathroom.

Just the thought of a cold shower began to cool me down. But it was not to be. I turned the cold water knob and received not the cool stream of water but *gurgle, gurgle, hiss*—no water.

Every curse word I could think of passed from my mouth. It was excruciating hearing that damn tap hiss at me as I stood there in my boxers. The doorbell rang.

"Of all the bloody things, now what?" I threw on my T-shirt. Opening the door, I was confronted by the stereotypical plumber, large and smelly in overalls that probably hadn't been washed in years.

"We gotta turn off da wadda till tomorrow, young fella." I thought he was going to hoark one at me. *That's "miss," you dumb shit,* I felt like saying.

"Yeah, OK." I slammed the door. "Great, just fucking great." No water, what to do? The heat seemed to seep into the house and soak everything, including me. All I could think about was water, cold water. The fridge held the answer, or so I thought. All the water in the Brita was gone and juice was nonexistent. Roommates.

I let the cool air of the fridge wash over me; temporary relief. I didn't hear the phone ring but heard the machine.

"Not home," my voice said, "leave message."

"Are you hot?" the disjointed voice questioned. If I weren't already, that voice made me hotter. I had met her a few weeks ago when she walked into my restaurant. Short blond hair, pale blue eyes. I screwed up the dish I was making just looking at her. She was alone, that I noticed. I sent her wine, she left, but came back the next night and the next. A week later we met; I introduced myself and finally learned her name. Ridley. She had weird parents. Coffee and talking followed. She was unsure of her sexuality and was full of questions. I was hoping I might stop answering and start showing.

I picked up the phone.

"Yes, very." I let the obvious show in my voice.

"What are you doing?"

"Cooling off in front of the fridge."

She laughed, "Why don't you have a shower?"

"No water. The renovations have screwed up the plumbing."

She paused, I waited.

"Do you want to come over for a shower?" Her voice was bold, but I sensed something else. Shyness maybe.

"Are you sure?" Suddenly I was nervous and hot.

"I'll come and get you." Before I had a chance to answer she hung up.

I had only been to her place once before; it was tucked in the back of a big old house almost as an afterthought. One plus in this weather was that it was very cool in the evening.

Throwing on a pair of clean shorts and a fresh shirt, I packed some clean clothes and walked outside to wait. The heat was unbearable as I stood at the end of my driveway. Sweat began to drip between my breasts and down my back. I was about to douse my head with the neighbor's hose when I heard tires squeal, and the now-familiar red CRX pulled up. I had to laugh. Ridley was…Let's just say she drove with a passion.

"Hey," she said through the open window, "hop in." I did just that, noticing the car smelled of her perfume mingled with her own scent. My heart fluttered and a warmth that had nothing to do with the heat spread over me. My shirt stuck to my back as I sat down. I could see a dark spot forming on the front of Ridley's shirt. My thoughts wandered.

"Want to have a shower right away or go for a quick drive?" A quick drive with Ridley really meant just that. I hated to admit it, but her driving really turned me on. Something about how she shifted; like I said, passion.

"Sure, down by the beach?" A long, straight road.

"Good idea." Into first and away we went.

It didn't take long to drive the four kilometers along the beach, windows down, the cool ocean wind blowing through the car.

"Shower now?" that big smile asked me. Before I could answer she did a U-turn in the middle of the busy road and we were speeding back. I watched her shift from first to second and into third. Suddenly we were turning, and I was glad to be wearing a seat belt. Parking was a fast thing too. She hopped out of the car and opened my door before I realized I was gripping the door handle, which almost yanked me out.

"Oops, sorry." The blush rushed up her neck.

"It's OK." I maneuvered my way out of the small car and grabbed my bag.

I was right; her apartment was cool and dark, giving instant relief from the thick heat outside.

"Are you thirsty? Water or juice?" She opened the fridge.

"Water, please." I dropped my bag in the living room and sat down.

"Here you go." The glass floated in front of my face. I took it and rubbed it over my forehead. The condensation dripped down my temple. I sipped the cool water and looked up to catch Ridley staring at me. She was standing in front of me, watching. I wanted to stand up and kiss those always-red lips. I made it as far as standing up, but doing so seemed to shock her out of a trance, and she moved away quickly.

"There's a clean towel on the toilet you can use; take your time." She sat down and looked away.

"Are you OK?" I put my glass down, unsure of what to do.

"It's just the heat, it's nothing, go have your shower." She still wouldn't look at me.

"All right, if you say so." I went into the bathroom and shut the door. I wondered what was wrong with Ridley. Had I said something? Done something? Taking off my sweat-drenched clothes, I turned on the water to a lukewarm temperature. I stepped under the flowing water and let it run over my face. I was worried. Had I screwed things up? I knew she was confused, but I had felt something since we first met, and the way she had behaved before tonight led me to believe that she felt something too.

I put my forehead against the tile wall and let the cool water flow down my back over my ass. It felt so refreshing. What had I done wrong? The water cooled my lustful thoughts, but they were replaced by worries.

I turned off the water after washing and reached for the towel. While drying off I realized that I had left my clean clothes outside. I didn't know what to do, so I dried my hair, wrapped the towel around my waist, and put my shirt on.

I opened the door and stepped out into the cool apartment. Ridley was still sitting in the same place, unmoved.

"Sorry, I forgot my bag—stinky shirt." I pulled at my T-shirt. No answer, just silence. I walked into the living room and picked up my bag.

"Are you sure you're OK?" She was still looking away.

"Is your shoulder still hurting you?" Finally, eye contact.

"Uh, yeah." My shoulder had been mildly injured at work a few days before. Without a word she stood up and walked toward me.

"Sit down, let me rub it for you." Next thing I knew I was sitting down with Ridley behind me. Her hands slowly massaged my shoulder.

"How does that feel?" She rubbed harder.

"Much better, you OK?" I winced but she didn't see.

"Yeah, I'm sorry. I was just thinking…" She began to knead the muscle.

"About what? Nothing bad, I hope." I tried to turn around, but her knees kept me facing forward.

"No, nothing bad. Just thinking." She pushed my head forward and rubbed my neck. "Does that feel better?" Her hands began to move forward over my collarbone. That warm feeling that had slowly been spreading since the massage began started to move faster over me.

I tried to turn around, and this time I was successful. Raising myself onto my knees, I looked her in the eyes. I searched those blue eyes, trying to figure out what it was she wanted.

Reaching my hand up, I cupped her jaw and received my answer when her head tilted into it, her eyes closing. I leaned forward and kissed her lightly on the cheek. Her hand slid into my wet hair as I kissed her lips. I pulled closer and slowly opened her lips with my tongue. The minute our tongues touched I felt her shudder just as I did. Whimpering noises escaped her as our kiss deepened. I slid my hand from her cheek into her short hair and pulled back her head. My kisses left her lips and trailed down her chin to that pale neck. I licked and bit, her hand pulling at my hair as I worked my way up to her ear.

"I want you," I whispered, "do you want me?"

"Yes." Her voice was raspy.

"Say it, tell me." Tracing her ear with my tongue.

"I want you, God, how I want you." She pulled my hair again and kissed me. I broke it off and reached under her knees.

"Arms around my neck," I ordered. She obeyed quickly. Standing, I carried her with me to her bed. Lying her down, I straddled her, leaning over to resume kissing her neck. Hands slid everywhere; I started to undo the buttons of her shirt with one hand and held her head with the other. Slowly I worked my way to her lips, then back down to follow the shirt as it slowly opened.

Ridley clutched at my head, at my shoulders. She called my name as I ran my tongue over her collarbone.

"Jane," a moan, "kiss me." She was almost begging.

"In time, in time," I murmured against her sternum. I licked her nipple through the silken burgundy bra. Her back arched to meet my lips, allowing me to reach around and release the thin material that held those small breasts captive. Freedom gained, I caressed them with my hands and mouth. Making my way up to her mouth we kissed; never had I experienced such passion. Deeply we kissed. Suddenly she stopped.

"What's wrong?" I hovered over her.

"I'm afraid, I'm nervous." She turned her head away.

"Ridley," I turned her face to me, "it's all right, if you don't want to."

"I do, I do, I want to." She reached for me but I held back.

"Are you sure?" I was worried, not wanting to push.

"Yes, make love to me, seduce me." I fell on her, crushing her to me. She began to pull at my shirt and to push against me. I sat up and pulled off my sweaty T-shirt. I allowed her to run those smooth hands over my breasts and stomach, pulling off the damp towel.

Grabbing both wrists, I pushed those hands above her head, lowering my naked torso to hers. The perspiration gleamed on her forehead; her neck tasted of salt and perfume. Holding her hands tightly I again kissed her breasts, bringing her nipples to a rise.

Ridley fought to be released, but I would not let go.

"In a moment, hold still." Our bodies slid against each other, our mouths kissed, and our tongues explored. I released her hands so I could taste that flat stomach and began to undo the buttons on her shorts. Sliding my hands around, I lifted her ass up to pull off the denim. Her underwear matched the burgundy bra, but had a touch of lace.

Lowering my mouth down I exhaled hot breath over her and licked the already-wet crotch of her panties. Her fingers entwined in my hair, her and breath came in gasps as I licked again.

I could feel her clit hardening beneath my tongue; her back arched and I took my chance, removing the barrier between us. Deeply inhaling the scent of her, I ran my tongue over and over her clit. My hands explored where my tongue already had and followed it into her softness. She tasted sweet and sweaty.

I began to suck and taste her as I moved inside; my tongue on her clitoris moved faster. I grasped a hand entangled in my hair and held it. Moving my middle finger down, lightly I touched the other sensitive spot. A throaty moan escaped her as I slowly slipped in my finger. Ridley began to buck and push against me. Deeper I pushed, licking faster and faster. Her breath came in pants and sobs; the hand holding mine gripped tighter. She let out a loud gasp and moan as she came, yelling my name. She lay still for a few minutes then sat up, pulling my face to hers. I looked into her blue, crying eyes.

"It's OK." Wiping away tears, I held her head to my chest.

"Thank you." Tears ran down her face onto my breast.

"For what, Ridley?" I was confused.

Pulling her face away, she looked up at me.

"From the first time I saw you, I wanted you; I wanted to let you seduce me, but I was afraid."

"I've wanted you since we met, but I wasn't sure…" I held her hand.

"Listening to you, hearing you, being around you, the way you looked at me—I just needed you to start. You must think I'm stupid," she said, her eyes downcast, "you were my first."

"Ridley," I said as I lifted her head, "Ridley, it's all right." I held her close.

The night had begun to cool, but it was still hot and we were both sweaty. I was about to suggest a shower when I felt Ridley's lips on my breast. Before I could ask what she was doing, she read my mind.

"Now it's my turn." I allowed myself to be turned and pushed back.

It was a long, hot night.

Pretty Please

by Debbie Ann Wertheim

I'm a virgin.

I'm not a virgin to finger sex, or even strap-on dildo sex, and certainly not a virgin to sex with women or sex with guys; nope, none of those.

I'm an anal sex virgin.

And Chessie, she's my girlfriend, she'd like to have anal sex. She doesn't really demand, she doesn't exactly push, and if she did, I'd probably resist. Instead she touches the desire in me, desire I didn't even know was there, and then suddenly I'm the one pushing her. Then she takes a step back and starts teasing me. She likes to know what I want, she likes to make me ask for it, she likes me wanting, and then she'll decide when and how. I allow her to decide when and how; I just make sure she knows what I want. There's this subtle push-pull going on just underneath the surface. In some strange way maybe that's why we've been together for five years. She's one of the few women I've met who knows how to play tug-of-war with me.

It feels like I've been thinking about anal sex for a while now. I know it will feel good, but I'm still scared anyway. I'm scared that my body will betray me, in a way that doesn't even seem possible in other forms of sex. We've done lots of spanking play, and plenty of her using a strap-on and fucking me from behind, so it really has been clear to both of us that my sexuality tends to be bottom-focused. She'll even put a finger or two in there, in that place, and I want it, I want those fingers, even though I still feel shy about it. Sometimes I'm terrified to look at her fingers after she pulls them out of me, but when I look, they are clean. She plays with that shyness, and she especially likes to play with that shyness in public. Sometimes we go to parties that fit right into her plans, like this last one.

Chessie picks me up and takes me to the party, and it is one long sweet tease. First she mixes up J-lube, but then we can't play with it. I watch her stir lube for a good long time. Chessie likes J-lube, or lubricant used by veterinarians, partly because it has no taste and no odor, but also because it comes in powdered form and mixes up with water to create vast quantities of thick lubricant. She's mixing it up to show other people what it is like, but our host doesn't want any sex happening. We've been talking about vaginal fisting, and we've been talking about anal sex, but we don't talk about either right now, she just keeps mixing the lube. People take out floggers, and say mine is thicker than yours, and test their floggers out, but nobody actually flogs each other. A well-secured chain hangs from the ceiling at just the right height, and I reach up and hold on to it. I flirt.

It is crowded, lots of pretty girls in small black leather dresses, lots of femme flirt energy. I am wearing a shirt, skirt, and shoes, and nothing else, and would like nothing better than to take this clothing off. Chessie reaches up under my skirt to wipe the lube off her hand, but since this doesn't make her hand any drier, she goes and washes.

I meet boys in the kitchen, and they are talking about bugs, and I really don't pay too much attention, because right about then Chessie takes out her four-foot whip, a signal whip, like the kind they use to make dogs pull sleds, and I say to Chessie, "Where do you want me?" Greedy little girl, but it's not my birthday, so I don't get whipped.

We leave. We leave because Chessie has decided we are going to leave. I think we leave because she wants to tease me more, and she can't do it here at the party. We come back to my apartment and mix up more lube. I put a towel down on the bed, and we flirt and smile and kiss and turn on the light. I pull my cunt lips open and Chessie starts playing, sliding fingers in and out, more and more fingers, sometimes it hurts and I'm supposed to say so, but I just want to push past this hurt. I want her fist inside me. I've never had a fist inside me. Greedy little girl.

We play this way for a while, and then she starts putting fingers elsewhere. I feel shy about this; even though I think, *I shouldn't feel shy,* I still do. Nice girls don't do this, we say. And we talk about the party, making up things that never happened, things that excite us both, we talk about putting me down on the floor in front of all those boys, and they watch Chessie slide in and out of me, and they get hard and want to play with themselves, and I want them to come on me. And Chessie holds me open, and they all look at me and want to touch me. And we keep talking about these things that never happened, and I get wetter and wetter.

Two fingers slide into my asshole, and they hurt. I look away, cover my eyes with my hand, can't talk very well, and still want more stories about how girls need to be trained, they need to be stretched and opened up, and I try to make my body relax, and then I think about how I want her to fuck me, and how much bigger the dildo is than her fingers, and my whole body tenses up again, but I'm told to turn over and stick my ass in the air, and I do, with lots of shy, insecure wiggles.

And then slowly, with all the patience in the world, at my pace, Chessie starts sliding the dildo into my asshole, and I try to relax and push and hide all at the same time. I just try to breathe and I feel hot, very hot, burning-up hot. And it feels so incredible. I think about how very much I wanted this. I feel too hot and nonverbal for stories, I just feel what this feels like, and I like it, and all I want is more. It feels like every single heartbeat is communicated. She's really not very far inside of me, it's not like she's fucking me, though it is closer than we've ever been before. Sometimes I wonder why it took me so long to get to this place, but nobody ever felt as right for this as Chessie does. She's safe. She pushes.

After a while she stops. I think I want more, but it's pretty clear that my body has had enough. Chessie rolls over on her back, spreads her legs, and starts to rub herself. I lean up on one arm and put my hand over hers. I look at her face. I love to watch her face. At first she looks dreamy, glazed over, and then as she gets closer to coming, her eyes squeeze shut in intense concentration. I can feel her body tense up as I lie there next to her. One of her hands holds her labia open while the other one rubs her clit. I hear her breathing getting faster, and then she comes hard and fast, spasms moving her whole body, and as she grabs my hand and pushes three of my fingers up into her, I push in deep. She's soaking wet, and I can feel her muscles tighten onto my fingers. I fuck her with my fingers, and she comes again, hard. Finally, we collapse in a heap. I'm a happy, content little girl.

Later, weeks later, we try again. I lie across Chessie's lap, and she squirts warm water inside my anus and then lets me up, and I go to the bathroom, close the door, and let all the water out of me, and then I come lie across her lap again. I like that. The water temperature is just right, and I feel so close to her, safe over her lap, like being spanked. I think about anal sex, and I think I'm scared of it being messy and the other person feeling disgusted. I think it makes me feel shy because I'm not as in control, I can't quite see what is happening, and I'm afraid of what my body might do. I'm scared and I want it all at the same time.

And then we are on the floor in front of my mirror, my head down, bottom up, legs spread, and she slowly, easily pushes inside of me, and I can't believe how good it feels. She is completely inside of me and I can feel everything. I can feel her body pressed up against mine, I can feel the dildo, hard and deep inside of me. Every time she starts to pull out I feel this small twist of anxiety that it is going to be gone, and I love how full I feel, how content. It hurts just a little bit, I feel stretched, but not too stretched. I think, *Why was it so difficult before and so easy now,* but then all thoughts are gone, and it is a wave of pleasure through my whole body. It feels emotional to me, like being home and safe and warm, like this is where I belong, and this is what I need. I can't believe anything can feel this good. I moan deep. It isn't like a rubbing-my-clit kind of coming, it is deeper inside of me, more depth, more resonance.

I try to look in the mirror, wanting to watch Chessie, and watch me and her, like all those gay-boy porn films we have rented, because I love to watch anal sex, but I can't watch, I can't be outside of my body, I need to be inside riding waves of pleasure and hunger as she pulls almost all the way out and then pushes in steady and hard and deep. I want her cock, her dildo, her, inside of my body, and I don't want to let go. The thrust in feels so good to me. I'm soaking wet with pleasure and delight.

I'm not a virgin anal sex girl anymore.

Two Virgins

by Charlotte Cooper

Mari and I met through a personal ad. I have done this many times before; it is nothing to me, I feel no embarrassment about it. This is not so for her. I can feel her prickling through the words in her letter of introduction. She wrote the ad; I answered it. On reflection she was pretty truthful; she said she was a novice, that she wanted someone with whom to explore S/M. In my reply I was honest as to my level of experience.

It feels strange writing this from the point of view of seducer. *Virgin* feels much more appropriate a label for me, especially at the time these events occurred. Rather than being banished in a pop, I feel as though my virginity is constantly being eroded by new sexual experiences: first time jerking off; first fuck with a man; first time a woman fucked me; first time I fucked a woman; first time I ate pussy; first fist; first time I fucked a faggot's arse with my dick; first piss scene; first public sex; first time I got whipped; first group sex. I know my sexual horizons are wider than those of many people, yet I often lack confidence in what I do, and I wonder if I will ever stop feeling inexperienced, virginal.

In the time since Mari, I have become more promiscuous, more assured of my ability to procure sex, and more secure in my attractiveness as a sexual partner. But at the point at which

I met her, I felt new and vulnerable. My lover and I had recently decided to become nonmonogamous, I had been beaten for the first time that summer, and now I had started to think about S/M. I wanted to put myself out there and live a new life. When you embrace new things, the old parts of you seem suddenly shabby, and I was eager to distance myself from that and become recast, though as what I am still not sure. I tried new roles, clichés really, as silent stud, willing myself to believe that I was hot, wondering if I was convincing, if I could play these parts and be human too. Mostly I felt impatient and annoyed that I didn't already know the scene, that I was going to have to start from scratch and make myself open if I wanted to meet anyone, that it would take time to establish myself. I was afraid that my naïveté would leave me defenseless and that I would get hurt. Nearly ten years younger than me, Mari was also starting out. The personal ad allowed both of us to reinvent ourselves, to leave behind our history and float into a new world, and with so few ties we knew that we could easily cut ourselves free from the wreckage if we crashed.

Mari told me she'd be at this meeting, and she was. This was the first time I saw her, and I don't know what I'd been expecting, but, yes, she was good-looking, kind of small and energetic. She opened the door and walked in; I knew it was her, but as she sat next to me I said, "Oh, are you Mari?" trying to sound casual.

"I guess you're Charlotte," she replied. Someone asked us how we knew each other. Mari smiled, "It's a long story," and I was relieved when she left it at that. Although we were involved in separate activities, I was super-aware of her presence and of her location in the room the whole evening. Was she playing the same games with me? I could see her looking at me from time to time, but I was too afraid to meet her eyes, although not too inhibited to show off in front of her and sass back at my friends who were also at the meeting. Would they notice what was going on? Mari left early, although we'd arranged to have coffee the next day. So she liked me too.

I made a mistake about the time, and I waited a whole hour before she turned up. The café was crowded, and I felt as though everyone was watching me as I grew more anxious about our meeting. And these thoughts were rolling around in my head: *I want a fuck, I want to fuck her, she will probably let me, I want pain, oh, God, but I want it.*

Mari showed, and her nerves made her cute. On reflection I think now that we really didn't know shit about what we were doing, it was as though we'd read the same how-to books, and that we were trying hard to behave in the way that we thought leatherdykes did.

I asked her about sex, I asked "Do you want to play with me?" with my voice shaking, to which she responded with a smile and a nod.

"What do you like?"

Mari said quietly, "I like being beaten and humiliated. It's only happened a few times, but I've loved it, and I want more. I like pain because it makes me feel invincible to be able to survive intense sensations."

My heart was beating fast; it was as though she had grabbed the words right out of my mouth. I knew we were going to be compatible, and I felt excited. Mari told me some private secret sex things: "Sometimes when I'm jerking off at home, I like to reach round under my thigh with my left hand and stick my fingers up my arse." She looked deliciously devious. We had to get down to specifics. She said, "I want to be blindfolded the whole time, I need to get into my own head."

"What about fucking?" I wanted to know. No answer. I continued, "How are we going to make it safe?"

"I want gloves," said Mari.

"OK, fine. What if there's blood?"

"Clean the wound, apply antiseptic, and cover. Don't worry, I've done first aid!" she winked.

"What don't you want?"

"No piss, no shit," said Mari, giving me a fake stern look. "Don't you want to know my safeword?"

I felt caught out; this was important, and I'd nearly forgotten to ask.

"It's 'Stop!'"

I felt like I'd done the right thing by such adult handling of my crazed emotions, but now I think I was just hiding my fear behind a set of rules because passion and spontaneity were too much for either of us to handle. It felt like a business arrangement. I guess it was.

We set a play date the following afternoon at my house. As Mari had never bottomed, and I had never topped, we decided to go with these roles. The horniness and fear that I felt at this proposition were, in truth, the sexual sensations that I was looking for, although they are a dizzying combination to live with. I tried to deal with my performance anxiety by making meticulous preparations: cleaning, sweeping, polishing my house and my body. I created weirdly obsessive lists of things I wanted to do; I thought they would help me pace the scene, which of course had to be perfect. I wanted so much to be the cool, controlling, capable bitch I believed all tops to be, but there's only so much pressure I can force myself to work through, and by the time Mari rang the doorbell my hands were sweating and my mind was racing.

In those first moments both of us were human and awkward, stumbling over my threshold. Mari looked so normal in her sunglasses and jeans, not the snivelling worm I imagined, although I was more in role than she. Immediately we started working through my mental list.

"Look at my front yard," I said. "Can you see the way the wind blows all the trash from the street under the hedge and all over the place? It's such a mess, isn't it? I want you get out there and clear it up."

Mari said "No." Was she playing, or did she really mean it? What was she really willing to do, compared to my fantasy? How could I handle this and still project my authority? Well, if she really didn't want to do it she could safeword. "If you don't clean up the trash," I countered, "you'll have to go."

She started cleaning, at the same time whining, "Why aren't you helping?"

"Shut up complaining," I answered, "I'm going to watch you." It felt alien playing mean, but satisfying too. She was pissing me around, not working hard enough, talking back. I grabbed her neck and looked in her face. "Stop wasting my time," I deadpanned, and it came out hard and right, and she knew it.

I invited Mari inside and asked her to sit on the floor and show me her toys. We were still kind of in the same conversational mode as we'd shared in the café, but now there were new feelings surfacing. As she pulled out a dick and harness from her bag, as she told me about her vibrator and how she jerked off in secret in bed at night, as she infused her words with a genuine confidentiality, I was just so charmed. My stereotypes of S/M are of a sexuality that is dour, pompous, and humorless, but Mari looked so fresh and eager down by my feet, and her sweetness in this position was something completely unexpected.

I don't know the point when I started to forget about my list of stuff. It probably coincides with the places at which I began to lose my fear and just take pleasure in the moment. This first happened when I blindfolded Mari and instructed her to remove her clothes. I had never seen a woman's body like hers up close. Until then my friends and lovers had been people marked with age and kinks and difference. Mari had smooth skin, no belly, strong thighs, high breasts; it seemed illicit. It felt so inappropriate to take pleasure from watching her undress. I felt confronted by my inadequacies of poverty, age, and fatness. How could she give me this sight? How could I deserve it? I felt seedy and had to leave the room to breathe. Mari was patting the floor around her when I returned; she was trying to find her jeans to fold them and place them on the pile with the rest of her clothes. In the sunlight, looking lost and tentative, maybe wondering what I was doing, she was so beautiful.

Mari had brought a crop with her. On her hands and knees I put the leather twist in her open mouth and told her, "Bite." In this fashion I led her crawling around the room and then down into my dusty basement. Later Mari told me that she had no idea where I was taking her, that she thought maybe it was some kind of garage, or even that we were out in the open. In my basement is a large wooden table to which I tied her very badly, my hands shaking, me panicking a little as I muddled through clumsy knots. I knew she could move quite easily, which was not the intention, but by her good manners she never showed me this.

I tied open her legs and began clipping away her pubic hair, then shaving the stubble. On another occasion I might complain that wet shaving takes ages, but this afternoon I was glad for the time it took as I became calm and mesmerized by the sound of the razor scraping across her skin, the smell of soap, small talk.

"How long did it take you to get here today?" I asked. "Tell me about your hometown, how is it different to London?" and "Are you warm enough?" and "What would you be doing if you weren't here?"

I am blessed with an ability to ask a never-ending stream of inconsequential questions. Every now and then this was punctuated by Mari requesting "a sip of water, please;" "Can you cover my legs? I'm shivering;" "My hand is starting to feel cold," and I would rub her hand back to life, and tend to her, help her feel all right. I was grateful for the chance to look at and touch her pussy gently, to take my time with her, and as I carefully removed her lovely thick hair, to see globs of wet appear from inside her, and I was moved that, in spite of my ineptitude, I was doing something that made Mari feel good.

I untied Mari and asked her to turn over so that I could shave her arsehole. Humiliated, she demurred until I gave my best matronly spiel about women "all looking the same down there" (even though I do not believe this for a second). I was humbled by the presence of a tiny piece of a tiny piece of toilet roll wadded tight and stuck to her anus. I knew she would have been mortified had I mentioned it, but I was comforted by that sight, which appealed to me as sweet, and funny, and unaffected.

By mistake I nicked the skin in the inside of her arse cheek. Mari got scared for real, but I apologized and tended to the tiny cut with antiseptic. I rolled her back over, inserted a speculum, cranked it open and had a good look inside. I had rehearsed a line for this moment, "You can't hide anything from me," and I said it out loud, but in reality it sounded flat and corny. I pulled the speculum out again awkwardly, its "beak" closing with an alarming snap. Mari lay on the table while I went upstairs to regain my courage.

Back downstairs I positioned Mari against the table and started beating her. Though she is an athlete, I am bigger and stronger. I had never been with someone as small as Mari. I became aware of my strength and worried that unless I restrained myself I could do some damage, I could mash her into a pulp, so I took it slowly and built it up. I used my hand to smack the skin around her shoulders and arse, feeling the heat rise and her flesh shake. I used a skinny little cane to work a line of tiny stinging red stripes down her thighs. I used a little plastic flogger, swinging and whizzing it past her ears, then making delicate fan-shaped scores, and then the crop. With each implement I worked a rhythm, beating hard and soft, alternating the tempo, playing with her expectation by withholding and then delivering.

As Mari's skin transformed from creamy-pale to red to welts, as the bruising started to rise, I began to concentrate only on the rhythm. I forgot about the people in cars on the main road outside my house; I forgot what I did yesterday, or what I planned for tomorrow; I slipped out of my skin, and my arm raised, her cringing body, the force of my blows was all it was. I was well on my way to a place where it didn't matter what Mari wanted, seeing her shift on her feet, arse rolling, rocking from side to side, seeing her body shuddering with the pain, I didn't care if she liked it or not, I was just going to take from her what I wanted. I wanted to fuck her but, you know, I didn't—it wasn't negotiated.

It was time to stop. I put the crop back in Mari's mouth and led her upstairs, took off the blindfold, and ran her a bath. We held each other tightly, she shaking and crying and laughing in an old T-shirt of mine, and me tired and overwhelmed by what I had done.

On that afternoon Mari and I rose above our fear, we transcended our self-consciousness, and we both took the leap to do what we really wanted to do. I saw Mari a few more times afterward, I developed intense feelings, which embarrass me in retrospect, and which I think intimidated her. She had to leave the country suddenly and go back to college. There followed months of silence, and then, last week, an E-mail, just saying "Hi."

Lovely Work

by Louye

"Thank you, Jesus, for that safe flight," I said out loud to myself as I spotted my car in the Detroit Metro's garage. *That damn seminar in New York was flaky. But the women were fine as wine,* I thought as I sat in the driver's seat. Looking in my rearview mirror to see what was around me, I pulled off, heading to work. "Gee, the streets are packed," I said while turning to get to Livernois Street. As I accelerated to go with the flow of traffic, I noticed some fool coming up behind me and trying to pass me. "Damn, what is this fool in the Beemer trying to do!" As I said that, the BMW whizzed by and almost drove me off the road. "Shit, that stupid ass, almost messed up my ride!" I started to yell, knocking off my cap in the commotion. The BMW sped away and disappeared over the horizon.

Finally I got to work. I put my hat on the hat rack and walked to my desk and sat. I looked up, and the director of my division appeared and stood in front of my desk, accompanied by a stranger I seemed to know or had at least seen before.

"Well, Terri, you're back from your seminar. How was New York?" the director asked.

"Great, Mrs. Bain," I replied.

"Please come and talk to me later about the seminar," she said. "And by the way, I would like to introduce Miss Diane Petersen to you. She will be working with you to set up the new federal guidelines that become effective in July."

"A pleasure to meet you, Miss Petersen," I told her.

"Likewise, Terri. You can call me Diane," she replied.

"Well, it seems like you both are on a good start, with that nice introduction," Mrs. Bain cheerfully said. In the back of my mind, I noticed Diane was a very fine black woman. She was coffee-colored, and her lips were full. She had medium-length, straightened hair. In the suit she was wearing, I could see she had a "phat" body. The thought "some of that" surely passed my mind. But it was quickly canceled because my intuition about women said she was straight all the way. And seldom am I wrong. *But on the up side, at least I will be around her every day or so,* I thought. *So I'll still be happy.*

"Oh, Terri, you and Diane can go to the cafeteria and take a break and talk a little. I have to go back to my office," Mrs. Bain told me as she slowly walked toward the door. "OK, Mrs. Bain. I will show her around," I eagerly replied.

When Mrs. Bain left, Diane asked me, "How long have you been working here?" "Ah, five years now," I answered.

"That's cool," she replied. "Well, I used to be a lawyer, but didn't like defending scum and playing too much politics. I got into social work as a duty to my race." She continued, "So, now I am here in Detroit. My boyfriend is going to University of Michigan, so it kinda worked out for both of us."

"Yeah, that sounds good," I told her. The thought of her having a boyfriend confirmed the fact that she was straight; well, at least acting straight. If not, she had a great facade going on. As I looked into her eyes, I saw she was a very warm and caring soul. And so dainty. She was almost unreal. I quickly got out of my daze.

"What do you think about welfare reform?" I asked her.

She took a breath and said, "I knew welfare reform was on its way. It will make or break a person in that dire situation. We have to realize that we are part of a system that is not going to change. So, we have to play in it or get off the pot. Meaning we have to get our education, and compete as a race, in this battle of survival. And I'm the motivator, that's the part I am playing."

"Wow, that was deep, I agree with you," I replied. "On that note, are you hungry, 'cause we're near the cafeteria. If not, we can walk around, and I'll show you to your office," I told her.

"No, I'm not hungry right now," she replied.

"OK, we can just go and check out your new office, then." We walked to her new office and investigated the surroundings. We both sat. *This woman is bad,* I thought.

She got up to put her purse on the table and dropped her keys. I immediately picked them up for her, but I noticed she had a gold BMW key ring. *Um,* I thought. *BMW, I know she isn't the fool who was in the Beemer earlier, who tried to sideswipe me on the road. She looks like that woman.* Suddenly I asked her, "Diane, were you on Livernois Street this afternoon?"

She replied, "Yes, about an hour ago. Why do you ask?"

"Oh, 'cause I was there an hour ago too. By chance do you drive a BMW?"

"Yes, how'd you know?" she said, surprised.

"Well, there was a person speeding up Livernois Street in a BMW who nearly killed me," I told her.

"Now I didn't try to kill you, uh-uh. That was me, though," she replied regretfully. "I remember you, I glanced at you when I passed by you," she said excitedly. "You were in the Lexus. I apologize. But didn't you have a hat on. I thought it was a man, but I now remember your lavender shirt you have on. I was trying to get here for my first day on the job."

I blushed when she said I looked like a man. I thought to myself, *I can act like a man if you wanted me too, though.*

"Oh, sometimes people think I'm a boy with my baseball cap, it's my security blanket of sorts," I began to explain to her. I looked up and there was Mrs. Bain.

"Terri, I have to borrow Diane for a couple of hours," Mrs. Bain explained. "We need her expertise. If you don't see her later, you will see her tomorrow." Mrs. Bain and Diane left quickly from the office. I sat awhile and thought about my newfound friend and coworker, Diane. She was a black woman; I was so pleased. I closed her office and returned to my desk to catch up on my work. And the time flew by rather quickly till I was ready to go home. My day was complete.

Here I was, back at my desk. It had been a week now since I'd seen Diane. However, she had left messages on my answering machine, but we'd been playing perpetual telephone tag. Mrs. Bain was using her for another project. *Oh, well, I will do my best on the guidelines until she comes.* To my surprise, I looked up and there was Diane. Fine as ever. I missed her. I just wanted to hug her, but I maintained my composure and just greeted her with a handshake. "So, how was your new assignment, Diane?" I asked her.

"Oh, it was nice, but do you know something… I missed you. It's so strange, but I have been thinking of you ever since I met you a week ago. It's weird, I can't explain it, and I've never felt this way toward another woman."

"Is that so?" I answered.

"But anyway, Terri, we need to finish our report, since I was not here to help you, and we have been unable to talk with each other."

I quickly gathered up my notes to show her what I'd done. She took the papers one by one and scanned them slowly. "This is excellent, I really don't have to do much more. You have covered all aspects of the initial shock it will have on the cut-off recipient." Continuing to read, Diane nodded her head to agree with what she saw. "Gosh, you are good," she interjected between the nods.

Meanwhile, I was feeling really butchy, because in front of me was a fine black woman, named Diane, giving me praises and admiring my work. All of a sudden Diane bent down to the chair to pick up a fountain pen she dropped. In that gesture she exposed her butt. I was glued to her ass. She turned to me and caught my eyes on her ass. *She dropped her pen to be naughty,* I started to think. I continued to look into her eyes 'cause I was feeling a little stir in my pussy.

She walked to the door and closed it very lightly. And she asked, "Are you expecting any clients in the next hour and a half?"

I was a little wary and said, "No, my time is devoted to this project with you. And I don't have to see anyone until 1:30 today." I kind of sensed she was flirting with me.

When I said that she immediately locked my office door. She told me, "OK, Terri, I want to feel your hands all over my body. I want you now." She went back to the papers and sat on the desk. She started to spread her legs and pulled up her shirt, exposing a body covered in a Victoria's Secret teddy with a garter belt and fine, silky hose. Her stomach was nice and firm, and you could tell she worked on keeping it flat and hard. As she sat there, she unsnapped the crotch, and there were two perfect lips and a very pink bump between them. It glistened as I stared at it. I quickly got on my knees and stuck my tongue on the tip of the bump, licking on each side of it. I got up quickly. "I just had to taste it, but I better stop now," I told her. She leaned forward and had a pout on her face, with begging eyes.

"Oh, Terri, please, I'll do whatever you want me to, just don't stop." She put her middle finger in her love hole and pulled it out, showing me the wetness from it. "See how you do me," she whispered. I just could not resist her offer. Between my legs I felt intense throbs. So I told her to pull her skirt up to her waist. And roll her panties down to her ankles and spread her legs out to as far as the panties would stretch. I told her to stand there so I could just see her from a different view. Her pubic hairs by her lips were stuck together, with her wetness as the adhesive. She looked divine.

I wished she could take off all her clothes so I could see her nipples and then gaze down at her private parts at the same time. I told her, "I want you to turn around with your back facing me, and keep your skirt up high. Now bend over so I can lick that butt of yours." She bent over and exposed brown and pink lips with a glistening spot near her asshole. Oh, it looked so good. I went to her butt and gently nibbled on each of her cheeks and rubbed my hand all over her lower back… Soft like a baby. She squirmed in pleasure and pushed her butt up higher. I took both my hands and spread her cheeks so I could lick up and down the crevice, while teasing her wet spot a little. I wanted this woman to desire the touch of a woman after I finished with her today.

I was in heaven as I licked her and stuck my tongue in forbidden places. She enjoyed it, 'cause she was pushing her rear closer to my face. I then put my two middle fingers into her hotbox, and they just slid in so smoothly. I took them out and she whimpered. I stretched my hand to her face so she would lick it. And she slowly licked her come off my finger. My fingers were ultrasensitive; I could feel her every lick in my groin. This girl had it going on for having never been with a woman before.

She pushed her bush up to my chin so my mouth would be right on her slit. I touched her clit, and it was on fire… It was so hot. I took my tongue and put it right down her hole, wiggling it around. That shit was good. I just wanted to stay in her pussy all day. As I continued I had to touch between my legs and rub my finger around my swollen lips. 'Cause I wanted to come now. This woman had me wanting to beg her to let me come. Right then the telephone rang. I had to take a deep breath and calm my breathing down and answered it. "Yes, Mrs. Bain, she is here. I will send her down to your office," I told the person who was speaking to me on the phone. "Damn," I whispered to Diane as I hung up. "Mrs. Bain has messed up my thing here, shit, she wants you to come to her office, now."

"But just let me lick between those hard legs before I go and make you come quickly," Diane begged. I thought to myself, *Mrs. Bain can wait.* The way I felt at the moment, Diane would just have to touch it and I'd come. So I sat on the edge of the desk and spread my legs open wide so they were suspended the in air. Diane got down in a squat and gently licked my bump up and down until it started to rise. I told her to go faster. She sped up, in the right sync, and my hips were starting to buck, so I was able to feel myself hitting against her tongue. I grabbed her head and just held it down to rub her face in my hotbox as I pumped my hips toward her mouth. I was losing control, 'cause I was ramming my small hardness in her mouth. Just messing up her hair. But it was so good. Each time my pelvis hit against her face, I wanted to hold it there and enjoy the reach for my orgasm, but I tried to hold on, and the waves of pleasure went through my stomach.

I hollered, "Oh, shit, Diane, damn you, girl… Oh, my God."

After hearing that, Diane came as she rubbed her wetness with her fingers and whispered in my ear, "Terri, I want you for mine. Never have I felt the oneness I'm feeling with you now. With no one, ever."

I responded, "You know what, Diane, I'm yours, and I love you for this."

The telephone rang again. I said, "Oh, shit, it's Mrs. Bain, you've got to go and get tidied up… put some perfume on, not too much now. I will see you later." Within minutes Diane was back to her coiffured self again.

Upon departing, she kissed me on the lips, wiped her lipstick off, and told me she loved me. She didn't return that day. But I've seen Diane since, 'cause we are committed lovers and very much in love.

Lori-girl

by M. Damian

"I love you." The soft sigh behind the words made me gently kiss my partner's warm, inviting mouth.

"I love you too," I breathed, savoring her nearness. We had just made love, yet I was loathe to stop. After all my years of torturous waiting, even a small respite was too long to be away from the sensual delights of Lori, my one true love. Cradling her in my arms, I began the sexual dance yet once again, kissing her eyelids, her soft sweet lips, slowly, lovingly moving down to nibble at the turgid tips of her breasts, treasuring their feel on my tongue, in my mouth. Lori's skin was velvety against my hungry mouth, a hunger which only total possession of her body could ease; never satiate, oh, no, never; only ease, temporarily.

Slowly, tantalizingly slowly, feasting on my enjoyment of her body, I eventually rubbed my cheek on the honey-colored patch between her legs, letting my lips linger on its fullness before moving on. A musky smell hit my nostrils at the same time as my tongue dipped into a sweet moisture. All my senses were heightened as I made love, hearing every moan, feeling every movement Lori made under my tongue.

I teased her with my mouth and hands until she was begging me. Slowly I brought her up, up, up with my tongue, ever higher, her body trembling, legs shaking, hands dragging through my hair, until finally, "Marie...Marie... oh! oh! oh!"

But it wasn't supposed to be like this.

I mean—*it was definitely not supposed to be like this.*

We weren't supposed to fall in love.

We met through an Internet posting board. Someone I had been going out with for six months had just more or less dumped me. Of course, "going out" is a relative term. Brenda lived in Indiana; I live in New York. But after stringing me along for those six months with promises of moving here, she reneged, and we parted. I didn't trust lesbians anymore, but I wanted to forget about Brenda, so I posted an ad, not with any real hope of scoring. I mean, that's how I had met Bren. But any action was, at least, action.

Lori answered the ad its first day up. Initially I was not interested because she was a bi-curious mom, but her honesty won me over. She wasn't interested in a relationship, she just wanted to have a sexual experience with a woman. Honest and to the point. Our E-mails for the first few weeks focused on her nervousness about being with a woman. Could she do it? Would she do it? But for all her anxiety, she was very graphic, very sexual. She had one agenda—and that was to get laid.

Hey, no problem! I certainly didn't want any entanglements. It was supposed to be a one-weekend-a-month meeting for sex. Just hot sex and plenty of it. I knew that a married woman would be an easy target. I mean, it wasn't as if she had ever really had *good* sex before, y'know? So I figured I'd dazzle her with incredible lovemaking—that appealed to my butch heart. "Show me the pussy!" became my battle cry.

After three weeks of E-mail and phone calls, we made an appointment to meet. She was driving her 19-year-old son down to see a specialist in Great Neck, so I drove over that night to her motel.

"Oh! I need a pin to close this blouse. Do you have a pin? I can't go out like this."

She was in a feminine tizzy about closing the top of her blouse. The low-cut neckline revealed too much if she bent over. She fluttered about the room, mumbling and searching.

I liked what I saw—a cute femme with red hair, nice shape, and *the* most incredible green eyes I've ever seen—and decided to reach out and touch it.

But luck wasn't with us that night. Except for some bump-and-grind, Lori's inquisitiveness had to wait until we could be a little more comfortable and have privacy. Her son had gone into NYC, and she didn't know when he was due back. She had gotten up the courage to explore: "Well, you said eating pussy is an acquired taste. I want to start acquiring it," but we had been rudely interrupted by voices outside the door. She quickly got up from the bed, and I just as quickly got dressed. But when it proved to be a false alarm, I backed her up against a wall, kissing her hard, plunging my tongue into her mouth as my fingers slid up deep inside her. Her knees buckled, but I held her up with my body, kissing and plunging. I wanted to do more, and I sure as hell know she did, but I didn't want to worry about being interrupted. And, I also wanted to wait until she got the results of her AIDS test back, so we went to dinner instead of dining on each other.

I didn't see Lori until May; the time in between filled with scorching E-mails and burning phone calls. Our initial rendezvous in the motel room whetted her appetite for lesbian sex.

She was ravenous to find out what happened next. "What else do women do, Marie? I can't wait to find out."

That night led to her coming down to see me three times in the month of May alone, each time more incredible than the last. Her one recurring theme when having sex with me was that she wanted me to be rough, to rape her. Even though I knew this was a fantasy of hers, every time I'd try to be rough with her, it didn't work. Lori needed gentle lovemaking, not getting thrown around on the bed.

But it took time for her to see that. She would drive the 400 miles down to Staten Island, and immediately we'd jump into bed. At first it was just sex—wet, satisfying, delicious sex. On her third visit, however, I fell in love with her. I knew I wanted to be with her for the rest of my life.

In June I drove upstate to meet her husband. "It'll be easier for him if he meets you." Against my better judgment, I went and met the guy who had thrown his wife at me. Because, in essence, that's exactly what had happened. Lori had been cruising the Net, found my ad, and responded. He took it all as a joke, told her to go ahead with it, that he wasn't worried about her leaving him because he was such a great lover.

Well, surprise.

Lori was in love with me also. Had been since the second time we had been together. Two days after getting back from meeting him, I called her up in the morning, and her husband got on the phone, telling me that my relationship with his wife was over. Stunned is a good word to describe how the news hit me, but I wanted to be fair. So at first I agreed that he and Lori should go for counseling, try to help their marriage. But when she called me four times that day, crying and telling me how unhappy she was, I relented. Of course, that made us both liars and cheats in his eyes.

He honestly believed that *three hours* was enough time for her to get over me. And as for my feelings? Oh, I should have been able to move onto the next bitch in my stable. I mean, it's a well-known fact (according to her husband, anyway) that gay women don't have long-lasting relationships, that we all hop from one bed to the next, not caring about who we hurt or leave behind. And when Lori didn't instantly obey him, didn't immediately cast me from her life and beg his forgiveness—well, that's when the problems really began.

But that's another story. This one is concerned with my having sex with a woman not previously initiated into the pleasures of woman-to-woman intimacy.

The first time she came down to Staten Island, I showed her exactly what came next when women made love to women. We didn't even make it up the stairs before I had her lying on them, blouse pushed up to her chin as I started playing with my two new toys, her huge nipples. Eventually, we made it to the bedroom and the mattress. That's when Lori's education officially began.

I leaned on my elbow, looking down at her, at the desire burning in those incredible green eyes of hers. "Make love to me, baby. Make love to me."

Five months later. I melted whenever she said those words to me, knowing how long it had taken her to be able to vocalize her need. Dipping my head down, I kissed her sweet lips. When she buried her hands in my blond hair, my tongue snaked into her mouth. She knew how turned on I got when she did that to me. I moaned with pure animal pleasure as I felt her fingers play with my baby-fine hair. I sucked on her tongue as my fingers strayed to her breasts. I stretched her nipples out, pulling on them, teasing the tips with my nail. She began to move, her hips rising slightly off the bed. Now it was her turn to moan. I knew what turned her on too.

"Ooh," she gasped, wrenching her mouth away from mine. "That feels *so* good."

Five months under my hands and tongue had brought the passionate side of my Lori-girl out. We had finally moved past the quiet foreplay and tame orgasm; past her fears of taking too long if she didn't come in ten minutes. Only by constantly reassuring her that taking her time was not selfish was she finally able to relax and enjoy having love made to her.

And there's nothing I enjoy more than taking my own sweet time with her.

I gave her a half grin, the one that drove her wild, because she knew all the lust, love, and teasing that lay behind it

"Yeah? How good? Huh? How good?" I muttered huskily.

In answer she took my hand and shoved it between her legs. "This good."

"Not so fast, Lori-girl. Not. So. Fast," I whispered, pinning her to the bed with the hungry look in my blue eyes.

Taking my deliberate time with her made her crazy. As my hands slid over her silky smooth skin, she shuddered—with delight, in anticipation, with lust.

But she knew it wasn't going to be that easy, knew that I wasn't just going to jump on her and "do" her. But it was the not knowing just exactly how long it was going to take that excited us both.

I lost myself in her eyes, seeing in their limpid depths all the love she felt for me. Because she was in love with me, had told her husband so, and was in the process of leaving him. "I can't live without you, Maria. You're the reason I wake up in the morning—because I know I'm one day closer to living with you."

Spurred on by that undying love, I eased myself between her legs, holding myself up on my elbows so I could see her face clearly, so I could see the changes of emotion rush across her features.

When my lips touched hers, she closed her eyes, losing herself to their caress. I kissed her eyelids, her face, drifting down to the satin skin of her lovely neck, alternating between barely brushing her skin with my mouth and sucking hungrily on her. Her submissive gasps of delight increased my ardor but not my tempo. I had my own sexual agenda in mind.

Trailing my lips down, I moved myself to her breasts, her glorious breasts capped with those huge nipples of hers. Nipples that were stiff with desire, waiting for my mouth. Glancing up, I saw her looking down at me, something else I had taught her. Lying with her eyes closed while in bed with her husband and several affairs she had had was in her previous life. With me, I told her how erotic it was to look at your lover while being made love to; it was part of the enjoyment. "Why keep your eyes closed? Don't you want to watch me as I make love to you? Watch as I enjoy you—and myself?"

She watched as I bent my head to pay homage to her breasts with their aroused tips. Gently tonguing each in turn, I licked the undersides of both breasts, trailing my tongue up to tease the swollen tips. Her moan told me how much she was enjoying this. Looking up so our eyes met, I lightly fastened my teeth around her right nipple, dragging them across it. She plunged her hands in my hair, keeping my head prisoner, not wanting me to relinquish her nipple. But she wasn't the boss in bed; at least not tonight. Shaking my head free, I strayed over to the left breast, fastening my teeth onto that little peak. Her moans deepened.

Leisurely, I moved down her body, delighting in feeling her soft skin against mine. No matter where on her body my lips strayed, they were met by silky smooth skin. I kissed her all the way down to her mound, rubbing my nose in the ginger patch of hair there, reveling in its soft fullness.

"Like this, baby?"

"Uh-huh," she affirmed enthusiastically.

I smiled, knowing she was at my mercy.

I moved a little farther down. Her inner lips were swollen with desire, peeking past her outer ones. Now it was my turn to gasp: I got so turned on when I saw that because I knew that it was my doing. I placed a lingering kiss on them before licking her entire slit. Her body stirred under my ministrations. My Lori-girl knew we were gettin' to the good part.

Using the tips of my fingers, I pried her lips apart, revealing her pink insides. When I saw her inner lips in all their glory, I almost swooned—one of the best parts of making love to her was taking them into my mouth and tugging on them, something that got us both hot. But that was for later. Right now, I just wanted to inhale her female scent, smell Lori's puss. She still wasn't quite over the fact that pussy smell wasn't nasty, as she had been told over the years. Still couldn't get over the fact that she didn't have to take a shower each and every time we made love. That I loved smelling her arousal. Her juice.

"You smell so good, baby," I said, lifting my head up. She looked down at me, her eyes like glowing coals in the lamp's subdued light.

"Good enough to eat?" she asked coyly.

"Oh, yeah," I said huskily, filled with desire. "Oh, most definitely yeah."

I lowered my head and lovingly began to suck on her inner lips, both together and then each velvet petal individually. Lori-girl arched her hips, trying to get more of my mouth on them, but I pulled my head back, mutely showing her who exactly was in charge. When she reluctantly subsided, I went back to my sucking, making smacking noises with my mouth and moaning deep in my throat, verbally showing the enjoyment I was experiencing at tasting her body. Her hands began to stroke my hair.

I licked her slit from top to bottom, enjoying the slipperiness of it against my tongue. When I got to the top, I intentionally avoided making any contact with her engorged clit; when I got to the bottom, I rimmed her moist opening, drawing a deep moan from her.

"Ooh, Marie."

My head bobbed up and down as I licked her sweet cunt, making sure to never touch the burning ember at the top. When I finally plunged my tongue deep inside Lori's puss, I thought she was going to explode.

"*Ooh,* Marie, no one's ever done that to me before!" and she arched her hips up again so I could go in even deeper. I gladly obliged, stretching my tongue as far in as it could go, rolling it around, feeling the inside walls. She kept up a steady moan as I sent my tongue exploring in that little cavern.

When I slid my tongue back up her slit, I knew her clit was near bursting. And so did Lori.

"Please, baby, please. Don't do this to me. Please, baby," she pleaded softly.

Something else I had taught her: "Verbalize your feelings, honey. Let me know what you want. You don't have to just lie there. Take part in what I'm doing." Now she knew asking me to pleasure her clit was OK.

But she also knew that I didn't like people telling me what to do. So instead of making a beeline for her clit, which I knew she was begging me for, I pushed its little hood off and started stroking her shaft instead. Another thing I know she adored. I was rewarded by a deep groan, replete with pleasure.

"Is that what you wanted, Lori-girl? Huh?" I teased.

"Bitch!" she shot back.

I laughed in my own devilish way, adding to the sexual tension. "Whadda want, baby? Tell Maria what you want."

Our eyes met—it had taken me months to get her to say the next sentence out loud.

"I want you to eat me," she said shyly.

"All you had to do was ask, sweetheart."

"Bitch!" and she pushed my head back into her cunt.

In retaliation I quickly flicked her ultrasensitive bud with my tongue and stopped, just to remind her who was the boss. And then I went to work.

I sucked on that delicacy, eliciting groans and moans.

"Oh, baby, it's jerking! Can you feel it?" she asked excitedly. I could. Every time I put my tongue on it, I could feel the little delight twitch underneath. "That's never happened before."

And I knew it wouldn't happen with anyone but me. Because me and Lori-girl brought synergy to the ruffled, perfumed sheets. We were the separate catalysts that ignited each other's sexual passion.

I beat up her swollen clit with my tongue, first stroking it up and down and then sideways. Each time I changed direction, she rewarded me with a moan. Those moans meant the world to me; they showed her appreciation of my lovemaking.

I took my time, circling her clit with my tongue, sucking on it, flagellating it unmercifully with the tip. As she got closer to orgasm, her hips started bucking up off the mattress. I knew instinctively I was in for a rough ride, one I had been waiting for. Reaching up, I gently grabbed her hips, holding on, not wanting to lose her clit with her ever-increasing frantic bucks. Each arching up was accompanied by moans, increasing in volume, with my name and "I love you" interspersed. I dug my tongue in, so to speak, and flicked it faster, keeping up a steady drumming on her clit. When I found the nerve, her hips shot up, muffling me in cunt. But I held on.

"Oh, Marie, oh, Marie, oh, Marie, oh, Marie, oh, Marie, oh, Marie," she chanted low.

I knew she was close. Burrowing my head even closer, I unmercifully let loose with my tongue, whipping it around her clit. Her thighs clamped around my head, keeping me prisoner. Like I wanted to go anywhere! I kept up the momentum, feeling her body reaching upward, upward, upward, reaching for release. I just kept working, stroking, feeding. Suddenly her hips arched up high; I held on, and her body spasmed, her puss jabbing into my face with her orgasming. She kept up her chant, but it slowly died out.

After several seconds she flopped back onto the bed, exhausted.

I could hear her panting, see her chest heaving with the intensity of her climax. Planting a chaste kiss on her now-satisfied cunt, I crawled back up alongside her body. She was covered in a fine patina of sweat. I kissed her; she could taste herself on my lips. I gathered her into my arms, holding her, telling her how much I loved her. She fell asleep listening to me croon my love.

I make love to Lori with my whole being, every fiber of my body coming alive as I roam over hers with my hands, my tongue, my mouth. I've shown her a new side of life, a side where sex isn't simply selfish fucking, rolling over, and going to sleep. I've shown her how hours of foreplay hone her appetite for when I make love to her, how caring she wants her lovemaking to be, and how special the time after intimacy truly is. And should be.

She says when I make love to her, I work magic, but magic is what she does to me. I have never experienced making love with a woman the way I have with Lori. Before her, I had been with seven women. Not even in my two long-term relationships did I feel such completeness, such joy at loving another woman. I've opened myself, both sexually and emotionally, to the only woman I know I can trust. We complement each other, both in and out of bed; in bed, the sexuality is pure synergy. Each time we see each other, it's more satisfying for both. It's amazing to me because this virgin, unschooled in the art of lesbian lovemaking, has shown me the true delights of being in and out of bed with a woman.

As time goes by, I'll introduce Lori-girl into more of the sexual joys associated with being loved by a woman. But for now we're both content to feast on each new facet as it presents itself. Because she's worth taking time with. Because she's someone who's worthy of having a woman in love with her. I've shown her what it's like to be a woman who's desired, loved and appreciated. She had no self-esteem when I first met her. During our months together, I've shown her that she's truly a special lady, one who deserves to have someone who's totally and completely head over heels in love with her.

And we all know how truly special that is.

Seek and Conquer

by C. J. Place

It was a lover's game. No rules. No principles. No time limits. The premise was to seek an opponent who aroused me, seduce her, conquer her, and then seek another. Over the years I learned to play the game well. I never considered that I might lose.

I first saw her walking down a corridor at the office. I immediately wanted her to be a player because her stride exposed a competitive spirit. Her hair was wild and unkempt. It suggested she didn't have time for haircuts and teased my curiosity. Who was she? Was she single? A virgin? A lesbian?

The next time I saw her, we were sitting across from each other in a meeting. I studied the sensual curvature of her lips; they begged to be bitten and sucked. Her eyes were curious and alert. Her nose turned up slightly at the tip. Her neck disappeared smoothly into a turtleneck. She caught me staring. Desire slapped my cheeks and left them burning.

I had to conquer her.

Months passed before I introduced myself and suggested lunch. Carefully she chose words, smoked cigarettes, and ate heartily. I watched her lips and imagined her sucking my neck, my breasts, my thighs, and my lips.

She was disciplined in the military and recently honorably discharged. I sensed emancipation made her nervous. Much of her life was new: boyfriend, apartment, job. Female companionship was a neglected luxury, men monopolized her time and squelched her need to share with a kindred heart.

I didn't tell her about the seek and conquer game—that it's been my passion for nearly 20 years, or that I wanted her to be a player. Instead I nodded my head and listened attentively while planning my strategy, choosing my tactics. Friendship would be my disguise, patience and understanding my secret weapons.

I increased my invitations to spend time together after work. Still, she suspended me at a safe distance—close but on her terms. Mostly, she accepted only when her boyfriend was busy.

Finally she agreed to visit my apartment. As I contemplated the possibility of victory, a rush of excitement tickled my stomach and settled in my womb. I envisioned her lying naked on my couch, inviting me to paralyze her nipples with ice cubes, taunting me to bite her frozen flesh.

She arrived, and I shivered when she asked for wine in a tall glass of ice. We sat on the floor around a coffee table and shared a pizza and laughter. For the first time, she removed a layer from her protective armor and revealed vignettes of her emotionally tortured past.

I wanted to hold her to my breast and smother her memories. How arrogant of me to believe I could mend the damage. I sat silent, sympathetic to her pain and suffering, enamored by her strength and courage. Exhausted by memories, she went home.

Two months later she failed to show up for work three days in a row. I called and asked if I could help in any way and she said she needed a shoulder to cry on. Once I arrived, she told me her job wasn't as promised, she hated the city, and she missed her family. Her new boyfriend didn't understand her and they argued most of the time.

I pretended to listen while a craving left my body, climbed over the table, undressed her, and consumed every inch of her body. I nodded when it was appropriate and asked questions to appear sympathetic. I wasn't. Didn't she understand? Men and women aren't compatible. Never have been. Never will be. How many times could I listen to the same old story: man charms woman, man is wonderful, man moves in, man is a pig.

I suggested she find a nice woman, settle down, and live in peace. She wasn't shocked. She explained "that lifestyle" wasn't for her; however, she could understand how women would be more compatible. That was all I needed to hear.

They are getting married. I'm supposed to be happy, but I'm not. I never understood the institution of marriage. A piece of paper cannot support a crumbling wall, and a promise cannot create love. For some couples marriage is a blessing. For most it is a curse. Little spats explode into wars, possessions expose obsessions, and pet peeves can fester beyond torment.

Usually I didn't play with straight or married women because it repulsed me to stick my tongue where a man's penis had been. My most fulfilling conquest was a virgin—cherry still intact, untouched by man or woman. I was jealous of the boyfriend's proposal. I didn't want her to strengthen her heterosexuality and settle for a man. I had accepted that she fucked men because instinct told me I would be her first woman. She was so alluring I decided I could make a concession for marriage.

The ceremony was small and unobtrusive. Vows were recited in front of a witness, followed by dinner with the parents. I never got to kiss the bride. The groom couldn't take time off for a honeymoon, so it was wham, bam, we're married, ma'am, gotta get back to work.

She wanted to quit her job and go to college. We joked that she could quit if she got pregnant; however, we agreed that was the wrong solution. Two weeks later she made the announcement.

I didn't flinch, which was amazing because my heart spiraled down to my feet and left a path of collapsed arteries. I knew a child would change our relationship, and the game would be almost impossible for me to win. By planting his seed, the husband ignorantly took control of the game.

We talked on the phone a little and saw each other even less. I stopped inviting her to go out, and I quit flirting. If she noticed, she pretended it didn't bother her. She became a ghost who haunted my soul and tangled my memory with fuzzy cobwebs.

Then came the phone call. It was a Saturday night. My latest conquest had come over to hang out for the evening. We fooled around a little, picked up some Chinese food, smoked a joint, and turned on the television. The phone rang.

I picked it up. "Hello?"

"Did I wake you? Are you busy?"

"Not really."

The voice sounded familiar and friendly, as if we talked often. I didn't know who it was, but I didn't let on. "I'm just watching the end of *Saturday Night Live*. What's up?"

"I'm so embarrassed." Sob, sniffle. "I've been thinking about you, wondering if you were thinking about me."

"Who is this?" I still didn't recognize the voice, although I could tell that it was a female's.

"You don't know?"

"No." I started to hang up but then wondered if it was mistaken identity. "This is 555-1234, is that what you dialed?"

"Yes. I know I shouldn't have called, but I couldn't stand it any longer." Sob, whimper. "I'm really attracted to you."

"Why are you crying? Do I know you?"

"Yes. I want you to talk dirty to me."

"Is this a joke?"

"I want you. I know you want me. Talk dirty to me."

"Tell me why you're crying?"

"Because I want you and I can't have you."

"Why not?"

"It's too complicated. I shouldn't have called… I'm so embarrassed."

"Why are you crying? Did someone hurt you?"

"No. You want me, don't you?"

An internal alarm screamed for me to slam down the phone. Instead I heard myself say, "Sure. Why don't you come over right now?"

"I can't. Talk to me. Be kinky."

"Tell me where you are. I'll leave right now. I don't want to do this over the phone."

"Do you want to touch me?"

"Yes." I held my breath.

"Do you want to lick my lips?"

"Yes." I became aroused.

"Do you want to bite me?"

"Yes." I melted.

"Talk dirty to me."

"OK." My inhibitions floated away. "You must do what I say."

"Talk to me."

"Are you naked?"

"Yes."

"Spread your legs. Can you feel the heat?"

"Yes."

"Are you wet?"

"Yes."

"Slide your finger…" I stopped. "I'm sorry. I can't do this. I have to see you. Tell me where you are."

"No. Don't stop now."

"I want to see you. I can't do phone sex."

"I shouldn't have called. I have to go."

"No, I'm glad you called. Call me tomorrow at 7."

"I have to go."

"Will you call me?"

"Yes."

I was stunned. I had never received an obscene phone call from a woman. I blushed when my lover touched my hand, which was between her legs. I hadn't realized I was massaging her. She asked about the call, but I silenced her with kisses. Physically I made love to her, but my mind made love to an embarrassed, sobbing, mystery woman.

At 7 the next evening I waited for the phone to ring. It never did.

I obsessed over the phone call even though I knew it wasn't worth my effort. Each time I heard a woman say she was "embarrassed," she became a suspect—legitimately or not.

The next week, I took a day off to see the woman who haunted my soul. I wanted to see and hear that she was miserable with her new life. Instead she talked enthusiastically about her new role as a wife and mother. I studied her profile and felt an unwanted wetness between my legs.

I told her about the phone call and my crazy obsession to reveal the caller. She listened attentively and then offered that because the caller didn't have the courage to face her own loneliness and homophobia, she called anonymously.

As I listened to her speak, I realized that my obscene caller was her! She had me talk dirty to her so she could masturbate at home, safe and sound with no embarrassment. All the pieces fit. It had to be her. That revelation rekindled my passion for the game. I let the phone call fade and became obsessed with fantasies of conquering her.

I called and invited myself over. I hadn't seen her for two weeks, and I ached for her physical presence. It was a Saturday night, and I arrived with sex, drugs, and rock and roll on my mind. She had been shopping all day and showed me her purchases while the husband sat in his chair watching television. I stood close to her—as close as I could get without invading her space—and devoured her smell, her voice, and her beauty. We ate dinner and counted the minutes until the baby went to bed.

By the time she uncorked a bottle of wine, the husband and I were comrades sharing a comfortable beer buzz. I assumed the role of DJ and used heavy doses of B-side mellow rock from the '70s to enhance the mood. The music stimulated memories, reefer sparked laughter, and alcohol drowned inhibitions.

We got into a heated argument about a parent's role in a child's education. The husband didn't offer an opinion. Instead, he watched us for a while and then taunted us several times to kiss and make up. She ignored him and kept talking. I didn't. His comment threw me off balance. Should I do it?

Would she let me? What would the husband do? Did he want to watch?

We drank more alcohol as the conversation drifted to sexual fantasies. She revealed that she would enjoy watching her husband make love to another woman. I offered that I only enjoyed watching two women together. The husband asked me if a big, thick, juicy penis excited me. I gagged and we all laughed. I restrained from saying it was his wife's thick, juicy lips that excited me.

He suggested that she and I have intercourse. She grinned at me. I squirmed as he motioned to where we should do it in the room. Neither of us moved. He became excited and danced in front of us like a stripper. She seemed embarrassed by his behavior, but soon we all laughed hysterically. I changed the music to an upbeat tempo and we all danced. All of a sudden she stopped dancing, and tension filled the room. I turned the stereo down but continued to dance. She said she was tired and had a headache. Party's over.

For three days I couldn't concentrate on anything except that night. I called her and asked if her husband had plans for the three of us. She was relieved that I brought it up because she wondered the same thing. She said I wasn't ready for three-way sex, especially because he would want to fuck me. I said no, thanks.

After we hung up, I wondered if they were in this together. Did she put him up to it? Would a ménage à trois be a safe introduction to bisexuality for her? Were they playing the seek and conquer game with me?

Flashbacks of the party consumed me. I hated not knowing their motives. In another phone conversation we talked about the night of the party, and she said the husband denied that he was provoking a ménage à trois. I questioned her about what his reaction may have been if we had kissed. She said we should have. Then she had to hang up because the baby was into something.

My bubble burst. I was close to telling her how much I wanted to kiss her. I was so afraid—afraid I might lose her friendship, or even worse, she might laugh at me. Besides, I didn't want to confess my feelings over the telephone. What if she felt the same about me?

A few days later I called and requested a time that we could talk. I arrived full of courage and grand intentions, and then I opened my mouth. Words lodged in my throat like a lump of oatmeal. I felt my face turn red and then white as my confidence drained. I had never faltered during the capture, but I also had never used words as a conquering tool.

I regained my composure, and she suggested I just blurt it out. So I did. I missed the reaction on her face because I couldn't look at her. She admitted that I was in her thoughts often, but her thoughts were platonic. She firmly stated she wasn't interested in a lesbian relationship. It would be too complicated. She was flattered, but wondered what brought this on. Had she done or said something to perpetuate my feelings? Was she serious?

That night I didn't dream or fantasize about her. The next day I called and during the conversation admitted that I hadn't dreamed about her. She said, "You didn't. Well, that's too bad." The game continues.

A month passed before I saw her again. She invited herself to my house and said she had a surprise. Habit forced me to prepare to conquer.

She looked angelic all dressed in white. A new haircut accentuated her profile, and I was overwhelmed with adoration and desire. How dare she tease me with her sexuality! But I would not relent. She would have to make the first move.

She began to vent about her husband and their inability to have sex regularly. It angered her that when they did have sex, it was because she initiated it and she did all the work. She missed the fun and spontaneity of the past—she remembered how they used to fuck on the vibrating washing machine, role-play, and lounge in the bathtub together. Lately her big thrill came when she put clips on her nipples and masturbated with a warm zucchini.

I savored that she wasn't being satisfied and sensed that she wanted me to make love to her but was afraid to ask. I teased her with stories that embellished my reputation as an ardent, intense lover, and I exaggerated graphic incidents that illustrated my passion for long, deep, arousing kisses.

She admitted we could easily satisfy each other because our techniques and passions were similar. I wanted her to put clips on her nipples and masturbate for me. I wanted to lick her clit while she sat spread-eagle on the washing machine. She didn't make advances, nor did I.

Several days later, I joked with her that I needed a guinea pig so I could research sexual short story ideas. She said I should come over right away, that I could experiment with her. Of course, I thought she was joking. She wasn't. I asked her if she was sure. She said yes.

I thought about how easily she rejected and teased me, and I took a rain check. I used the excuse that I wanted to be tested for HIV. She was disappointed but said she would rather be safe than sorry. After three and a half years she finally admitted that she wanted me! I performed a little victory dance and made plans to visit her in a couple days.

The next day came the painful rebuff. She called, full of apologies and said she couldn't go through with it. I pretended it was OK. I said I understood and cut the conversation short. I cursed at her, shed some tears, and then I vowed to stop playing the seek and conquer game. I realized she was playing her own game with me, and I didn't like it. I surrendered.

I thought of her constantly for a month. Finally, one morning, I could stand it no longer. I had to see her so I called. She said she had hoped it was me and asked if I was coming over.

I arrived at the baby's nap time, and she suggested I come upstairs while she prepared the baby for bed. After finishing she shut the door, and we moved down the hall to her study—the room she often slept in because she couldn't stand to sleep with the husband anymore. The room was decorated with colors of pastel green and off-white. A floor-to-ceiling bookcase overflowed with books and stood at the foot of a queen-size bed. Several fluffy pillows lined the headboard and a thick comforter was drawn down as if to invite a weary visitor.

Our nervous conversation flitted from one subject to the next. Soon we were lying on her bed, side by side on our stomachs, looking out the window. We talked as if we were two schoolgirls with nothing to do on a rainy day except stare out the window and wish for better things. I was aware of our legs touching and the heavy sexual tension.

As I babbled on, she interrupted me in mid sentence. "I want to rub my pussy against your pussy."

I sighed and dropped my head. "Damn, this is hard. I'm going crazy trying to fight temptation."

"I know. We shouldn't have sex. It won't strengthen our relationship. We will always be best friends. It won't prove anything."

I thought for a moment. She was right. I could walk away. We could both walk away. We had come so close and fought our urges each time. Nothing had to happen. "You're right, but who would it hurt if we kissed? If you only knew how long I have fantasized about kissing you." I looked at her and smiled. "Could we do that?"

"It wouldn't be enough…for me. I couldn't stop at a kiss."

"We can handle it. It's just a kiss."

She laughed nervously and started to rise from the bed. "I'm getting too excited. We have to stop."

As I watched her rise from the bed, three and a half years of obsession raced through my mind. It was now or never.

I jumped up and grabbed her shoulders. I pressed my lips against hers and guided her down on the bed. She resisted a little and then I felt her lips shift and give way to desire. I felt her whole body stir when my tongue searched for hers, and I heard a faint groan when the tips of our tongues touched. She was right, a kiss was not enough. I wanted all of her!

I moved my arms under the pillow that held her head and raised her deeper into our kiss. I opened my eyes to make sure she was really lying under me and that this wasn't just another fantasy. Her eyes were closed, and she looked sensual and more beautiful than ever. I rubbed my cheek into her hair as I inhaled her smells, and I let our bodies breathe together. She made little grunting noises, and her breath quickened while she caressed my hair and face. I pressed my lips into her strong, tender neck, kissing and sucking her beautiful olive skin while my hands began to explore. My hands found bare skin, and she responded by removing her blouse and bra.

Her hungry lips found mine again. We melted into each other, our lips fused so tight that no air or sound could escape. We kissed that way for a long time, until I was dizzy with lust. I traced the curve of her shoulders with my fingertips and followed their contour to her nipples. I flicked them with the tip of my tongue and pinched them into hard little mounds of pleasure.

Slowly I unzipped and removed her jeans while I danced my fingertips gently over her newly exposed skin. I began to massage her feet, ankles, calves, and I worked my way to her thighs. I rubbed the inside of her thighs and felt the warmth radiating between her legs. I slipped my finger in between the elastic of her panties and tangled my finger in her pubic hair. I looked at her face and saw her devilish grin as I pushed my finger deeper into a pool of come. She began to move her pelvis, and I heard her mutter "Teach me, teach me." I slowly removed my finger and quickly slid her panties off.

I slid my palms over her stomach and down her hips, inching closer and closer to the wetness that I knew was there waiting and begging for me. Over and over I glided my fingers along the fold between her leg and her hips, each time letting my fingers rest momentarily on the lips of her vagina. She began to lift her hips so that each time I pushed in, my fingers would go a bit farther. Each time I withdrew my fingers far enough that I was not touching her but close enough that she barely could feel me when her hips pushed upward.

I continued to tease her while I watched her for a few minutes, and I felt my own cunt throbbing. Soon she was breathing hard while grinding and lifting her hips as she strained to force my fingers deeper inside her. She was sweating and crying, "Fuck me, stick it in, fuck me." But I wasn't ready yet. I wanted to drink her come. I spread her swollen lips with my tongue and thrust into her. Her taste was exquisite—nectar of the goddess. I bit her lips, licked her walls, and sucked her juices while she squirmed and writhed in pleasure. I massaged her breast with one hand as I slid two fingers from the other hand under my tongue. She gasped and spread her legs farther.

I explored her pink folds, tickled her labia, wiggled her clit. She shivered and arched her back. Her arms were over her head and her hands climbed the wall as I massaged and slipped my fingers in and out of her hole, lubricating my fingers with her come. She moaned "Faster, deeper, harder" as I felt her expand, and she invited my whole hand to explore her inner sanctum. I plunged inside of her and felt her suck me in, holding me with her pelvis, never wanting to let me go. I synchronized to her rhythm as we swayed to the lover's dance. She whispered, "Don't stop, don't stop, please don't stop."

I watched her face as she neared orgasm. I could see in her eyes she was ready to go over the edge. She was ready for that spark that shot from head to toe and settled in her heart, throbbing, dripping, and panting. I quickened my thrusts, and she exploded in ecstasy and shivers. I saw desire dilate her pupils and make them dance with contentment and joy. Her eyes pleaded with me to never stop touching, licking, sucking, and loving.

Then she cried. That was a first for me. I wrapped her in my arms and comforted her and asked why she cried. She told me it had been four years since she had an orgasm, since anyone touched her with tenderness. She sobbed because her husband didn't care enough to learn how to please her.

We lay quietly until she broke the silence. "Where did you learn how to do that?"

"It's simple, I love women." She got dressed while I washed. We kissed and hugged, and without another word, I left.

I backed out of her driveway and drove down the street. While sitting at a stop sign, I performed the victory dance.

I stayed away from her because everything had changed. I was madly in love with her—a married woman! Eventually I became so crazy with desire that I called and asked if she would see me. She agreed.

I became extremely nervous as I drove closer to her house. I had no idea what either of us would say. I knew if she consented, I would make love to her again.

She looked great. We didn't hug, and I felt tension immediately. She came right to the point and told me lesbianism wasn't for her. Sex between us would never happen again. She had only agreed to it because she felt it was easier to just let it happen than to try to stop me. As far as she was concerned, it never happened, and we never had to talk about it again.

Rejection all wrapped up in a tidy package.

I listened while my heart wept. I didn't protest or beg.

A short time later I sat in my car in her driveway and waited for the engine to warm. I stared at the living room window but I couldn't really see in. I was numb. I backed my car down the driveway and glanced again at the window as I drove by. Through the sheer curtains I saw her outline—in the middle of the living room—performing a little victory dance.

Over the years, I learned to play the game well. I never considered that I might lose.

High School Sweetheart

by Paula C. Bowden

I would like to begin this as a story of two healthy, sexy young women discovering hot, passionate love together. But I can't. It would be a blessing if I could tell it as the love affair of a lifetime. But I can't do that either. This instead must be told as the story of one budding young lesbian coming into her own, however painfully. I can, however, tell this as it is: the seduction of a virgin. The virgin in this story is Lee. Well, that's not her real name, but given the outcome of this tale, it is better her that true identity remain unknown.

Our mystery girl, Lee, is someone I met in high school French class. She sat behind me, so conversation was strained, but we would pass notes back and forth. During class, when the teacher wasn't looking, I loved to turn and watch Lee pronounce the French pronoun *tu* as she pursed her lips for that perfect nasal tone. We really had nothing in common, Lee and I. She was butch, beautiful and athletic, three inches shorter than I, with short blond hair and blue eyes. Lee was a science fiction freak, and I a band fag, as we were called. French class was our only common denominator, but it didn't take long before I was in love.

Lee and I slowly became friends. Extending our friendship outside of French class, we would eat lunch and go to the movies, and I would occasionally be invited to her home. I was impressed with the hand-built models of various famous starships she had made. She liked me because I could keep up with her intellectual conversation. Other high school students just weren't interested. When we went to the mall to ice skate and shop, she would loop her arm in mine and we would walk arm in arm with sisterly camaraderie.

As our friendship grew and we spent more time together, I became increasingly aware of my excitement when she was around. My heart would beat hard in response to her beautiful smile and the rare touch with which she would grace me. Our friendship became more and more important and more and more frustrating as my feelings for her grew. Lee had no idea what I was feeling for her.

I was miserable. I was also a born-again Christian, which I am sure added to my misery. Here I was, 15 years old and beginning to be aware of my physical attraction to another woman and unable to act on it. Night after night I would lie in bed thinking of Lee. Staring up at the ceiling, holding my pillow tight against my chest with one arm and using the fingers of my other hand between my legs to stroke my furry wetness, I would imagine it to be Lee's hand in its place. In my mind it became her hand; her body on top of mine; our young supple breasts pushing against each other. Stroking, petting until I came, so very quietly so no one would hear, but breathing hard, just the same.

After the orgasm I would admonish myself for "sinning." Not just for masturbating, which was bad enough, but also for fantasizing about a woman. For shame! The next day, when I would see Lee after a night of intense solo passion, I would blush and stumble over words. Lee had absolutely no idea.

This terrible crush continued. I was especially tortured at the end of our sophomore year together. Lee's family had to move away. The school year was nearly over, and Lee wanted to finish it at our high school. My grandmother (with whom I lived) got wind of this and offered Lee our house (and my bed) as a place to stay for the two weeks left of school.

Sharing a room with her was both joyful and hellish. Lee felt totally safe with me. Since she was so comfortable around me, she would change her clothes in front of me without hesitation. I had the opportunity to see her small, beautiful breasts and fluffy pubic hair. This could have been my chance at total happiness and sexual satisfaction; however, I was just too confused with my religion and my intense sexual feelings to do anything but dream during Lee's stay with me.

Now that I had seen her nakedness, I had a physical image to accompany my nighttime fantasy. When we crawled into bed to sleep, I would again lie on my back, only this time I had no physical outlet with Lee so near. I was sure she could hear the throbbing of my wet and swollen clit. Out of desperation I would stretch my long body toward hers. As I settled back into relaxation, part of my leg or arm would just happen to touch Lee's side or hip and just by chance I would fall asleep so the errant limb stayed put, basking in the warmth of Lee's body.

After the first week of sleeping together, Lee would let me spoon up behind her. I was so glad I wasn't a man. My own protrusion was nearly big enough for her to feel through our pajama bottoms as it was. Despite my seemingly obvious infatuation, Lee continued to be clueless about my feelings.

I let no one know about my private love affair. I began to talk about a fellow clarinet player as though I had a crush on *him* just to save my hide as the other girls talked about boys. I even created a false attraction for him in my journal, trying to convince myself (and everyone else) that I indeed was far from being a homosexual. After all, this was just a phase, wasn't it?

Lee moved away, and we continued our friendship long-distance. I would stay with her family during the winter holidays and for part of the summer. We would share a bed, and as I became more aware of my sexuality, my attraction became much more of a burden. I caught myself "accidentally" bumping up against her breast, and as her nipple grew hard from the contact, my lips and tongue would ache to taste it.

Upon my graduation from high school, my grandmother asked me to leave the house. She and I were arguing all the time and I was preparing to go to college. I had nowhere to go, so I turned to Lee's family. By this time they treated me like one of theirs. I called her parents Mom and Dad. With such closeness already established, they took me in and gave me a job and a place to stay (Lee's bed).

Before I actually moved in, Lee's mom sat down with us and asked if our friendship would survive living together for three months. We both assured her we would be fine. I had my doubts, but by this time I was positive I was straight. Lee and I did share a bed, but we worked different shifts so our actual time together in the bed was cut short. I had started dating a male coworker, which proved to me I was in no danger of being lesbian. Still, I would wake in the morning only to roll over and smell Lee's scent on the pillow. My nightly fantasies continued, and I feared Lee was beginning to suspect. My favorite fantasy went like this:

Lee, who had never been sexual with anyone, who never even thought about sex, spends the night. We have a nice evening watching science fiction and eating dinner, occasionally feeding each other ketchup-laden french fries. After a proper amount of time, I would fake sleepiness. Going to the bedroom first, with the excuse that I wanted a shower before bed, I head to the bathroom. Bathing quickly, ignoring the feeling of the hard water against my skin, I jump out of the shower, towel off, and run to the bed to slide under the silky blue cotton sheets, totally nude.

When Lee comes into the bedroom, we begin talking. As she is crawling into bed I say, "Lee, can I cuddle with you tonight?"

"Sure," she replies, oblivious of my intent. Lee rolls on her side and I curl my naked body against her, pushing my supple breasts and bare tummy into the soft flannel of her pajamas. I ask her if she wants a massage. "Sure," she replies again, ever so casually.

"Well then, take off your shirt and roll on your belly, silly." In the darkness she is unaware of my nudity as I straddle her muscular butt. I knead the tight muscles in her back and make my way down to the sensual skin at the side of her breasts. As she relaxes into the massage she begins to sigh, "Oh, this feels so good." Then I would slowly lower my torso so my swinging breasts and perky breast buds tickle her skin.

To continue the seduction, I kiss her neck, pressing myself deep against her. Being shy, my inevitable lover takes her time turning to face me. When she begins to move, I slither off her butt and lie at her side, continuing to kiss and caress her soft skin and strong back. Lee's earlier sighs of relaxation turn to deep moans of desire. "I've never had a back rub quite like this before, Paula." Slowly, slowly, I ease her pajama bottoms down her hips and begin telling her how handsome she is, how beautiful. As her pants come off, I knead the hard musculature of her now naked rear and slide my hand down her thigh to where she is warm and wet. Her eagerness surprises us both. She turns completely over and lets me finish undressing her. My kisses follow the descent of the pants. Stroking and petting, finding her clit with my tongue, I lie stretched out between her legs, my hands beneath the small of her back. My tongue and teeth nibble and lick till quite suddenly she arches her back with orgasm, dripping delicious fluid down my chin.

At this time in my life, I had had little to fill in the details regarding how a woman came. I knew about orgasm by playing with myself in shame and what I had read in *Wifey* by Judy Blume when I was 12. My lack of knowledge was a superficial concern at best, as everything I was doing with Lee was only fantasy.

Fortunately the summer ended quickly. I moved to the dorms at college and met other lesbians. I came out two years later, when I was 19 and had transferred to a private university. In the meantime visiting Lee at her parents' house was becoming more difficult. Even giving her a simple hug was now an erotic experience. Lee had started playing softball. Her arms were defined and strong, her hips wide and full. I had had a couple of experiences by this time and though they were with men, I had discovered the feeling of just how wonderful it could be to make love with my friend. I was moving away though to the new school. To ask Lee to start anything at that time would have been tough. I moved the 200 miles away, and we kept up our friendship again through letters and phone calls.

One of the special things about Lee and me is that our birthdays are only three days apart. We always made it a point to spend our birthdays together. As December approached and Lee had time off, she made arrangements to come see me. By this time I was going nuts. I had come out with a bang. Once I realized and accepted my sexuality, there was no going back for me. I was politically active and around other lesbians most of the time. Seeing Lee for the first time since my second rebirth, I realized how much like a butch dyke Lee appeared.

I hadn't had a love relationship with anyone and had never had sex with a woman. I knew that more than anything I wanted to make love to Lee. I was positive that if only I could convince her to go to bed with me, she could see the love I had for her and we would live happily ever after. I had created scenes in my head where we had a house and a big dog. Our days together could be filled with making butter and feeding cows; our nights could be filled with endless nakedness and sweat. I would trace my finger down Lee's side as she lay in bed next to me, a big flowered comforter keeping us warm. My hand would slyly slip. Suddenly it would be on her breast. Her nipple would rise under my touch, simply inviting my warm mouth. With my tongue busy, my hand would continue to snake its way down to her inner leg, trace circles on the hot skin until it found its way to the jungle maze of tangled fur. Pausing a moment, just to feel her squirm in anticipation, I would dive into the pool of wetness that awaited.

So the fantasy was cliché. It was the best I could do at the time. The important thing was that though my studies were suffering due to my imaginings, she was coming to see me, and I had finally acquired the nerve to tell her how I felt.

Why is it that the most important part of a story is the hardest to tell? I can remember each detail designing the years surrounding the blessed day, but the memory of this day is as pale in my memory as a rainy November day.

Lee arrived at my humble student apartment about an hour before we had to leave to see a play in the city. We walked around my pseudo college town looking for a quick bite. All I had in mind was *how* I wanted to share my "quick bite" with

Lee. The conversation was hesitant. Lee was tired from the drive and didn't have much to say. I was too scared to think and blamed that on tiredness as quickly as I could.

After dinner we left immediately to see the show. I was so riddled with anticipation that I am unable to remember what we ate, the long drive there, or even the show we saw. I had thought about it long and hard. I had the evening planned out and figured that the long drive back home would be the best time to finally tell my love of the oh, so many years that I wanted to bear her firstborn, or something like that. This way, if she was totally freaked, our evening wouldn't have been ruined and if she was excited, we would have a wonderful night to look forward to.

I had told Lee that I was gay about six months before this evening. At that time, she seemed nonplussed by the fact that her best friend liked to "lick pussy." Well, given her virginal status, it is very possible that she never gave that aspect of my life a second thought. She said she had suspected that I was gay for a while, anyway.

I started the conversation that night by reminding her that I was gay. I proceeded to tell her my coming-out story and how I knew I was gay that summer before college when I had had to share a bed with her. I was even supposed to go to New York with her about a year before but explained that I had been unable to make the journey, as I was afraid of what could happen.

I was driving my '72 orange VW bug with tears streaming down my face, explaining my love and how it had deepened over the years. I don't know what was wetter, the windshield from the rain or my face from the tears.

Lee had never had a relationship or sex before in her life. She explained to me that it wasn't anything she was interested in. As my tears slowed, Lee began to talk. "I have never really thought about sex much. I have always been interested in other things. Sharing my life with another person doesn't mean anything to me. The idea of dating and spending my free time with someone feels like it would grate on my nerves." The talk continued in this vein until we reached my house. She didn't say anything else about what she was feeling, which was typical.

I was a nervous wreck. We were pulling up to the house, and I didn't know what to do with myself. I parked the car and sat a moment in the cold, listening to the fast rain beat down on the roof in rhythm with my heart. Then Lee said, "I am not sure why, but I am willing to give it try."

Feigning nonchalance I said, "Well, we'd better go in before we freeze."

Lee turned her head toward me and smiled, her teeth gleaming in the half-light of the street lamp. "Yeah, I already need a hot shower just to get warm!"

I thought of all the witty comebacks I could make like, "I could make you wetter and hotter than some dumb shower," but instead I turned to kiss her. Of course, before I could make my move she started to get out of the car. All I could do was follow. "Race ya!" shouted Lee, jumping out to dodge the rain. I followed, letting her win.

She waited for me under the eaves and laughed as I fumbled for my keys, dropping them on the wet cement. Once in the door Lee sprinted for the stairs and the warm shower. I knew better than to ask her if we could shower together; however, a nice thing about our friendship was that we often shared the facilities. After she undressed and stepped under the spray, I followed her into the bathroom to brush my teeth. The way the mirror was set up, I could look at myself watching her take a shower in the reflection. She was standing behind the rainbow-patterned shower curtain, legs slightly spread, back and neck arched, allowing the hot water to hit her chest. My fumbling fear at the front door melted into lust, watching the droplets drip to the end of her now hardened nipples. I could nearly feel my own tongue at the tip catching the water as it fell. Sometimes she would lick her full, pink lips to catch errant drops. I was getting as wet as she just watching the shower take place.

To not give myself away, I soon left the bathroom, making sure Lee had a large towel to wrap herself in. I had showered before she arrived and didn't want to waste any time, so as quickly as I could I got ready.

My room was long and narrow. I had a futon on the floor at the left and a bookcase on the right. There was a closet and a chair, which I generally used as a clotheshorse. Despite my student income, I loved little bits of luxury. I had maroon, 200-count cotton sheets on my futon and at least five pillows. The sheets were clean and good-smelling. Sliding between them was a sensuous experience all its own. I took advantage of the five minutes I had to remove my clothes, throw them on the chair, and slide beneath the sheets to warm the bed. I heard the shower turn off, and a couple of minutes later the bathroom door opened. I lay in the bed waiting. My previously calm heart began a belly dance in my chest.

All the fantasies I ever had flooded my memory. This was the night I was waiting for, and I was going to make it right. Then, to my disappointment, Lee came through the door dressed in her old worn out pj's! Not quite the sexy image I had had of her wrapped in my big towel, but I knew she was scared, so I let it go and moved on to the next part of my plan by inviting her to bed.

Lee's pajamas consisted of a battered, very soft gray sweatshirt I had seen her wear since high school, and boys' flannel, plaid pj bottoms that had the handy opening in the front. I kept this in mind as she lowered her body down to me and slithered beneath the sheets.

"Hey, the bed's warm," Lee commented.

"I warmed the bed for you like you warm my heart for me, dear," I returned. Lee graced that banal comment with a smile. Lee by nature was quiet. "So how are you?" I asked stupidly. "Oh, fine," she replied with equal intelligence.

I rolled my eyes in frustration. "Well, what would you like to do?" I have no idea where my years of preparation for the moment had gone.

"Well," Lee said, matching my hesitation, "we could make love, but I have never done this before. I don't know how to start."

"OK, sweetie, just lie there and let me do my stuff!" I retorted cockily.

Lying next to her on my side, I began the seduction by stroking her hair and face. She began to relax into the futon, turning her face toward me. I moved my hand down her neck and found her right breast. My hand was outside her shirt and she began to move ever so slightly with either pleasure or repulsion. I banked on the former as she didn't protest, and continued. My hand crept to the bottom edge of her shirt, paused for a moment, and made its ascent on the inside of the soft material. Lee hadn't been making much sound, but when I touched her waiting nipple, it immediately sprang to life. Lee's eyes widened and I heard the faintest of gasps escape from her. "Is that OK?" I asked with some hesitation.

"Hmm, feels nice," she murmured. Lee let me explore her body further.

Lying on my side, I was propped on my left elbow, so I had only the one hand free to roam over her nakedness. Goose bumps formed under my hand. The luxury of her silken skin under my fingertips was driving me wild! My heart was pounding, but this time with desire. I looked into Lee's blue eyes and saw the matched desire there. She wanted me, and I wanted to feel her nether lips, I just couldn't wait.

Finding that handy doorway of her pajama bottoms, I sneaked my fingers through. I kept my eyes on Lee's face in case she wanted me to stop. "That's really nice," she said, her voice quivering. Getting up my courage, I searched further and found one damp, curly mass of tangled fur. I didn't waste much time. My middle finger found Lee's hardened clitoris. I stroked the soaked sides of her lips and watched her respond. Her eyes closed, and her head tilted back. Her breathing deepened. She was actually enjoying this! I snaked my way back to her waiting bud and continued. The desire to seduce her was gone. I just wanted to make her come and come hard.

I began a rhythmic stroking of Lee's clit with my index finger on one side and thumb on the other, indulging in her silky wetness. Looking at her face again, she opened her eyes. I could see that for that moment she totally trusted me. I increased my strokes and called her name. Her hips arched. Suddenly her eyes flew open and her body began to shake. "Hey, what's happening?" she startled.

"Does it feel good?" I questioned, sustaining the rhythm. "Do you want me to stop?" "No! Don't stop," she chopped, then more quietly, "please, it feels so good, I have just never felt this before." Lee's orgasm came to its crescendo with her riding all the way. Lee muffled a cry behind her hand, then the orgasm began to wane like waves upon the sand. As Lee's breathing calmed, I held her, once again stroking her hair and face.

"Can I touch you like that?" she asked, stretching her body. "Can I make you feel good too?" I was nervous and scared. I didn't want Lee to touch me.

"I just came too, touching you," I lied. "Don't worry about me."

"OK," she said, bewildered, but accepting. To this day I regret that decision.

Lee and I lay in comfortable silence for a while, our bodies adjusting to the moment of passion. Lee then surprised me by asking what life was like as a lesbian. I was pretty militant at the time. I told her of my feelings of solidarity and sisterhood. After a moment Lee told me her mother had always known I was gay. "I wonder what she would think if she knew this had happened? She wants me to marry a man and have kids, you know." Suddenly there was a pause as if Lee got it for the first time what it meant if she decided that making love to me was the best thing in the world and she had to live life as a lesbian to do it. Something changed in her eyes. A light went off inside her. "Well, I don't think I am a lesbian, Paula."

My heart audibly broke. I cried for a year.

Leave-taking the next morning was awkward. It's true that if I made love to a woman now as I did to Lee then, no self-respecting lesbian would have me. I don't think that was what turned Lee's head from a life of lesbianism, though. Sometimes I wonder if it would have been different had I let her touch me. Perhaps she was afraid of her mother's alienation. I probably will never really know.

Lee and I tried to be friends for a while. We managed for about five years with a strained and painful dignity. I haven't seen her now for over a year. We talked once on the phone, and even though it has been ten years since our sexual experience, our friendship has never recovered. I don't know if she has ever had sex since then. She likes to listen to Rush Limbaugh. She still looks like a dyke, walks like a dyke, talks like a dyke, and I still think she is a dyke. Maybe someday I will get that phone call where she says, "Hey, Paula, guess what!" Until then I have only memories.

A Brief Musical Interlude

by Rebecca O'Bryan

As I slammed the door of my truck and ran across the parking lot of the San Francisco airport, I was worried about just two things. How did I look, and would she show up? Checking my watch, I noticed that I was two minutes late, and hoped like hell that Rachel's plane was running late too.

This was turning out to be more stressful than romantic. I slowed down and looked at the arrival board in the terminal. The plane *was* running late, and I had another half hour to kill before Rachel arrived. What the hell was I doing here, meeting a woman I had only talked to on the phone? Why was I so hot to have an affair with someone I'd never met?

Why was I having an affair at all?

Granted, my current relationship was rocky, but it had always been rocky. Cindy and I never saw eye to eye on any issue except sex, and even that was becoming boring. After four years of confrontation and neurotic arguing, I was ready for a change.

In the midst of this chaos, I was given Rachel Callan's name as a contact person at a record label I was wooing. The first time we talked on the phone, we clicked. This woman knew exactly what I was talking about. We discussed the difficulties of being women in the very male-dominated music business, the necessity of schmoozing people you really didn't care for but needed, and the long, long hours it took to nail down a deal in a business where most deals are as fluid as the endless cups of coffee we downed all day.

To say that I enjoyed our first conversation would be an understatement. The only flaw in this sea of perfection was the fact that I hadn't come out to Rachel during our long talk. However, I decided that since future conversations were obviously going to get even more personal as time went on, I should tell Rachel right up front that I'm a lesbian. Kiss me or kill me, but don't accuse me of being in the closet. So a couple of days later, when Rachel called to confirm some information on our project, I managed to work the conversation around to a more personal note.

"I can't imagine having to live in L.A. How do you stand it? I can barely tolerate a week down there, and I feel like I have to detox when I get back to the Bay Area," I gracefully inserted into the conversation.

Rachel just laughed. "Hey, it's no big deal to me. I was born in the Valley, and I've lived here all my life. You get used to it. And there are lots of great places to go and things to do down here. In fact, next time you come down, give me a call and let's get together and go out."

Bingo! I segued into my next line, "Well, I don't know if you'd want to go to any of the clubs I hang out at."

Rachel laughed and said, "Why, where do you hang out? In strip clubs or something?"

"No," I said deliberately, "I usually go to Girl Bar when I'm in L.A. Sometimes The Palms if I'm in a sleazy leather mood."

There was a short pause, and Rachel said, "Girl Bar. I think I've been there. It's on Robertson, isn't it?"

"Yep. So, are you family then?" I asked hopefully.

"Family?" she repeated. "I don't understand. Who's family?"

I stammered, "Ah, family—you know, gay."

She laughed. "No, I'm not gay, but a lot of the people I work with are, so I've spent a lot of time in West Hollywood. Actually, one of the women in my department is a lesbian, and she took me to Girl Bar one weekend. It was great! I love dancing with women."

Now, I have been an outrageous flirt all of my life. Having found out that Rachel was open to at least talking about lesbians, I decided to find out if she'd ever considered it as an option for herself.

"So, if you love dancing with women, how do you feel about dating them?" I asked her. There was silence as I sat and mentally pounded myself over the head for coming on so strong.

"I've thought about it a few times," she said slowly, "but I've never met a woman who interested me sexually. I mean, I just don't know what you do sexually, you know what I mean?"

I laughed. "Hey, next time you're in West Hollywood, stop into A Different Light bookstore and pick up a book on lesbian sexuality. Then you'll understand the mechanics of it, if not the reality." I paused a beat, and then added in a lower voice, "Of course, we could go over the realities next time I'm down there."

She stopped for a moment, then said, "I don't know where this conversation is going, but I don't think I want to continue it at work. Can you call me at home tonight? I'll give you my number."

Later, as I sat in my office with hundreds of erotic scenarios running through my mind, I realized that I didn't even know what this woman looked like, let alone anything about her personal life. I also realized that this was part of what appealed to me about Rachel. We had connected on a workplace level, but we had very little personal knowledge of one another. Having sex with her would bring back that feeling of being young and hot and having sex with women I'd pick up in the bars and then very likely would never see again. I wanted that feeling of uncomplicated sex again. And I decided that Rachel needed to find out just what lesbian sexuality was all about.

Over the course of the next two months we spent hours every evening on the phone with each other. During the day when I'd call her about project details, we were all work. But at night our conversations got more and more intimate; within a month we were having phone sex. For a woman who'd never been with another woman, Rachel was ready to try.

Both of us were going crazy with this tease, yet our schedules were such that we were never able to get together. Finally, after a couple of months of this, Rachel took vacation time and made arrangements to fly up to San Francisco, where we planned to spend two days in a hotel. Literally. We had no plans to sightsee, go out to dinner, or visit any friends. We wanted to spend two days in bed, exploring one another.

And so here I was at the airport, having serious second thoughts. *What if my lover finds out about this?* I had told Cindy I was attending a music conference in The City, and I wasn't sure where I would end up staying. At that low point in our relationship, it was fairly obvious that she couldn't have cared less where I was staying, or with whom. *What if Rachel wants more than just an affair? What if I fall for her and I end up wanting more than an affair?* I spent the next 30 minutes driving myself crazy with questions that had no answers. By the time they announced her flight arrival, I was ready to call my therapist and ask for an immediate session.

Too late. My feet were walking to the arrival gate, and I was scanning the crowd looking for Rachel. We had never exchanged photos, so I was going on the basic information I had about her: 5 foot 6, long dark hair, fairly thin, and dressed entirely in black everything. I had described myself to her: 5 foot 10, long blond hair, muscular (all my sexual frustration had been recycled into gym time). I watched every dark-haired woman come off the plane. Was that her? No, she'd never mentioned wearing glasses. Nope, too tall, too fat, not wearing black. Finally I saw her. It had to be her. Our eyes locked, and the smile on my face threatened to stretch my ears around to the back of my head. *Oh, my God, she's gorgeous!*

I waited for the crush of passengers to clear the walkway, and watched as she came towards me. "Rachel?" I asked.

"Rebecca!" she said, smiling. "My God, you're really tall!" I took her hands and pulled her toward me.

"I need to feel my arms around you," I said. "I need to know that you're real."

"I can't believe I'm here," she whispered. "I can't believe we're finally together."

I smiled and murmured, "I'd really like to kiss you right now, but I want our first kiss to be special. So how 'bout if we get the hell out of here and go to the hotel?"

Rachel laughed, "You're right, let's get the hell out of here."

We went out to the car and zoomed off toward the City. Luckily, traffic was light, and 20 minutes later we were checking into the hotel. I tipped the bellman, hustled him out of the room, and turned to look at her. Petite, with finely drawn cheekbones and beautiful eyes, she was absolutely stunning.

"Come here," I whispered. "I want to kiss you." She moved into my arms and I kissed her lightly, moving my lips to her neck and back up to her earlobes. Trembling with excitement, I told her, "I want you now, but I need to know that you're OK with all of this. Tell me if you're not."

"Oh, yes," she said, "I want you too. I've wanted to make love with you for weeks. But you have to show me what to do."

We kissed for what seemed like hours. Tongues sliding in and out, over teeth, lips, sucking gently on her tongue, touching her everywhere, teasing, making her want me as much as I wanted her. Slowly, so slowly unbuttoning her shirt, my tongue running a path along the top of her breasts, down the underside of her arms. I sucked gently on her fingers while I unhooked her bra; beautiful firm breasts with tiny brown nipples already so hard that I just had take one into my mouth and lick and suck it, trying to make it harder. She rose up as if to fit her whole breast into my mouth. I moved over to the other breast, gently massaging the nipple I'd just taken out of my mouth. Rachel was moaning and pushing my head down as if to say "Suck harder." I reached down and undid her pants, sliding my hand inside to feel how hot and wet it was.

"Oh, God, baby," she moaned, "please, please, I want you inside me."

I rolled off the bed and took off my own clothes. Then, kissing and touching everything I could reach, I took off her shoes and pants. She was wearing a tiny green satin G-string. I snapped it in two and slid my body on top of hers.

She felt so fine, soft and silky, and oh, so wet. I sucked a nipple into my mouth and slid my fingers inside her at the same time. Rachel gasped and held me tight against her as I moved my fingers very slowly inside her. She whispered and moaned and thrashed as my thumb moved on her clit. Finally, when I couldn't wait any longer, I moved down between her legs. Gliding my tongue up and down, sucking her clit into my mouth, she practically screamed.

After about half an hour, it was becoming clear to me that Rachel was enjoying all this, but she was not even close to having an orgasm. I moved up on the bed and pulled her into my arms. "What's the matter?" I said. "Is there something that you really like that I'm not doing?" I laughed lightly. "Just tell me what it is. I'm not the sensitive type, I don't mind a little direction."

Rachel was almost in tears. "It's not you, Rebecca, it's me," she said. "I can't have an orgasm." I held her in my arms and kissed her forehead while she cried a little. And then she told me. She'd never been able to have an orgasm with a man, so she had always just assumed that she couldn't have one, period.

"Oh, honey," I sighed, as I held her tight, "there's nothing wrong with you. There's nothing wrong with not having an orgasm. This isn't a goddamned soccer game or something. We're not scoring goals here, we're making love. I'd love to be able to give you an orgasm just because it feels so wonderful. But if you enjoy our lovemaking, that's good enough for me, with or without the damned orgasm."

Rachel kissed me. "I always fake it with guys because if you don't have an orgasm they'll keep pounding away at you all night, trying to make you come, or they tell you there's something wrong with you. I still don't know if I can or not, and I'm too tense now to do anything."

I hugged her tight. "Honey, I have the perfect prescription for tense. Follow me."

Lighting a small candle, I filled the Japanese-style bathtub and handed her into the bath. Sitting on the side, I reached down and massaged her neck and shoulders. No conversation, nothing sexual, just relaxing warm water and massage. "This feels so good," she whispered. "I can't believe you're doing this for me."

I smiled and kissed the top of her head. "I can't believe that no one has ever tried to help you relax before, babe. Just enjoy it."

I was starting to get a little chilly, so I stepped into the tub, situating myself behind Rachel, letting my breasts rub against her back, enfolding her with my legs. "You don't mind if I join you, do you, baby? It's cold out there!"

"No, no, that's fine," she murmured, "just hold me." We sat in the tub for another 20 minutes, just being warm and close, and then suddenly Rachel stood up. "Let me sit behind you now," she said. I moved forward and let her slide in behind me. I leaned back against her as she massaged my breasts and played with my nipples, which were rock-hard again. Her hand slid down between my legs, and I felt a feathery touch on my clit. "Let's go back to bed," she whispered in my ear, nibbling my earlobe and kissing my neck.

Rachel pushed me down on the bed and lay down on top of me. "What do you like?" she asked. "I don't know what to do."

I ran my fingers through her hair. "Suck my nipples, baby. That's what I really like. Suck 'em hard." Rachel's head moved down, and she sucked and licked my nipples, all the while touching me with her soft, gentle hands. She was driving me crazy. "Put your fingers inside me, honey. Feel how wet I am for you." She moaned and moved her fingers into me. She continued to suck on my nipples and I thought I would die from feeling this good. Suddenly she moved down between my legs and began licking my pussy. I was so wet, I was dripping as she moved her fingers in and out and sucked hard on my clit. I turned underneath her and ran my tongue inside her as she continued to lick and suck my clit. I could feel my orgasm coming, so I moved my mouth away and put my fingers inside of her. Her breathing heightened, and then I couldn't think about anything except coming.

At last, my breathing slowed and I realized that I still had my fingers inside Rachel. I turned her on her back, and moved my head down between her legs. Moving my fingers inside her hard and fast, I sucked and licked at her clit. She began whispering, "Yes, yes, oh, yes, baby, make me come." She grabbed my hair and pulled my face even deeper into her, and I concentrated my entire being on giving Rachel an orgasm. She let go of my hair and grabbed the pillows, scream-whispering, "Yes, yes, yes, oh, yes," and then she came. Wetness poured over my face, and I licked it up as fast as I could.

"Oh, God, baby," I whispered, "you taste so good."

Suddenly, in between heavy breaths, she began crying and giggling. "I did it! I did it!" she yelled. "I can have an orgasm!"

"Hot damn!" I started laughing, and Rachel pulled my hair.

"Don't laugh, goddamn it! This is a big deal for me!"

"Oh, honey," I chuckled, "I'm not laughing at you. I'm happy because you finally got to experience something that feels so fucking good. I think you're great!"

We ultimately ended up spending almost five days together in San Francisco, hanging in the Castro, sightseeing, and always, ending up together making love in our room. When I finally called Cindy one night to let her know I'd be gone for more than a couple of days, I got the answering machine. I left a message and my cellular number, but Cindy never bothered to call.

Rachel went back to L.A., and our relationship continued to evolve long-distance. Even though we didn't see each other often, we stood by each other as we made important decisions and changes in our lives. Rachel was a constant source of strength as I ended my relationship with Cindy and struggled to deal with living alone. I listened to her agonizing over coming out as a lesbian. We loved one another without being in love.

After about a year, Rachel called me one day to tell me she had "met someone." "Someone" turned out to be a woman named Gail, a friend of one of Rachel's coworkers. I've never been very good at being alone, and I have to admit I gave Rachel a hell of a hard time about her new relationship, trying to convince her that we really belonged together, and that Gail was just a temporary fling. But being the patient sweetheart that she is, Rachel made me see that I was just grasping at her so that I wouldn't have to be alone, that a love relationship between us would ruin the friendship that we had; and she was right.

Rachel and Gail have been together for over three years and live just a few miles from my house in Los Angeles, which I share with the love of my life, Isabel. Every now and then, when I see Rachel at a party or at the bar, our eyes will lock and we smile, remembering San Francisco.

Every Inch of Her Face

by Shelby Lee

It was a typical hot day in Arizona. There was nothing unusual about the 102-degree heat of late June, but her presence, her aura, made it seem at least 200 degrees.

I had just picked her up from the airport, and we were headed to Sedona for our first weekend together. It had been six months since we had seen each other, and that trip was filled with too much business and too many people for us to spend any time alone. Previous to that we had simply been long distance friends, never revealing any sexual feelings for each other. This weekend was a big step for her and for our relationship.

The hours spent on the phone during the previous months could not have prepared me less for the tremors that her mere presence brought to my body. Nothing could have prepared me for, nor could my memory do justice to, her beauty, the softness I felt when I looked into the green of her eyes, or the comfort brought by simply holding her hand. She had been telling me for months that she couldn't explain why she adored me so or why she wanted me to be her first. She couldn't even tell me what it was that had sparked her feelings to flourish into more than just friendship. I knew without a doubt why I wanted her: She epitomized my every dream.

All the way to Sedona, we talked, we held hands, and we sang along to the radio. We appreciated the same scenery. We laughed a lot. Our belief that we were meant to be together was solidified. Our comfort with verbal interaction had long been established through endless phone calls. Now our comfort in each other's presence was without doubt.

Once we arrived in Sedona, we checked into our hotel. I would have been happy never leaving, but she wanted our first time to be just right. I thought maybe she was nervous since she'd never been with a woman before. I didn't want to rush her. I too wanted it to be just right.

We did some sightseeing, had dinner, and picked up some essentials, including bubble bath, grapes, Cool Whip, and wine. It was starting to get dark as we headed back to the hotel. She found the perfect spot and stopped the car. We were on a mountain overlooking the city. Just above was the biggest, brightest moon either of us had ever witnessed. She left the radio on while we walked around admiring the view. A favorite song of hers came on and she began to dance. I sat on the hood of the car and watched her move in the moonlight.

As I watched, I was aroused. Not only sexually, but emotionally. I loved the way she moved. She was sensual, confident, exuberant. She smiled as she danced. She looked, and I presume felt, as free as a bird flying in the night under the moon.

She approached me, still dancing. She stretched her hand out to me, encouraging me to dance with her. She moved her body enticingly. I blushed and slid off the hood of the car. Obviously more self-conscious than she, I simply leaned against the car, saying, "Go ahead. I like watching."

"It will be more fun if you dance with me."

How could I say no to her? I began moving to the music with her. Our bodies immediately fell into sync without conscious effort. She felt soft and warm. I could have melted right there. As our bodies rubbed together and our breasts touched, I could feel myself getting wet. Her blond hair shimmered in the moonlight, creating a glow around her face like the halo of an angel. I wanted to kiss her lips, full and rich with color. I touched the soft, smooth skin of her face and lightly rubbed her bottom lip with my thumb.

I wanted to go to the hotel room. I wanted to make love to this woman dancing in my arms. She turned her face toward me and kissed my ear. As if reading my mind, she whispered, "Let's go to the room."

I knew she felt the excitement, the electricity, too. I wondered if she wanted me as badly as I wanted her. My quick agreement to her suggestion brought laughter to her. I loved the sound of her laughter. She knew I wanted her. She was self-assured. I couldn't believe I was the one who was scared. She was the virgin, but I sure felt like one.

During the car ride she asked if I had ever had a massage—a real one. I was taken by surprise.

"No. I haven't."

"Good. I want to give you your first. When we get to the room, you get undressed."

She had my curiosity aroused, but also my nerves. As I spoke, my voice quivered. "You want me to just get undressed?"

She laughed a little at my surprise. "How else do you think you get a massage? Don't worry, I'll cover you with something."

I watched her, so confident and still so free. "I don't know about this." I was still nervous.

She looked at me with those beautiful green eyes and said, "It's me. It's just me."

How could I say no to her? So I did exactly what she wanted when we got to the hotel room. I took my clothes off and lay on the bed while she prepared. She came out of the bathroom with only a towel wrapped around her trim body. I wanted to take it off. I wanted to see her body. I reached for the towel and tugged at it a bit. She softly pushed my hand away. "No, not yet."

She was so sexy, even in the way she pushed me away. "Now turn over on your stomach. I'll lay the towel over you to keep you warm." I obeyed.

She climbed onto the bed and sat next to me. I watched her, but she told me to close my eyes and relax. Closing my eyes did anything but relax me, but once again, I granted every wish she had.

I felt the towel lift up from my shoulders. The air in the room was cool. As her hands lightly fell upon my shoulders, I got goose bumps all over. She giggled softly. I just lay there, her captive. Her hands squeezed at my tense shoulders, first softly, then more firmly. "You're supposed to be relaxing."

"Sorry."

"It's OK. I'll take care of it for you." She continued rubbing my shoulders and neck. It felt amazing. Her hands slowly began to go down my back. They were so soft, with just the right amount of pressure. As she rubbed over my shoulder blades, I was aroused by the feel of my breasts pushed up against the bed and by the idea of her touching my breasts. She smoothed the concoction she had developed all over my back. It felt like honey, warm and rich.

As she moved down my body, she used another towel to cover my upper back and shoulders. "This will keep you warm." I had other ideas about how to stay warm, but I was surrendering to her.

She began caressing my lower back and focused on the curve in it. "Ooh, I love this." She kept running her fingers over that curve.

"Why?"

"I don't know." As she touched me, she said, "It's just really nice." We both laughed a little bit. My laughter stopped abruptly as I felt her fingers on my buttocks. She caressed, squeezed, rubbed, and tickled all at once. I was self-conscious but thoroughly enjoying it.

"I like this too," she whispered as she bent down and kissed my right cheek lightly.

"Oh." The moan came out of me from nowhere, uncontrolled and unexpected. "Me too" barely came out of my mouth. I'm not even sure she heard it.

Slowly she moved farther down my body, uncovering my thighs. She rubbed the back of my thighs and then spread my legs ever so slightly. My head was swirling and getting hot. As she massaged my inner thighs, and I felt her fingers only inches from my pussy, I wanted her. I wanted her to touch my pussy. It was wet and hot and calling for her. I moaned a little, hoping she'd get the point. She tapped me on the back of the leg as she moved down to my calves and said, "That part comes later." I couldn't believe the self-control this woman had.

She massaged my calves and then my feet. She kissed each toe individually. Then she sat on the bed beside me again and said, "OK, turn over."

"What?"

"Turn over. A massage is not complete unless it's on both sides, so turn over." Seeing my hesitancy, she said, "Didn't it feel good?" She sounded so sweet.

"Well, yeah, but…"

"But nothing. It will feel better on the other side. I promise."

Slowly I turned over. I tried to hold onto the towel, but as I turned it fell, exposing my breasts. She just sat watching me. I quickly grabbed the towel and covered myself. She smiled at me.

I was flat on my back in front of her. She began with my shoulders again, but this time she worked her way out my arms and massaged my hands and fingers. The best thing about lying on my back was that I could watch her. I could see those lips that I adored as they softly kissed each of my fingers. I could watch her face as she touched and looked at almost every inch of my body.

She began rubbing my upper chest. She carefully avoided my breasts at first. Then she uncovered one half of my upper body, revealing my left breast. She rubbed down my side to my hipbone and then over to my stomach. Slowly she moved her hands upward toward my breast. When she got almost to it, she retreated back down my stomach.

Oh, what a tease, I thought to myself. I kept watching her as she looked at my exposed breast. She was intense. She was almost studying it. Her hands came back up my stomach toward my breast, and this time they didn't stop. A shot ran through me as her hand covered my breast. Again, a moan from some hidden cave inside came out of me with invitation only from her. She smiled. She enjoyed the power she held over my body.

She caressed my left breast only for a few seconds before covering that side of my body again and uncovering the right side. Again she teased me. She rubbed her hands up and down my side, stroking the side of my breast casually, lightly. She made me want her more with every stroke. Then she suddenly covered my breast with her hand. Again a moan, this time more quiet, more controlled.

She looked at my face. I was looking at her. "Don't hold it in. If it feels good, let me know." She gave me such total freedom. Freedom of expression, freedom to feel.

She covered my upper body again and uncovered my thighs. She massaged them tenderly and firmly. As she let her hands run up them, she touched the hair around my pussy. Again I felt a shot through my body and moaned uncontrollably. "You like that, huh?" She smiled at me.

"Oh, yeah." I couldn't help laughing. This was as new a situation for me as it was for her.

She finished massaging my legs and then sat on the bed beside me again. She put her hands on my face, rubbing my temples, the curve of my nose, my eyebrows, my lips. She was a master of the art of touch. I knew this for sure.

When she stopped she said, "OK. You're all done. How do you feel?"

I looked at her. "I feel wonderful. I'd like to try to make you feel this good."

She plopped facedown on the bed and said, "Go for it."

I let my towel fall as I sat up. I removed her towel and covered her legs and back. I started with her shoulders. I tried to mimic what she had done to me. As I rubbed, she moaned and said it felt good. I removed the towel from her back and massaged from her shoulders to her lower back. She too had a nice curve in her lower back. "Oh, I see what you mean." Her skin was so soft and so white. Its delicacy demanded gentleness.

As I moved down her back, I removed the towel from her buttocks. They too were soft and white. As I massaged them, I squeezed, tickled, and lightly ran my fingers along her crack. I bent down to kiss her buttock, and my breast rubbed against her thigh. I couldn't take it anymore. I had to have her.

I softly kissed her left buttock, then her right. I let my tongue touch each one lightly and then the top of her crack. I moved to her lower back and kissed the curve that she had so adored in me. I nuzzled my face into that curve. Her skin was soft and warm against my face. As I crawled up so that my body was even with hers, I kissed her back all along the way. Occasionally I let my tongue do the walking. I nuzzled my face into the back of her soft blond hair. I whispered, "I can't take it anymore. I want you so bad." With that I let the rest of my body lay down on top of hers.

We were definitely the perfect fit. My breasts were on her shoulder blades and my pelvic bone fit perfectly under her buttocks. I kissed her cheek softly. Her skin was like a feather. My lips had never touched anything like it. I pulled her hair away from her neck and kissed it softly. Then I opened my mouth and firmly took as much of her into it as I could. She tasted so good I wanted to eat her up.

She reached back to touch my hips. She was moaning from the feel of my body and kisses. I moved my body up and down. She moved with me. I continued kissing her neck and face. Her moaning grew louder. I wanted to see her face, so I turned her over. Again, I lay my body down on her. I had never felt such warmth and comfort. I put my right leg between her legs and I could feel the heat coming from her pussy.

"You are so beautiful," I couldn't help telling her. The words did not do justice. I looked at her lips, and I longed for them. I slowly and gently brought my lips to hers. They felt just as soft as they looked. At first we kissed tenderly, then more firmly. I opened my mouth and let my tongue enter hers. The kiss became a longing one. Our tongues fondled each other, they played, they explored. We moaned and our bodies moved closer together and became in rhythm with each other.

I kissed her face, every inch of it. I adored her beautiful face. I treasured it. I kissed her eyelids and her nose. I kissed her chin and just beneath it. I kissed her neck, down the center, then around to her right side. I held her head in my hand. I continued moving my body. Our pelvic bones were rubbing. She arched her back just a bit as I let my tongue run along the center of her neck from bottom to top. Then I looked her in the eyes and repeated, "You are beautiful."

She smiled and touched my face. "You are the beautiful one, my angel."

I kissed her lips, delving my tongue into her mouth. Her tongue met mine and sent sparks through my head. The situation, the kiss, and the warmth of her body were all perfect. She was perfect.

I wanted to explore her body, so I moved from kissing her mouth down to kissing the left side of her neck. I kept my body tight to hers and inched my way down her neck, past her shoulder and collarbone, kissing them along the way, to the curve of her breast. I kissed all around it, slowly, with each round getting closer and closer to her nipple. I kept my eyes open. I liked looking at her. She was watching me kissing her breast. Her nipple was hard with excitement. I stopped just beneath it. Her nipple was the prettiest shade of pink I had ever seen. I let my tongue touch it softly. She gasped as if the breath had been taken from her. The sound brought a smile to my face. I slowly covered her nipple with my entire mouth. I sucked it softly. I tickled it with my tongue, and I kissed it with passion. She moaned and closed her eyes as I began my path farther down her body.

I kissed down her rib cage to her stomach. It was soft. I loved the curve of her waist just above her hips. I caressed her hips and thighs with my hands. I explored her navel and the curves of her hips. I kissed a path from her hipbone to her inner thigh. I could smell her ripe, wet pussy ready for my tongue. I loved that smell.

I slowly turned my face toward her pussy. I looked at her. She was red and juicy with anticipation. I let my nose brush against her hair. I heard the breath come hard out of her. I touched her softly with my tongue. I started with the sides, moving up and down, then came over to her clitoris. I touched it lightly and gently and then wandered down to her vagina. She moaned, "Oh, baby," as my tongue trailed down her pussy. She was the sweetest thing I'd ever tasted. As she moaned, I touched her with more pressure. I let my whole tongue touch her pussy and move up and down. I took her juices into my mouth. I moved up and down and all around as her breathing and moaning became increasingly faster. Her body began moving with excitement, and I followed her rhythm. I closed my mouth over her pussy and sucked on her clitoris. I explored every part of her pussy, growing more and more wet myself.

I moved farther down to her vagina again. She was open and ready for me. I let my tongue enter into her. It was even sweeter than the outside. She moaned from pleasure. Her legs came around my neck, and she grabbed my hands. She held tight to my hands as my tongue went in and out of her wet vagina. She began moaning, "Yes. Yeah, baby." Her body was moving along with my tongue. Suddenly I felt the tremors inside her vagina. I had never felt anything like it. It seemed a miracle created by my tongue. Her vagina was tremulous for what must have been a full minute, and then it released. I felt the last tremor come down the canal, followed by a rush of juice. As she came her vagina tightened and pushed my tongue out. She let out a shriek. She was mine, mine completely.

She reached for my head and pulled me on top of her. I kissed her neck and wiped her pussy juices from my mouth. I lay on top of her for a few minutes while she enjoyed the moment. "I love your pussy," I couldn't help telling her.

She rolled me over onto my back and said, "Let me get to know yours." She kissed my neck and then my breast. I was ready for her. I almost came just from the feel of her kissing my breast. She rubbed her hands along my stomach and thighs and then began her descent. She kissed my body along her way. Once she arrived at my pussy, she pulled my legs apart and settled in between them. She opened my pussy with her hands and looked at me. She said, "You are so wet."

I was embarrassed, but so excited it didn't matter. I held her head in my hand as she came toward my ripe pussy. The breath rushed out of me as a shot of fire ran up my body when her tongue touched me. I grew increasingly wetter. She let out a moan as her tongue delved deeper into the folds of my wet forest. I knew I had never felt such joy. My head felt as if it would fly off my body at any moment. She moved her tongue softly around my pussy, exploring every crevice. I held her hand and her head, and suddenly my body began moving up and down. I felt like I had been invaded by an unfamiliar force. She licked me harder and faster. I moaned and squeezed her hand tightly. No control was left in me. My head was swirling, and I was coming. I felt a tremor run from my vagina all the way up my body. I came with her mouth still on me. My orgasm rushed me with such force and emotion that I began to cry. She had crawled back on top of me and was holding me when the tears started.

"Why are you crying?"

Through my tears I looked at her. I held on tight and said, "Because I've never felt this way before. Because you are perfect."

We lay there together, naked, holding each other until we fell asleep. The next morning I awoke and looked over at her beautiful face. She was sleeping soundly, but with thoughts of the night before, I couldn't resist waking her. I leaned over and kissed her face, every inch of it.

That was five years ago. This morning when I woke I looked over at that same beautiful face sleeping next to me, and I couldn't resist waking her. I leaned over and kissed her face, every inch of it.

My Side of the Bed

by Veronica Holtz

I have never in my most preposterous fantasies ever desired a virgin. They may be anxious, but not passionate; desirous, but lacking style and finesse—the qualities that bring the depth of living and female carnality to fiery consummation. That's why I decided to pursue Trish, the community poster dyke. With dark hair and lustrous brown eyes, she strolled down the streets like a mayoral candidate, greeting every lesbian she passed with a kiss. And this was quite a feat in a big East Coast city.

I tested the waters by suggesting we take in a movie. It had been a particularly stressful work day, and Trish welcomed the chance to relax. There was no mention of lovers, roommates, or any circle of friends with whom she had to confer. Then again, I had purposely asked her out on a Monday so that any conflict in plans would be remote.

I intended to put my arm around her exactly 21 minutes into the movie. This, by my calculation, was the normal amount of time it took to place all sodas and snacks under the seat and settle in comfortably without any latecomer disturbance. But just as the opening credits dissolved into the screen, I felt her arm slip around me. The gesture was warm and easy; it was a confirmation that we had a good beginning.

Afterward, as we walked to my car while conversing, Trish treated me to a private concert of tonal flirtation. She had a casual and open manner of speaking, which came across as a hedonistic melody to me. Some lesbians like legs, some lust after breasts; a fluffy pillow of a woman; a thin and lengthy feminine outline. Being an audiophile, I sensed Trish's deep, succulent voice sending shivers down to my G spot.

Before it became embarrassingly late, she pecked me sweetly on the cheek and said, "Call me when you get home, so I know you've arrived safely."

This was enough for me to floor it across town and burst through the door of my apartment in record time. I waited a minute for my blood pressure to settle and decided that a short, pleasant good night call was the most appropriate next step.

This strategy may have been sincere, but when she answered the phone, my Achilles' ear bloated to its height of vulnerability. Any resolve to cut the conversation short disappeared when she offered to recite something she had written. It could have been homely, quaint, or otherwise. Anything. I didn't care. I just wanted to hear her voice a bit longer.

It was a tale of two women in a crowded four-star restaurant, groping underneath the white tablecloth for a dropped spoon. Coming in contact with a bare, feminine leg, one woman slowly made her way upward, massaging the other's knee while the waitress took their order. Pushing into a softer thigh, she reached the moist entrance of longing. Eyes locked across a candlelit table; asking; daring her to go inside. She stoked the flames of a famished heat and watched as her woman slowly singed the edge of her chair with the deep clutch of fingernails. Stroke after stroke became burning pleasure, and her lover swallowed her cries like a secret banquet until she finally erupt-ed underneath. Emptied. Satisfied. The couple dismissed dessert as a pale redundancy.

The story held me in wet silence. I wasn't sure whether I should light a cigarette or hop into my car and race to Trish's doorstep back across town.

"Are you there?" asked that silken voice through the phone line.

I still couldn't answer.

"Hold on," she said. In the background, I heard the distinct voice of another woman. Though Trish muffled the phone receiver first, raised voices filled my ears, followed by the slam of a door.

"Sorry about that," she said congenially into the phone. "That was just a friend who comes in once in a while to use the shower before work. I've been meaning to get the key back from her."

I glanced at my watch. Just a friend at 2 in the morning? Thrust into girlfriend alert, I said a very quick good bye and decided she was one of smoothest, most unabashed polylover lesbians I had ever met.

Perfect, I decided. I had been accepted at a university in San Francisco and already knew that my future would be on the West Coast. With only a few months before my departure, a last noncommitted fling with a beautiful woman seemed the perfect send-off.

That's why, when we were at my apartment the next Saturday, I couldn't stop myself. Her closeness was too appealing. The smell of her hair too magnetic. I kissed her on the back of her neck. Sensing no resistance, I brought her face around to meet my lips and pulled her down to the carpet. In one moment, I climbed on top of her, pressing my body against a womanly heat in constant motion.

I didn't recognize it as evasive maneuvering until Trish dashed sideways like a frightened crab, leaving me with carpet fibers on my lips. When I looked up, she sat balled-up on the far side of the room, clutching her knees. The only other time I had seen such a sight was when I accidentally held a hetero female's hand a bit too long, and she reacted as if I had LESBIAN LUST HOUND tattooed across me. I deliberately slid in the opposite direction to ease the petrified look on Trish's face and waited for an explanation.

"I cut myself shaving," she offered. "I didn't want you to see the scar."

She must have realized this explanation was insufficient; after a moment she blurted out, "I've never done this before."

"You have someone?" I declared more than asked.

"No," she answered feebly.

"That time of the month?" Not that it mattered to me. I had my red wings.

"No."

The embarrassed tone in her voice made me suspicious. "That was your story you read to me over the phone the other night, wasn't it?"

"Yes. Well…it doesn't mean I actually ever…I read a lot of lesbian anthologies."

The implication was becoming all too clear. "You kiss every damned lesbian you meet."

"Just a friendly peck on the cheek. That's all."

"You give women the keys to your apartment."

"Just one. She works late at night and needs to use the shower. She has her own lover."

I pulled a lingering piece of carpet out of my mouth and stood up. Any desire of mine had disappeared. My sole thought was to rid Trish's face of the torment that now pervaded it. I suggested we go get something to eat.

Her relief turned to calm during the appetizer. When the main course was served, she became a friendly resemblance of herself. By dessert, Trish was positively enchanting. This was enough to sustain me, but evidently not her. Only a few days later, she gave me the sweetest gaze, while she uttered the most horrific phrase ever invented by virgins: "Teach me."

I stopped dead in my tracks. In my view one can be trained to ride a bike, instructed to drive, or educated in any number of subjects. But it was sacrilegious to reduce a natural instinct to a mere learned science.

It wasn't that I was totally unsympathetic to virgins. I had been one once; throwing myself, heart and soul, at Marta. Lapping after her every whim. My paradise had quickly become her boredom. And I never forgave her for dumping me.

If Trish hadn't looked so inviting, I could have easily passed up the opportunity. As an experiment, I walked over to her and brought my lips within range. She immediately responded by opening her mouth into a tense, wide circle. Wiggling her jaw out of its starkly hinged position, I gave her a kiss and stepped back to observe her reaction. She smiled back with the excited anticipation of a freshman moving into her first dormitory.

I had my doubts when she took two hours to pack her overnight bag. I hesitated when she limited our first weeks of romance to hit-and-run nibbles disguised as kisses. My reluctance grew when she consulted her lesbian sex guides to make sure I wasn't overstepping the bounds of proper massaging. And I gave up any thought of morning bliss when I woke to find her clinging to the far edge of my bed. But most frustrating was when I dared to move my hands close to her wonderful breasts.

"I don't let anyone touch those," she declared, flicking my fingertips off to the side.

Now this bordered on blasphemy. She was taking away my natural habitat. Surely, there had to be some lesbian law against this. Confronted by an impenetrable mental chastity belt, I was tempted to buy a lesbian sex guide of my own to prove to Trish that this was permissible. I kept reassuring myself that this was just a phase. Yet even when she became comfortable enough to float leisurely about the apartment in the buff, she did not equate her unmerciful display with any weakening of the ground rules.

I felt like the winner of an all-expenses-paid trip to the Caribbean isle of dyke caught in a freak snowstorm. It was inconceivable to me how a lesbian could touch a woman without every pore becoming a heated rod of explosive sensitivity. Trish must have sensed my poise waning. For just as I had lost all hope of ever moving beyond the outskirts of the platonic, she offered her whole body to me. I gazed at her in disbelief, aware that she had never let anyone "down there," as she put it. To convince me, she lay herself out like a sacrificial lamb and pulled me close.

I knew I had to concentrate on gentle self-control, something I had always previously disposed of whenever lovemaking started. I began to massage the back of her neck, the one small fleshy spot I was absolutely sure of being sensual. Hearing a corresponding murmur, I kissed my way down her smooth, untouched skin; caressed her soft, candy-scented flesh. She became a jewel, rare and precious, slowly melting into my lips. I coaxed her over and pushed my body into the flame. The intensity was overwhelming.

Her nakedness took hold of my breath. Like the devil dancing across my carnal dreams, I greedily demanded her mouth and took possession of her womanly frame. The mesh of her nipples against mine drove my hand to her breast. But she tensed, with a quick, rigid whimper that forced me to retreat.

Denied, my desires spun back on themselves. I felt an inner tidal wave that threatened to crush me unless I could find relief. Selfish. Unrelenting heat. I struggled to slow my touch; rubbed lower, gripped longer, until she threw open her physical being. Pressing myself between her legs, my tongue reached out like a ravenous divining rod in search of a mountain spring. Each shake of Trish's giving body drove me deeper, until I felt us both moving in mutual pleasure. I rode her to and fro; absorbed her lush moans into my body and gave them back again. A liquid wildness was unleashed. Raw and flavorful. It splashed across my face; swept through every nerve. Spiraling past each urgent breath, this pitiless torrent flared inside until a prolonged gasp held Trish in mid motion. Her body jerked to its fullest height and yielded to its completion.

We had passed a milestone. We both knew it and lay in silent celebration of the moment. She was happy. I was relieved. The worst was over...or so I thought. Trish spread out over the middle of the bed and purred the words that replaced "teach me" as the champion of horrific phrases.

"I love you."

Once spoken, that all-consuming declaration instantly became a lethal roadblock I would have to maneuver around before reaching any sensual destination. My face buckled in on itself. Her tone seemed to denote my obligation rather than hers, even though I felt like an extracurricular part of the emotion.

After all my cajoling and patience these past weeks, suddenly her voice didn't sound sultry anymore.

"You don't have to say anything."

I didn't. It had never been my style to mislead anyone for the convenience of the moment. I went out to the living room and immediately chain-smoked three cigarettes. I thought again of Marta. And it occurred to me to phone her, wherever she was now, to tell her that I finally understood.

I stubbed my cigarette out in the ashtray and returned to the scene of the crime. Slipping under the portion of blanket that had been left for me, I clung to the far edge of my side of the bed.

Seduction of An Attorney

by Bleau Diamond

If I concentrate on the first feeling, the first vibration, I can tell you what I felt and you would understand. I am a paralegal and had just started working at this particular law firm in Phoenix.

The first time I saw her, she was walking down the hall at least 20 feet away from me. She looked stunning in her dark blue skirted suit and high heels. Her brown hair was cut short, almost tomboyish. I felt an immediate attraction to her, which was a combination of physical attraction and spiritual attraction. It was as if a huge "attraction vibration" hit me like a brick, and I literally fell to one side of the hall. I said softly out loud, "I have got to get a closer look." She had a confident walk that must have come from getting what she wanted. And how could she not get what she wanted—she looked gorgeous.

So I went down the other hall to find her, but she was gone. Disappeared. My heart was racing, and my palms felt moist. I went to the ladies' room to look for her, but she wasn't there either. I threw some water on my face to cool me off and started thinking about who she could be. I knew she wasn't an attorney with the firm, because I was introduced to all the attorneys when I started. Maybe she was a client or someone in for a deposition.

I left the ladies' room and walked down the hallway, still looking, feeling obsessed with my mission to find her. Having no luck, I went down the elevator looking for her, but she wasn't in the lobby. She was nowhere to be found.

I pondered at what effect seeing her had on me. She startled me with her beauty, sophistication, and style. But there was so much more. I felt a real psychic connection to her.

I saw her again after two weeks when I was walking in the hallway. I practically ran right into her because I was taking a corner too wide. She just looked at me and smiled. I introduced myself to her, and she said her name was Susan. I later asked a coworker who she was and found out that she was a newly hired attorney. The first day I saw her must have been her interview day. That made sense. Realizing that she was now a permanent fixture of the firm made me nervous and uncomfortable. I felt something for her. And I felt alone in my desire. That made me more uncomfortable. Throughout the next couple months she said hello to me when we passed in the hallway, but generally she was aloof with me and kept me at a distance. Maybe I made her as uncomfortable as she made me.

Since Susan avoided talking to me, she sent me E-mail messages and interoffice memorandums. I tried to get to know her secretary so I could maybe learn something about her—and I learned more than I wanted. She was engaged to be married. I was surprised. She seemed like she could be gay. Or maybe I just wished she were.

One day I went into her office to deliver something to her, and her secretary said she was out at a meeting. So I dropped off the information on her chair and casually looked around her office. I noticed her CD collection, her neat and tidy office, her diplomas, and then I saw pictures of her in Hawaii, on the beach, with a man, presumably her fiancé. While in her office I could smell her perfume, even though she had been out of her office for hours. I took a deep breath and fantasized that she and I were in that photo. I imagined her perfume in all the right places, a dab between her breasts and a dab just below her belly button. I felt a little dizzy from my fantasy and from the perfume, and so I left to ponder what she was like on vacation and what she was like in bed.

Trying to seduce an attorney is not an easy task. They have their guard up at all times and are usually so stoic that they don't even notice when you are making a pass at them. I knew I would have to meet her after work in order to get her full attention.

One day I was standing at her secretary's desk, talking about hiking, when Susan came out of her office and joined in the conversation.

"I like to hike too," Susan said. She beamed an air of confidence.

"Really?" I said, in a questioning tone. I knew she worked out because she was in exquisite shape, but I had no idea she liked the outdoors. I continued, "And where do you hike, Susan?" I was trying not to give her any eye contact. Being that close to her made me nervous, and I was afraid she would be able to read my eyes and see how lustful I was feeling toward her. So I kept my eyes moving around, but eventually my eyes stopped right on her breasts. She had a long strand of pearls around her neck and she was fidgeting with them. It just so happened that her breasts and the pearls were located in the same place. I could not help that my eyes were following her movements. She caught me looking at her breasts. I could not move my eyes quick enough. *Damn,* I thought. But she just continued talking, as if she was kind of intrigued by my boldness.

"Oh, I hike Squaw Peak or Camelback Mountain, and there are a few other mountains around Phoenix. And whenever I go out of town, I like to find a place to hike." As Susan was speaking, she was twisting her necklace so tight I thought the pearls were going to fall off. She was totally unconscious of her nervous behavior. But I wasn't.

I looked at her and realized my desire for her was stronger than ever. And for the first time, I felt an air of sexual energy coming from her that I had never felt before.

She looked radiant. Her brown eyes were full of wonder and excitement. I didn't know she liked to hike. I was so happy she came out of her office to be included in the conversation.

Her secretary tried to make a few comments, but Susan and I were in a rhythm, totally in sync, talking about hiking, and no spectators were allowed to join in. I am sure her secretary felt a little left out, but she did not leave. I did not want her to leave. I needed her there so the tension between Susan and me did not escalate. Her secretary was like a buffer. As long as she stood there with us, everything looked innocent. And in a law firm, appearances are everything.

Susan said, "Let me know when you want to go hiking." I said OK and walked back to my office. *I cannot believe she wants to go for a hike with me. She cannot be serious. She is opening the door as wide as she can, letting me in, telling me she is interested in spending time with me.* I was surprised.

That night when I was leaving work, I stopped by the door to her office and said good night. She said, "Are we going hiking soon?"

"Yes," I answered. "We can go this week if you want to." Susan smiled at me like I had just given her a box of chocolates. Her eyes, which usually looked so mysterious, now looked very calm and inviting.

"Good," she replied. Then she added, "Why not tomorrow after work?"

I was stunned.

I thought about how fat I felt, how I would need to shave my legs, how my car needed to be washed, and I just felt rushed and a little lost. "OK, after work is good," I heard myself say before I could catch myself.

"Great, I'm looking forward to this," she said with an anxious look on her face.

The next day I could barely work. I sat at my desk and stared at the wall. For months I had been attracted to this woman, and now she wanted to spend time with me after work, hiking, alone, just the two of us. I couldn't eat my lunch. And I had to force myself to eat my protein bar before I left for the hike because I was afraid of running out of energy.

We met at South Mountain, which is the world's largest municipal park, located in South Phoenix. I arrived before her and wrote in my journal until she arrived. I was incredibly nervous and excited, and when she pulled up in her sports car, I wanted to climb in and kiss her. But I showed restraint and greeted her with a hello. She seemed nervous too and greeted me with "Let's go."

We had decided to take the National Trail to Hidden Valley. The trail is moderately difficult and also can be isolated in the evening. We started on the flat trail that winds down an unpaved road for a mile before heading up the mountain. The road was pretty busy with runners and bike riders, but I noticed that once we started up the mountain, no one was on the trail behind us, and we didn't pass anyone for the next hour. As we hiked, we talked casually about ourselves, our likes and dislikes, and about work. Sometimes we hiked in silence, due to the elevation and the intensity of our pace. I felt like we were competing, in a sexual way. Who would show they had the most endurance and strength? It was typical of an attorney and a paralegal to have that competitive spirit.

I was ahead a couple paces when she said, "I need to ask you something."

"OK, go ahead," I answered, as we arrived at Hidden Valley. Hidden Valley is an area of South Mountain that is hidden from other trails and other hikers. It is a really secluded spot, and I had picked it as our spot to watch the sun set. We entered the valley and continued hiking up through a ravine. I was patiently waiting for her question, which I thought came at a great time. We were off the trail and in the valley, and her question seemed to need the intimacy that our hike had led us to.

"When did you first know you were gay?" I stopped, turned around, and looked at her. I had not discussed anything personal with her, so I was curious how she had gotten to that conclusion. In fact, I thought my long blond hair hid my identity at work pretty well. I even wore dresses to work, which I thought was going one step too far.

"When I was 17," I answered. "I was taking a photography class and my girlfriend came over, and we kissed while we were developing photos in my bedroom, which was also our darkroom." I looked at her for reassurance and continued, "I knew then that I loved women." I waited for her response.

She had a familiar look on her face, that same look she gave me at work on occasions when no one else was around and we were talking. She would look at me as if she were looking into my soul.

She didn't answer me, and I felt an uncomfortable silence, so I continued walking up through the valley, hearing her a couple steps behind me. We came to a place where we had to crawl through a small opening or try to jump over a huge boulder. Since I had hiked through Hidden Valley before, I knew the only reasonable choice was to crawl through the small, cavelike opening.

"We have to crawl through here," I told her, motioning to the opening.

"This is our only option?" she asked.

"Yes," I said. "It only looks difficult. You'll need to take off your pack and throw it through the opening, and lie on your back and slide sideways through. I've done it before. You can do it."

"OK," she said, "do you want to help me get my pack off?"

Do I ever, I said to myself. I walked over to her, her back to me, and I reached around her waist and unsnapped the belt to her pack. I was close enough to taste the sweat off her neck. As I pulled the pack to the side she turned around and faced me.

"Kiss me like you kissed her, the girl in your darkroom," she said. I looked into her eyes and saw incredible passion rising. She was trembling. I reached up with both hands and touched her face and placed my lips on hers. She was explosive. Her lips opened and closed, pulling my tongue in and out, sucking on my tongue, kissing my lips, and kissing my face, my cheeks, my neck. She started for my breasts, when I stopped her.

"Let's sit in the crevice," I suggested.

"OK," she agreed. Luckily I carry an emergency blanket as part of my first aid kit. I quickly opened my pack, opened the silver blanket, and laid the blanket out on the rocks inside the crevice. Susan lay down on the blanket and motioned for me. I took a moment to look at her. She looked incredible and I wondered how long she had desired me. She was not at all what I thought she would be like. I thought I would have to seduce her. I don't know how to seduce a woman. I have always been seduced. And the times that I needed to seduce a woman, I don't think I ever really said anything, I just did it.

I lay on top of her, fully clothed, and started kissing her, like I kissed a woman when I was 17, the kind of kiss that is endless and exploring, and gentle and aggressive.

She said she wanted for me to talk to her and I thought, *I will talk to her and seduce her by believing that she has fantasized about me before, and therefore, in her mind she has already made love with me.*

I began, "Have you ever been with a woman? No, I don't have to ask you that. I know the answer. You have. Tell me, what was it like when you unbuttoned her pants, when you reached in to feel her wetness. Did you like that?" Susan started to squirm, and wrapped her legs around my leg and pulled me in closer to her. I didn't know for sure if she had been with a woman before, but I thought she probably had fantasized about women, and maybe even me, so I continued.

"Tell me what it was like when you unbuttoned her shirt, and you kissed her breasts. And you wanted to unbutton her bra but you were too scared. Tell me, did she unbutton it for you and let you suck her nipples?" Susan was breathing out of control, pulling at my purple polo shirt. She pulled my shirt off and started kissing my breasts. When I unhooked my bra, she pulled one nipple at a time into her hot mouth, and sucked until I almost reached orgasm.

I continued, "Tell me about when you kissed and licked her neck. Did she moan, did she talk to you, and did she tell you what she likes?" Susan stopped sucking on my breasts and moved to my neck. By now she was sucking on my neck so hard I thought she was going to leave marks.

I continued, "Did she like it? Did you like it? Tell me. Did she ask you what you like, and what did you tell her? What do you like, Susan, do you like it soft and slow or fast and hard? Did you like her whispers or do you like the silence? Did you touch her soul or just her body? Tell me, did you come? Twice? Three times?" Susan unbuttoned my Levi's shorts and almost had her hand inside my underwear when I continued.

"Did you want her again? What did she look like? Did she look like me?" Susan pushed into my jeans shorts, and I felt her finger inside me. She was kissing me everywhere, on my lips, my neck, my breasts. I reached down and pulled my shorts to my knees and pulled her elastic-waistband shorts down. We were naked enough.

I sucked on her breasts, pulling one nipple in my mouth and running my tongue over the tip, circling and sucking. My other hand was holding me up because the rocks were definitely not soft.

I felt her finger gliding in and out of me, slow and deliberate. I pushed up to meet her thrusts into me and felt a little lightheaded from the hike, from the passion, and from the newness of the experience. She whispered in my ear, "Fuck me." I gently thrust my finger in her and noticed she was so wet, so open, I added another finger. She moaned as we were fucking each other in unison. I felt her swell inside while my fingers delved deeper and pulled back just before exiting her wetness. My thumb massaged her clit as my fingers moved in and out. I wanted to pump her forever, but her clit was ready and I was ready, and we came together in an explosively loud movement.

Afterward I laid next to her, and she looked at me and started to tell me about her desire for me and how she liked me when she first saw me but didn't know what to do, how to get close to me. She recited some sexual harassment stuff about her being the attorney and how she had to wait for me to make my move on her. She told me how my perfume drove her crazy, and I told her I loved smelling her essence in my office, in the hallway, and everywhere that she had been. She beamed hearing that I was so attracted to her. I guess I really had hid my desire for her as she had hid hers for me. She said she finally answered her questions of why do I arouse her and why do I make her smile and laugh and feel so good. She knows now.

Susan looked into my eyes and said, "You are wonderful. I love you," and she giggled.

"You are wonderful too," I said and placed a kiss softly on her lips.

We got up and out of the crevice in time to see the sun set, and we hiked back to our cars. I looked at her and she said, "So what do I do now that I am in love?"

I smiled and said, "Same time tomorrow?"

She laughed and said, "Yes, that would be great."

I saw her for several months. We hiked after work and on weekends. We took trips to Sedona and Flagstaff. Sometimes we hiked and sometimes we stayed in our room and talked. On those days, she would ask me to repeat "The Story," which was the words of seduction I had used at Hidden Valley. She just loved for me to talk to her when I seduced her. I enjoyed my days with her until she got transferred to another law firm and moved to another state.

Today, when I hike alone through Hidden Valley, I always think of her. She never did get married.

Rising East

by Fletcher Mergler

The road that cut through Setauket and headed east toward Port Jefferson gave a traveler a straight shot to the Elk. It was a beautiful road, lined with cottages and covered by a canopy of leafy maples. During the summer months the scent of honeysuckle filled the air. Even on rainy days people would ride with their windows wide open just to catch the fragrance. And riding the road made one feel unfettered because of its proximity to the bay. Even on the bitterest of winter days, completely encased under layers of clothing and with no thought but to survive the stinging cold, one would feel alive from the smell of the salt air whipped inland by the wind.

It was on such a wintry day that I stopped my car at the last intersection before Port Jeff and, casting back, was glad to remember what a favorite spot of mine this had been. It's from the memory of this vantage point—that is, being able to see the Elk Inn—that I revisit this story.

Having peaked in popularity with the townsfolk some ten years before I came to Setauket, the Elk Inn had since declined. Taken over by students, the place featured during the day a handful of bleary-eyed patrons who, surrounded by a half-dozen empty coffee cups, would sit for hours over plates of congealing eggs and toast or thick burgers with grilled onions, thinly sliced fried potatoes, and garlic pickles. At night, though, it took on a different life as a favored haunt that bustled with the animated hum and rattle of student talk and clinking bottles. With its dim lighting, dark paneling, and cloth chairs, we could feel that we were more than simple students from a public university—that we were more brilliant and worldly than the people who knew us could ever suspect.

One night a new student joined the crowd I often ate with. She had just entered her first year at the university and so was a few years younger than I, but her beauty and reserve made me and others notice her immediately. She was slender, with thick auburn hair that fell in waves to her shoulders, and large blue-green eyes that looked out, somewhat warily, from under naturally dark lashes. She seemed to keep her distance from the crowd, but carried herself with a confidence and grace that belied her shyness. She was rumored to be taking a load of biochemistry courses. Her mother, I learned later, was English and had died of cancer a year earlier; her father, a businessman; and her older brother, a medical student at NYU, lived in Brooklyn. This was her first time living away from home. My interest was piqued and, watching her across the table, I felt a little protective of her.

On this particular night more snow had fallen, so shortly after dinner I announced that I was leaving to dig out my car. Once outside I began as I always did, with the fun stuff first. In this case that meant kicking the frozen snow from the wheel wells. As large chunks of dirty snow flew to pieces with each kick from my boot, I turned to find this young woman standing behind me.

"May I help?" she asked. Feeling appreciative and flattered, I smiled and nodded. As we dug a path out of the icy snow around the car, I couldn't help looking at her. She seemed intent on getting more snow cleared than I did; she looked like a worker determined to complete an assignment.

"I've never seen this much snow. I mean, it rarely snows this much in the city," she said quietly while brushing off the back window.

"That's quite possible. I think cities are generally warmer than the outlying areas." I too kept busy.

"Hey!" she said suddenly, and I looked up to glimpse her raised arm tossing snow at me. I turned to let it strike my shoulder and in the same motion scooped a handful of wet snow and charged toward her. She didn't try very hard to get away. I caught her as she tried vainly to open the door, pinned her lightly against the car, and held her arms down to her sides. Pressing against her slight form, with my leg between hers and our breath merging in the cold night air, I felt my instinct, like a faint sexual throb, urging me to subdue her. Instead, after a moment we laughed and slid down with our backs against the car. She took a piece of ice from my glove and held it up to my lips. For a few moments we didn't speak but sat close together on the snow bank next to my car.

"Come on," I broke the silence, "can I buy you an Irish coffee at Gertrude's?"

It occurred to me too late that she might be too young to be allowed in, and I was right. We walked to the bar, which was packed, only to be turned away when my young friend showed her identification to the bouncer. Embarrassed and apologetic, she seemed as much a child as an adult.

I waved it off and said, "Not to be discouraged. Let's go somewhere else." Pretending that we each needed the other for balance, we held tight to each other, arm in arm, and carefully negotiated the sidewalks back to my car.

She stood next to me and watched as I unlocked and opened her door. Before I could move away, she reached out and drew my hand to her mouth and kissed my fingers. "Thank you. I didn't think they'd ask me for ID."

She looked delicate in the night.

"May I ask how old you are?"

"Eighteen. And you?"

"Twenty-one."

She continued the conversation when we got in the car. "I've heard a lot about you. I think most people feel intimidated by you. You seem serious." She went on. "That group of women from the school does nothing but talk about you."

"Oh. really?" I feigned surprise. "Yes, I know…I think it's my eyebrows. They make me look more serious than I am, I guess—or maybe it's the other way around—first I was serious and then my eyebrows grew this way."

"Eyebrows or not, from what I've heard, you are the stuff that scandal is made of," she said, looking directly at me, and my eyebrows began to itch.

"If you believe that, why are you here?" I asked, feeling some discomfort.

"Because I believe hardly anything I hear. Who I see now is very different from what people say you are."

"What do they say?" a sort of morbid curiosity compelled me to ask.

"Well, one woman said you were supercilious, and another called you self-centered. I heard that you were banned from a consciousness-raising group. And someone else said that one woman so desperately wanted to meet you that she got tearing drunk at a campus dance and did a striptease for you in front of half the gay community."

"Sure you're not leaving anything out, just to spare my feelings?" I asked, half smiling, when she finally paused.

"Only one. The story about the seminude photos of you and a girlfriend taken surreptitiously by a photographer from the women's center."

"Yes, that was a shocker. I should've sued her ass..." I looked into her eyes. "Will you come have tea with me despite these stories?"

As we drove to my apartment, I felt a pleasure that rarely graced my heart. For this night, at least, this small, quiet woman beside me was my asylum—she would keep from my door the dark of loneliness, the chaos of the stories that swirled about me. Perhaps she sought sanctuary too. I wanted to be strong for her, to protect her.

Settled in my small front room, surrounded by stacks of books and half-written papers, we sat on the couch, facing each other with our feet touching, and talked for most of the night. Her blouse, open at her neck, draped loosely around her shoulders. Candlelight bathed her neck and breasts. Her long body—the body of a dancer—was soft and supple. Despite her innocence and reserve, I felt an erotic tension from her. And I could feel the raw edge of my own emotions growing, pulsing in my heart, my arms, my legs, a sexual electricity that tensed and vibrated through my body.

During a lull in the conversation, when our tea had grown cold and the candle had gone out, we sat for a moment in the snowy light of the streetlamp. Then she said quietly, "You asked me earlier what I was interested in, and I told you a number of things—do you remember?"

"Yes, of course I remember."

"Well, one of the things I've become interested in lately is you." She leaned forward and kissed me very gently. Her soft lips tasted like chamomile, and her blouse held the faint but spicy scent of patchouli. She trembled as I lightly stroked the back of her neck. I imagined making love to her, and with that the taut thread of my control began to unravel.

"Have you ever made love with a woman?" I asked.

"No." She paused. "Neither a man nor a woman. I've never found the right one."

I don't know whether I thought I could show her I was the right one, or that women were the right choice for her; but some unspoken question needed to be answered. I leaned forward and, with my hand gently under her chin, brought her face to mine. She closed her eyes and I felt her mouth give way under mine.

I intended to go slow so as not to overwhelm her, but her breathing quickened, and I felt her press her breasts to me. She wrapped her arms around me and pulled me to her. I adjusted my weight and laid her down gently on the couch. She hardly let my mouth leave hers, sucking my tongue, her hips rising to find mine, little moans escaping between breaths.

I was hot already but wouldn't come until I'd given her pleasure. I slipped my warm hands up her shirt to caress her breasts. She put her head back and whispered, almost inaudibly, "Harder." I watched her upturned face as I squeezed one small firm handful and took the other nipple between my thumb and finger to twist gently. She arched her back.

That was all I needed to know. I took the nipple in my mouth and pulled, swirled, tugged, sucked, and nibbled, while pinching and massaging the other. Her hips were gyrating under me, almost rocking me off, and her breaths were long and gasping. Her hands ran the length of my back and clutched my ass, her lean muscled legs entwined around mine and held me to her. Her whole body begged, racked with wanting. With my mouth still on her breast and my eyes raised to her face, I slid my hand slowly, tauntingly, down her smooth flat belly and—needlessly—felt her crotch. Her jeans were soaked. I crept my fingers back up and undid the fly one button at a time. She shivered involuntarily when my hand slipped beneath her waistband to the tender flesh of her lower belly.

Her hair was damp. I imagined its salty taste as I slipped her jeans from her hips. I nuzzled the soft skin of her belly, breathing in her musk and sweat, and slowly inched my way down to taste her liquid gold. I could feel the heat between her legs and struggled to pace myself. My tongue designed moist traces around her belly and thighs, promises of what I was about to do. She tried in vain to stifle her moans, while at the same time thrusting her pelvis up to meet my mouth.

With my tongue I lightly outlined her swollen lips before pushing her legs apart and parting her labia to seek out her hard clit. My face was quickly bathed in her juices and I smeared them over my nose and chin as I pushed in, lapping and sucking, drawing the sweet flow out of her and drinking it up. I teased her clit, swirling around it, back and forth over it, pulling at it, nibbling it with my lips, feeling it swell in my mouth as her excitement grew and she writhed more urgently.

I didn't want her to come yet—I wanted to see her face when she gave in. With a last lingering lap I left her ready and straining for release, and slid up to let her taste her sweet scent on my face. She was breathing so hard I hardly dared kiss her.

"Baby—" I whispered in her ear before filling it with my tongue. She thrashed with the surprise of the sudden pleasure.

I nibbled her earlobe and neck as I cupped her ass and pressed into her crotch.

"Please—" she murmured between gasps.

With one arm cradling her, I slipped the other down her arched torso. I cupped her mound but couldn't linger there as she thrust her wanting, hot cunt into my hand, voicelessly demanding—pleading—to be taken. I was overwhelmed with waves that pushed my body onto hers as I entered her with first one finger, and then two, and then rocked her as I fucked her with my arm pumping her and my fingers drawing back and forth against the inner wall behind her pubis.

"Oh, my god!" she shouted. "Ooh—" The words became a rising pure wail that peaked as, with one final arch and her legs flung straight out behind me, she filled my hand with come.

I don't know whether she decided to go on to love other women, or created her own trail of stories at the university, or got married, or became a doctor. We didn't become lovers. I wouldn't have wanted to. But I relish the memory of her in my fantasies.

STATE OF GRACE

by L.A. Livingston

"Nice nails. How come only on one hand?"

The voice, young and absolutely innocent of all innuendo, scarce in this jaded summer resort town of incestuous community, cut through my silent, in-my-head monologue. "What?"

"I said that I like your fingernails and I was wondering why you only have one hand long and painted. Oh, and what flavor did you say you wanted?" The exchange, so direct, so *earnest* in its delivery, gave me pause for thought. Contemplation. And almost instant rejection. No way. There are just some places you don't go. And I had learned, the hard and expensive way, that one simply does not play in her own backyard.

"Coffee. Yes, they are real. And I only grow the left hand long because of my lifestyle." And left it at that.

Or so I believed at the time.

The time being the early '80s. The place, Provincetown, P-Town. The outermost tip of the Outer Banks of Cape Cod, Massachusetts. And the summertime playground for all that was queer and gay. A party place, a resort town—and my home, year-round, for the past nine years. I'm a writer by work, a sometime horse trainer, sometime bartender, and I've been known to wait tables in a pinch toward the end of the season, which runs, approximately, Memorial Day through Labor Day in this New England fishing village turned artists' retreat.

Mostly I'm respectable, I "clean up well;" and when I play—well, I play hard. I have a bit of a reputation in this (at the time) politically correct town of Real Lesbians. A dark hint of leather. A shadow of steel chain. Telltale sign of a bulge in leather jeans—if you're interested in being read *that* kind of fairy tale, pun very much intended. Yes, at the time, a time before AIDS and before crack cocaine, I worked hard, drank hard, and played hard within the sandpapered walls of the S/M community and was deeply addicted. To addiction. My philosophy was, "If you're not living life on the edge, you're taking up far too much room."

And there was not a lot of room in my life for a sweet, "straight" girl from Virginia, spending the summer before entering college (Bates, in Maine) on the Outer Banks of Cape Cod. Scooping ice cream for a new name in town, a little down-home operation out of Vermont called Ben & Jerry's, after its kooky—and brilliant—founders. Yes, she was cute and had a voice like spiced apple cider, with cinnamon *and* nutmeg. Yes, it *was* true that my ethics had been described, by friends, as "various moral shades of gray." And no, I most definitely was not going *there,* in word or action. I bought my ice cream, one of my top three passions, and left without a backward glance.

The mind, however, is a curious organ and often (I've learned in retrospect, hindsight being *better* than 20/20) not easily dissuaded from its pursuit of hedonistic pleasures. Over the next several sweltering days in August, I found myself consuming more Ben & Jerry's coffee ice cream than even my normal intake. And polishing my nails. Left hand only. Come Fuck Me Red. I learned her name—Belinda—through casual sugar-or-waffle cone conversation and her place of summer residence: Wellfleet-on-the-Bay (more modestly known to locals as Wellfleet Harbor) at her grandparents' home. And that she recently had broken up with her boyfriend (he didn't understand her, apparently) and that she was majoring in women's studies (uh-huh), and that she had these most incredible eyes (gray-green) and the bone structure of a Siamese cat (meow). And that she was 17 years old. Just. (Early acceptance to college coupled with skipping third grade at some private school on Philadelphia's Main Line.)

Seventeen. I left town. Three days to Boston by ferry to play in the dungeons of Dorchester with mistresses and slaves and editors of local S/M rags. I jumped out of a birthday cake to celebrate some bitch's birthday, sans clothing. I masterminded a brilliant scene against a backdrop of fish netting and iron shackles. And I drank Glenfiddich scotch and thought about Belinda; she of the sea-colored eyes, angles and planes body. And thought about Belinda. And listened to all my friends, they of the 9-to-5 jobs and American Express cards by day, the weekend riding crop set, and decided to play it safe and avoid the little shop next to town hall that housed two of my most pressing passions for the remainder of the season, when the shops would close and little wayward—and altogether too innocently curious—college coeds would be off to pledge Sigma Kappa Phi or kama sutra or whatever.

Back in Provincetown and on a diet of sorts, I conscientiously avoided daytime and Commercial Street by Town Hall and continued my writing and drinking, watching the weeks of summer play themselves out in the dramas and romances of my friends around me. With the coming of Labor Day, the day that traditionally marks the close of the summer tourist season, the pace, the eternal energy of the town was picking up, and you could fairly feel the buzz and hum, the pulse of late summer in the day's exchanges, the locals, and the weather as it began to turn.

If the end of August on Cape Cod is traditionally the close of summer, it is also the height of hurricane season; days of sunlight and heat changing dramatically to high winds and heavy rains. Generally such storms will blow themselves out to sea off George's Bank or into such a chaotic swirl that they become little more than warm northeasters or, at worst, tropical storms. Occasionally, however, the Outer Banks will be threatened with a full-fledged fury, a hurricane blowing up the coast from the Carolinas, sending the Portuguese fishing fleet and private yachts alike scurrying for the comparative safety of harbor and dry dock. If you're not a boat owner and have not much to lose, that is, no shop or house along the shore to board up and sandbag, the storms can be an exciting and invigorating experience. Town becomes a madcap flurry of activity, and the atmosphere becomes almost partylike in its doomsday feel. Once you're boarded and bagged, your stock of flashlights, drinking water, and batteries set in, the switch on your emergency generator primed, there is nothing much to do but sit back, drink heartily, and enjoy the ride.

And fasten your seat belt.

If you're me and already a little crazy-by-rule, you head off to a deserted beach, being careful to avoid the roadblocks and rangers from the National Seashore whose duty it is to keep you safe from yourself. And that's just what I did: I donned an old marine all-weather parka that I kept handy for such occasions, complete with a thermos of Bailey's and coffee, and headed for Coast Guard Beach in North Truro, the most deserted beach I knew of in times like these. The access road to the beach often would wash out in all but the gentlest of April rains, and at that time, most of the road ran through Cape Cod National Seashore property and so was not occupied by either houses or tourists. Of course, all that has changed now; almost twenty years later the area is built up and upon, but that's another story. Suffice to say in that August of the early 1980s, it was fairly deserted.

Fairly.

As I drove slowly through town, watching the last of the nails being hammered into plywood boards protecting plate glass and wrought iron, I thought of Belinda and where she was weathering the storm onslaught. Most likely at her grandparents' "cottage" in Wellfleet, or perhaps she had already left for Maine and college life. I felt a short, sharp pang of regret as I passed the already storm-fortified Ben & Jerry's storefront and shrugged it off as quickly as it had come. Some places you just don't go. Though it was clear I might be placing myself in physical danger by riding out "The Storm" at the beach, I understood it in no way to be on the same level as the danger presented and successfully avoided these past weeks by the underage temptation serving summer slurpies. Yes, while it may be true that if you're old enough to sit at the table, you're old enough to eat, where I'm from, 16 will get you 20 and 17—and "straight"—is just a hairbreadth too close for safety, not to mention comfort. No, Belinda was my ice cream-covered fantasy this summer, and it was just as well she stayed that way for her sake and mine. Still, I was a bit wistful—and lustful—as I steered the truck out of town, down the back roads toward the woods and shoreline of Coast Guard Beach and the hurricane with the jagged, female name, already roaring in from the Atlantic.

Coast Guard Road was long, dark, and windswept—and already more than a little under water as I made my way to the beach. The pines along the road, really hardly more than a rutted cart path, sheltered me from the worst of the storm, and so I was unprepared for the fury that was Grace as I drove out from under the cover of conifers and into a maelstrom. My vehicle was powerfully sandblasted as I gave up any hope of exiting it and hunkering down between bluffs to experience a furious Grace. Who was I kidding? At that moment I felt the first twinges of alarm; maybe I shouldn't be out here in 120-mile-per-hour wind and rain? Perhaps coffee with my intellectual Harvard cousin in the kitchen of his worn and weathered saltbox a few miles away from the surf was not such a bad idea… I warmed to the idea as the heavy wind buffeted my truck, rocking it to and fro. With difficulty and a bit of disappointment as I was anticipating a Hemingwayesque evening alone in the dunes, I wrestled the steering wheel around and headed for higher ground, noticing as I did so the not-so-slow approach of the headwaters over the reef below me. A killer storm!

As I maneuvered my truck, nearly nonexistent shocks groaning in protest, my peripheral vision caught a flicker of light, and I found myself wondering what idiot would venture out on a night like this one. I knew it had to be someone wandering about, as all the seasonal cottages were much farther up the read, not to mention deserted at this late date, and the old Coast Guard barracks were uninhabited and scheduled for demolition later this fall. The barracks, a bunch of old, graying shacks, are a mute and decaying reminder of the days when the lighthouse at Nauset was manned and sailors and rescuers alike would take refuge during big northeasters, after being washed up and, if lucky, pulled from the cold Atlantic. *But who would be there tonight?* I thought. There was a lengthy craft advisory yesterday an this morning, with plenty of warning to come ashore and beach one's boat, and anyway, the shacks were all boarded up and closed off to trespassers. Vandals? Nothing left to vandalize. Someone lost? Unlikely; Cape Cod National Seashore is hardly a wilderness, with STAY OFF THE DUNE GRASS signs at every turn and a large population of skateboarders on its bike trails these days. Someone as foolhardy (I prefer to think "daring") as me? Though I dismissed the idea almost instantly, my adventuresome spirit (lack of sound judgment?) pulled me toward the flickering light at the far end of the barracks. Throwing caution to the wind(s), literally, I drove my truck up and over the embankment, safe from all but the flashiest of flash floods, and climbed out of the cab.

And almost instantly regretted my decision. The wind grabbed me with an intensity that I had not imagined, and the rain, surprisingly cold for so early in autumn, soaked me through in a matter of seconds. I thought about turning back, of that hot coffee, now laced with brandy in my imagination, with my cousin in front of a roaring fire, but something propelled me forward, head down and blindly reaching out for the boundary of a wall, a door, a tree, anything within the increasing force of the storm. I touched hard, rough shingling, and then a door opened and a rush of warm air enveloped me—and a strong hand reached out and pulled me across the rotting doorjamb and into the shack.

I stumbled into the room, for I guessed it was a room, though the water pouring off my head, streaming into my eyes, made it impossible for me to see anything. I would have fallen but for the hand that guided me toward what sounded like a fire (did these old places even have fireplaces?), and as I felt the first tongues of heat against my skin, I began to shiver violently. "Here, you had better take those clothes off and wrap yourself in this." The scratchiness of a wool blanket against my face, put into my hands. That voice. Main Line Philly meets South Boston, Victoria's Secret with a baseball cap. Bailey's and coffee. *Belinda?*

I blinked rivers of water out of my eyes and looked up under a mane of dank wetness and was not surprised to see her kneeling a few feet away, adding another log to a cheerfully crackling hearth. Apparently these shacks, or at least this one, have fireplaces; a broken down affair with crumbling mortar widening the cracks, a firetrap, no doubt, but at the moment an architectural delight. She watched me watch her—and continue to shiver—and again suggested I remove my soaked clothing and wrap myself in the blanket I was holding against me. And (no kidding) she was wearing a Ben & Jerry's hooded sweatshirt. The kind that advertised all the flavors spelled out on one's arms and across one's shoulders.

I had to laugh. And once I started, I couldn't seem to stop. I mean, here I spent the better part of a perfectly good summer avoiding this underage temptation the way a Weight Watchers advocate will avoid anything buffet, and here she was, sitting, no, *kneeling* at my feet offering to remove my clothes. Well, not exactly but close enough… My laughter slowed to low chuckles as I realized that while I knew what was going on, she had not a clue. And, by the way she was looking at me, was more than a little curious. Outside the wind howled and shook the building with such force that our eyes widened at the power of this storm. The fact of this shared situation, coupled with the knowledge, or lack thereof on Belinda's part, in regard to my sexuality sobered me quickly. We weren't exactly trapped here but to drive out at this point seemed reckless, she had no idea that I was a lesbian, and what the hell was she doing here anyway?

With those facts at hand, I felt myself experiencing a very rare (for me) moment of shyness as I finally began to remove my clothes. Modesty or no, however, I was freezing, and as I stripped off my layers of clothing, it was Belinda who turned away, ostensibly to stoke the fire, poking at the embers with studied concentration. I wrapped the blanket around me, unmindful of the scratchy wool and grateful for its warmth, and hung my clothes, wringing wet, over the broken arm of an old kitchen chair that stood propped against the wall to my right. As my eyes adjusted to the comparative gloom of the room, I began to take stock of our accommodations.

When built in the early 20th century, the Coast Guard barracks were meant to house crews that were used to rescue hapless sailors washed aground on the natural sand-and-rock bank that surrounds the tip of the lower Cape. Since that time, with lighthouses becoming automatic and radar taking the place of viewed search and rescue, the barracks have been used as both a summer residence for rangers of the National Seashore and conservationists gathering data on the flora and fauna of Cape Cod. The living quarters had been used up until last summer, and the remains of austere furnishings, as befitting both the government and military, were scattered throughout the cabins/shacks. This one was fitted with a small sink and stove, both long unused and with fixtures disconnected, an old-fashioned icebox, a table and two chairs, one of which was doubling as my clothesline, a rather lumpy-looking single bed—more like a cot with aluminum legs, more than likely where the wool blanket had come from—and a small room beyond the fireplace, which no doubt housed what passed for a bathroom, probably a toilet and maybe a stall shower. That and the hearth made up our hurricane sanctuary. Musty. A bit dirty. But warm and dry. And from the looks of it, recently inhabited. By Belinda.

"What are you doing here?" she asked, eyes a bit puzzled and definitely green tonight. Emerald green by firelight.

"I might ask you the same question, Miss," I countered, trying vainly to avoid being captivated by the shadows her lashes created across that angles-and-planes bone structure of hers. "Looks like you've been here a lot longer than me."

"I..." she flushed and looked away, an utterly charming combination of tilted head and blunt cut, honey-colored mane falling across—you guessed it—those incredible feline cheeks. "I've been coming here all summer," she continued, unmindful or unobservant of my mesmerized stare. "I sometimes stay here to just get away, have some peace, some solitude. To think," she added. She paused and looked as if she might continue with something else, but she stopped herself, bit her bottom lip slightly, and fell silent. Again, I watched her and was reminded of a cat, graceful, slightly arrogant in stance, and completely unaware of its nature. Or perhaps completely aware and accepting. Matter-of-fact. Did this woman really have no clue what she looked like right now, by storm-induced firelight and what her presence in my life was doing to me? (That's a question...)

"How did you find me?" She broke the silence between us by giving voice to the assumption that I was looking for her. In a manner of speaking, I was, and as I explained the events leading up to my invasion of her solitude, she nodded knowingly. "Yes, I also came tonight to be in the storm. My grandparents are in Virginia, visiting relatives, and they think I'm in Boston with friends this weekend, having one last hurrah before leaving for school in Maine. I hopped the bus from South Station to Hyannis this morning and caught the last connecting shuttle to Provincetown this afternoon, got off in North Truro, and walked from Route 6 in before the worst of the storm hit. In Boston they're calling this a tropical storm, but on the Cape and Islands, Grace has been upgraded to a full-fledged hurricane," she finished.

Again, after she had concluded her conversation, she looked away from me, deliberately, it seemed. Did I make her nervous? As nervous as she made me? We spoke for a few more minutes about the intensity of the storm, something about the electricity in the air or some such nonsense, our mutual need to seek solitude during such an event as Grace was turning out to be, then we both fell silent. And it was a silence born from acceptance, comfortableness. We were both more than OK about each other's presence in the shared space, despite our respective desires for aloneness.

I don't know how long we sat there, without the need for conversation, with only the fierce wind howling outside, causing the salt spray and sand to rattle against the graying wood of the shack and the lone pane of glass set high on the far wall. Occasionally she or I would add a log to the fire from our dwindling source of cut wood stacked under the window, stirring the embers with a crackling hiss.

It was a very companionable silence, the kind I do not feel often, preferring true solitude to senseless chatter. I found myself relaxing and was almost dozing when her voice, Jack Daniels-with-hot-honey-and-lemon stirred in, flowed across the space between us in the deepening darkness.

"About your fingernails, the long ones; what's that about, really?"

Without hesitation, with a courage born from the boxed-canyon effect (I was trapped, really; I mean, what could I say? That I broke all the nails on the right hand? That I ran out of money when I was having them done? That I type a lot—with only my right hand?), I replied, "I'm a lesbian, pretty heavy into the S/M scene, and it makes it a bit difficult to, ah, perform (I may have blushed a *little* at this admittance) with long nails on both hands. But I like the look and, at this point, it's kind of my, um, signature of sorts." (I definitely colored here, but it was probably too dark in the room for her to notice.)

Quite matter-of-factly, those Siamese-cat eyes betraying no guile, "Why didn't you just tell me that when I first asked you in the beginning of the summer?" she queried.

Why didn't I tell you—when? When I was so captivated by your eyes, your smile, your voice that I could hardly state a flavor of ice cream, much less my sexuality? When I thought you would have avoided me like the proverbial plague if you even suspected my dealings with women (and still might; we hadn't even touched on the whole S/M thing yet)? When, in theory, your age added to my thoughts could have me making license plates up there in Framingham along with the likes of Pam Smart? Yeah, right! All that came out of my mouth, however, was a rather lame, "I dunno."

"Tell me about it; what it's like with women," Belinda requested. "I never have (*no shit!*) but I'm—curious," she finished, her voice drifting dangerously downward on the last word. I swallowed hard. Once. And then that calmness settled over me. You know, the calmness, the deliberateness of thought and word that sometimes translates to action, which steals over you when you are sure of yourself, sure of your ability to commit to the risk, if not the risk itself. It happens in my writing, that turn of a phrase with a comma, an adjective skillfully placed that makes all the difference between reading the words and knowing the meaning. It happens in my riding, when my horse sidepasses or shoulders-in because we are communicating in a way that has nothing to do with semantics. And it happens in flirtation, when you know, beyond a shadow of a reasonable doubt, when the sexual friction in the air will become action on the sheets. Or floor. Or up against the hood of your car in the parking lot of Wal-Mart. Whatever, wherever.

I looked at her and put my hand up, palm stretched up to her. Left-hand nails glistening in the firelight. Come Fuck Me Red. (Thankfully, I had just repainted them yesterday.) She reached out and laid her hand against mine; I covered both with my right hand. And pulled her over to me. No resistance, she came willingly enough, although she looked a little scared. I sat like that for a while, her twisted against me so that her body was up against mine, her back against my chest, our hands entwined. I could feel her tenseness, her shoulders taut, her palm sweating just slightly. Truth to tell, I was a little nervous myself at this point. Sex was something that was pretty rough with me, fairly animalistic in its rutting, and this tenderness, this romance, if you will, was something I was unfamiliar with. Unfamiliar with and willing to explore.

I was all too aware of the fact that I was clothed only in a blanket (and a scratchy one, at that), and as Belinda began to relax a bit, she pressed harder against me, causing that familiar tightness in my chest and wetness between my legs. I must have uttered some sound, a groan or sharp intake of breath, perhaps, because she half turned toward me with a questioning look. It was just too much; a scene out of any Bogart and Bacall movie; all that was missing was the music. If it hadn't been so serious, I might have laughed, but there was nothing funny in the intensity between us as I placed my hand behind her neck and pulled her into me for what I imagined would be a first, tentative brushing of lips (hers) against lips (mine). I truly was ready to let go of her in an instant, at any sign or hesitation or display of coerced confusion. Truly. I need not have worried. Belinda twisted in my arms and kissed me, softly at first but then with tongue and teeth busily working across my mouth and down my throat, it seemed. Virgin? Maybe, but an eager one, to say the least.

Some minor adjustments and Belinda lay on top of me, full-length, her long and lanky body pressing into mine, her legs naturally falling one between mine, the other half-cocked, cat-like (no surprise here).

The implications of the top/bottom stereotype flashed through my mind, and I rolled her over onto her back, losing most of my blanket cover in the process. I had forgotten about my body piercings, and as I knelt over her, the firelight reflected off my nipple ring (left), catching her attention. "Did it hurt?" she asked in wonder.

"A little," I replied, adding that my piercings (I noticed she caught the plurality of the word and wondered what she would think about *that*) were part of a vision quest and were spiritual rather than sexual in nature. She smiled slightly at that statement and leaned upward, caught the gold ring between her teeth, and tugged lightly—and caught me off guard. I gasped audibly and fell on her neck, biting easily, holding her hands down and behind her head. She writhed under me, leaving me no doubt as to whether she was a willing participant in her own experiment, and I paused momentarily.

"Do you know what you're doing here?" I asked her. "Are you sure this is what you want?" Her eyes, unblinking, caught mine in a stare that was unreadable. "We can stop anytime you want," I added—the prerequisite statement before moving into uncharted territory. She continued to stare. "Belinda?"

"Unzip my pants." It was a command, a directive.

"What?"

"Unzip my pants." I sat up and reached down and first unbuttoned, then unzipped her well-worn Levi's. For a minute, the storm stopped, the wind and rain ceased, and the only sound in the room, in the world, was that zipper moving south. Then my hands moved, as if of their own volition, to lift her hips and ease her jeans down and off. She reached forward and moved my hands against her skin, under the elastic of her underwear (Victoria's Secret?), and through the wiry fur that lay underneath. She was so hot I could smell her, her scent equal parts nervous musk and Love's Baby Soft. I pushed her hands away and pushed up her sweatshirt, exposing an undershirt the likes of which, in my circle, is called an Italian tee. No bra. Very butch. Great breasts. I paused to admire the effect for an instant before the T-shirt joined the sweatshirt up around her neck. I attempted to pull both off her—but for some reason, about which I could only speculate, she resisted my attempts to totally bare her body. I contented myself with her bare flesh from her neck to her slim waist, my hands disappearing under the frayed and open waist of her dungarees.

Belinda lay under me, panting slightly, perspiration making her skin glow with a bronzed sheen, reflecting the remains of her summer tan. I remember thinking she reminded me of honey; thick and warm and golden in color—and oh, so very sweet. She lay under me, simple and uncomplicated, her eyes wide and questioning. I was hyper-alert to any sign of fear or doubt on her part (I knew what I wanted), and so paused before doing anything more than brushing my fingers over her pubic hair. She sensed my hesitation and urged me to explore her more intimately by putting her hand over mine and not so gently exerting pressure. I lowered my mouth to hers and simultaneously worked my fingers through her now-drenched pussy hair and against her outer lips, rubbing slowly at first, then faster to match her movements under me. My index finger found her clit and circled it while I moved my mouth from hers downward to gently lick and tug at her nipple with my teeth.

At this point she was literally growling underneath me, her body beginning to buck, with the first strains of "Yes, you're doing this right" starting to hum under her skin. I didn't know how much longer I could continue; at this level I had been somewhat dispassionate about my own body and was craving attention, aggression, release. Belinda's sexual rhythm was a lot like her personality; easy, uncomplicated, and I could feel her begin to tighten and strain under my hand, her clit hardening and disappearing under its hood, preclimax. What I really wanted was to rip her clothes off her body and bury my head between her thighs, my mouth working over her greedily like some starved street urchin gnawing on day-old bread. I risked a sharper-than-previous bite on her nipple, the flesh puckering in immediate response, and was rewarded by her back arching and a quick intake of breath. Heartened, I continued to bite and moved my other hand to the waistband of her dungarees. And pulled downward. Almost involuntarily, she lifted her buttocks, and her jeans and now-soaked underwear moved satisfyingly southward. I didn't bother with shoes and socks; I used one hand to bunch the interfering clothing at her ankles, continuing my clit-teasing with the other.

I reached up and pinched her nipple between my thumb and forefinger as I moved my mouth lower. Navel. The downy line of hair, a treasure trail, that mapped the way to her wet cunt. My teeth pulled at her wiry hair and she lifted her head to watch my progress, offering no resistance. I wondered if her boyfriend had ever done this and if he was able to get her off, and then my rational thoughts ceased as I inhaled her muskiness. I moved my fingers off her clit and to the entrance to her pulsing hole, and she moaned in protest. Before she could stop me or utter a denial, I extended my tongue and replaced my hand with my mouth, eager and almost drooling. Honestly, I was beyond caring about anything at this point; I am one of those who can get off on touching my partner. The feel of her, the smell of her, the sounds of my mouth against her skin, teeth finding and teasing her clit into attention; all of this took me dangerously close to the edge. My edge. Where I abandon all that is gentle and loving for the hard and forceful slamming of flesh against flesh, flesh into flesh, taken rather than offered.

The heat coming off Belinda was a telltale sign of her approaching orgasm, and mine was not too far behind. I steeled myself for one of those rub-up-against-you-and-come, sort of, fucks and began my own countdown-to-breathing, circling Belinda's clit faster with my finger and beginning to push one, then two of my fingers inside her, first slowly, then more rapidly to match her insistent body motion. As we both began the upward ascent into the downward spiral of precome, she frantically moved her hand from where it was lying, inert by her side, to my back, my ass, and pushed me up on one knee, her fingers searching for my wetness. At least, it sure felt like that, and I promptly forgot about her virginity, her inexperience, her "straightness." *Be careful what you ask for…*

I used my other hand to push hers through my tangled and matted crotch hair, bypassing my aching clit, and against my swollen lips. If there was any hesitation, I didn't feel it, and as she bucked and strained under me, I used her wrist as leverage and pushed her hand, that same hand that scooped copious quantities of Ben & Jerry's ice cream all summer (and did God knows what to her boyfriend's dick), into my expanding and contracting cunt. She gasped but whether from the feel of her fist in my pussy or my mouth against her quivering clit, fingers fucking her furiously at this point, I don't know. I winced as I closed her fist against her fingernails, thumb joint pushing past the ridged wall to bring her fully into me; it felt like she was in my throat. She began to shake in earnest under me, and as her climax pulled her over whatever cliff she stood at in her psyche, I allowed myself to be pulled over with her, the force of our mutual orgasm drenching us both and expelling my fingers from her vagina—and trapping her hand within me.

We lay together, locked for a few minutes while I tried to relax enough for her to remove her hand from my pussy, finger by finger. The removal of her fist from inside me was enough to generate another small shudder from me, and I watched her through open eyes, wondering what she thought of all this—and for the first time in some minutes, really caring.

"Are you OK?" I asked her, watching for her emotional as well as physical retreat from this scene.

"Yeah, I think so…I mean, yes, I am," she answered, at first with hesitation, then decisiveness. And then as she lay there with me in the murky gloom, Hurricane Grace howling her intent outside our door, the firelight making dancing shadows on the moldy walls, she laughed. Not a giggle or an uncomfortable, break-the-silence kind of sound, but an out-and-out laugh, deep from her belly. I sat up and looked at her, quizzing with my eyes the reason for her expression of humor.

She extended her right hand, the hand that moments ago was buried to the wrist inside me, clenching and unclenching with the force of my cunt muscles and the heat of my orgasm, and uncurled her fingers, her Philadelphia Main Line French manicure glinting in the flickering light. Crimson wetness, drying and crusted against her fingers, stained her nails and left trails of red-tinged wetness over her knuckles and upward to her wrist. Apparently, she raked me with her fingernails as she pushed her way inside my pussy, her inexperience showing in her negligence to curl her fingers inward on her own palm as she fist-fucked me. In an odd turn of events, she lost her virginity, so to speak, by letting my blood flow.

"Now I understand the reason for your unorthodox manicure," she replied to my questioning gaze.

As Grace climaxed and descended into her own wet aftermath, flooding the Cape in her bath of passion, all I could do was laugh.

Contributors' Biographies

J.M. Beazer's short fiction has appeared in the anthologies *Best Lesbian Erotica 1996* and *Girls* and the magazine *Pucker Up*. A MacDowell fellow with an MFA from Sarah Lawrence College, she's currently revising her first novel, *The Festival of Sighs.* She's also started work on a second novel, which is based on the early life of one of Sigmund Freud's patients, a lesbian who at age 19 was sent to Freud to be "cured" of her homosexuality and whom Freud discussed in a 1920 case study. Finally she's working on a collection of stories called *Ten Little Nasties.*

Paula C. Bowden is a psychic dyke and fifth-generation Californian living in Sacramento. This is her first opportunity for publication, though she has been writing lesbian erotica for many years and enjoys the play the words inspire. Paula makes her money doing clairvoyant readings, massage, and computer repair. Second to meditation (and sex), writing is her favorite form of expression and release.

Lori Cardona is of Puerto Rican and Mexican heritage. She was born in Spanish Harlem, grew up in suburban New Jersey, lived in the Carolinas for 11 years, and currently lives in Fort Lauderdale, Fla., where she works as an administrator in a mental health agency. Her work has been previously published in the magazines *The L Connection, The Fountain, Esto No Tiene Nombre,* and *Conmocion,* and in the anthologies *Speaking Heart to Heart, Poesia,* and *My Lover Is A Woman: Contemporary Lesbian Love Poems.*

Paula Clearwater is a former psychotherapist living in the foothills of the White Mountains with her partner of 12 years and her faithful dog of seven. Her work has been published in several anthologies, including the upcoming *Best of Lesbian Erotica, 1998.* She has lived in just about every part of this big country, and is grateful to all the women who ever laid down their virgin souls for the possibility of love.

Charlotte Cooper is a kinky bi-dyke who lives in the East End of London, England. You can read more of her stuff in her heavily censored book, *Fat and Proud ;* the Alyson anthology *Generation Q,* in a variety of queer rags such as *Fat Girl,* and in her own 'zine, *kink.*

Caitlin S. Curran lives in the Los Angeles area. This is her first erotic publication.

M. Damian lives in Staten Island, NY, and is currently working on a lesbian detective novel. She was the first person to write an ongoing gay soap opera on the Net. She is in the process of renovating a new house—and waiting anxiously for her Lori-girl to come join her so they can begin their life together.

Jennifer Delamer loves women, writing, and walking in the romantic Seattle rain.

Bleau Diamond was born in England and currently lives in Scottsdale, Ariz. A Capricorn who preserves her soul by writing erotic poetry, she is a paralegal, a skip tracer, and an investigator. In her free time she writes short stories, and she is a screenwriter and a filmmaker. Her mission is to write, direct, and produce lesbian films that depict a positive image.

Alison Dubois is a widely published freelance writer in poetry journals, magazines, and anthologies, still pursuing that elusive dream: a book of her own.

Rebecca Faurer says, "Although time has moved on, the memory of the woman in this story has always held a special place within my heart. It was a magical, carefree time. I'm 33 and finally learning to live my dreams. Denver is where Sue, my partner of six years, and I call home. Without Sue's unconditional love, encouragement, and unending support, this story would not have been written. The deepest thanks also to momma Linda. Because of her trusting guidance and love many, many years ago, I am happily who I am."

Marylou Hadditt, Crone, lesbian, grandmother, lives and writes in Sonoma Valley, Calif. "Cowgirl" is from her Southern memoir in progress. Hadditt has contributed to *Women of the 14th Moon: Writings on Menopause* and *Sexual Harassment, Rebirth of Power: Overcoming the Effects of Sexual Abuse Through the Experiences of Others,* and *Readings for Older Women.* She wrote and performed *Garden in Second Bloom,* a play about menopause, and regularly contributes to *Women's Voices.* This was her first adventure in erotica, and she loved it.

Lou Hill lives with her partner and their son as well as a house full of pets. Writing has always been a passion, although she didn't actively seek publication until she was in her 40s. She has published several fiction and nonfiction stories in anthologies and magazines.

Veronica Holtz was born in Philadelphia, Pa. She studied and worked for several years in Europe and now lives back in the Delaware Valley area. She has written two plays, a novel, and several sort stories.

Myra LaVenue says, "By day I am a technical writer by profession, writing multimedia training and Web training in Portland, Ore. By night I write poetry and fiction. I have had poems published in the Los Angeles *Girl Guide* and nonfiction published in the Alyson anthology *Early Embraces,* which came out in November of 1996. Currently I am living with my partner, Tracy, in a newly purchased 1929 house in North Portland, which we are striving to make the new gay neighborhood."

Shelby Lee is a freelance writer who lives happily with her partner of five years. They share parenting responsibilities for their dog and two cats and are soon to be parents of a new baby.

Jennifer Lindenberger says, "Well, I'm still in Smalltown, Pa. I work in accounting, and it's going well enough that I hope to save money and move to the Southwest. I love the sunshine, and I enjoy pushing myself to the limit by hiking and climbing mountains; I'm definitely in the wrong place! I've written for *Hecate's Loom, Options,* and *Perceptions,* a short-lived but lovely gay and lesbian quarterly. My nudes have appeared in *Eidos* and other erotic magazines."

L.A. Livingston is a New England-based writer who shares her life with her Arabian stallion, Walden, and her chow dog, Cheyanne. When she is not writing, she trains horses, and while her work has taken her all over the United States, she knows "There's no place like HOME." She is currently working on a book project, slowly and diligently, Yankee New England-style.

Louye says, "This work, 'Lovely Work,' is the result of my love of women and the inspiration that it has given me. Living in this world as a closeted lesbian, and only revealing this aspect to the women I have loved and the current one that I love (L.P.), I feel this would be a great time to start having fun. For years I have written just to put my concealed thoughts to hard copy. Now it's time to let the public in on them. Enjoy."

Fletcher Mergler is a curly-headed humanist and linguist who fled the classroom as a language teacher to toil as an interloper in the sciences, an area in which she has had no training since high school biology. As vouched for by those who call her "friend," never once has she hopped off a teeter-totter, nor ever given any indication of a tendency to do so. Fletcher lives on Capitol Hill in Washington, D.C., where she works and plays in the company of her three dogs.

Jen Moses divides her time between Austin and Chicago. Though primarily a writer, she is also an actor and producer for the Hidden Theatre in Chicago. She is the author of a screenplay, *Saturn's Return,* as well as numerous short stories and pieces of erotica, and is currently working on a spec script for *Ellen.*

Rebecca O'Bryan has worked in the music industry for 15 years and is currently sampling the delights of working as a film extra. She lives in the Los Angeles area with her lover.

Jesi O'Connell spends her time writing, taking pictures, and hoping to be published again soon. She lives in California with her partner and a collection of pets lovingly called "the farm."

C. J. Place is a freelance writer and graphic artist. Her writing has appeared in *Lyrical Iowa* and *Writer's Forum.* Originally from Chicago, C.J. now lives near Iowa City where she is working on her first novel.

Jane Sebastion has no formal training in literature, but she has spent much of her life writing stories. Sources for these stories include her frequent traveling, her unusual family, and her sexuality, which she confirmed a few years ago. Other interests include classical music and jazz, carpentry, painting, and consuming mass quantities of coffee with friends. "Summertime" is a fond memory in Jane's life, although she is currently involved with a different, amazing, woman. Jane lives on the West Coast of Canada.

Rosanna Sorella was born in San Francisco and has been writing creative nonfiction for ten years. She is currently completing a book on contemporary women writers of Italian and Sicilian descent.

Inspired by the red rock of the Southwest, **Kanyon Sweet** is the pen name chosen by this author to represent a deep and delicious persona not available to the public. Her professional and public persona encompasses roles as licensed counselor, trainer, writer, and student of shamanic healing. She writes topical columns for a prominent gay newspaper, conducts women's workshops, and writes periodically for a metaphysical journal. At the height of the lesbian/feminist movement in the late '70s, her critical and provocative Master's thesis in clinical psychology settled the issue for once and forever that lesbians as a group are as well adjusted as their straight sisters. Her work was reprinted in a premier women's psychology textbook published by St. Martin's Press almost two decades ago. Kanyon Sweet has devoted a substantial part of her professional career to women's treatment issues. She helped establish the first two rape crisis centers in her state, directed a program for displaced homemakers, and published a treatment guide for working with adolescent victims of sexual abuse. For fun she studies Indian art and artifacts and does long-distance cycle touring. Kanyon Sweet is a mother and grandmother of two, who is settled comfortably with her dance partner of six years in their home in the rural Northwest.

Jules Torti says, "In the darkness before the breath of dawn, there is an intimate voyage of infinite possibilities. Inches apart, eyes closed with dreams, this is where lovers speak. The words I write happen in the thick velvet of night. Embrace the words, the feeling, a world of whispered thoughts. This is why we live…to love."

Debbie Ann Wertheim would like to thank everyone involved in the production of "Pretty Please." Her work can also be found in *Sex Spoken Here: Good Vibrations Erotic Reading Circle Selections* and *Sex Toy Tales.* She lives and plays in San Francisco and will always be a greedy little girl.

Gretchen Zimmerman is a binational boy-identified transgendered bi-dyke who hates labels. Her fiction has appeared in *Queer View Mirror 2: Lesbian and Gay Short Short Fiction, Countering the Myths: Lesbians Write About the Men in Their Lives,* and *Beginnings: Lesbians Talk About the First Time They Met Their Long-Term Partner,* an Alyson publication. She teaches creative writing in Seattle and is building an arc.

AFTERGLOW, edited by Karen Barber. Filled with the excitement of new love and the remembrances of past ones, *Afterglow* offers well-crafted, imaginative, sexy stories of lesbian desire.

CHOICES, by Nancy Toder. *Choices* charts the paths of two young women as they travel through their college years as roommates and into adulthood, making the often difficult choices all lesbians will understand. "Nancy Toder's first novel really is a classic lesbian love story. The outstanding thing about *Choices* is that it is a good story." *—Off Our Backs*

THE FEMME MYSTIQUE, edited by Lesléa Newman. "Images of so-called 'lipstick lesbians' have become the darlings of the popular media of late. *The Femme Mystique* brings together a broad range of work in which 'real' lesbians who self-identify as femmes speak for themselves about what it means to be femme today." *—Women's Monthly*

HEATWAVE: WOMEN IN LOVE AND LUST, edited by Lucy Jane Bledsoe. Where can a woman go when she needs a good hot…read? Crawl between the covers of *Heatwave,* a collection of original short stories about women in search of that elusive thing called love.

THE LESBIAN SEX BOOK, by Wendy Caster. Informative, entertaining, and attractively illustrated, this handbook is the lesbian sex guide for the '90s. Dealing with lesbian sex practices in a practical, nonjudgmental way, this guide is perfect for the newly out and the eternally curious.

THE PERSISTENT DESIRE, edited by Joan Nestle. A generation ago butch-femme identities were taken for granted in the lesbian community. Today, women who think of themselves as butch or femme often face prejudice from both the lesbian community and the straight world. Here, for the first time, dozens of femme and butch lesbians tell their stories of love, survival, and triumph.